BOOKS BY

Lori L. Lake
====================

The Milk of Human Kindness:
Lesbian Authors Write about Mothers & Daughters

Stepping Out: Short Stories

Different Dress

Gun Shy

Under the Gun

Have Gun We'll Travel

Ricochet in Time

Romance for Life

Advance Praise for *Snow Moon Rising*

"Lori Lake is one of the best novelists working in the field of lesbian fiction today."
   ~Midwest Book Review

"*Snow Moon Rising* provides nail-biting action, strong emotional impact, and a judicious balance of suspense and breathing space. People of older generations will remember the era and relate closely to it, but *Snow Moon Rising* should appeal to anyone with an appreciation of history, belief in the sustaining power of love, and a vested interest in tearing down the walls of prejudice."
   ~Nann Dunne, author of The War Between the Hearts, and editor/publisher of Just About Write e-zine (www.justaboutwrite.com)

"*Snow Moon Rising* is a book that shines. It shines with love—for family, for friends, for lovers. It shines with compassion for people caught up in the convulsions of war and for the forgotten victims of the Holocaust. It shines with humanity. The characters, the story, the emotion, tragedy upon tragedy all leading eventually to a triumphant of human spirit – all flawless. Lori Lake has reached beyond herself and written a modern classic."
   ~Ruth Sims, author of *The Phoenix*

"Magnificent storytelling! *Snow Moon Rising* is an epic historical saga with rich, well-rounded characters and a plot that totally captivates. Following the story of two families brought together by war and tied together by love and friendship, it's about two women who find the strength to survive and to love."
   ~Verda Foster, author of *Graceful Waters* and *The Gift*

Snow Moon Rising

Lori L. Lake

Regal Crest Enterprises

Nederland, Texas

ISBN 978-1-932300-50-5

First Printing 2006

9 8 7 6 5 4 3 2 1

Cover by Donna Pawlowski

Published by:

Regal Crest Enterprises, LLC
4700 Hwy 365, Suite A, PMB 210
Port Arthur, Texas 7764

Find us on the World Wide Web at
http://www.regalcrest.biz

Printed in the United States of America

Acknowledgments

Every book presents its own unique difficulties, and this one was no different, turning into an unexpected marathon that has lasted nearly four years. Thanks especially to Betty Crandall, Ellen Hart, Patty Schramm, Katherine Smith, and my lovely partner Diane for cheering me on through a race I thought would never end.

For early manuscript advice, a hearty thanks to the following: Brenda Adcock, Betty Crandall, Kim Miller, Patty Schramm, Katherine Smith, and Jane Vollbrecht. Also, Betty Crandall, Nann Dunne, and Patty Schramm did careful readings of the revised manuscript, for which I am grateful.

Marvelous proofing was completed under dire pressure by Brenda Adcock, Betty Crandall, Nann Dunne, Verda Foster, Ann German, Tama Huang, Joyce McNeil, Mary Phillips, Patty Schramm, and Ruth Sims. Thank you all for your attention to detail.

A big thank you to editor Jennifer Knight for astute attention to substantive and structural issues, and to Nann Dunne for amazing work on the line edit. Thank you to Donna Pawlowski for yet another exceptionally beautiful cover, both back and front.

Individual thanks go as well to:

Caro Clarke—for so generously sharing her vast knowledge about WWII and for supplying the much needed statement, "Well, Lori, you do realize that *some* people actually lived through the war." Without that comment, I might still be floundering.

Bonnie "Berlinpup" Glaenzer—for info on Poland, France, and Germany, and for German translations. Thank you for being the eyes and ears over a land I hope to one day visit.

Patty Schramm—who read every version and heard about every incarnation of this large and complicated book but never lost enthusiasm for the story. I'm gonna love ya forever for that, pal!

I hope I haven't forgotten anyone. Many people have encouraged me over the last four years, and without that interest and support, I might never have made it through this long journey. Thank you to everyone who sent good wishes or said prayers. I needed them!

If your curiosity is piqued by this story, at the back I've included a guide to the Roma Moons and a Select Bibliography of books about the Roma.

Happy Reading!
Lori L. Lake
Snow Moon, 2006

Dedication

To the women who remember the early part of the 20th Century
but especially to my octogenarian friend
Betty J. Crandall
who brightens my life on a daily basis

And with respect and awe for my septuagenarian friend
Nann Dunne
who really knows her way around words
and generously shared her talents

And in memory of my mother
Sylvia Palm
who didn't make it out of her sixties
but will always be remembered with love

Chapter One

New York City, November 1989 (Snow Moon)

HER HEART POUNDING, Mischka lay in bed and held her breath, straining to listen. The sound, whatever it had been, didn't come again. But something had awakened her. She remembered that visitors had come to stay. Was one of them up so late?

She gazed across the dim room. A tiny shaft of light slipped through the slightly parted drapes at the window, barely enough to see by. She fumbled for her wire-rimmed glasses on the bedside table.

There it was again—a whumping sound. It came from the kitchen. Careful not to wake her partner, she slid out of bed, pausing for a moment to be sure she could trust her arthritic knees. She found her slippers and eased them on, then shuffled to the door where her terrycloth robe hung. Freshly laundered, it smelled like roses. She snugged the belt around her waist and crept out of the bedroom.

Moonlight shone through the bay window at the far end of the living room. In the bay alcove, a kneeling form with broad shoulders showed in dark relief against the window. His right hand, gripping a half-glass of milk, rested on the sill. As Mischka drew nearer, she saw by the shock of white-blond hair that it was Tobar. Her relationship to him was complicated and made more sense when diagrammed on paper, but she considered him her grandson. He was family; that was all that counted.

She wondered why he was awake after midnight. Unaware of her approach, he made a sniffing noise, and she stopped halfway across the room. She reached out and steadied herself against the rough material of the couch arm, all the while wondering if she should intrude on him.

When she was much younger, Mischka believed in a free

exchange of thoughts and ideas and emotions. Everyone should feel the love, enjoy the exhilaration life afforded. She smiled to think how naïve and full of zest she had been then. Into her early teens, she had maintained such innocence. But eventually reality hardened her, and over time she came to realize that each soul needs its own private place and solitude to nourish both joy and pain.

Tobar was young, but from what she'd seen the night before, when he and his family arrived, he carried more than his portion of sadness. She'd been curious then, but who was she to pry? Perhaps she should spirit herself away and let him have his peace and quiet.

She stepped away from the sofa, not making a sound, but somehow the boy sensed her presence. He turned. "Mom?"

"No, it's me. Are you all right?"

"Yeah. Sure." He sniffed again and wiped his face on the sleeve of his white t-shirt.

Mischka heard the bleakness in his voice and instead of retreating, she strode across the room, shifted the nearest easy chair so it faced the window, and sank into it. "Were you having trouble sleeping?"

"A little. I'm not tired at all. The time change is weird. My body still thinks it's seven hours earlier." He took a sip of the milk. "I was thirsty, though."

"I'm glad you located the milk. We laid in quite a supply for you and your family. Would you like me to make you some toast or find you a fritter?"

"Oh, no, that's okay, *Beebee* Mischka. I'm not that hungry."

In the silver light, she could see the misery etched into his face. His blond hair was tousled, his bangs falling into his eyes, and the sadness came through to her. She envied his ability to kneel on the carpet so casually. His limbs were long and lean, the muscles not filled out yet, but the promise of a handsome physique was apparent. He had just had his fifteenth birthday and had already grown much taller than Mischka.

"You look so much like your grandma's brother Emil."

"I do?"

"Yes, you most certainly do."

"I don't remember him very well. What was he like?"

She looked at Tobar closely, and it was as if she were meeting Emil as the boy she had never known. "He was brave. He was strong in all ways, the most important *gajo* in my life."

"*Gajo?*"

"Means he was not Roma. I was younger than you are now when first I met him. He was a soldier then."

Tobar set his empty glass to one side and leaned forward, his forearms on the windowsill. Outside, the wind blew cold and blustery, and a rime of frost encircled the window frame.

Mischka rose with effort and peered up at the night sky. "Soon the snow will fly. Look how icy the world has become." She pointed. "And see the snow moon as it waxes."

"Why is it a snow moon when there isn't any snow?"

"There will be, soon enough. Many of the Roma moons are a time to prepare and plan. During Snow Moon, we ready ourselves for the winter. November is the month of my birth."

"What's the Christmas moon called?"

"Oak. But it has nothing to do with Christmas. The moon cycles are older than this society and its holidays. They are timeless. You are born in April, correct?" When he nodded, she said, "Seed Moon. Time to plant, time to think of tending fields. We don't follow the moon as we used to. Big buildings block it from our sight. But a very long time ago, we did."

"I wish I lived then instead of now."

"It was a hard time. You are better off now, with food and clothing and a roof over your head. There was no chance for education then, and there was war. You are so lucky now to have a good school."

"I hate school."

Surprised, Mischka said, "But your papa says you are a wonderful student, very smart."

"It doesn't matter how smart I am. I hate the new school in Germany. I want to go back to the one in Norway." His voice sounded weary, like an old man's.

She longed to take him into her arms, this boy-child whose voice and demeanor and blue eyes reminded her so much of Emil, but she had only begun to reacquaint herself with him after an interlude of nearly four years. His father and mother taught English and German in various countries around the world and had just moved to eastern Germany. Each posting usually lasted two to four years before they moved on. Though of course he remembered his great-aunt, *Beebee* Mischka, she wasn't yet sure that the childhood connection had survived. "Is it the coursework? The teachers?"

He didn't answer right away. He leaned toward the window until his forehead came in contact with the cold glass and let out a sigh. "I miss my life. I miss my friends."

"Someone special?"

"Yes. A girl I liked a lot. Nobody likes me at the new school. They make fun of me, call me names."

"Names? Why? What names?"

Tobar turned to look up at her, his fists clenched and his face full of fury. The silver light drenched his face nearly white. She was struck once more with how much he resembled Emil, and a strange tearing in her chest made her feel as though she might cry.

"They make fun of my name. Toe in the Bar, they say. Toe Jam. Toe Head. You're not in Kansas anymore, Toto Brain. Stuff like that." He brought his fists up to his eyes and held them there so his next words were muffled. "Jeez, I hate my name."

"Oh, my. I see." Mischka sank back into the easy chair and thought of the man for whom Tobar was named. Wide red smile. Black beard. Crinkling, happy eyes. Such heft and size. An image came of him standing motionless, arms out from his sides, his face marked with anger but showing no fear as he spoke his last words. She cut off the memory. She didn't want to remember that. Not now.

She took a deep breath and looked toward the clock above the end table. Nearly one a.m. but she wasn't tired, and the boy needed something from her. "Do you know anything at all about Tobar, son of Chal and Elena?"

He shook his head. "Only that he was someone Uncle Emil and Grandma knew. Grandma told me once they named me after him because he was strong and brave and was Uncle Emil's best friend. Oh, and that he died too young. I don't know what happened to him."

"Nobody knows much." She paused to think, and her next words came out in a whisper. "Nobody except me."

Frowning, Tobar turned and sat back on his heels, his left arm stretched out along the windowsill. "Tell me about it, will you, *Beebee?*"

Mischka gazed at his face, at intent eyes and a mouth set in anger. He's only fifteen years old, she thought. Too young for the weight of the world. As if to emphasize her concern, he scooted over close to the chair and leaned into her legs, his blond head near her knee. She reached down with a stiff hand and ruffled his hair. He was still just a boy.

"*Beebee,* if there is some reason I should like this awful name, I want to know. Otherwise, when I grow up I'm going to change it."

"To what?"

"I don't know—maybe Bruce Wayne or Han Solo."

"Who are they?"

"What? You don't know about *Batman?* Or *Star Wars?*"

His tone was so incredulous that she had to smile. "Hmmm, yes, I have heard of them, but I know little."

"You gotta see the movie, and then you'll know what I mean. At least those guys are cool. If I had a name like Luke Skywalker, nobody would make fun of me."

Mischka sighed. To tell, or not to tell? Would his parents approve? "Aren't you tired?"

"No, not at all. Back home it's seven hours earlier."

"Oh, yes, I see. This is a story, Tobar, that I cannot tell fast. But I guarantee you that the men and women in it were much braver than your Bruce Wayne or your sky heroes. And the story is real. It's true. Not made up."

"All right! That's what I want to hear." He popped to his feet and took her hand. "Let's go over on the couch."

Mischka let him pull her up, feeling every bit of the ache in her hips and knees, and she followed him to the couch while she had second thoughts. He settled in the middle, turned, and sat Indian-style, his face eager. She grabbed for the afghan lying across the back of the sofa and placed it over her lap with enough left to flap over onto his legs.

"I still get nightmares from parts of this," she warned.

"Tell me," he said in a firm voice.

Unsure where to begin, she squeezed her eyes shut. Memories surfaced, and pictures rose up from hidden recesses, not in the sepia tones she so often remembered, but stark, bright, vital, and as colorful as modern photographs. She cleared her throat.

"When you first come into the world, Tobar, if you have a *kumpania*—an extended family that loves you—you have no idea that anything terrible can happen. Bad things don't have the same effect when there is so much love and care surrounding a child. Much later a person begins to understand the world is not a very nice place and everyone does not survive. This is, perhaps, the end of childhood. I don't want to end your childhood with sad stories, but remember, after darkness there is always light. Just like after the moon disappears, the sun always rises. *Yes?* You can remember that?"

He nodded solemnly, and she stepped back into the past.

Chapter
Two

Southern Poland, September 1918 (Barley Moon)

FACES AROUND THE roaring campfire were dappled in flickering orange and yellow and white light. Voices rang out in harmony, singing a Roma nonsense song for the children. Overhead, a canopy of partially denuded oak tree branches formed a variegated pattern through which the light of September's Barley Moon shone. Tilting her head back, Mischka saw traces of moonbeams among the thick branches. The sight made her happy, and when she looked again at the singing people all around her, she felt contented. All was right with the world. In the nine years of her life, she had always been most comfortable at the fire circle, huddling with the other children and listening to the jokes, songs, and conversation of the adults.

Tonight, she sat cross-legged on the ground beside her father's left leg. He rested upon a fallen tree trunk next to her mother, who was clapping excitedly to the music. Nadja and Mimi, two special friends from their leader's family, were so close at Mischka's left that she could feel warmth from Mimi's body along her side. Somewhere in the large circle of people, Mischka's brothers Gyorgy and Stevo were singing. Gyorgy's bass voice always sounded slightly flat. In the distance beyond the fire, she heard Stevo's high tenor, always on key, but he was hidden somewhere in the crowd.

If Mischka were an eagle sitting on a tree branch above, her eagle eye would see a circle of fifty men, women, and children — and two dogs — around the fire. A dozen nickering horses, two goats, and eight tents, punctuated by *vardos* — traveling wagons — in various stages of disrepair, formed another wider circle some twenty feet behind them. The occasional cluck of a chicken came from a coop in a smaller dogcart parked closer to the fire than the other *vardos*.

The new encampment bordered a sleepy Polish town. They

had reached it only yesterday, and everyone's spirits were high. They hoped to stay for some time to replenish supplies and prepare further for their southern journey to warmer climes. The stream ran clean and cold, and much wildlife had already been captured to cook or to make jerky. Dinner had been unusually varied: pulled pork, green chili stew with chicken, cooked cabbage, floury bread, and applesauce. Everyone around the fire had a full belly.

As the song ended, Stevo rose and lifted a scarred guitar above the heads of those seated. He moved to a place near Mischka's mother.

Stevo's best friend Tobar called out, "Sing a fighting song for me."

"No," another voice said, "let's sing something in rounds."

Stevo laughed. "No, no, no. Tonight I have something new." He put his foot up on the trunk of the fallen tree a few feet from Mischka and strummed the guitar, then began a sweet melody.

The children loved him, for he often composed songs especially for them. Some of his ditties were clever, some naughty. Many he had been singing since he was a small boy. The second son in the Gallo family, Stevo was the middle child, and while his older brother Gyorgy drew respect for his physical strength and stamina, Stevo often got teased for being a dreamer. He was also a favorite of the adults—especially the young women. Though only age sixteen, with his dark, soulful eyes and a ready smile he had already captured the heart of more than one young girl. His tenor voice shifted from humming into words.

> *I look at the moon up above*
> *I sing a song to my long-lost love*
> *I sing in tones of —*

"*Essen*," a loud voice shouted. "*Gebt mir sofort was zu essen!*" Stevo broke off the song, his mouth open. Out of the corner of her eye, Mischka saw a dark figure come hurtling from outside the circle. At the same time, one dog growled and the other barked frantically.

A pale-faced scarecrow of a man stood next to the fire, his eyes wild as he spun 'round and 'round, flinching, and looking as dangerous as a wild boar. The dogs advanced, barking viciously, their faces and fangs monstrous in the firelight. The stranger held his right arm out straight and at first Mischka thought he was pointing a sharp stick. Then it registered. *He has a gun! The man holds a gun.* A thrill of fear coursed through her, and she sat glued to the ground, hardly breathing.

The man wore dark boots, tattered stockings, and the shabby, unbuttoned remains of what appeared to be a German soldier's uniform. As he spun about in a strange, herky-jerky fashion, mothers and fathers pushed their children behind them or off to the side. Mischka's father shifted above her, but the tree trunk prevented him from doing any more than sheltering her behind his legs.

One of the biggest men, Tobar, put his hands up, palms out, and shouted over the barking, "Please, put the weapon away," but it was clear the soldier couldn't comprehend Romany. The madman roared out further guttural words with a raspy voice Mischka didn't understand. She felt her father's leg move. She gasped when he rose and stepped forward.

"Papa," she said, fear in her voice. "Be careful, Papa..." and then her mother's warm arms pulled her up and held her close.

In an authoritative voice, Mikhail said, "*Soldat! Wir haben etwas zu essen. Frieden. Frieden.*" He turned and gestured toward the barking animals. "Tobar! Stevo! Call off the dogs. They're scaring him." Immediately the shepherd dogs were pulled from the middle of the circle, but Mischka could still hear them growling ominously.

The soldier let out a sigh. His pistol arm dropped slowly. Mikhail advanced toward him, continuing to say "*Frieden.*" Intuitively Mischka knew it meant something calming.

"Welcome," her father said in Romany, then, in the strange tongue Mischka knew she had heard before but didn't quite understand, "*Willkommen.*" With a sweep of his arm, Mikhail said, "Welcome to this circle of peace. *Frieden.* Peace!"

The soldier said, "*Frieden? Hilfe?*"

"*Ja!*"

The intruder's legs gave out, and he fell to the ground, nearly rolling into the flames. In an instant, Gyorgy, Tobar, and two other men grabbed the soldier's limbs and dragged him away from the fire. Mimi and Nadja's father, Gunari, who was their leader, dove into the fray and emerged from the huddle gripping the pistol. In the confusion, Mischka slipped from her mother's arms and moved closer so she could watch the leader pull at the gun's mechanism. It made a clicking sound, and then in exasperation, Gunari said, "This stupid fool had no bullets in his gun!"

The murmur of voices rose, and various adults shouted comments and questions.

"What do we do with him?"

"We ought to shoot him with his own gun."

"What did the *gajo* want?"

"Who is he?"

"What did the *gajo* say?"

Mikhail held up a hand. "Before he fainted, this man asked for *hilfe*, for 'help.' Before that, he demanded food. I think he's weak from hunger, perhaps sick from some ailment, too."

Gunari said, "Carry him over to my *vardo*. We will minister to him there. And we need for someone to keep a watch on him through the night to see that he does no further harm."

Mischka squealed out, "Me! I will. Gunari, I shall keep watch." Quiet snickers and loud guffaws burst out, and she felt her face flame.

Her father put a hand on her shoulder. "Thank you, Mischka, but Gunari is thinking more of large, strong men just in case the soldier attempts some harm. Besides, you need your sleep. You can help in other ways in the morning."

She backed away, her face burning with embarrassment, and watched as they carried the man away. All around the circle, people spoke with excitement, and Mischka tried to listen to everyone at once. Soon, Mimi sidled up and slipped her cool hand into Mischka's. Knowing that they'd be banished to bed before too long, Mischka allowed Nadja and Mimi to lead her off to their bedrolls, happy that she could hear what was going on much better from her sleeping spot under her family's *vardo*, adjacent to the *vardo* of Gunari's family.

BEFORE THE COCKS crowed, long before even the slightest hint of dawn marked the sky, Mischka awakened and stared blearily at the underside of the wagon above her. Mimi lay on one side and Nadja on the other, both with their heads buried in their bedrolls. Warm and cozy in her blankets, Mischka turned over and peered into the darkness toward Gunari's *vardo*. All was quiet. Across the encampment, in the center of the clearing, warm embers glowed from last night's fire. During the night, one of the women always rose to tend the fire—usually more than once. Sometimes soft voices wakened Mischka, but usually she slept through it. She would take her turn at fire watch eventually, but for now, at age nine, she wasn't expected to bear such responsibility.

She ran her tongue over the spot where her eyetooth should be. Her adult teeth were inching in, and she pressed her tongue against the sharp edges. A part of her wished her teeth would never grow in because now she could make a louder whistle than any of the boys. She knew that wouldn't last, though.

Half asleep, she lay on her stomach, hearing and feeling it

growl insistently. To take her mind off her growing hunger, she thought about the wild man and wondered if he were crazy — somehow unbalanced. Who would be so foolish as to charge into a circle of so many people and threaten them with a gun? She didn't know how many bullets the pistol could hold, but even if it were loaded and he shot all the bullets, he couldn't kill everyone. The men in her *kumpania* would never have let him get more than one shot off. Besides, the soldier was small and weak compared even to young men like Stevo and Gyorgy. She thought Tobar could crush him with one large hand.

Above her, the wagon shifted and creaked. She heard a soft thud then saw her mother's boots and long skirt as she moved toward the fire. Luminitsa, called Lumi, carried two large water jugs, one on either side of her belly, which was still distended from a recent stillbirth. Mischka understood that the baby her mother had carried had somehow died, but she didn't know why it had happened yet again. Lumi's last three pregnancies had ended the same way. Mischka was glad to see that her mother's sorrow had lifted in the last few days, but she was still not back to her old self.

Lumi was usually the first in their family to rise. With smooth steps, she moved past the fire and through the grove of plum trees. The *dikla* knotted on her mother's head was the last thing Mischka saw before she disappeared from the dim light. Beyond the trees, the ground sloped to the river. Lumi would wash up there, then move upstream and gather water for cooking and dishwashing.

Mischka turned on her side and slipped back to sleep. Then the first cackling noises of the morning came from the chicken coop, and her eyes popped back open. The two roosters vied for the most irritating call as the chickens hopped around in their wood cages and made squawking noises.

Thin light permeated the campground as Lumi made her way through the plum trees again, lugging the now-full jugs. From the corner of her eye, Mischka caught sight of several other women emerging from their *vardos* or tents. They greeted Lumi with a wave and disappeared into the stand of plum trees just as her mother had.

Lumi set down the jugs by the fire near several coffeepots and moved off to gather wood from the edges of the clearing to build up the fire and begin the day's cooking. They had set up camp so quickly the night before that much work still needed to be done. Later in the morning, Mischka and most of the other boys and girls would collect kindling and fallen branches. The older boys and men would chop up fallen trunks and put it all under dry cover. Wood detail was one of Mischka's favorites. She loved to walk among the trees.

Once the fire was glowing, Lumi strolled back toward the wagon. She stepped up on the wooden stair, and the *vardo* shifted as she rooted around for something. Mischka heard her father's deep voice rumble above. Her mother whispered back, then stepped away from the wagon carrying the coffee grinder and an apron to cover her long, flowing skirt.

For as long as she could remember, Mischka had watched her mother make coffee before the men awakened. While the pot heated on the fire, Lumi ground the coffee and then added it to the boiling water. She squatted by the pot and watched the coffee cook, preventing it from boiling over and squelching the fire.

A rich, aromatic smell wafted toward Mischka, and now she knew she was awake for good. From the bottom of her bedroll, she retrieved a pair of brown woolen pants, socks, and a sweater, and wriggled in her warm pouch to put them on. She slipped from the heat of her bed into the cool September air and reached for her leather boots.

They had become tight. All she had to do was say something, and another pair would be found for her, but she was unhappy that these would soon be too small. They were the first pair of boots made especially for her. Instead of Mischka wearing hand-me-downs from the other children, Gyorgy had cobbled the boots to fit her feet exactly. It had been a lot of work, and she was not sure he would want to go to the time and trouble again—but then, perhaps he would. In another moon cycle, snow would fly, and if they didn't get a lot farther south soon, they would all have a great deal of unproductive time on their hands while waiting for winter to pass. Gyorgy might consent to making her a new pair then. She hoped today the weather would warm up so she could go barefoot, but that remained to be seen.

She crawled from under the wagon, and the crisp morning air tickled her nose. With slow, quiet steps, she wandered past the opening of Gunari's *vardo*, but the curtain was closed, and she couldn't see in. Silently she cursed her bad luck. The soldier could have died in the night, for all she knew. She hoped not, but who could she ask? Sighing, she turned and strolled toward the fire.

Two full days passed before she found out more about the strange man.

Chapter
Three

Southern Poland, September 1918 (Barley Moon)

THE FIRST TIME Emil Stanek woke in the night, his head pounded and he was disoriented and woozy. Awareness returned bit by bit, and he discovered he lay on his side, wrapped in blankets. His stomach hurt. His ribs ached. His hand throbbed. The familiar feel of socks and boots on his feet was gone, but even barefoot, he was toasty warm in his undershirt and coat, blankets bundled around him. The confines of a small room swam into his vision, and he gradually recognized he was lying on the floor of a dimly lit wagon. A foggy lantern hung in one corner beyond his feet, and the slight amount of light it cast hurt his eyes.

Emil sat up, but a dark-haired figure at the rear of the wagon raised a hand when he tried to rise. "Nah, nah, nah. Shhh..."

The man was so big that his over-sized boots touched the wall of the wagon on the right while his upper torso lounged against the wall on the left. One ham-sized hand reached for a mug that sat on a long shelf running along the edge of the wagon. He passed the mug to Emil, who accepted it after a brief hesitation. The lantern shed such feeble light that Emil couldn't see the contents, but he detected a spicy aroma. Heart beating fast, he poked his tongue down into it, and the moment his tastebuds touched the thick, warm broth, his stomach erupted into flips. Without further suspicion, he sucked in one mouthful, then another.

Once he had slurped through half of the rich, garlicky liquid, he found chunks of vegetables on the bottom. He bit into a marble-sized piece and sighed with gratitude. Peppers...and chicken! The fragrant stew disappeared as fast as he could chew and gulp it down. He wanted more, but didn't know how to ask or whether it would be an acceptable request. After all, he had not been very mannerly upon first introduction to these people. He wiped his lips on the back of his right sleeve and met the Gypsy man's eyes, then looked away in embarrassment.

The man said, "*Dosta puyo?*" and waited. Emil stared at him. The man frowned. "*Komi?*"

Still, Emil had no idea what to say so he handed the mug back. The huge fellow nodded, then folded aside a heavy curtain, poked his head through, and spoke a torrent of foreign words in a loud voice.

He should make his move now. Emil imagined himself leaping up and across the wagon to launch himself out the back. He could roll and be up and running before this giant of a man knew what happened. But no, he was barefoot and barelegged. He also had a fever. The cold ground and chilly September weather would slowly sap away his strength, and before he made it to safety, he would freeze to death. His shoulders sank, and in despair, he wondered how to get out of this mess. Who were these people? The stew was a kindness, but was he safe? *Oh, God*, he thought, *what had he gotten himself into?*

Two nut-brown arms bearing a flat wooden board reached through the back curtain, and the Gypsy man took the board and passed it to Emil saying, "*Bogacha. Puyo.*"

Emil accepted the wooden slab, surprised to see that the foot-square cutting board was finely crafted with a soft finish. On it sat the mug from which he had eaten before — again filled with that delectable stew — and some chunks of what looked like floury bread. The Gypsy man rolled to his side and then up on his knees to lean across the length of the wagon. He pointed at the bread and said, "*Bogacha.*" He looked at Emil and his eyes widened as he pointed to the stew: "*Puyo.*" His large finger pointed again at the bread, "*Bogacha,*" and back to the stew, "*Puyo.*" Emil nodded and smiled. "I understand. *Puyo. Bogacha.* Chicken pepper stew and bread. Thank you."

The Gypsy man patted the flat of his broad chest and said, "Tobar."

Emil introduced himself the same way, adding, "German. I'm German. You are Gypsy?"

Tobar's eyes narrowed and his entire countenance changed. In a hissing voice, he said, "Roma!" Even on his knees he towered over Emil, who couldn't prevent himself from cowering as he pressed the wooden tray tightly against his thighs and waited for a blow that never came. Tobar growled, "No Gypsy!"

At this point, Emil expected Tobar to lash out or take the food away. Looking the dark man in the eye, he said. "I apologize." He patted his chest, "Emil — German," then pointed to Tobar. "Tobar—Roma."

Tobar smiled broadly, the apology apparently accepted, and Emil shuddered with relief. That was one mistake he wouldn't make again. As he focused once more on his stew, he hoped there wouldn't be too many of these terrifying lessons while he was accepting the hospitality of the Roma.

THE SECOND TIME Emil awakened, it was as though he were being sucked up into a nightmare vortex in hell. Fire. Bright lights of explosions. Screaming men. He heard his own voice and felt the rat-tat-tat of his heart, which he first thought came from a German Maxim machine gun.

Pressure on his left leg brought him fully awake. Tobar's big mitt had hold of his calf, and he spoke words Emil didn't understand. The tone was comforting, reminding him of his father sitting at his bedside when he was ill as a small boy. Gradually, the staccato of his heart slowed to a normal pace.

The pain in his right rib was acute, so Emil shifted carefully to the left, turning his hips, and pulling his knees toward his chest. Tobar gave his foot one final pat, then let go, and in moments, Emil was drifting again. His last thought was that he wasn't hungry for the first time in many nights.

The third time Emil awakened, he lay on his back and bright light poured into the cave of the wagon. As though from far away, a soft babble of voices ranged back and forth over his head—on the left, a deep rumble of words; on the right, a higher, softer woman's voice.

Surely he was dying—perhaps dead. They must be conferring about disposing of his remains. He could not force himself to care. His skin didn't feel sufficient to hold him, and with each breath, he became lighter, as though ready to leave his unresponsive body. His lungs burned so badly that he nearly lost consciousness. Shivering and racked with coughing, he couldn't prevent tears from oozing out and dripping down his cheeks in runnels of heat. Soft hands touched his forehead, his face, his chest. Someone removed the bandage on his left hand. A woman half-sang soothing words in soft tones. Something hot and flat was pressed inside his shirt, and he passed out.

A FAINT LIGHT sliced in through the crack of curtain at the rear of the wagon, and Emil heard cocks crowing. He sat up, feeling muzzy-headed and confused. His tongue was as dry as a log. Coughing and clearing his throat, he realized he was as thirsty as he had ever been. More coughing brought up phlegm. He picked up a rag lying next to him and spat in it. His hand throbbed, and he touched the smooth material wrapped around his palm. Someone had changed the makeshift bandage. He closed his hand, not quite into a fist. Without his little finger, it was never going to be the same, but perhaps he would not lose the hand after all. He no longer felt fire and sharp tingling from his palm and up his arm, only an uncomfortable pulsation.

He was alone. In Tobar's place sat a pile of clothing. Emil found a button-up shirt, knickers-length pants, undergarments, and long socks, darned many times. But no shoes or boots.

The back curtain whisked open, and a vaguely familiar-looking man leaned into the wagon and smiled through his thick beard. "*Droboy tume Romale.*" In German, he said, "That basically means good morning. Are you feeling better?"

Emil hesitated, then said, "Yes, sir."

"Are you as crazy today as you were that first night?"

Blushing, Emil shook his head. "No, sir. I am not. I apologize—"

The man cut him off with a wave. "My name is Mikhail Gallo, and I believe I'm the only one here who speaks sufficient German for you to communicate. If you stay with us, you must learn the Romany language."

Emil gulped. "Stay?"

"Why, yes. You are a man in trouble, are you not?"

Emil sat, swathed in blankets, wondering if he had talked in his sleep. "How do you know that?"

Mikhail raised his hands, palms up. "I know a man in trouble when I see one. Besides, you are a soldier, and soldiers do not travel alone so far away from the battlefield unless they have a problem."

Emil let out a groan. He didn't wish to think of battlefields, nor of trenches and mud, of screaming, nor of flying body parts after bombs crashed down upon him. He didn't ever want to think of any of it again, but this man would expect it. He met the other man's eyes. "You would not believe me if I told you."

"*Si khohaimo may patshivalo sar o tshatshimo.* That means 'there are lies more believable than the truth.' You will tell us more after we breakfast. First, you must gather your things." Mikhail slung a green knapsack over the wagon's gate. "We found this pack down near the river."

"Thank you. There's not much in there."

"I saw that." He gestured away from the wagon. "In a few minutes, the women will be done washing at the river, and you and I shall go to wash. Wait here."

He disappeared, then returned a moment later and offered Emil a mug. "It's only coffee, but it's warm and contains some milk. Your response, in Romany, is *gestena*. That means, simply, thank you."

"*Gestena*, Herr Gallo."

"No 'Herr' or 'Master' here. You know me by Mikhail, and I know you by Emil, if I may?"

"Yes, sir—I mean, yes, Mikhail. *Gestena*, Mikhail." He took a sip of the coffee, and it was like nothing he had ever tasted before. The coffee flavor was there, but so was a pungent sweetness and some sort of strong spice. Though hot enough to bring tears to his eyes, he couldn't keep from slurping at it as he discovered he was, again, ravenous.

"I shall return in a few moments. Please do not speak to anyone until we are around the fire to eat. In fact, disregard the entire *kumpania* until you have washed."

"All right, Mikhail." Emil was more than glad to steer clear of the rest of the group. His mouth tasted like he had dined on a dead dog, and from sweat and illness, his body smelled like one.

Mikhail disappeared, then strolled by a while later and tossed boots into the wagon. Emil, who had by then drained his coffee, scrambled forward and grabbed at the black boots. Though barely recognizable, they were his. Someone had worked saddle soap and boot blacking into them. The leather, which had been stiff and dry when last he wore them, was now soft again. After pulling on the clean pair of pants, he slipped his feet into the boots, leaving them unlaced. Dressed in his dirty shirt and soldier's coat, he would make his way to the river to wash up, but once there, he planned to change into the new set of clothes.

Today, he was a new man.

MISCHKA FINISHED EATING the porridge in her clay bowl and waited for her father and Gunari to return from the river with the strange man. Not a single boy was anywhere to be seen. It wasn't fair. Even the small boys could go down to the river to watch the soldier, but she was stuck here, feeding and watering the chickens. Most days it was merely an inconvenience to be a girl; today it was a true impediment.

Mischka twisted a piece of leather to release the slatted wooden door, and Khania, her pet chicken, squawked and stepped out of the cage. She had trained the little hen from birth, and as far as Khania was concerned, Mischka was her mother. The chicken allowed Mischka to pick her up and cradle her in one arm as the girl set about letting all the chickens out. Their wings were clipped to prevent them from flying away, but Mischka didn't think they would ever go far. They knew a good meal when they saw it.

"Chook, chook, chook," Mischka said. The last chicken popped out of the coop. She hurried to clean out the soiled straw, then scattered feed, knowing that at any moment the men could return. She didn't want to miss one minute of watching them eat breakfast.

She wondered what Gunari would do with the wild man. A tiny village nearby would likely take him in. He could also stay with the *kumpania*. A fair number of runaways had joined their caravan over the years. Her own father had, in fact, run from an oppressive foster family when he was only fourteen, and Palko, who had been the leader before Gunari, had adopted him as his own.

After she finished putting new straw in the coop, Mischka raced across the clearing, taking an alternate path down to the river so as not to run into the boys and men. She had never washed her hands and arms and face so quickly in her life. Before most of the other girls and women arrived, she was drying her hands with a cloth hanging on the branch of a sapling. She ran back up the slight incline, burst into the clearing, quickly located the soldier, and skidded to a stop. She wanted to watch his face, to see whether she could detect guile in his heart. Her father, when pressed, had told her earlier in the morning that the man was not an evil spirit. He had merely been ill and hungry. She wished to determine for herself if this was so.

Mischka's mother and the other cooks served the men first, then the children and themselves. Mischka squatted far enough from the fire to avoid the heat, but close enough to see the soldier's face. Holding her bowl of scrambled eggs and lamb to her chest, she propped herself against a fallen tree trunk, and studied him as he ate. Since he didn't speak their language, various of the women began speaking of him as though he weren't there.

Gunari's wife Tshaya said, "He seemed a lot larger when he burst upon us."

"It's true," Jeta said.

Mischka's Aunt Patia said, "He's not so much now, is he, Lumi? Your Stevo is bigger than he is."

"You have to remember how he startled us," Lumi pointed out. "And the gun — well, that would make Lenner look big." The women tittered.

"He's not so bad looking," Jeta said. "Perhaps, if he's a good man, he might be interested in Drina or Tawni."

Both girls were of marrying age, but their parents had yet to find husbands for them. At the next big summer encampment, many marriages would be arranged. Mischka thought that no one would be interested in Tawni, who was petulant and cranky most of the time. Mischka wouldn't be sad to see her go and hoped someone would come up with a dowry for her. Tawni's cousin, Drina, was a different story. No one ever knew what she thought or felt as she was so quiet all the time. She went about her business, doing her work, keeping her own counsel. It seemed to Mischka that Drina spent more time talking to the horses than to human beings.

She would marry Drina, Mischka thought, but there wasn't enough gold in the world to make her marry Tawni. Upon reflection, it occurred to her that in six or eight years, she would be expected to accept a suitor from the pool of boys, not the girls. She frowned, dropped her spoon in the empty bowl, and looked around the fire at the boys. She would never marry Boldor or Zurka. Maybe Milosh — but *not* his brother, Cam.

She and Cam had a contentious competition. He had been born half a year after her, but he tried to act like her superior. She could run faster, throw more accurately, and pin him to the ground any time they wrestled. He didn't take too kindly to her besting him.

She rose and took her bowl to her mother. "Do you want more, my little Mischka?" Lumi asked.

"No, Mama, but thank you. It was good, and I am full."

Lumi smoothed thick black curls off Mischka's forehead. "You must be growing, child. You eat as much as me."

"Soon I will be as tall as Papa."

Lumi laughed. "Perhaps. Perhaps not. We'll just wait and see."

Mischka leaned into her mother, her head against Lumi's arm. "Mama, what will happen to the man?"

"I don't know. That is up to Gunari to decide. Do you have any thoughts to share?"

Mischka shook her head. "He doesn't seem like a bad man."

"No, he doesn't."

Chapter
Four

Southern Poland, October 1918 (Blood Moon)

THAT HE COULD speak so little Romany embarrassed Emil. Of course he had been trying to learn the language only for a fortnight. He clutched at the words, the intonation, the phrasing, but most of it ran through his mind like dreams that flit away upon awakening. He didn't know why it was so difficult. After all, he was conversant in French, knew a smattering of Polish, and his German syntax and usage had been perfect in school. Though he tried hard to understand what the talkative troupe was saying, their words ran together in one fast, long string. To make matters worse, half the time, three or four were talking at once, and then he was lost completely. Mikhail had to translate, which made Emil uneasy. If he didn't learn the rudiments of the language soon, he worried they would put him out.

Then Mischka took him under her wing. At first, he held himself aloof from the women and children, but Mischka was relentless. After a time, he came to understand that she wanted to teach him Romany nearly as much as she wanted to learn German. He thought it odd that this slim, dark-haired girl was named Mischka, which meant "Little Mikhail." But she idolized her father, and the name suited her. She also looked exactly like him, though softer and much leaner.

She was an unusual child, different from the others in the *kumpania*. Today she stood beckoning him from across the clearing. Her black, wavy hair hadn't been tamed in days. A hint of gold, nearly lost in the tangle of hair, glittered in earlobes pierced by hoop earrings. Dressed in boots, brown breeches, and a long-sleeved yellow blouse stained with fruit from the morning breakfast, she looked like a wild boy. If her hair were cut short, he would have a hard time guessing she was a girl, but that would change, of course, as she grew into a maiden.

She opened the coop and tossed out a chicken. "Look," she

said to him in German. *"Khania."*

He knew the word meant chicken. He'd eaten a lot of it lately. *"Khania.* That means chicken in German."

"No," she said, shaking her head. "Khania is her name, her own special name."

"Ah, I see. You named your pet chicken 'Chicken.'" He grinned and pointed toward the shepherd dog frolicking with the boys on the other side of the clearing. "Is the dog's name 'Dog'?"

A look of sheer delight came to her face. "Spike! The dog is Spike!" Now it was his turn to laugh. She had learned the German word for dog and easily constructed a sentence. With her free hand, she pointed beyond him at the forest. "That is a tree." Next to the cooking pots over the flames, she said, "Fire."

He strode toward the chicken coop, indulging her, as they exchanged words in both German and Roma.

He tried not to laugh, but he, too, felt the glee that she displayed. Mischka was one quick study. If she was going to work so hard to learn his language, he was definitely going to learn hers.

"Stop," he said. She stood by a huge bay mare. He pointed at the dark horse and in Romany said, *"Grai."*

"Pferd!" she said back in German, excitement in her voice.

He gestured to her, and as she drew closer, he pointed to his left hand, but before he could say anything, she said, *"Hand!"* Her black eyes shining, she advanced, grabbed for his left hand. "Bad hurt." She traced the scar on his palm and shook her head sadly at his lack of a little finger.

"Yes," he said. "Ouch."

She gave him a beseeching look, but he chose to ignore it, not wanting to explain how he'd lost his finger and permanently scarred his hand. The skin was still tender and his grip uncertain. A heavy weight settled in his stomach, but when he met her eyes, he could tell she wasn't pressing him.

They continued around the clearing naming everything in sight, much to the amusement of Mischka's mother, Lumi, and her Aunt Patia. When he or she didn't know a word in the other's language, they stopped to figure it out, then repeated it over and over, and he had no doubt she would remember it. He decided he had better pay close attention or this young girl was going to get the best of him.

Mischka's father emerged from the forest, followed by Gunari and two older men, Nicolae and Nanosh, whom Emil didn't know very well. Mikhail came toward the coop as the others headed toward the fire. In German, he said, "I see my daughter is keeping you busy, Emil."

"That she is, Mikhail. I've never seen anything quite like it."

"Yes, she picks up words very quickly. Already she understands some of your German. She knows a smattering of Hungarian, many Polish words, and even some French, though she has never been to France yet. Right, my Mischka?"

She squinted up at her father, a wide grin revealing her two half-grown front teeth. "*Oui, Papa.*"

MISCHKA HAD NEVER been fonder of wood detail than during the late October days. She hastened through the trees, picking up sticks and chunks, keeping busy as she worked hard to memorize the various moon celebrations. October was Blood Moon, a time to remember all that the Old Ones, alive and dead, had passed on to the wanderers who were left behind. For her mother and father, their parents, her grandparents' parents, and back further than she could logically understand, travel had been a way of life. She knew that in one day, depending upon the terrain, the troupe could cover fifteen miles—or as little as four or five if the ground was rough or an axle broke. She couldn't comprehend that the Old Ones had traveled thousands of miles.

But the Blood Moon occupied only one part of her mind today. She also dwelt on the fire that burned about a hundred yards from the regular campsite. No small children were allowed to sit at the ceremonial fire, and the older girls and women were required to stay around the main fire where they talked and laughed as they prepared the coming meal. Mischka's older brothers were allowed, as were Tobar and any other young men who were interested.

Every young man was acutely interested.

Mischka wished she could attend, especially tonight, when Emil would be answering some of the questions everyone wanted to ask. The thought stayed with her as she finished wood collection, and when no one was looking, she crept to the east and doubled back and around, inching along from tree to tree until she was within earshot of the ceremonial fire.

Eight men, heads of the families, were seated on logs and stumps that formed a circle. Emil sat with them. Slightly behind the older men, a dozen young men sat cross-legged. Wineskins and tobacco changed hands, and much light-hearted teasing went on, particularly toward Gunari's adult son, Bersh, who was struggling with discipline for his little son, Lennor. The six-year-old had recently wandered away by himself without permission and fallen into the remains of a dead skunk. Everyone could tell when he was in the vicinity. For a moment, Mischka thought she smelled the sour odor, but then she decided she was imagining it.

Gunari said, "Let's get to the business at hand. Mikhail, would you be so kind as to exchange places with me so you can sit next to our young friend and translate?" The leader patted Emil on the thigh, which seemed to surprise the soldier. From her post behind a tree and shrouded in low brush, Mischka saw he looked nervous.

"It's time for you to tell your story, Emil." Gunari took a deep draw from his homemade cigarette and passed it to his left. "Tell us of the land from which you come and the cataclysmic events that have brought you to us."

Emil blanched and looked down into the fire, then around the ring at the calm faces there. Beyond Gunari sat Gyorgy and Tobar. He met Tobar's eyes, and Tobar nodded in encouragement.

Gunari said, "Don't worry, young man. Just start at the beginning, perhaps with the circumstances of your birth."

Emil hesitated, as if to gather both his thoughts and his courage. "I was born in 1899 in a farming village outside Reims, in the Champagne-Ardennes region of France." He looked around the circle, then at Mikhail. "Do they know where that is?"

Mikhail shrugged. "We have rarely traveled that far northwest, but I will try to make it clear to them."

"All right then," Emil continued, pausing every few sentences for Mikhail to relay his words. "My father's parents were German and French. They lived in France, in a city called Reims, for many years until they died. My mother is German, from the Strausbourg region. Her parents still live in Germany. The first time I remember visiting them, I was five. That was just after my brother Hans was killed when a coach and horses ran him over in Reims."

A chorus of voices rang out. "So young."

"Dreadful misfortune."

"That is a terrible thing to happen to a child."

"Yes, it was," Emil said. "My sister, Pauline, who we nicknamed Pippi, was born when I was six. Shortly after, my father fell ill and could no longer work the farm. We moved from Reims to live in Germany, near my mother's parents. It was difficult for me at first. I didn't know the language, and I didn't have near the skills for learning it that Mikhail's daughter Mischka seems to have."

Mischka smiled with delight at the unexpected praise and

crawled closer to the group, not wanting to miss a single word.

"I, of course, learned German rather well after all. I was fond of school, so much so that I determined to be a teacher of history and geography. Then two years ago my father died, leaving my mother, sister, and me alone. We had some money, but not enough. My mother is a fine seamstress, and my sister and I did whatever work we could. But then the officials came and took me into the military." He shuddered. "I thought the training phase was barbaric, but it was nothing compared to the infantry. We were transported east, far into Poland, and then marched miles and miles over hills and through forests, lugging equipment and supplies, stopping in villages and seizing their stores. We finally came to the front and settled there, under fire. When we advanced, we dug ditches and foxholes and made them our homes. By the time a fortnight passed, much of our battlefield had been bombed. I spent more time helping to carry the dead and injured than actually shooting."

He shuddered again. "After a time, I don't even know how long, I knew that there was no way I would get out of the war alive. We were strafed and shelled, and one by one, my comrades died ugly, horrifying deaths. The rain poured down, the skies bled upon us, and I stopped caring whether I lived or died."

Emil's face twisted in pain. He gestured toward the wineskin Gunari held loosely in his lap. "Would you mind, sir, if I had a little of that?"

Gunari hefted the wineskin into the air over the fire. Half-standing, Emil caught it with shaking hands and settled back into his place. After taking a couple of deep pulls, he passed it to Mikhail then stared vacantly into the fire for a moment. When he spoke again, his voice was calm and mechanical.

"Then came the worst day. Bomb after bomb fell. Explosions and debris. Blood and dirt and body parts. So many bombs from such tiny little craft." He sighed. "I had already sent goodbye letters to my mother and to little Pippi, my sister. We held our position, praying that reinforcements from the north would come in time. They did not. Once, I looked up, and through the smoke, I could see the outline of the pilot in a British aeroplane. And then more bombs fell and there was screaming...someone crying for help. An officer's head blew off, and I screamed out myself. Gunfire took the rifle right out of my hands. The barrel was ruined, so I picked up the dead officer's pistol. There was so much roaring and rumbling and flames..." His voice was filled with bewilderment. "So much fire. I don't know how that could be, since we were up to our ankles in water and mud. But the fires of hell sprang up all around me. I crawled to the end of the foxhole. They were all dead. To a man. Dead."

Panting as though he were about to pass out, Emil said, "I crawled out of the foxhole and ran away from the shooting until I came to a stand of trees. The noise of the aircraft above was deafening. I looked back and saw a bomb falling. It blew my foxhole to pieces. All I could see was a huge crater and — and — " He leaned forward and looked like he was going to pass out.

Mischka felt sick for him. She almost wished she were not hearing this story, but at the same time, there was no way she could creep away and not hear the end.

Mikhail handed the wineskin to Emil again, and he downed a sizable gulp. When he started to hand it back, Mikhail shook his head. "No, you keep it. You need it more than any of us do. Please go on when you're ready."

Emil sat for a moment, the wineskin clutched to his chest, then said, "You can't imagine how it was — like I'd been transported into a strange nightmare. The dust and dirt rained down like a blanket of fog. I fled through the forest...tripping over logs...slipping in mud. I didn't even know my little finger was gone and my palm was chewed to the bone. When I noticed blood dripping all over the place I took off my pack, found a handkerchief, and bound it up. I threw out everything I didn't need. All I kept was rations and a shirt and socks. And then — I just ran."

He paused, looked around the circle. In a bitter voice, he added, "I kept on running like the coward I am. Days I hid and slept. From dusk until dawn I kept moving, continually orienting myself into Poland as far away from battle as I could. I don't know where I thought I would go. Who would want a man like me?"

He passed on the wineskin and waited for Mikhail to translate. To Mischka it seemed that Emil's sorrow carried through the forest to her, where it lodged in her throat and chest like a heavy stone.

"After a time, I had consumed all the meager rations in my pack," he said. "Then I ate berries and used the gun to shoot whatever I could. I had some sort of hedgehog on a spit once. It was bitter and tough, but I had to eat. And then I ran out of bullets. I may be wrong, but I think I had traveled for ten — no, perhaps eleven — days without anything more than apples, plums, dying berries, and stream water. The nights were cold and so damp, and I lacked warm clothes. By the time I discovered your camp, I was out of my head from pain and hunger and lack of sleep. Perhaps you will one day forgive me for my terrible behavior."

He hung his head, and all was silent around the fire for a few moments.

Mario, partially blind and the oldest man in the troupe, cleared his throat. In a slow, deep voice, he said *"Jek dilo kerel but dile hai but dile keren dilimata."*

Mikhail nodded. "He says 'One madman makes many madmen and many madmen makes madness.'"

"Is he speaking of me?"

Mikhail smiled. "No, of course not. He is speaking of those who make war and send young men to their deaths. You have emerged from madness, Emil. To do anything but run away would have been foolhardy. You are alive now because you were smart enough to flee."

Mario spoke again, *"Kon del tut o nai shai dela tut wi o vast."*

"Just so you know, Mario tends to speak in riddles and adages," Mikhail said. "What he is saying now is, 'He who willingly gives you a finger will also give you the whole hand.' I think what he is getting at is that you have given up a finger for the madness of the war, and it is not cowardice that you did not give the whole hand. You were prepared to fight and die. You bore the horror as long as you could, and then you decided 'Enough!' None of us—" he swept his arms out in front of him "—faults you for what you have done."

Speaking in Romany, he spent a minute relaying this latest part of the conversation. All around the circle the men grunted their assent. If she could have, Mischka would have leapt up from her hiding place and added her own agreement. Wisely, she kept out of sight.

Gunari tapped some tobacco into a scrap of paper and carefully rolled a cigarette and twisted the ends. He struck a match on his shoe and lit the cigarette, sucked in a deep pull, then rose and passed it to Emil. "Now I believe I understand your nightmares, soldier. Were I you, I, too, would dream as you do." He paused. "What you need is a woman."

All around the circle the men grinned. Emil hung his head again, and Nicolae swatted him on the shoulder, obviously teasing him, though it was clear Emil didn't understand his exact words.

"Well," Mikhail said, "without a woman, we can always sing some of your pain away tonight, Emil. We will drink more wine and get out the violins and guitars and bells and every rhythm instrument we own."

One of the boys, Branko, called out, *"Mulengi Djilia! Brigaki Djilia!"*

Mikhail laughed. In German, he said, "Branko is calling for

dirges and sorrow songs. Don't ask me why, but that's what he likes. I was thinking more in terms of *Patshivaki Djilia* — friendship songs."

Mischka wasn't sure what Gunari meant about Emil needing a woman, but she knew that she would one day be a woman. As it was, she was currently a girl. She decided right then and there that Emil could count on her. If he needed someone female, she filled the bill.

"One more thing," Gunari said. "About these nightmares. Some nights they cause you to disturb the camp. I think they will decrease over time, but until they do, there is no use in your needless suffering or in the waking of the *kumpania*. Tobar — and Kako's sons as well — are light sleepers. I propose each night you place your bedroll near one of these young men. They can take turns beside you, and if you call out in the night, they can wake you to let you know you are safe. How is that, boys? Would you do that for Emil?"

Tobar said, "Of course," and the other young men echoed his agreement.

Mischka longed to dash into the circle and inform them all that she, too, would sleep next to Emil and soothe his nightmares, but she restrained herself. The eight men in the inner circle rose. Her eyes widened. If she didn't leave soon she would be caught. Already Nanosh's sons were tramping in her direction, and she knew they were seeking a private spot to relieve themselves.

She wormed her way backwards, crawled behind another tree, and slithered into a patch of brush and away from all of them. Cloaked in the forest, she walked a long way, threading a path through brush and over fallen logs until she looped around west to the stream. She squatted on well-worn stones next to the water and tried to understand the meaning of war. She knew what death was and how the body of the person or animal joined the earth while most spirits returned to live again in some other form. She also understood killing animals for food. Though she hadn't yet wrung a chicken's neck, her mother had explained that it must always be done with respect for the creature and only when the animal's meat was needed.

She understood anger and how one person could enrage another. Many times she had had to stop herself from tackling Cam and bashing his head in. The few times they had tussled, though, she hadn't actually wanted to do more than hurt him enough to make him stop his teasing. Whoever struck first was usually sent to the tent to cool off for hours, which was a worse punishment than teasing.

But that was different from gathering together all the men of a town and going after another town. What could be so important that men would use guns and aeroplanes to kill one another? The worst violence that Mischka had actually seen happened on the road when a Polish horseman started an argument with one of Nanosh's sons, claiming that someone had thrown something at his horse. He dismounted and pushed Simionce to the ground. When Gyorgy intervened, the Pole had slammed a fist in his face. Gyorgy struck him back, and suddenly there was blood everywhere and a pile of men on top of the Pole. When they let him up, he got on his horse and called them "dirty Gypsies" and other names. He rode away screaming that he hated them.

At the time, she had thought the man mad, like a dog bitten by a skunk with rabies. No sane person would attack a group of others — it made no sense.

But she did understand hatred. Often, as they traveled through towns, people called out rude names and shook their fists in the air. She didn't know what her *kumpania* had ever done to deserve that, and it occurred to her that perhaps wars were fought over the same mistaken kind of hatred. Perhaps Emil and the *gajos* had done nothing to deserve the treatment they got. After all, how could Emil have done anything wrong? He was her friend.

Chapter
Five

Southern Poland, October, 1918 (Blood Moon)

THE WEATHER GREW colder, and Mischka was happy they were ready to move south. After a hasty breakfast, the *kumpania* packed up and prepared to leave. From their time at the clearing, they had gathered two cartloads of wood, six metal containers of drying deer jerky, a variety of fruits, and enough stewed rabbit to last days. Although they had often stopped over the years in the nearby Polish town, Gunari decided not to go there after scouts came back and reported that they saw soldiers in the distance. Gunari's decisions were usually sound, and it was rare that any of the men disagreed. Occasionally one of the wives brought a vision or dream to her husband who then relayed it to him. More often than not, Gunari listened to the man and took heed of the woman's advice or intuition. This time, there was nothing to share.

Mischka worked quickly to stow the chickens in their coop on the dogcart. Her pet hen, Khania, complacently allowed Mischka to put her in the coop, but the two roosters were less than cooperative. Mischka was pecked twice before she got them tucked away. The hens with the new chicks were no trouble, but one hen persistently eluded Mischka. After a time, she grew so frustrated that she just wanted to kick the squawky little chicken, but she couldn't get close enough for that. Finally, she closed up the coop, helped her mother carry the last of the cooking pots to the *vardo*, and climbed in.

Wagons packed, tents stowed, children accounted for, and all but one chicken collected, the caravan pulled away from the clearing and rolled slowly down a narrow track. Their leader sat in the front wagon urging on his two horses. The Gallo horses and *vardo*, sixth in line, rolled merrily along pulling the chicken coop behind. Mikhail and Lumi sat up front to guide the horses, and Mischka lounged on the rolled-up tent in the back, eating a thick slice of bread covered with honey. The other two *vardos* trailed them, followed by the people who chose to walk. At this slow pace, not much dust rose, but once they got into flatter, less rocky land, it would be no fun to walk in the wake of the churning wooden wheels.

They had progressed less than a quarter mile when Mischka heard a cackle. A white bundle of indignant hooting streaked by, low to the ground. She rolled her eyes and sighed. That cursed chicken. If she ever got her hands on —

"Mischka!" Her father's voice was sharp.

"Yes, Papa?"

"Why is that chicken loose?"

She scooted forward on her knees toward the flap at the front of the wagon. "Papa, I hate that chicken. Every day I chase her. Every day she dodges me. She is more work than she's worth. I couldn't catch her this morning, so I left her behind."

Mikhail handed the reins to his wife and turned in his seat to look down into the darkened opening. In a firm voice he said, "We leave no one behind, Mischka, not even a being no more significant than a chicken. You will get out of this *vardo* now and find that chicken, even if it takes you days. We will all wait." He reached up high, to a nail set into the wood of the wagon, and removed a whistle strung on a leather cord. He blew two short, high-pitched blasts as Lumi slowed the horses. The caravan ground to a halt. Mikhail hopped down and gave a wave to Corin ahead of him. "No problems, my friend. Just a lost chicken." Corin passed the word to Kako ahead of him, and the news spread about the *kumpania*.

It took her five minutes to corner the stray hen, and only with the help of Emil, Branko, and Tobar was Mischka able to capture her. Red-faced and angry, she stuffed the chicken into the coop and looped the door shut. When she climbed up into the back of her family's *vardo*, her father grinned down at her through the open flap.

"We might have to get a leash for that one, ay?"

She settled onto the rolled-up tenting, her face set in embarrassed indignation.

"Tut, tut, Mischka. You are more like that chicken than you would care to admit, and we haven't leashed *you* yet."

Her mother called out, "Though sometimes we'd like to," laughing as she said it.

As he turned, Mikhail said, "And we don't ever plan to leave *you* behind." He blew three short toots on the whistle, and the caravan moved on.

THEY CONTINUED AT a leisurely pace for the rest of the day, passing two bands of Polish travelers. The first group hurried by, barely giving them a wave, but in the forenoon, they came to a talkative bunch made up of six young men on horseback. A hearty-looking lad named Budzyn, who said he hailed from outside Jaroslaw, led the conversation with Gunari, Mikhail, and Koloro, who spoke the most fluent Polish. Budzyn was so friendly that the Romany leader asked the young men to join them for a meal.

In short order, the horses and wagons were pulled to the side of the road, and the men set out rugs to sit upon while the women prepared a cold repast. The Poles contributed a gunnysack full of pears and apples, and when everyone had slices of fruit and pieces of lamb jerky and *bogacha* bread with honey, Gunari asked their guests, "What news have you of the war?"

"Depending on the side you favor," Budzyn said, "it is either very good or very bad. The Germans were prevailing, but the Allied forces are winning now. Many terrible battles have occurred. You may have heard that in mid-summer, the Russian tsar and all of his family were assassinated by Russians."

Gunari said, "Tsar? Their leader and all his family have been killed?" Budzyn nodded and Gunari shook his head and relayed the information in Romany.

Mikhail said, "I could understand the political overthrow — even the killing — of the leader, but to kill his family, too? That's barbaric."

Budzyn went on. "The British and French and their Allied forces are driving out the Germans. It's only a matter of time, and the war will be over. The western front crumbles. Too many have died. The support for the Germans has disappeared."

"How is it you men have avoided the soldier's role?" Gunari asked.

Budzyn grinned, showing crooked white teeth. "Poland is a land divided. The Germans have conscripted many into their army. We do not share their political views. We went north, to Prussia, and worked in a factory there."

"I see," Gunari said. "We must admit to sharing *your* point of view. The Roma are a people unto themselves, too. We're not considered a part of the nationalities among whom we travel, and yet we are partly descended from all these nationalities."

"We understand," Budzyn said. "In Prussia, Gypsies — or as you say, Roma — are persecuted and, in fact, outlawed. Special laws against your people have been passed. You have to have a permit to travel there, and it's no longer safe. You would do well to avoid that country."

"We became aware of these new laws some years ago," Mikhail said. "We avoid Prussia and all other lands where we are mistreated. We have an old saying, 'Bury me standing—I've been on my knees all my life.' My people have never been well-respected, I'm sad to say. Thank you for your concern."

Obviously seeking to break the tension, Budzyn elbowed the man sitting next to him. "Rakoski here has come into some money from his family. We may all end up working for this famous new Polish robber baron."

Rakoski laughed and made a circular motion near his temple with his index finger. "The man's gone crazy. My grandfather has died and left me, the only grandson, a house and farm. These miscreants have agreed to help me work it. I am no robber baron."

Gunari smiled. "Don't worry. We didn't see you as such. You have a long distance to travel now?"

Budzyn nodded. "Yes, we are traveling carefully, though, working hard to avoid conflict. Please do not mention our passage."

"We will keep this visit among ourselves," Gunari said.

Koloro, who had been busily translating, asked a question of his own for the first time. "You say the war is soon over. When?"

Rakoski said, "In the letter from my family, my father said that many predict by year's end."

Mikhail translated this information for all the travelers, and the Roma let out a whoop of excitement. Mischka understood this announcement—whatever madness had caused Emil so much pain and suffering was ending. She looked for him and saw with surprise that he was no longer sitting with the group. She moved from her cross-legged position and up on her knees to survey the area. In the rear of the caravan, she saw him with Drina, sitting on a log by the last *vardo*. Mischka was torn between curiosity about what had drawn him away and the desire to listen to more of what the Polish men had to say. When Budzyn spoke next, she turned her attention to the group.

"Many of the villages ahead are tolerant of your people, but I would suggest you send a vanguard to ascertain this. You will also find another caravan ahead of you perhaps some seventy or eighty miles. I don't know if you will catch up with them, but they, too, were kind to us."

Gunari said, "It is our pleasure. *Latcho drom*, meaning we wish you a safe journey."

The men rose and shook hands. Budzyn beckoned to Gunari, and the elder followed him to his horse. "Perhaps you could use

this?" He withdrew a six-inch jackknife from the depths of a
saddlebag.

Gunari's eyes lit up. "It is fine!"

"Yes, it is," Budzyn said. "I have more than one. This is
what we made at the factory."

Gunari opened the first of two blades and touched the edge
to his thumb. "Very sharp. Very fine. *Gestana.* Thank you. Let us
give you sufficient food for your journey."

Following the final exchange of gifts, the Poles headed
north, and the *kumpania* resumed their southern trek.

After the first mile, Mischka grew bored. She slipped over
the wagon's gate and onto the narrow running board, let go of
the *vardo,* and leapt into a patch of weeds off to the side. She
landed and rolled, popping up before her mother had even
noticed her absence. Grinning mischievously, she stepped out of
the weeds and brushed twigs and moisture from the seat of her
pants. Her body was alive with heat. All around the air smelled
sweet, and she heard the cry of a hawk. Far above and off to her
left, a woodpecker made a rat-tat-tat sound into the wood of a
tree, and when she licked her lips, she could still taste honey
from a slice of bread she'd eaten earlier. Her stomach was
pleasantly full.

Out loud in Romany, she said, "Magical." Then with a smile,
"*Magique.*" She skipped a pace. "*Mágikus.*" Another pace.
"*Zauberisch.* Magical, magical, magical," she said in every
language she knew.

She jogged toward the rear of the procession, wondering
how to say 'magic' in Polish. No matter how hard she willed the
word to surface in her memory, it would not. She decided that no
one had ever told her that word, and she wished she had thought
of it when Budzyn and his Polish friends were still there.
Perhaps it was a word her father or Gunari might know. She
resolved to ask when she got the chance.

She found her brothers leading horses, as were Drina and
Emil. Cam and Milosh rode the horses Gyorgy and Stevo led,
and Mischka held back her disappointment. How did Cam get
there before her? His *vardo* was ahead of her own parents' and
she hadn't seen him slip away. Oh, well, she could ride one of
the other mounts. Emil held the reins for a big, black bay named
Harman as he and Drina walked down the middle of the road.
Harman's brother Samuel, who looked almost exactly like him,
walked sedately along the edges of the road ahead of four roans.

When Mischka asked if she could ride Samuel, Emil hoisted
her up onto the tall horse, all the while smiling warmly at Drina.

Mischka landed with her face in Samuel's mane and the

front of her pressed against his broad, warm back. She squeezed with both legs and arms and let out a humming noise of pleasure as she sat upright, hoping Samuel understood from her hug how much she liked him. "I love to ride a horse," she sang in a droning voice.

Emil gripped her calf and said, "You are happy."

"*Tak. Ja. Oui.*"

In German, he said, "You are incorrigible, Mischka."

"I don't know that word."

"You *are* that word." He let go of her calf and left her wondering.

THE CARAVAN WOUND its way down an incline as the warm sun gradually receded, dropping low behind the trees. Some time earlier, they'd spied a grove far down in the valley, and Gunari now led them toward the spot, which everyone agreed was less than an hour away. Mischka saw children playing in a field outside a small town they were passing and asked if the caravan could stop. She longed to go ask the children how to say 'magical' in their tongue, but had to satisfy herself with waving at them as the convoy moved on.

She glanced over at Cam. He looked tired. His eyes drooped and his body sat like a sack on top of the stallion he rode. Milosh had dismounted at the last little village and retreated to a wagon for a nap. Mischka refused to miss out on anything, so she ignored her increasing fatigue. Emil and Drina still walked beside Samuel, and Mischka was surprised to hear the gentle murmur of Drina's shy voice, and especially surprised that she was speaking to Emil, not to a horse. She tried to hear the conversation, but their voices were too soft.

Ahead, some of the men were singing, and their happy voices floated back. Mischka thought she heard drums, but the beat wasn't right. She had never been able to carry a tune, but her rhythm was good, and whoever was keeping time was terribly off. For a moment, she wondered if it was Cam, but then she realized that the drumming was not coming from ahead of her at all, but from behind and it sounded a lot like fast-moving horses.

She glanced toward Cam. He was fully awake now, and they both turned and gazed back. Two men on horseback approached at a gallop. Before she could think to say anything, the men, dressed in gray-green soldiers' uniforms were upon them. Their horses skidded to a stop, and a fair-haired young man holding a rifle dismounted.

The other soldier, a man so fat that his belly lapped over his belt, stayed on his horse and said in Polish, "You will stop. Now."

Mischka understood the insistent man as did her brothers and Tobar, and they slowed the horses to a halt. In broken Polish, Stevo said, "What is the trouble, officer? How can we help?"

The man on horseback said, "We have a report that you are harboring army fugitives. You criminals will stop immediately."

The caravan continued rolling. From her perch, Mischka looked ahead. She could hear the singing voices wafting away as the wagons moved on, and it was clear that no one up ahead knew what was happening.

The man on the ground leveled his rifle at Stevo, who stood slightly ahead of Tobar and Gyorgy with his hands up, palms facing out. "Stop the caravan and bring us all of your young men and the coward malingerers."

Nobody understood the meaning of his last two words. He shouted again, and Mischka looked around, her heart beating madly. She didn't know what to do. Emil stood behind Samuel, shielding Drina, out of sight of the soldiers. The stallion shifted and Mischka realized Emil was bringing him around as the others gradually moved the Roma horses closer together.

The man with the rifle continued to shout commands, then he said to Stevo, "You will kneel. Kneel! Hands behind head!"

Mischka's beautiful dark-haired brother sank to the ground. She opened her mouth to shout, but Tobar, wide-eyed and with his own mouth gaping, caught her eye and shook his head emphatically. She prayed to the goddess of the moon as the soldier held the muzzle to Stevo's head saying over and over, "Where are they? Where are they?"

The soldier on horseback said, "Private Chudak! Wait." He nudged his horse and came closer. Waving a big hand and pointing toward Emil, he said, "You! Behind there. You come out. Her, too. Bring out the girl."

Drina stood in Emil's shadow, peeping around his shoulder. The horses nickered and moved uncertainly. The soldier paid no attention to Mischka or Cam, perhaps because they were clearly small children.

Emil strode forward. "Stop this. These people have done nothing wrong." His Polish was halting, but Mischka and the soldiers understood him clearly.

Private Chudak said, "You must be a deserter. You aren't one of them, and you speak Polish with a German accent. All of these people are cowards. Where are the young men? They will become soldiers. And where are the others?"

Emil said, "Others? There are no others."

"Liar! You will explain fully or I will shoot this man. You have to the count of three. One, two—"

Chudak's rifle made a clicking sound as he shifted and pushed the gun closer to Stevo's head. A flash of movement...a throaty shout...he pulled the trigger...a roar blasted so loud it hurt Mischka's ears.

Emil screamed. He and the private gripped the rifle between them, shouting. Emil brought his knee up. His opponent shrieked and lost his grip with one hand, but he didn't let go. He bent and charged head first into Emil, and they tumbled to the ground.

Tobar and Gyorgy sprang into action. As the mounted soldier reached for a gun in a holster on his hip, Tobar grabbed his leg and pulled. The horseman lost his balance, and the men dragged him to the ground near Emil and Chudak. He rolled to the side. Tobar's fist crashed into the side of his head. The big soldier barely paused.

Chudak and Emil still struggled. Emil wrested the rifle away, and the soldier struck him in the face. Emil raised the gun to protect his head from a second blow. Chudak knocked him to the ground and kicked and punched him.

Gyorgy and Tobar flailed desperately with the huge man, trying to take his pistol. A fist struck out and connected with Tobar's nose. Blood flew everywhere and Tobar fell back. The soldier shouted something guttural and pushed up to his feet, waving the pistol. He aimed the gun at Gyorgy's chest.

With a panicked yelp, Mischka dug her heels into Samuel's side. The horse bounded forward and knocked the soldier to the ground. Screaming, he rolled away from the big hooves, scrambled to his feet, and pointed the pistol at Gyorgy again.

An explosion concussed Mischka's ears, then another. The fat soldier dropped the pistol with a surprised look on his face. A bloom of red spread on his chest. When he opened his mouth to speak, only a gasping sound came out and he crumpled to the ground.

The acrid smell of smoke drifted toward Mischka, and she slowly took in the tableau from left to right. Private Chudak lay motionless on his back with a big hole in his chest. Gyorgy and Tobar, faces bleeding, sat on the ground near the fat soldier, who was also dead. Stevo lay curled in a fetal position on the ground.

Emil had always looked pale, but Mischka thought he had gone even whiter. He lowered the rifle he was holding as though it weighed a hundred pounds, then dropped it and stood, staring, unmoving.

Mischka slid off Samuel, down to the bloody ground, and ran to Stevo. In an instant, Gyorgy was beside her, turning their brother over. A dent in Stevo's forehead seeped blood. Dirt in the wound made it look black, as though red blood and black tar leaked from his brow.

"He's still breathing." Gyorgy cradled the limp body. "He's not shot."

Tears clouded Mischka's vision, and the next thing she knew, strong hands seized her under the arms, and she was clutched to her father's chest. People swarmed all around her. Even half-blind Mario, Tobar's sixty-eight-year-old grandfather, had run to help and was breathing as loud as a dying cow. He held a hammer in his right hand and muttered death curses.

Mischka looked up into her father's face to see it twisted with horror and something else—a kind of helplessness she had never seen before. She squirmed in his arms. "Papa, I am fine. Put me down and see to Stevo." She gazed beyond the horses and saw Emil, frozen in place. "And to Emil," she whispered as he set her gently on the ground.

Everyone shouted and talked at once.

"What happened?"

"Who did this?"

"Who are these men?"

Lumi shrieked, her voice high and frightened. "Tobar!" She fell to her knees in front of him. He sat splay-legged in the dirt, his head tipped back, trying to stanch the blood flow from his nose. He looked as though someone had poured a bucket of red pepper sauce over his face and down his beard and chest.

A blood-red sun shone through the trees as dusk drew near. "It's not so bad, Lumi," he said. "At least I'm not dead like them."

Mischka stepped to the side of the road and squatted down, her knuckles in her mouth. Suddenly she didn't feel it was such a magical day after all.

STEVO DIDN'T AWAKEN for fifteen hours. By the time he did, the soldiers and their weapons were buried far off the road, their clothes burned, and their horses set free. The caravan traveled all night, making no stops, and continued at the speediest pace possible until noon the following day. They paused to sleep for six hours, then resumed travel after dinner until midnight and commenced again at dawn. For three full days they journeyed as far and fast as they could. No fires were set, and they ate bread, fruit, and jerky on the run.

Finally, over a hundred miles later, the caravan came to a stop on the edge of a great forest. As soon as the leader said that they would break their journey, Mischka awakened, wrapped in a blanket in the *vardo* with Stevo nearby. She poked her head out. Grim-faced, Lumi stood on the narrow track next to the furrow of a wagon wheel rut, one hand on her lower back.

"Mama, are you all right?"

"Just sore and tired." Lumi's voice was soft, almost sorrowful. "How are you feeling?"

"I'm hungry."

"I'm a starved bear," Tobar called out. "Stevo! How goes it?"

Mischka looked back at her sleepy brother. The left side of his face and brow were black and blue, and his left eye showed no white, only a swelled up, bloodshot mess.

"I have a headache with no end," Stevo said in a soft voice. He pulled his knees up to his chest and cradled his head in his hands. For a moment, Mischka thought he looked like a small boy.

"I don't blame you," Tobar said. "Come out and go for a walk. Get some water. Move around. It will help, I think. Come out in the light and take a look at my nose. It's as big as a horse's rump!"

That got a laugh out of Stevo. Tobar's big mitt reached in to help her brother down out of the wagon, and Mischka followed them. Everyone was worried about Stevo, and she was, too, but she was even more concerned for Emil. For three days he had followed the caravan on foot or horseback, refusing to rest in any of the wagons. When they stopped to sleep, he laid out his bedroll far apart from the others, and all efforts to engage him in conversation failed. Earlier in the day, Mischka heard her father tell her mother that something would be done once they were safe. She wondered if that would be tonight.

"Nah, nah, nah, Mischka!" Cam pointed and jeered, his dark eyes merry. "You're walking like you have a stick up your behind."

She scowled at him. She was, indeed, walking stiffly. "You have the nose of a dead chicken and the stench to match."

"And your stink is greater than ten dead chickens."

A wicked grin lit her face. "Yours is worse than all the papas breaking wind at once." Both of them stifled giggles, and as they passed next to Nanosh's *vardo*, they bumped shoulders, jostling one another with determined pleasure. She stepped around him, still grinning, and set her sights for the man standing near the horses at the rear of the train. Road dust covered Emil's pants and jacket, and his face and neck were streaked with dried rivulets as though he had sweated and the dust had stayed once the moisture evaporated.

Mischka moved closer and caught a glimpse of his bruised eye, still black and blue from the struggle with the soldier. "Why are you so sad?" she asked, taking his hand. It was limp and dry, like sandpaper, and she could feel the scar that bisected his palm. "Are you worried the *mulé* will get us?"

"What?" He looked at her blankly.

She stepped closer and whispered, "The *mulé*—the ghosts of those bad men." When he shuddered, she hastened to assure him. "Papa says we have outrun them, Emil. Don't worry. They won't haunt us." Hugging his hand and arm to her chest, she said, "Forget about that. Come help set up camp. Come with me."

He didn't budge. She waited, imploring silently until he glanced down at her. Stunned to see a tear on his cheek, she realized the tracks on his face were from crying. She didn't know what to say. Gripping his hand tighter, she said, "You are my friend always, Emil. Please, let's go talk to Papa."

He shook his hand free. "Yes. I will. Go on now. I'll catch up when I have seen to the horses." He turned away and stood outlined against the setting sun, its rays blood-red and gold around him. For the briefest moment, Mischka thought that the sun's beams shone right through him, as though he were disappearing into thin air. But then he moved, pulled a blanket off the horse, and became solid once again.

With a sinking feeling, she turned and scuffed her way from the back of the entourage to the clearing off to the right. She paused next to a fir tree and touched its rough bark. She wished she knew how to make Emil feel better, and she decided she would talk to her mother.

She waited until the sun sank below the horizon and the last light faded. Close to the campfire, Mischka sat on a wooden box next to Lumi. Both of them munched on apples and spooned up *mamaliga*, a warm cornmeal porridge, which was the first hot food that had been prepared in days.

"Mama," she said, "something is wrong with Emil."

"Yes, I imagine so."

"What shall I do?"

"Nothing, child. Leave him be and let your father and Gunari handle it."

"Will we stay here for a while?" She leaned into her mother's warm skirt and set the empty bowl aside.

"I think so. It would be nice to let the chickens get settled. They've laid no eggs these last three days. I'm hoping we'll get a nice batch in the morning."

"I'll go have Khania let her sisters know that we are done running." Mischka rose and slipped an arm around her mother's neck. "Will you tell some tales tonight?"

"Maybe — maybe not. It depends on whether the men wish to talk. You go check on the chickens, and I'll let you know."

As the various families congregated around the fire, Mischka could see, even from a distance, that everyone was tired and preoccupied. The usual joking and boisterous conversation was lacking. Emil sat apart, across the clearing, opposite from the chicken coops. All of the women, even Lumi, avoided him, and Mikhail was the one who brought him a bowl of *mamaliga* and some flat bread. Mischka's heart went out to the ostracized man.

After the meal was finished and the bowls cleared away, Koloro said, "Gunari, we must decide what to do now. He's not one of us, and he has blood on his hands."

Many of the men nodded. Mischka closed the door to Khania's coop and crept closer. She tried to see across the circle where Emil sat on a log near her father's *vardo*. In just the short time he had traveled with the *kumpania*, the German had learned a lot of Romany. She thought he would understand what they were saying, and even though she was bone-tired, she wanted to be able to rise to his defense.

"Yes, it is true," Gunari said. "But without his actions, the lives of Mikhail's sons and daughter, of Tobar, of Nanosh's sons, and perhaps even Nicolae's Drina would have been lost." He paused, then said softly, "Not to mention the rest of us and our fate."

"I do not wish to entice the *mulé* by my statements," one of the men said, "but it would seem to me that the only man suffering is the German. I have no nightmares. My wife and children are not haunted by the ghosts."

"Very true." Gunari pulled at his beard. "He is *gajo*, though, an outsider to us. He is among us, but not of us. What curse could he bring to us as such?"

"What about the soldiers?" Koloro asked. "They seemed to be looking for him."

Tobar said, "Actually, they wanted *all* the young men. It wasn't just Emil they were after."

The elder, Old Mario, spoke. *"Te shordjol muro rat..."*

Everyone waited for Mario to finish. *May my blood spill...* Mischka wondered what he meant by that. She had been told that Mario was close to seventy years old. At age nine, it was hard for her to understand the concept of seventy years, but his wrinkled face, sparse hair, and lack of teeth had always led her to believe he might be the oldest man on the planet. She kept this observation to herself.

He coughed and spat into the fire, then choked out, "May my blood spill before that boy is harmed." No one spoke. The only sound was the crackle of the fire and the quiet whimper of one of the dogs lying asleep near the old man. "Tobar, my loving grandson—he is all I have left. My Tatoya died so many years ago. My son rests in peace. My sisters and brothers are long gone." He cleared his throat again. "May my own blood spill in gratitude for the life of my Tobar. I am sorry the soldiers are dead, but they attacked us. It is regrettable that they would not listen to sense. His God will forgive Emil, or, if He sees fit, he can take me in the German's place as a sacrifice."

He settled back, having spoken more than usual. For the better part of a minute, no one said a word.

Mikhail rose and took in the faces of Mischka's friends and family, aglow in the firelight. Beyond them, Emil sat alone, stiffly, his arms crossed over his chest as though he were cold. Mikhail said, "When I was fourteen years old, I ran away from the beatings my cousin dealt to me. My parents were dead. I had no brothers, no sisters. I was alone. I begged for asylum from a passing group of Roma. Gunari, you know well that your father, Palko, became my father. Lumi and I named Mischka, our little daughter, after your mother, Marona. I honor the memory of your father and mother every day of my life." He gazed up at the sky for a moment before continuing. "This man," Mikhail said and waved a hand to direct the *kumpania* to look beyond the circle to Emil, "is not yet twenty summers old and he has been wounded by the world in a way that resonates with me. He is a brother of the spirit, and I would like to claim him as my own."

Before he could speak further, Gunari rose and put a hand on Mikhail's arm. "Wait. Wait, Mikhail," he said. Standing in the middle of the group, the two men held a whispered conference and when Mikhail sat down he looked satisfied.

The leader of the *kumpania* tapped his toe on the ground and surveyed the open faces all around the circle. His gaze came to rest briefly on Mischka, and she grinned up at him, just barely containing her excitement. If she was understanding things correctly, Emil was about to be adopted into the *kumpania*—and as her brother, no less. She squirmed her way through the people around the fire and made her way to her father, took his hand, and squeezed in next to him, quivering with glee.

Gunari spoke. "Is there anyone among you who opposes the idea of offering the German more than temporary asylum? Take some time to consider."

He removed a cigarette from his pocket, leaned down to the fire, and lit it. While he smoked, the men whispered to one another.

Eventually, Koloro asked, "Do we invite in his *mulé* if we invite him in, too?"

"I don't think so," Gunari said.

"How can we be sure?"

"He has been among us these many weeks, and no *mulé* have haunted any of us. In these past few days, no *mulé* have materialized. They are outsider ghosts — *gajo* ghosts. They'll not trouble us."

Koloro stood for a moment longer, then with an awkward sign to ward off evil spirits, lowered himself back to the log. Taking that as assent, Gunari said, "All right then. Well... Emil Stanek!" His voice thundered across the clearing, obviously startling the German. "Do you understand what is happening here?"

Emil rose as the words were translated. His face was pale, and he shivered from the cold. "No, not entirely."

Gunari squared his shoulders and raised his chin. "I, Gunari Camomescro, son of Palko, grandson of Gunari the Elder, and leader of this *kumpania* ask you to honor me by becoming my adopted son."

Mikhail continued his quiet translation, but there was little need. Emil's eyes widened in understanding, and if it was possible, his face went paler than before. He put his fist to his chest. "I am not worthy." He looked to the ground.

With his hands behind his back, Gunari asked, "How did you come to us?"

Emil swallowed. "By accident. I came upon you in the woods. I was ill and hungry, and you gave me food and care."

"Why have you stayed with us?"

Emil bit his lip, then stammered. "I have nowhere to go. I'm an army deserter. I can't go home to my mother and sister without putting them in danger and facing death or prison. I'm an outcast."

"Where is your father?"

"Dead. He died of a blood disorder some time ago."

"I see." Gunari tapped the tips of his fingers against his chin. "Tell me, why did you kill the two soldiers?"

Emil folded in on himself as though in pain. "I thought we were in mortal danger, that they would kill us."

"Do you wish you could change what happened?"

"Yes."

"If you had it to go back and do again, would you have acted differently?"

Emil sat, his arms folded tightly over his middle. He did not answer right away. When he did, his words came out slow and measured. "Under identical circumstances, no. I would have done the same thing. They were going to kill Stevo. We had to stop that man Chudak. Then the officer in charge aimed for Gyorgy. I saw no other choice."

"And you cannot accept this choice?"

Emil put his elbows on his knees and his head in hands. "No."

"Because they were fellow soldiers?"

"No," he whispered. "Because it's wrong to kill. That's all. It's wrong."

"Yet you would shoot them again, should the same situation present itself?"

He stuttered. "Y-y-yes." More firmly, he said, "It was either them or Stevo and Gyorgy. I chose to let Stevo and Gyorgy live. But that should be God's job, not mine."

Gunari smiled. "Is it not possible that God sent you to us to ensure that Mikhail's sons were not harmed? Is it not possible that you did God's will?" The leader put a hand on Emil's shoulder. "You are haunted by the past, by war, by death. There is only one way to heal from that. You must forgive yourself. You did what you had to do." He removed his hand and stepped back. "We are seldom presented with easy choices. That is part of what manhood is about. I give you a choice now. You have no father; you have no nation, no *kumpania*. It should not be so. You will be my son, live by our laws, protect and be protected by this extended family." He made a sweeping motion with his arm. "We will be your people now, yes?"

Emil looked around at all the faces staring at him. Mischka wanted to leap up and run to him, tell him to agree, hug him tight and tell him all would be well. Instead, she looked up at the moon happily, waiting for the answer she was sure Emil would give.

"Do you find me unfair and dishonest?" Gunari asked. "Will you argue that my judgment is wrong?"

"No. No, sir. I would never insult you in any way."

"Will you then accept my judgment in this matter?"

Emil hesitated, then nodded. "Yes." It came out flat, as though he wasn't sure he could believe what Gunari was offering.

"Then I ask you again, will you accept my guidance, as both father and leader."

"Yes."

Mischka let out a squeal of delight, which she quickly stifled. Gunari laughed. "I think it is time for the women and little ones to go to bed. We men have much to discuss, and I suspect we will be up far into the night."

"Mama," Mischka whispered when Lumi came to claim her. "This means Emil is now my cousin!"

"Yes, I believe you are right." Lumi led her away from the fire and toward the tent.

"I wanted him to be my brother."

"You've already got two brothers."

"True, and I surely wish I had a sister."

"Give it time, Mischka. Give it time."

Chapter
Six

New York City, November 1989 (Snow Moon)

THE SOFT, REPETITIVE murmurs seemed so far away that Pippi incorporated them into a dream of journeying on a train. The clickety-clack of the rails jarred her while the hypnotic motion of the car and the rise and fall of a voice she couldn't quite identify made her feel edgy and nervous. She rose from the scratchy coach seat and gazed out the train window, a portal through which she saw the rolling Polish hills.

She lifted her hand. How strange. Where was her ring? The touch of her index finger to the clear glass left an oval smudge rimmed in red. Her heart beat faster, and her breath stopped in her throat as the fingerprint gradually turned scarlet, thickened, and became liquid. It formed a bead that broke away from the smudge and dripped down the pane.

She stepped back, unable to breathe. The other occupants in the train car slept, but as she hurried to the door, she glanced at a gentleman with slicked-back hair. His face looked gaunt and gray, his mouth twisted in pain. All of her fellow travelers were dead. The decay of many days had set in, and she smelled something rancid, worse than rotting chicken.

Pippi wrenched open the door and burst into the tiny passageway.

The train shook and the engine roared like the din of a thousand machines straining in unison. Pippi no longer controlled her own movement. She floated through the train, followed by the ghosts of people whose voices she could almost recognize. They called to her for help, but she was filled with far too much terror to stop. Panting, sweating, she flew headlong through the empty dining car. At the door, her bare feet touched down, and she felt cool metal against her soles. Where were her shoes? Why was she here?

The cold steel handle of the dining car door spun in her

fingers. With a mighty pull, she ripped the door away. It detached from its hinges and fell against her. With a shriek, she sloughed it off to the side. It fell with a mighty crash that sounded louder than the engines and echoed in her ears.

She heaved herself through the doorway onto the edge of a cold metal platform that swayed in the darkness. The ground streaked by at a dizzying pace. The train jerked rhythmically. Each revolution of the wheels made an unearthly sound, a command she knew she had heard before but defied. *Jump. Jump. Jump. Jump...*

The old hopelessness engulfed her. She put her hands to her face and screamed. A whoosh of wind. The screech of brakes. She lost her balance and tipped forward, and the vertigo became unbearable as she fell, twisting, grabbing for anything, and finding nothing to slow the free fall. She opened her mouth to cry out for help.

PIPPI AWOKE ALONE, her fists tangled in the sheets and pressed to her face, which was wet with tears. Her feet felt as though she'd been walking on an ice floe, and she shook from the cold. She reached out and didn't find the familiar warm figure next to her.

She took deep breaths. Her ribcage rose, and she marveled at how rapidly her heart pounded and how long it took for it to slow to its normal rate. She heard the faraway murmurs again and lay on her back, listening for a little while before creeping from the bed to make her way down the hallway, past the guest rooms and bathroom, and into the living room.

On the sofa, Mischka sat with François and Maria's boy, Tobar. He was positioned sideways on the sofa, his back to Pippi. Moonlight poured in through the front window and bathed his hair in a silver glow. He'd been much younger last time his family had visited, and Pippi hadn't noticed anything special about him then. But this time, his resemblance to her brother Emil struck her as uncanny. She hadn't consciously realized until just now that since Tobar and his family had arrived the day before, she had kept a distance from the boy. Because his younger brother and sister were so rowdy and loud, that hadn't been hard to accomplish, but suddenly she was well aware of the reason why. She waited a moment longer, listening to the lilting tone of Mischka's voice, then stepped into the room.

Mischka's head popped up. "My dear, what are you doing awake?"

Tobar squirmed to his knees, turned, and leaned over the arm of the sofa.

Pippi shrugged. "How can I sleep when I might be missing something of interest?" She shuffled forward carefully and lowered herself into a wooden rocking chair.

"We thought we were keeping our voices down, love."

"You know how I never sleep much anymore. Not at night, anyway." Enough light came in the window for her to see Mischka's smile.

"Tobar and I are talking about old times — long ago, far away old times."

Pippi stiffened. "Why?"

"Tobar is curious about the man for whom he is named and about his ancestors on both sides."

"This must be boring for you, young man." Pippi grasped the front of her robe and twisted it in her hands. "No one cares to hear of old-fashioned times."

"But I do, Grandma. I *do* want to know."

Mischka shot Pippi a pleading look. Pippi wanted to ignore the appeal in Tobar's voice and in Mischka's expression. Lately, the more she tried to block the memories of the past, the more nightmares she seemed to have. To speak of the unspeakable past — to dredge up the anguish, the shame, the gut-wrenching sorrow — this made her feel light-headed.

Tobar hunched down and pulled a corner of the afghan over his lap. "Tell me about the olden days, Grandma, about when you were a little girl. Where did you go to school? What was it like in Germany?"

"Happy times. I am speaking only of the happy times."

"Good," he said with a smile.

There it was again — Emil's grin — and the intense way her brother had focused on other people when he found them delightful. How could she resist?

"Tell me about the happy times, then." With his legs crossed Indian-style, he leaned into Mischka and gazed expectantly at Pippi. "Tell me about one of the happiest days of your life, okay?"

"All right, then. Since I am surrounded by you night owls, I will share a few stories. Let me see. I was born in January 1906."

"Wolf Moon," Mischka said.

"*Ja*, Wolf Moon, and I grew up in a small village in Germany, outside Eisenhüttenstadt, near the border of Poland. My father died when I was young, and my brother Emil who was six years older than me became the man of the house. We lived an ordinary existence, well, until Emil was sent to the war..."

Chapter
Seven

Eastern Germany, May 1920 (Hare Moon)

EAST OF BERLIN, the town of Eisenhüttenstadt sat in the fertile Brandenburg valley near the Polish border. Across the countryside, farmers plowed vast fields, and the hum of insects droned in the early morning light. Farther south, a small village nestled along the edge of a bubbling river. Most of the village's nearly four hundred occupants had been awake and about their business for some time, but on Feder Street, the Stanek household was quiet, the windows still shuttered against the previous night's chill.

A bright sliver of light pierced a crack in the shutters of their bungalow into a tiny room behind the kitchen. The sun's beam was persistent, and Pippi gradually awakened. She lay in her cozy bed in the dim room and listened for her mother's soft footfalls in the kitchen. No sound reached her ears, and she didn't smell coffee brewing or breakfast oatmeal cooking.

With a sigh, she sat up and brushed her hair back and out of her eyes. Her braid had come out, and her thick blonde hair was a wild tangle. She slid out of bed and sought a pair of leather slippers and a thick robe that hung on a peg to the left of her bed.

The door squeaked open, and Pippi stepped into a short hallway. To the left was the doorway to the small room that used to be her brother's. Next to it the washroom door stood open. She passed it and in two steps had a clear view of the narrow room that abutted the wall of her bedroom and served as a larder. Past it, the kitchen was open and more spacious. A bare table, clear counter, and cold stove were proof that Pippi's mother had not yet risen—again. Pippi put her palm to her forehead. Mother, mother, mother... She let out a sigh as she moved through the kitchen to the front room.

After the death of Pippi's father, the tiny upstairs had been turned into a flat, which they rented out to an ancient widow. At one time, the door to the street had opened into a large, welcoming parlor, but now the entire front area of their house had been made over into a sewing room. A treadle machine, racks of thread, and rolls of material were organized all about the room. Partially finished projects covered most of the divan. Stacked bolts of cloth nearly hid the upright piano in the corner. On a tall table near the front door, a clear glass vase sat upon a delicate white lace doily. Cherry branches poked out of the vase, and tiny, decorated eggs dangled from strings, leftover remnants of the recent Easter celebration. That table remained the only surface in the room that resisted being taken over by sewing items.

In the center of the room, a low table held an array of the nearly assembled cloth pieces for a wedding dress. Small imitation pearls in teardrop patterns adorned the bodice, and the expanse of satiny material for the skirting reflected in the dim light. When Pippi had retired the night before, the dress wasn't anywhere near its present state, and she guessed that her mother had stayed up until the wee hours of the morning working on it. Yet there was no rush—the wedding wasn't scheduled until late June.

Pippi thought about her mother's increasingly crazy hours and the moody spells she had been suffering of late, and a feeling of helplessness came over her. Camille Stanek had suffered from insomnia for some time, but ever since their ten-year-old cat, Ludo, had died before Easter, she had slept even less. Their sewing work kept Camille and Pippi busy all hours of the day, and Camille had become a veritable night owl. Pippi, on the other hand, rarely managed to stay awake past ten o'clock.

A handsome wooden clock sat atop a cabinet next to the archway leading to the kitchen. It made a quiet tick-tock sound, and she squinted toward it, remembering that a customer was due at nine. It was only seven-thirty, so she had plenty of time to wash and dress before waking her mother.

Pippi chose a bright blue dress with white trim. She liked it because the sleeves were roomy and it was easy to move in. It also flattered her fair complexion. With a sturdy brush, she combed her hair. The thick, wavy blonde tresses were a constant trial, and it was all she could do to manage an English braid. On festival days she often wove in multicolored ribbons, but today her spirits were far too low to even consider it.

Once her hair was arranged, she went to her mother's door and tapped. No answer. She turned the knob, stepped into the shadowy room, and moved to the side of her mother's bed. Flat grayish blue eyes exactly like her own opened to examine her.

"Pippi."

She lowered herself to the edge of the bed. "Good morning, Mama."

Her mother's arm emerged from under the covers and smoothed a lock of hair over Pippi's ear. "Did you sleep well?"

"Yes."

"Good. We have much work to accomplish today. What time is it?"

"After eight."

"Oh, goodness. The Fleischers will be here soon." Camille tossed the covers off. "We'll take care of them, and then you must go to the market."

"We need another block for the ice box."

Camille agreed. "You can order some later today from Herr Huber." She swung her legs over the side of the bed and rose. Reaching for a light wrapper, she let out a loud yawn. "I certainly could use more sleep."

Pippi studied her mother's lined face. Camille was obviously fatigued and looked older than her forty years. She had aged—almost overnight—upon learning the news of her son's death twenty-two months earlier. She had not been the same since. Distant. Depressed. Preoccupied. Shortly after Easter, Pippi had refused to go to school any longer, staying home instead to keep her mother's spirits up. But she, too, felt the anguish of their losses. *First Papa, then my brother, and now my little Ludo.* She had cajoled her mother about acquiring a kitten, but her mother resisted the suggestion saying that it would be just one more thing to grow dear and then be lost.

On the verge of tears, Pippi didn't stay to watch her mother dress, but went to the kitchen to prepare oatmeal for breakfast. As it simmered, she stood gripping the stove's enameled edge, forcing back her tears. If something happened to Camille, who would take care of her? They were a long way from her father's family who lived far off in the Champagne-Ardennes region of France. How could she live? How would she survive?

IT WAS LATE morning before Camille and Pippi completed the measurements for Frau Fleischer and her daughter, and once the customers had departed, Pippi threw herself on the divan and let out a gasp. "How can you stand it, Mama? I have never seen such rude and presumptuous people in my life!"

Camille looked up from her hand-sewing. A grim smile graced her tired face. "Ah, but they pay well, and to be honest,

Pippi, I double their bill to make up for their discourtesy."

Pippi laughed. "Are you serious?" Her mother's unashamed nod brought out another laugh. "Now I don't feel so bad."

After a simple meal of bread and butter, cheese, apple slices, and tea, Pippi prepared for a walk to the general store three blocks away. She had written a list to which her mother added only one thing: sleeping draught.

Pippi didn't comment when she read her mother's spiky lettering, but she swore her heart skipped a beat. The summer before, their neighbor, old Frau Metzger, had downed two bottles of sleeping draught and passed on into dreamless death. Pippi was sure there was already an entire bottle of the mixture in a small cupboard in the washroom. Before leaving, she checked and found she was right. She concealed the bottle in her room before picking up her basket and bidding her mother farewell.

A blue sky, warm breeze, and the sight of new plant shoots greeted Pippi upon her exit, but she noticed none of it. A block of ice exactly the size of her stomach pressed against her spine, and she felt afraid for herself and her mother. She stumbled on an uneven spot in the path and chided herself to stop worrying.

As she walked along the lane, a horse and rider trotted toward her, and she recognized the farmer who lived several miles outside the village.

He tipped his hat and called out as he passed, "Gypsies! The Gypsies are coming! Lock up your valuables and hide your livestock!"

Pippi sighed and swung her empty basket, the braided handle feeling warm and slightly damp from the sweat of her hand. Various Gypsy troupes came through the village many times each year, and she and her mother never had any trouble. In fact, two years earlier, she'd managed to sneak away after school and have her fortune told by a heavy-set, black-haired Gypsy woman who had set up a little tent on the outskirts of the village.

For three small coins, she smoothed warm fingers over Pippi's palm and in broken German, said, "Long life. *Many* troubles. Two true loves. No trust the fisher." Brushing a soft hand along Pippi's cheek, she smiled. "Is all, little one. Godspeed," and Pippi tumbled out of the tent, breathless from the smell of burnt strawberries that pervaded the dim interior.

She was glad that she was to have a long life and true love but was still puzzled about the fish. Had she misunderstood? Fish? Fishermen? Well, she had never much liked seafood anyway, so she rarely ate any, and she had no intention of marrying a fisherman.

Pippi passed the town meeting hall, which was little more than a large ramshackle shed. As she drew near the blacksmith hut, Gregor, the smithy's son, emerged into the afternoon sunshine, wiping his hands on a cloth. He waved when he caught sight of her. Hesitantly, she waved back. Gregor was ten years older than she and had obviously taken a fancy to her. To her dismay, he ducked back into the hut, then emerged bright-eyed, without the cloth. Groaning, she quickened her step and headed as swiftly as she could toward the store, all the while observing him from the corner of her eye.

She paid no attention to the couple crossing the dusty horse track.

MISCHKA STRODE DOWN the street holding her adopted cousin Emil's hand. She knew her father and brothers were watching from the trees, and a thrill of excitement coursed through her. The men had trusted her to go with Emil into the village. Not Cam or Simionce or Aladar, but Mischka. With her free hand, she mashed down a dark brown hat that hid her long, wavy black hair, and lifted her head high. She puffed out her chest, then looked down and let out some air at the depressing sight of the two small buds, just beginning to grow.

This unwelcome change had ended the long summers of denial where she believed that one day she would awaken and be the boy she had always dreamed she was. She dared not tell anyone about her dearest wish, certainly not her male playmates. They would tease her and she couldn't bear that, not when the indignity of approaching womanhood had already hurt her pride badly enough. Soon she would be forced to don the long skirts all Roma women must wear, and she wouldn't be able to move so freely around the men of the camp.

The thought made her tighten her grip on Emil's hand. In German, she said, "Papa, how are you?" Calling Emil by her father's title induced a giggle she only barely managed to suppress.

In Romany, he replied, "I'm fine, little one. What is it you want?"

She smiled up at him, taking in his darkened skin. Ever since the incident with the Polish soldiers, he had been applying a tincture that made his face, neck, and arms look a dark red-brown. He didn't exactly look Roma, but he also didn't appear German anymore either. "I like you as my Papa," she said.

In his low, deep voice, he replied, "I am glad for that,

Mischka. Now mind your words and pay attention. And don't speak unless I ask for your help."

A granary and a mill sat on the stream among a grove of trees at the outskirts of town. They passed and drew near the first small structures at the edge of the village, some of which were little more than large sheds. A man in a gray fedora sat whittling outside a lumber store. He didn't look up when they went by.

A man walking two horses ambled down the center of the hard-packed dirt road and stared at them with curiosity etched on his face. They passed a two-story building spewing smoke from double chimneys, and Mischka wondered who could live in such a giant place. Or was it a building for some other function? There was no sign on the front, so she couldn't tell.

The first row of houses were small and had thatched roofs. The farther they walked, the bigger and more solid the houses became, some with shingled roofs. Soon they came upon a group of shops, their storefronts whitewashed and welcoming.

Ahead and across the dirt track a young woman walked toward them. She wore short brown boots and a blue dress darker than the sky. The round hat on her head looked to be made of straw. Emil tugged at Mischka, and she was suddenly propelled across to the other side of the road. The woman was halfway up the stairs leading to Grewe's Grocery when Emil halted and muttered, "Pippi?"

The girl hesitated, her back to Mischka and Emil.

"Pippi," he said in a hoarse whisper, "is that you?"

She spun around and stared, her mouth slightly open as though she were about to say something. She shivered, held the basket more tightly to her, and brought a hand up to a beaded necklace at her throat.

"It can't be. Are you—are you a ghost?"

"No, I'm real, and we need to talk." Emil looked swiftly left and right. "Not here, Pippi. Not now. Meet me at home when you're done shopping. I'll come after dusk."

From behind, Mischka heard a man clear his throat and whirled to see a tall fellow with a thick, pale brown beard. The heavy apron he wore over his bare chest was dirty and so were his pants and boots.

He said, "Pauline, are these people troubling you?" He pulled his fists against his chest and flexed his biceps. Mischka watched as his arms bulged and relaxed, bulged and relaxed.

The blonde girl stood, transfixed—and a girl was all she was. She had the figure of a young woman, but Mischka didn't think that Pauline—or Pippi, as Emil had called her—was more than three or four years older than she herself.

A tense moment of silence passed, and then Pippi spoke. "No, Gregor. They merely asked for directions to — to — well, I'm not sure. I couldn't understand them." Her eyes darted from side to side as though she were praying for rescue.

Emil's grip was so tight that Mischka thought her hand would be crushed, but she choked out a word. "Salve." It was the first word that came to her mind, perhaps because she was sure she would need some to repair her broken hand. "We need some healing salve." She purposely spoke broken German and pointed to Emil's hands with her index finger. In Romany she said, "Let go of me and show them your palm."

Emil kept his head down but did as she said and turned both palms up. The right was red and creased with calluses, but the left was covered with scars, and his pinky finger was gone. A healed scar near the base of his left thumb looked worse than it was, but it did the trick.

Pippi gasped. "That looks terrible!" She turned, hurried into the shop, and the door slammed behind her.

The big man let out a sigh, and his eyes narrowed as they swept from the closed door to the two people before him. Mischka didn't know if he would recognize Emil, so she put herself between the two men and in purposely halting German, said, "Well? Have you...some salve?"

For a moment it seemed he was going to ignore her. Then he strode off toward his shop. Placing a warning hand on Emil's chest, Mischka said, "Stay here. I'll be right back."

She darted out into the lane and caught up with Gregor as he reached the blacksmith's hut. She did not follow him inside, but when he reappeared, she bowed her head and thanked him for a square of dirty cloth which he folded and handed to her.

As she crossed the road again, she heard him call out, "Now don't be stealing tools or anything from my shop. You hear me, boy?"

She waved over her shoulder, calling out thanks once more, her gaze fixed on Emil all the while. He looked frightened, and when he spoke, his voice shook. "I know him. He was three years ahead of me at school. How did he not know me?"

"He only had eyes for the girl. Come. Let's get out of here."

He rose slowly from his seat on the stairs. "Right. We should go lay low until later today."

As they moved over the same ground they had just traveled, she peeled open the dirty cloth. Inside was a congealed glop of salve. She raised it to her nose. "Good stuff, Emil. Dab a little of this on your hands."

He reached over, scooped some on his finger, and rubbed it in as they walked. "Germans have always produced the best salve."

BEFORE THE MOON was up, but after dusk had darkened the skies, Emil set out. Mischka watched him go, her heart heavy. No matter how much she'd argued and reasoned, she could not convince her father to allow her to accompany Emil to his mother's home. What would happen if he were captured? What if he decided to stay in the town instead of coming with them? What if? What if?

She carried several freshly chopped logs to the fire, where Drina squatted, stirring a pot of goat's milk. When the older girl glanced up, Mischka was surprised to see misery etched into her face. She set the wood in the pile and squatted next to her. "That looks good."

Drina's voice was so soft, Mischka could barely hear her. "The littlest ones want spiced milk with their supper."

Mischka examined Drina's face, her dark hair, her worried eyes, and suddenly the words tumbled out. "You love Emil."

"Shhh." Drina averted her face and her long hair obscured Mischka's view. Her spoon made a tink-tink sound against the side of the pan, and Mischka could tell she was in tears. So, Drina loved Emil. What about Emil? How did he feel? And what about *her*? With a sigh, Mischka smoothed her shirtsleeves and stood up. She wanted to say something that would comfort Drina, but she had a feeling she would only make matters worse so she headed for her family's *vardo*, climbed up on the back step, and crawled in, settling on a thick, folded square of canvas. Little light shone in, and she thought she was alone, but then a soft voice interrupted her thoughts.

"What is it, Mischka?"

She jumped and let out a squeak, then realized Stevo lay in the shadows. "Sorry if I woke you."

"I wasn't really asleep. Just thinking. What's wrong?"

"What makes you think something is wrong?"

"It's not like you not to be out in the thick of things."

Mischka thought about that. She could hear happy voices teasing, talking, singing. All over the campsite, wood was being gathered, food prepared, tents going up. Usually she would be helping, but right now, her heart wasn't in it.

"Stevo, what will happen to Emil?"

"What do you mean?"

"Will he stay behind in this village?"

"I think not. It's not safe for him."

"Then why is Drina upset?"

Stevo didn't answer for a moment. "Like you, she is unsure, Mischka. Unsure of Emil."

"She does love him then?"

"Yes, but he is *gajo*. Nicolae intended to seek a husband for Drina in another *kumpania*. These things are complicated, and you probably don't realize she was already betrothed once. The arrangements fell through when the young man eloped with someone else. However, Nicolae has heard that there is another son, and he is waiting to find out if there is sufficient dowry."

"Did Drina want to marry with this other man—or his brother?"

"Not really. She didn't want to leave her favorite horses, and she doesn't know either of them at all. Nicolae and the boy's father talked of it last fall—remember when we had that celebration in the woods with those other four caravans?" She nodded. "No *pliashka* for engagement has been held, and no bride price had been settled. And now Emil goes in secret to his people to ask for his father's legacy to use to buy a *vardo* and persuade Nicolae that he is worthy."

"I have some coins. Should I give them to him?"

Stevo's voice was filled with mirth when he answered. "Emil will need a lot more than a few *zloty.*"

"Oh." She sat back, wondering how she had missed these details. She had no idea how marriages were arranged, and she was curious about the older girls she knew, all of whom were at or near marrying age. For the first time ever, she seriously considered what would occur when she was older. What would happen if her father picked out a husband for her whom she did not like? And would she have to leave her family?

"But Stevo," she said in a rush, "if Emil married Drina, they would have to stay with us! She cannot go live with his people, right?"

"Right, and the fact that our papa married into this *kumpania,* is an advantage."

Now she understood why Emil had been grim and full of worry lately and Drina was so tearful. "Oh, Stevo," she said. "How can we possibly wait to discover how this will turn out? I simply cannot wait!"

Stevo laughed. "My little sister. She wants her finger in every pie."

THE SMELL OF baking bread and the pungent aroma of cooked pork wafted in the night air, and Emil's mouth watered as he made his way up a slight incline to the grove at the end of the village. He stood in the shelter of the trees and scanned the road ahead. Back when he was trapped in the foxhole at the front, he had dreamed of reunions, but sneaking into town like a criminal was not the triumphant return he'd had in mind. He looked down at dark hands sticking out of the long-sleeved white shirt he had borrowed from Stevo. He was as clean as he could get, but the tincture he used on his face and arms could not be easily removed. He had to leave it on anyway, just in case he was stopped.

Pippi had been so overwhelmed this morning that he wasn't sure she really believed he was alive. He hoped the advance knowledge of his return would reduce his mother's shock. He remembered far too well how ill she became when his father died. He didn't want to be the cause of any more pain and anguish, especially since he couldn't stay.

He crept along a hard dirt sidewalk, staying close to houses, ready at any moment to run. A hundred yards ahead two men stood on the road talking, so Emil cut along the side of Galt's shoe shop, crossed through a dirt track of an alley, and slipped into the shadows next to a tall house with white framework, tarred beams, and a thatched roof. Before he left for the army, the occupants had moved away, and he had no idea who lived there now. The house was dark, so he assumed no one was home. He crept through their yard and went over a waist-high fence.

As a boy, he had run through every yard, every garden, every lane. He knew the village well enough to navigate with closed eyes. Up ahead, a dog barked behind Frau Neuberger's house. He paused, wondering if the little mutt, Bello, would remember him. He had spent many a day playing with and walking the pup. He itched to round the corner and call him, but what if the dog didn't recognize him? Would his smell be as different as his looks? He couldn't take the chance to find out, so he avoided Frau Neuberger's place.

Passing a three-story brick house with a flat pasteboard roof, he noted the peeling green gate and smiled. When he was fourteen, the owner, the village postmaster, had hired him to paint it, and if Emil knew the frugal official at all, nobody had scraped and painted it since. That morning's work had earned him enough money to buy Christmas gifts for his parents and sister and still have ice cream and candy money left over for weeks.

With every step he was reminded of some childhood friend

or event. Recognizing so many familiar sights was bittersweet. All of that was lost now. Perhaps this would be the last time he would stand in the physical place where such memories arose. Once he made arrangements with his family, he knew he should never again return. A lump rose in his throat. He pushed it down and moved on, cutting along a path and around a hedge, and there it was—the family home. Pale light shone out from the main floor. In the upstairs of the gabled house, the windows were dark. Whoever rented the tiny upstairs "mother-in-law" flat now must be away—or sleeping. Either way, Emil intended to be silent in his approach.

The backyard was slightly overgrown, but his mother had put in a garden of colorful flowers next to the stairs along the back of the house. He examined the entire yard, the back alley, and the homes on either side. Bello still barked in the distance, and he heard far-off laughter from down the road, but otherwise it was quiet. He stepped carefully around the flowers and lifted the window to his sister's room. The casing was narrow, but he had no trouble pulling himself up. The wood floor on which he landed creaked so loudly he was sure the neighbors could hear. Shivers descended his spine as he looked around the dim bedroom. Like the postmaster's gate, Pippi's room needed a coat of paint. Her slippers were tucked half under the bed, and the coverlet hung crooked on one side. Three dresses hung from hooks behind the door. He moved soundlessly and turned the knob.

The smell of baking hit him: cinnamon and yeast. He moved down the hallway by his old room, past the bathroom and the larder. "Mama? Pippi?"

A sharp intake of breath. The squeak of a chair. Thumping noises, and then his sister rounded the corner from the living room and wrapped her arms around his middle.

Camille Stanek approached more slowly, her fingertips to her mouth and tears running down her cheeks. "Oh, my son. It *is* you. I didn't know whether to believe your sister."

Emil let go of Pippi and took his mother into his arms. "I'm sorry," he said. "So sorry."

Pippi attached herself to his side, and the three of them stood embracing in the kitchen, all of them crying tears of pain and joy.

After a few moments, Camille sobbed, "Why—why? Why didn't you write? Why didn't you let us know you were alive?" Red blotches mottled her face, and he felt her tremble.

"Let's sit down, Mama." He gestured to the kitchen table, and she lowered herself into the nearest chair.

Pippi said, "I will make us tea. Is that all right?" When he nodded, she busied herself at the stove.

Without letting go of his mother's arm, Emil pulled a chair close to her, and sat. He kept his hand on her shoulder and wiped his tears away with the sleeve of his shirt. "I couldn't take the chance to write. It's a small place, Mama. The postmaster is in everyone's business. Listen." He leaned in to meet her eyes. "I am a deserter. I ran away. If they find me—if they ever learn I'm alive—I'll be captured and executed."

She gasped. "No."

"Yes." With a sad half-smile, he reached over and gently tipped up her chin. "But it will be all right. Don't worry."

Camille took his good hand. "Pippi said your hand was scarred."

"I was wounded in the final battle—the one I ran away from." He moved his hand from her shoulder and tightened it into a fist in front of her, then turned it over and opened his fingers slowly.

She let out a whimper and started crying again. "Oh, Emil..."

"It doesn't hurt. I can use it fine." He waggled the three remaining fingers. "It *doesn't* hurt, Mama. It's healed and I have adjusted to it. Please—please, don't cry."

With an effort, Camille straightened up and composed herself as Pippi set the table for tea. With shaky hands, Camille proceeded to pour three cups.

Pippi settled in the chair across from her mother and spooned sugar into her tea. "We will have cold chicken and vegetables for supper, Emil. I made some apple tarts, too."

"I thought I smelled cinnamon." He beamed at her. "You have grown so much, little sister. I can't get over it. You're fourteen now?"

"Yes. And you're almost twenty-one."

"Yes."

Pippi pursed her lips. "If you're a fugitive, then you can't stay here with us. Are you saying you can never come home?"

"Yes. But we can figure out ways to visit sometimes. We will settle upon another name for me to write under, and then I can send you letters."

Camille said, "Where have you been living? France? You are so dark." She stifled a laugh. "You don't smell, Emil, but you look—well, you appear to be rather dirty!"

This made him chuckle. "It's not dirt. It's a stain. I am also tanned from the sun, but Mikhail and Tobar helped me apply this tincture as a disguise. How should I explain? Mama, I don't have a home anywhere. I travel with the Roma. The Gypsies." At the startled look on her face, he added gently, "This is truly a day of shocks for you, isn't it?"

She didn't reply for a moment, then said, "I keep reminding myself that you're alive. That's all that matters. The rest is merely details."

"Good thinking. I'll try to explain the details." He met Pippi's eyes. She seemed calm, her fingers laced together on the wood table and her gray eyes twinkling in the warm yellow light. "The people I'm with—they are Gypsies—though you must never call them Gypsies to their faces. They are the Roma, and they saved my life. Who could ever have expected such a thing?"

Camille, still pale, bit her lip. "If they saved your life, then I'm in their debt."

"Mama, they are nothing like you have always been led to believe. I belong to them, and they belong to me now. They are my family, so they are your family."

Both Camille and Pippi had numerous questions for him. He answered as best he could, explaining all that had happened to him since he'd run away from battle. He told them about Drina, about Nicolae's concerns, and about his plans. After more than an hour, Pippi laid out dishes and silverware and prepared their meal as Emil continued to talk.

"Both of you will like these people," he said. He rose and washed his hands at the kitchen sink. "Their ways are different, but not so very different. They are kind and honorable and fun-loving."

He watched his mother's face as he dried his hands on a towel. He could see the concern written all over it.

Before their meal, Camille prayed, "Bless this food, Lord God, and let it nourish us and make us strong as we confront all of the new things presented to us. I pray for my children, that they may make the right choices and be happy. Keep us all healthy, and bring Emil safety and comfort all the days of his life, no matter where he travels. Amen." Her voice broke at the last. She squeezed his hand, then excused herself and hastily left the table. A second later, Emil heard the bathroom door click shut.

Brother and sister met one another's eyes. Pippi was the first to speak. "This has been a strain on her, but she'll be fine. She's happy to know you're alive. You don't know what it's been like for her. For us."

"I have a general idea."

They busied themselves with dishing up their plates, and soon Camille returned to the table and peppered him with more questions. After the meal, Emil and Pippi tidied up. He returned the clean plates and pans and cups to the same places in the cupboards where they had always been kept, then swept while Pippi held the dustpan for him. For a short while, it was like old times. The only thing missing was his stack of schoolbooks on the table near the doorway.

"Pippi," he asked, "how are your studies?"

An odd look passed over her face, and she didn't meet his eyes. Camille answered instead. "She hasn't been attending."

"What? Why? You always liked school."

Pippi shrugged. "I'd rather keep Mama company."

"She takes good care of me." Camille's eyes narrowed. "But Emil is right, Pippi. You need to go to school, get an education."

"But Mama, I don't need school! I want to be a seamstress, just like you. Where better to get the training?"

Emil smiled. "You need to be a Renaissance Woman, Pippi. You'll need many skills. I wanted to be a history and geography teacher, and all I cared about was reading about the past. As it turns out, the geography has been somewhat useful, but I would have benefited from having learned many other subjects."

Pippi crossed her arms. "Like what?"

"Oh, animal husbandry, horticulture, botany, farming, carpentry, horseshoeing, playing instruments, a little about medicine—and other languages. I have learned much Romany and a bit of Polish now. I wish I remembered my French better, and Czech and Hungarian would be most useful."

"You couldn't have learned any of that in school," Pippi protested.

"Sure I could. Even an introductory book would have helped. Instead, I've had to learn a lot of things the hard way."

Camille asked, "How do you survive? What work do you do?"

"Anything and everything. We travel near a city, set up camp, and then come to town to ask for jobs. Any kind of labor, painting, digging, plowing, chair repair, blacksmithing. Some of the *kumpanias* do a lot of fortune telling and palm reading. Some of our women do, but we rely more upon singing and dancing. I am not much help there. Somehow, the waltz doesn't seem to fit in."

Camille laughed for the first time since he'd arrived. "All those lessons I gave you on the living room carpet, they have come to no use whatsoever, then?"

He grinned. "No, Mama. But if they ever do, I'll be most grateful to you."

"What next, my son? I take it you cannot stay with us more

than a few days."

"Actually, I dare not stay here that long. I must leave tonight."

"What? You've only just arrived. You can't leave already!"

"I must."

"At least spend the night."

He took Camille's hand. "No, I can't. I have to go before it's light out." Tears came to her eyes. "No, wait, Mama. Listen. I have a plan. I want you to be at my wedding. I want to marry a girl from the *kumpania*. Drina is her name. I need some things, though. I need to know if—" Embarrassed, he looked down at the table. In a quiet voice, he went on. "Once upon a time, Papa said he had set aside money for me with which to start a business or buy a farm. Is this so?" Before his mother could answer, he said, "If not, it's fine. Perhaps you needed it for living expenses or for the future. I just thought I should ask, that you might, might—" He stopped speaking, flustered, then met her eyes.

Camille nodded once. "Yes, indeed, your father left both of you a legacy. Pippi can have hers in a few years, and you can have yours now. It's not so very much money, but you could buy a shoemaker shop or a small store with it."

"Really? What I should like to do is buy a *vardo* for Drina and me—that is, a wagon in which to live. And it would allow me to provide a dowry. I really *could* marry her! Oh, Mama!"

Camille said, "A wedding. Oh, my. You mean off in the woods somewhere without us?"

"No, of course not. I want you and Pippi to get away and join the *pliashka*—that's an engagement party—and the wedding, which is called an *abiav*. Can you come? Will you?"

Camille frowned. "What happens at this *pliashka* thing?"

"The groom's father brings a bottle of fine wine wrapped in a brightly colored silk handkerchief. And also, the groom's family makes a necklace of gold coins. Then everyone in the *kumpania* assembles around the fire. On his son's behalf, the father puts the necklace around the bride's neck, then drinks from the bottle of wine and passes it around to all the guests." He saw the look of pain on his mother's face as though she was going to start crying. "What's wrong?"

"What if you have no father?"

He put his elbows on the table and took a deep breath. "When they accepted me into their group, the leader of the *kumpania*, Gunari, became my father."

Camille's face crumpled in shock. "And your mother? Who became your mother?"

"No, no, no, it's not like that. Gunari took me into his clan as his own, like a son, but there is no equivalent for a mother. A man can adopt a son or a daughter, but it's an honorary thing, like having a guide or a mentor. *You* are my mother, my only mother. You will be honored and treated with respect because of it. And you, Pippi, you will be welcomed as well."

Camille rose and moved away from the table, stumbling toward her bedroom. Emil felt a shiver of cold apprehension run through him. What if his mother didn't accept this? What if she rejected him? Before he could carry the train of thought further, she emerged from her bedroom and set a rectangular jewelry box on the table. He recognized it immediately. Made of solid mahogany-finished elm, the top was inlaid with birds-eye maple. Even after all these years, the finish was still glossy. When he was a small boy, he used to sneak into her room and look at the shiny baubles and jewelry inside.

Camille shook out a silk handkerchief with a swirling pattern of blue, yellow, and black. "This was your father's. In fact, I think you two gave it to him long ago." She raised it to her nose and inhaled. "He didn't carry it. Thought it was too wild. Will that work for the wine bottle?"

"I remember when we got him that. Papa always carried white hankies."

Pippi reached for the handkerchief. In a dreamy voice, she said, "I wanted him to have some color in his pocket. He always wore black and gray and white."

Camille hunted through the jewelry box and finally lifted a gaudy-looking gold ring between thumb and finger and held it up to the light. "This wedding ring belonged to your father's grandmother."

"Let me see." Pippi took the ring and slipped it on her left ring finger. "My, she had big hands." She passed it to Emil.

"Drina would like this, I think." He looked at his mother. "But what about Pippi?"

"When Pippi marries, her husband will be responsible for the wedding ring, but let me see." Camille fished around in the jewelry box. "Here it is. This is my grandmother's ring. You shall have that."

Pippi slipped it on. "This fits much better — almost perfectly. It's only a little loose."

"That's good, then. Your hands might get bigger over time, but probably not smaller. You may have that now if you wish. I have also this locket." Camille pulled out a golden oval on a gold chain. "See, there is a photograph of your grandfather and grandmother."

Emil leaned over her shoulder, squinting at the tiny photos in the open locket. "Oh, my! Your mother looks exactly like Pippi, only a little older!"

"I never knew that." Pippi laughed with delight. "She does look like me. May I wear this?"

"Yes, my dear. I have been waiting to give it to you. Now is as good a time as any. Well," Camille said and gazed from one child to the other, "you both look happy. Tomorrow we shall make an appearance at the bank to get gold coins and withdraw Emil's legacy." When he gave her a startled look, she went on. "Don't worry. You don't have to come with me. When is this *pli-pli—*"

"*Pliashka.* I hope it's soon. I must now return to Drina's father, and ask for her hand. As soon as I know, I will send word to you."

"All right. In the meantime, what about a wedding dress?"

"Oh, Mama." He held a hand to his forehead. "I am so glad you said something, or I would not have thought to tell you. The Roma dress their dead in white, *not* their brides. They marry in bright and bold colors. If you could help me, I should like to wear a bright blue jacket to match my eyes, and if it would be all right, could you get some red material for Drina to fashion her own dress? There is one and only one time in a Roma woman's life when she wears a red dress, and that's at her wedding."

"If you like, I can help with the sewing. I'll need Drina's measurements."

"I don't know how to get her here so you can measure her."

"You can send her here, son. She'll be safe."

"All right. I'll try. But we've put the cart before the horse. Nicolae first has to accept my proposal on her behalf."

"Stop worrying. It will all be fine. You love this girl, right?" He nodded solemnly. "God has a way of working out the details. Leave it to Him, and with our prayers, you will soon be with your love."

Pippi asked, "Who will be your maid of honor and best man?"

Emil shook his head. "It doesn't work quite that way. I've only been to one big wedding celebration. Last fall, five *kumpanias* came together, and seven couples were married. Three of the girls were from our families and now live with other caravans. I am so grateful that Drina wasn't one of them!"

Camille patted his hand. "You send word when the marriage arrangements are made, and Pippi and I will come."

"Oh, I hope that happens. I need to warn you in advance, though, that you will have to travel a distance. And you will have to sleep in a tent out on the ground. You may be uncomfortable."

"So what." Camille shrugged. "We'll bring extra pillows and pretend we are on an African safari."

He laughed a full-throated, body-shaking guffaw, his first such laugh in many months.

Chapter Eight

German/Polish Border, June 1920 (Dyad Moon)

LATE THE NEXT morning, Emil kept his promise and told Mischka—and everyone else who wanted to hear—what had happened in his reunion with his mother and sister. Then he and Nicolae went for a walk along the road. Mischka had a fleeting idea of following them, but one stern look from her mother killed that thought. Instead, she went into the nearby woods to play hide-and-seek with Mimi, Nadja, and Lennor. Before long, Cam, Tsura, and little Mario joined them, and an entire afternoon passed while they played tag, ran, climbed trees, and shrieked in the forest.

They were hungry and thirsty when they descended upon the camp later. Mischka was thrilled to find Emil and Drina sitting on the back step of her family's *vardo*. One look told all. She raced up to the two of them, skidded to a halt, and stood panting with an expectant look on her face. "Well?"

Emil grinned up at her. "The *pliashka* will be in a few days, as soon as my mother and sister can get away."

Mischka let out a whoop of joy and did a cartwheel. Her mother, standing a dozen feet away, laughed and marched over to her daughter. "Marona Lovell Gallo! Emil and Drina's *pliashka* will be significant in more ways than one."

"What do you mean?"

"It marks the day you get out of breeches and begin wearing girls' skirts."

"What? Oh, no, Mama." She backed up, shaking her head vigorously.

Lumi crossed her arms, and tapped her toe in the hard-packed dirt. "Don't argue, little one. I have been stitching for days for you."

"You have?"

"Yes. Now, leave these two alone and go wash up. You look starved."

IN EARLY JUNE, ten days after Emil first appeared in the little village outside Eisenhüttenstadt, Pippi and her mother set out to meet Emil's new family with two suitcases and a sack full of food and wine bottles.

"Try not to look so excited," Camille said. "We don't want to call a lot of attention to ourselves."

They'd already attracted some curiosity when Camille asked to borrow a wagon and horse from a neighbor, Heinrich Hofstetter. It had taken considerable determination to dissuade him from coming along with them.

"It's just over the border, Heinrich," she'd said. "We will be on our own for only a few miles, and then we meet up with my cousins and travel just a short distance. Please, don't be concerned."

"I worry about two women on the road. Sometimes there are crazy automobile drivers out and about now, you know."

She put her hand on his forearm. "You are a wonderful neighbor, Heinrich. Thank you so much for caring."

Luckily, he was overwhelmed with spring business and couldn't afford the time to escort them anyway. "Your husband, rest his soul, will come back to haunt me if anything happens to you, Camille."

"Don't be silly. Now you give Brigitta my regards, and I'll bring back something for her sweet tooth. We'll be careful, and you'll see us back here in no time at all. I will personally see to your mount and cart." Grudgingly, he'd let her go.

Two miles outside the village, a cart heaped high with hay came toward them, and Pippi recognized the two Strasbach boys driving the cart. Dieter, who was in her grade at school shouted, "We missed you at school!"

She put her hand on her hat and called, "See you next year, Dieter."

"Yes, that's right," Camille remarked. "I don't know what I was thinking, letting you drop your studies. Once this summer is over, you must return to school and get an education."

Pippi relaxed against the low wooden back of the seat. "That'll be all right, Mama. I think I'll be ready for it."

Before long, they reached a copse springing up from a wide gulley on the right side of the road. Pippi heard a shrill whistle and scanned the thicket. In the dim brush she made out her brother and some other figures.

Her mother reined the cart to a halt. "Anyone behind us, Pippi?"

"No."

"Get out then."

Pippi clambered down. Before her feet hit the ground, Emil and a huge man stood next to the cart. Emil said, "Meet Tobar."

She nodded. "Hello, I'm Pippi." He laughed with glee, and his bushy beard bobbed up and down. She pointed at her mother and said, "This is Camille—Emil's and my mother."

He lowered his eyes and lifted two suitcases from the back of the cart as though they were no heavier than dry kindling. Two other young men materialized out of the copse. Emil beckoned them down a deer path while the other men guided the horse and cart over the lumpy ground and down into the grove. They unhitched the horse in seconds, rolled the cart behind the trees in thick brush, and covered it with branches cut and prepared in advance. Emil took the suitcases from Tobar, strung a rope between the handles, and laid them over Herr Hofstetter's horse's back.

"Will the ropes hurt the horse?" Pippi asked.

"No, we haven't far to go. I'll carry that bag for you, Mama. What is this?"

"Wine, sandwiches, cheese—lots of cheese."

"No wonder it's so heavy." He hefted the bag into a comfortable carrying position. "You've met Tobar. This is Gyorgy and his brother Stevo." Both men bowed, which Pippi thought was elegant.

"This way." Emil pointed into the thick of the woods, "It's not far—just to the next road over."

It wasn't long before they emerged from the thicket into a meadow of calf-high grass that caught at the hem of Pippi's dress. Though she wore wool stockings, the tips of the grass swayed in the breeze and tickled the backs of her calves. On the air, the scent of lilacs came to her. With the sun on her back, the wind in her hair, her brother safe ahead, and her mother right behind, she felt her eyes fill with tears, then laughter welled almost immediately. She hadn't been out of Eisenhüttenstadt since long before her father died, and then she'd been so young, she didn't remember much. An adventure. They were going on an adventure!

The ground sloped downward, and she hurried to keep up with Emil. Behind her, the three men laughed and talked in the strange tongue of the Gypsies. Roma, she corrected herself. She listened to their lilting intonation, but not one word was recognizable to her. Oh, she hoped she didn't go through this entire adventure not understanding anything anyone said.

A sharp incline rose ahead. Emil paused and insisted, "Take my hand, Mama. It's steep here."

Before Pippi realized it, Tobar had slipped his large hand

under her upper arm, and she fairly flew up the hill, propelled by the strong man. They came to the top of the rise, and a handsome older man stood waiting in front of a tall wagon hitched to two horses, his thumbs hooked in the armholes of the black vest he wore over a red shirt. His black pants were rumpled, but Pippi thought he looked rather dapper.

He bowed deeply. "You must be Fräulein Pippi. And you are Frau Stanek."

Her mother stood very upright, hands laced together at her waist. "Please, just call me Camille."

"And you must call me Mikhail."

Pippi marveled at his near-perfect German. She understood every word he said. A dark-headed imp peeked around the haunch of one of the horses, and Mikhail swept his arm to the side in a flourish. "And this is my only daughter, Mischka."

Pippi felt a flash of recognition as Mischka came forward. *Daughter?* This was the young boy she'd seen with Emil that day in the village, but...it couldn't be. How could he have grown so much wavy dark hair in so short a time?

Mischka said, "Hello. I am honored to meet you. Emil is my cousin, so I believe that makes you my Aunt Camille."

"You speak German!" Pippi had not expected this at all. In fact, she was almost ashamed to acknowledge her thoughts, that she had expected this Gypsy—Roma—child to be uneducated, certainly not fluent in more than one language.

"Why, yes. Your brother is a good teacher."

Emil put the bag he carried into the back of the wagon. "We've little time for chin-wagging on the road. Let's get home. Mama, will you and Pippi ride in the cart while Mikhail leads the wagon?"

"Certainly," Camille replied.

Mischka piped up. "Pippi, would you like to ride this horse?"

Pippi's heart thudded almost painfully in her chest, but she shrugged to hide her nerves. "I can do that. I don't ride well bareback—not in this skirt anyway."

"This horse has a saddle. Here let me help you. He seems tall, but he's not easily frightened. His name is Samuel."

"Is Samuel your horse?"

"No. I'm not sure who owns him. He just belongs to all of us, isn't that right, Tobar?" She restated her comment in Romany, and Tobar nodded assent.

For the next hour, Mischka chattered as they rode. Pippi found Samuel's gait smooth and with Tobar on her right, and Mischka on the left, she felt somewhat protected. In the course of their conversation, she discovered Mischka was almost eleven years old and born under the Snow Moon. Her mother was due to have another baby in mid-summer. Much to her surprise, she learned that at Emil's wedding ceremony, three or four other couples, including Gyorgy, would also be marrying. She asked why nobody was sure of the number, and Mischka informed her that the bride price must be paid first. Until then, nothing was settled.

Pippi had to answer a lot of questions, too, but she thought she learned more about the Roma in general and Mischka in particular than the other girl learned about her.

"Do you ride much?" Mischka asked when Pippi shifted a little in her saddle to relieve pressure.

"Sometimes. I've gone for pleasure rides with my friend, Suse Schonecker. But the Schonecker horses are ponies compared to Samuel."

With an air of satisfaction that made her seem older than she was, Mischka said, "You would be so sore after a whole day on a horse that you wouldn't be able to stand up, much less walk. So it might be best if we ride in the *vardo* – the wagon, I mean, once we reach the camp."

Pippi raised no objection. Her legs and shoulders were already tired. She glanced toward Gyorgy and his brother, Stevo. Mischka had been quick to tell her that Stevo wasn't married. She was surprised since he was so handsome. He had dreamy dark brown eyes, curly black hair, and the smoothest tan complexion she had ever seen on a man. The only thing marring his looks was an odd indentation on his brow at the top of his hairline. She didn't know how to ask what had happened to his forehead, but sooner or later she thought she might get it out of Mischka, who was currently yammering on about chicken pepper stew.

"...and do you enjoy food that is spicy and hot?"

"Yes, I think so. Unless it's so spicy that it burns your esophagus."

"Esophagus? What is that? I don't know that word."

For the first of many, many times in the coming days, Pippi defined a new word for Mischka's collection.

"Esophagus. Now that's an odd word. I like it. Thank you. Know any other good new words for me?"

Pippi giggled. "Since I don't know what you do and don't know, how can I decide what is new and what's not?"

Mischka thought for a moment. "You are correct. I shall have to ask as we go along."

PIPPI STOOD IN the middle of a dim tent next to her mother. With one hand she steadied herself against the center pole where there was plenty of room for her to stand upright. Though the front entrance had been tied back to let in light, the tent was stuffy and dark. Outside, the constant din of people talking and laughing drifted in. Each time Pippi emerged from the tent's gloom, she felt the eyes of countless strangers upon her. Today, for the weddings, there were more people than ever at the camp, and she was reluctant to venture out.

A thick rug lay on the ground beneath her feet, and bedrolls for her mother, Mischka, and herself were stacked in the far corner. Camille stood behind a cane chair combing Mischka's thick hair. The younger girl had spent the past half an hour chattering about various aspects of the wedding ritual.

Pippi asked, "Does the king of the Gypsies — of the Roma, I mean — oversee the exchange of vows?"

Mischka laughed. "There is no king, Pippi. We have no king. Whatever gave you that idea? We have a *bulibasha*, a man who is respected for his wisdom. He is the *Kapo* for those of us who travel in this area. Whenever two or more *kumpanias* meet up, we have a big celebration for friendship and unity, and he will lead tonight."

Camille tucked the comb in the belt of her dress and removed the *diklo*, which was a special head scarf, from where it lay over the back of Mischka's chair. She slipped it around Mischka's head, but couldn't get the knot in the back right. "Your hair is so thick and curly," she complained with an indulgent smile.

Mischka nodded. "And Drina's is, too. If you can handle mine, you will manage hers. So, we must practice."

"Mama, let me try." With a few quick twists, Pippi had the *diklo* knotted and properly adjusted.

Mischka reached up and touched the scarf. "Yes. Perfect. This is exactly right. Let's keep working on it, Camille. You'll get it." She untied the scarf and handed it back.

Pippi took the multicolored *diklo* and held it up to the light. The silk was old, but the scarf was sturdy. "Why don't you wear one of these, Mischka?"

"I don't have to until I get married."

Camille took the scarf from her daughter and smoothed it over Mischka's head. "I'm a widow, but have been married all the same. Should I be wearing one? Is it offensive that I'm not?"

Mischka giggled. "Camille! You have no husband now, so you can marry again. You need not wear a *diklo*."

"Oh, well, I thought I'd better check." She gently patted

Mischka between the shoulder blades so that the girl leaned forward in the chair, and this time the knot was easier to get. "There. I think that's right."

"Yes, it is." Mischka popped out of the chair and turned around. The button-up shirt she wore bagged over her breeches, and she was barefoot.

Pippi still thought she resembled a boy. She moved around the chair, untied the *diklo*, and smoothed back Mischka's unruly curls. "You have lovely hair, you know."

Mischka smiled at her. Though younger than Pippi, she was the same height and looked her in the eye. "You, too. I have never seen such gold." She reached out and ran her fingers through the long tresses. "*Pakvora.*" When Pippi frowned, she said, "That means beautiful. *Pakvora* is beautiful."

Mischka's open admiration made Pippi's stomach do crazy flips, and she felt a blush suffuse her face. "That's nice of you to say."

"Not nice. Just the truth."

"Shall we change?" Camille asked. "Won't the ceremony start soon?"

As if to answer, Lumi poked her head in the tent, and Mischka translated her message. "The *Kapo* is ready for the weddings, and then for the celebration. I must go with my mother to dress, but I will be right back." Lumi held out a hand, and Mischka took it. An impish smile was the last Pippi saw of her as she vanished from the tent.

"Are you ready for this, Mama?"

Camille sank into the cane chair. "I thought the *pliashka* was stressful. I can only imagine what this next part is like."

Pippi put her arm around her mother's shoulders. "I thought it was perfect. The fire and the singing and the wine...it made my head feel light when I drank it! And even though she's so shy, Drina is beautiful. Can't you tell how much Emil loves her?"

"Yes, you're right, sweetheart, but it's all so new and strange, and I can't help but feel that we don't exactly belong."

"Oh, Mama, they *want* us here. Emil wants us here."

"I know, I know. It's just—well, I didn't expect my son's life to turn out this way."

"He's alive and he's happy."

"True, and that should be all I care about. Still, don't you go falling in love with a Gypsy, Pippi Stanek. At least one of my children ought to live in a house!"

Pippi hugged her mother. "Stop worrying, Mama, and consider this all one fine adventure you will someday tell your great-grandchildren."

BEFORE DUSK, CAMILLE and Pippi assembled among the Gallos, the Lovells, and the Romany of the four *kumpanias*. The circle was huge, and in the middle, piles of logs and kindling had been arranged, ready for a bonfire to be lit. Near the unlit wood stood four couples, holding hands. The men were dressed in slacks, vests, and suit jackets, and each woman wore a red dress and a great deal of jewelry. Pippi thought they all looked gorgeous — and nervous as well. She was so glad she had brought her mother's costume jewelry. Drina looked wonderful in the bracelets, necklaces, and earrings she had shared with her.

Pippi took her mother's hand and glanced over at Mischka who looked entirely different now, no longer the slim, boyish imp. She wore a long brown skirt, a slightly over-sized blouse of many wild colors, and small gold hoop earrings. Pippi had given her two gold-colored bracelets, a small gesture that seemed to thrill her. Tobar and his fiancée, Vadoma, went first, standing before the *Kapo*, heads bowed. Mischka took Pippi's hand and whispered in her ear, "Here they promise to be true to one another." Lumi glared at her daughter but Mischka merely gave her a smile.

Then in the silence around the circle, the *Kapo* spoke words in Romany that Pippi didn't understand, and Mischka mouthed, "Later."

The couple sat in chairs and their families surrounded them. Vadoma was given a small piece of bread and a salt shaker, which she held out to Tobar. He salted the bread, tore it in half, and ate one portion, then fed Vadoma the other. Tobar took her hand, the *Kapo* shouted out some words, and Mischka whispered, "That means health and harmony to them."

An older woman who looked very much like the bride leaned over the girl and kissed her, and suddenly the sound of weeping came to Pippi's ears. Vadoma would be leaving her *kumpania* and her mother and father. In the future, she would see her birth family only when a celebration happened to bring them all together. Pippi could understand why she seemed so apprehensive. Vadoma's mother and younger sisters unbraided her hair, and Tobar's mother, Elena, moved forward to tie the bride knot in the *diklo*.

Cheers came from the guests, and Tobar rose, gently drawing his wife to her feet. Even from across the circle, Pippi could see her trembling. He put his arm around her, and she melted against him. Pippi looked around the circle at all the faces watching so intently, and she decided that any sort of wedding ceremony would be frightening.

They stepped back, and the couple from the other caravan

went next, then Gyorgy and Tauna, and last of all, Emil and Drina. Much to her surprise, Pippi was crying by the time her brother and his bride sat in the chairs. Mischka pulled her forward, and a horde of people stood in a half-circle behind the bride and groom as Emil salted the bread and ate it. Drina's sisters and aunts unbraided her hair. Unlike the other three families, their relative would not be leaving. Instead, in an unusual reversal, Emil had to leave *his* family, and for the first time, Pippi's tears were from grief.

Drina's black hair flowed free in the evening wind, and Camille and Lumi wrapped the tresses in a silk *diklo*. In one smooth motion, Camille tied the knot and stepped back to the cheers of the Gallo family. Pippi jumped up and down next to them as the entire entourage continued to clap and cackle and laugh.

In the rapidly diminishing light, the four couples listened to some final words from the *Kapo*. Then, from outside the circle, several men threaded their way through with smoking torches, which they tossed onto the logs. The dry kindling caught fire and as the flames rose, Pippi dried her tears and searched for her brother in the crowd. He was holding Drina close, her arms wrapped around him and her head tucked in next to his neck.

A shiver ran through Pippi, and then a feeling of longing. She hoped one day someone would hold her like that.

THE DANCING AND singing, drinking and music-playing went on and on. Mischka showed Pippi some dance steps, and though she felt awkward, Pippi joined in twice when the women and girls rose to dance. The rest of the time she marveled at Mischka's spirit and the way she knew the rhythm and the steps, never faltering, never running out of energy, her dark brown hair tossing and the bracelets flashing in the firelight. Pippi didn't think she would ever have the smooth, feline agility that the other girl so naturally displayed. She swayed. She twirled. She clapped and gamboled with glee. Pippi watched her face, entranced by the energy and delight that poured from her.

At first, it was all very new and exciting, but as the evening wore on, Pippi grew fatigued. She had eaten her fill of pork with whiskey sauce, lamb and rice, garlic chicken, stuffed peppers, and slices of apples drizzled in some sort of cinnamon sauce with nuts, which Mischka told her were a delicacy. Camille sat near the fire watching the festivities. Pippi went over, gave her a hug, and told her she was heading to bed. She was surprised when Mischka immediately announced she was also tired and

would retreat to the wagon with her to lie down. They picked up
an apple as they passed a table laden with food and also
managed to make off with two huge mugs of wine.

Sitting on the rug just inside the entrance of the tent, they
sipped the rich, tangy wine until both of them were light-
headed. Even though their tent was well away from the bonfire,
they could hear the fiddle music and stamping and hooting quite
clearly.

Mischka pointed through the tent flap and up at the slice of
moon above. "Isn't that excellent? It's the month of the Dyad
Moon—perfect for weddings. At least that's what my mother
says."

"What does dyad mean?"

"Two—it means two."

"But there are never two moons."

"No, that's not the meaning. I think it has to do with how
people have two sides and how two can become one. But I'll ask
my father. He can explain it better than I can. The waning moon
is beautiful. Aren't we lucky that the night is clear so we can see
it?"

"I was born in January. Do I have a special moon month?"

"January? Which is that? I can't keep track of your people's
moons."

"The first month following the end of the year."

"Oh. When it is cold and snowy still? After the month of
your Christmas?"

"Yes, that's it."

"I was born during the Snow Moon, then comes Oak Moon
during that time when Christmas falls. The next moon is Wolf
Moon. That's your month. If I'm remembering right, that's when
we pray for protection for the weather and for wayfarers."

"So this Wolf Moon is not a happy time?"

Mischka let out a howl, like a wolf, then laughed and took
another swig of her wine. "Wolves are beautiful animals. Have
you ever seen one?"

"I've seen photographs."

"Not the same at all. To see a wolf lope past, leaping over
logs, stopping to peer at you... A wolf brings—how would you
say it?—*baxt* is the word. Hmmm...good luck. *Baxt* is good
fortune."

Pippi shivered. "But aren't they frightening?"

"Not really. They usually stay far away from people."

"I see." A cool breeze carrying the scent of burnt wood
wafted into the tent. Pippi yawned. Her limbs felt heavy.
"Mischka, what work does your father do? How does he earn

money to support all of you?"

"We all work together. As we travel we have places we go to help with harvesting, to build things, fix chairs. There is hunting for game. We dry fruit and venison for the winter. We go to towns and dance for coins, and some of the women tell fortunes. Gyorgy can cobble some wonderful boots." Her voice took on an excited tone. "You want me to have him make you some?"

"Maybe. I'll ask my mother."

"I love his boots. They always form to fit my feet so perfectly."

Pippi set her empty mug down and shivered again, this time because the temperature was dropping.

Mischka must have noticed, for she got up and disappeared into the recesses of the tent, returning with a blanket that she draped over Pippi's shoulders. Lowering herself, cross-legged, next to Pippi, she snuggled in under the blanket with her. "Is that better?"

"Yes. Thank you." Pippi leaned her head against Mischka's shoulder and yawned again. "I can't believe I'm so exhausted."

"It's late now — close to midnight."

For a short while they watched wisps of clouds scud past the quarter-moon. They could hear the strum of guitars out at the bonfire, and the women sang a melodic call that the men responded to with a rousing line.

"Do you usually stay up into the wee hours of the morning?" Mischka asked.

Pippi laughed. "No, never."

"We can sleep now, if you'd like."

Pippi nodded and rose. She slipped out of her shoes and dress and fumbled around in the darkness until she found her nightgown rolled in with the bedding. She and Mischka worked together to lay out the bedrolls and blankets, and she snuggled down into the coolness which quickly warmed to her legs and torso. Casting about one-armed, she located a roll of clothes to use as a pillow and tucked it under her head. She felt hands at her waist, and Mischka whispered, "Are you warm enough?"

"Yes." She shifted closer to her companion, then felt fingers at her neck.

"What is this necklace? I noticed it tonight. Very pretty gold."

"It's a locket. From my mother. I'll show it to you by the morning light."

"Yes, you must. I'd like to see it."

Hands kneaded her shoulders, then slipped around her neck. Pippi could feel Mischka caressing her back, and it made her shiver.

"You *are* cold."

"No, I'm fine. That—that just feels good—you touching me, I mean." Pippi eased herself closer and wrapped her arms around her young friend.

Mischka let out a sigh. "*Te' sorthene.*"

"Hmmm?"

"*Te' sorthene.* It means 'friend bonded by heart and spirit.' I feel it in my soul."

"I'm glad you're my friend, Mischka."

"*Sutho.*" Pippi waited for a translation. "*Sutho.* Means forever," Mischka whispered. "*Te' sorthene sutho.*" She kissed Pippi's forehead and lay back. "A promise north, south, east, west, by the sun and the moon—especially the moon—and inside my heart."

Mischka's breathing evened out, and Pippi lay in her arms feeling a soft, warm breath against her neck. She'd never met anyone like Mischka. She seemed older and wiser than her years and so full of life, so happy. What would it be like to live as a traveler? To wander the land? Pippi had a hunch it would be a lot of work. The men seemed to enjoy themselves, but the women had a lot of work to do just to make meals.

She didn't fall asleep right away. Instead she thought about the people her brother lived with and how they were nothing at all like the townspeople had made them out to be. She couldn't imagine Gunari or Mikhail or any of the other men, young or old, kidnapping children. From what she had learned, they rarely stole anything—and then only if the children were hungry. She liked these people, and it pained her to think of leaving them in a few days. She pushed the thought out of her mind and let herself float off to sleep, warm and secure in Mischka's embrace.

Chapter
Nine

New York City, November 1989 (Snow Moon)

TOBAR SAID, "YOU'VE known each other a long time, way longer than I've been alive."

"Yes, we have," Mischka said.

"Must be nice," he said in a bitter tone, "being friends over the years and hanging out together. I wish I didn't always have to leave my friends behind."

"But we did not hang out together, as you say. There were years and years that Pippi and I never saw one another, and I had no way of knowing where your grandmother was."

He looked at her blankly. "How did you keep in touch— phone calls?"

Mischka laughed.

"Tobar," Pippi said, "you have to remember that this was the 1920s. My mother and I didn't have a telephone, and Mischka's people, out on the road, certainly didn't either."

"Oh. I didn't know that. How did people keep up with each other then?"

"Letters. Word of mouth. But it was hard for me to track down Emil, much less Mischka. The Roma were always on the move."

"And it got even more difficult," Mischka said, "when I was married off into another *kumpania*. Away from Emil, I had no way of easily reaching your grandmother."

Tobar looked back and forth between them. "But you managed somehow, right? I mean, you must have since you're sitting here right now, but how exactly did you two stay friends then?"

Pippi said, "Not an easy feat."

"Not at all," Mischka said.

"What about your husband, *Beebee* Mischka? Nobody ever told me you were married."

"It's not something you would be interested in," Pippi said hastily.

"What? Of course I want to know. Tell me."

Mischka listened to him reason with Pippi and wondered who would win. She knew Pippi didn't like to hear about this time in her life, but it had happened so many years earlier. She paused and calculated. Sixty-three years ago. How could so much time have passed so quickly?

She recalled most of those events in sepia tones, not in the bright colors she associated with Pippi, and because they occurred so long ago, they had ceased to hurt her.

"All right then," Pippi was saying. "But *Beebee* Mischka had better tell this part."

Tobar met Mischka's gaze. "Go on, then. What happened?" He looked at her eagerly, his eyes clear and face unlined. He was so young—and yet he had those old eyes, eyes that seemed understanding beyond his years.

"I was sixteen years old in early 1926. Two moons before the yearly summer meeting of *kumpanias,* an emissary from a distant tribe came to see my father bringing a request from Luciano and Zigana, the parents of a man named Arben. I'm not sure how, but they had heard that I was strong, healthy, well-mannered, and that I possessed domestic skills."

Pippi giggled, and Mischka shot her a look.

"Perhaps they were misinformed, but they offered a sizable dowry for my hand in marriage to their son, and Papa and Mama were thrilled, especially because I am not a full-blooded Roma. Remember, my father was adopted by Palko over thirty years earlier, but his ancestry was Hungarian. If I married a Roma, any children I had would be considered one hundred percent Roma just as Gyorgy and Stevo's children were, and this made my father happy."

"Did you have children?" Tobar asked.

Chapter
Ten

Central Poland, April 1926 (Seed Moon)

MISCHKA HAD ALWAYS hoped no one would ever show up to ask to marry her. Even though her good friends Mimi and Nadja had been married since age fourteen and reported that all was fine, Mischka wasn't interested. She knew she was headstrong and overly tall, both factors that had made her less desirable than some of her childhood friends. So she hadn't counted on a marriage proposal.

She dared not protest to her father, but Mischka talked at length with her mother to explain her misgivings.

"What do you mean, you don't want to get married?"

"I want to stay with you and Papa. You need me here. Drina needs me to help with the horses." Drina was with child and confined to her tent, unable to do her chores.

"Don't be foolish. If this boy is suitable, of course you shall marry."

Mischka felt torn. "But what about my little sisters? Who will take care of them?"

Her mother's exasperation was plain. "I was able to raise you perfectly well, was I not? I'm sure Liza and baby Elena will turn out fine."

Mischka shuddered to think of leaving her family — not to mention Emil and Drina, Tobar and Vadoma, and her nieces and nephews. Her sister Liza was not quite six and Elena was soon to be a year old. She couldn't bear the thought of picking up her few personal belongings and leaving with some strange *kumpania*. Perhaps if someone she knew were a member of the troupe...but no one was. She would be alone with strangers. "What if he's not suitable?"

"Oh, Mischka, why wouldn't he be?"

And the conversation was over.

Her *kumpania* traveled along the Vistula River, and Mischka became increasingly forlorn. Each day she awoke and looked around the camp, memorizing the faces of those she loved. One day, after they'd stopped in the late afternoon, she sat on a low-hanging branch of a stately oak tree and watched the river run. Two ducks paddled by. A flock of black-necked grebes tittered in the trees across the river. An osprey flew in the drafts high above the trees. What if she never saw this again? She couldn't help but feel a painful sense of foreboding.

Several weeks later, during June, they reached the enormous clearing where the yearly celebration was to be held, and she accepted that she was in deep mourning. Always in the past, the summer festival had been a joyous occasion — games and dancing and food galore — but not this time.

Her parents met with Zigana and with Luciano, son of Grofo and father of Arben. Their *kumpania* was large, some thirty *vardos* and nearly as many carts. Their group had come far southwest of their normal traveling grounds to join the festivities, and the clearing that had always seemed so enormous was dwarfed by the numerous *vardos* and carts and tents. The bonfires were huge, and the dancing was wilder than ever.

On the fifth day, a ceremonial celebration was held in honor of Mischka's family. She was introduced by her given name, Marona. The men were fed, then the women and children ate off to the side while the men smoked pipes and cigarettes. Once she had eaten, Mischka was sent away with her mother. When her father returned many hours later, all he said was, "The wedding arrangements are complete. All is well."

All is well? Mischka kept her tears in check, held her head high, and slipped off to bed.

The next days passed in a blur. Drina helped fit her for a red wedding dress, and her friends and family gave her little gifts. Each coin, each piece of jewelry plunged a knife to her heart. She was being tossed away in return for a dowry. Her father would buy a horse, a goat, a new *vardo*. He would have money to spare for some time.

The night of the *pliashka*, Mischka went through the evening like one asleep. Once, as her mind wandered, she wondered what would happen if she ran away, but she had nowhere to go. Her whole world was her *kumpania* and her family. No one noticed the tears that brightened her eyes and threatened to fall. She returned to her tent with the customary necklace of gold coins around her neck. She wrapped them in a kerchief and hid them in her bundle of clothing.

Seventeen couples were marrying the next day. When Mischka rose the day of her wedding, she helped serve the *kumpania's* morning meal for the last time. Tobar and Emil and her brothers sat on a log across from the fire and laughed and joked. Gyorgy and Stevo were happy with their wives, and they were teasing a friend who had finally managed to scrape up enough money for a dowry. He was getting married as well, and the joy he displayed was a remarkable contrast to Mischka's feelings. She wished she were a man. Her wife would come to her *kumpania*, and Mischka would have all the say-so. Why did it have to be this way?

She attacked a bowl with a dishrag, then a disturbance broke into her thoughts. On the western side of the campground rose a plume of dust. A farm wagon, shepherded by a pack of small children, came to a standstill two hundred yards away. Mischka shielded her eyes with a damp hand and squinted. A man strolled to the wagon, then turned and pointed toward Mischka's family's camping area. The wagon rolled forward, pulled in near Nicolae's *vardo*, and stopped.

Emil stood with a smile on his face, then gave Mischka such a triumphant look that she knew something was up. All the women around Mischka called out questions.

"Who is it?"

"Who is our mystery guest?"

"Why, look, it's two women!"

Mischka was stunned to see Camille and Pippi Stanek alight from the wagon. Her knees felt weak. For a moment she let herself imagine that the Staneks had arrived to spirit her away, but her fantasy was short-lived.

Emil called out, "Mama! Pippi! I'm so glad you could come for Mischka's wedding."

He hugged them in the *gajo* way, clasping them each to his chest in turn, and the Roma, who never permitted adult men and women to hug, politely ignored that social blunder. Emil turned, his arm around his mother, and called out, "Mischka, look who has traveled from far for your wedding." Pippi waved with one hand while mashing a round straw hat down on her head against the breeze.

Mischka moved in slow motion, feeling as though she were marching toward a firing squad. Some response was needed, but what should it be?

It had been six years since Mischka and Pippi had last seen one another at Emil's wedding. At that time, Pippi had been a girl rapidly changing into a woman. Now Pippi was a full-grown woman. She wore a pair of stout walking shoes, a long, pleated cotton skirt with tan and green stripes, and a lightweight, white, long-sleeved blouse. The straw hat obscured the upper half of

her face. Not until Mischka was a few strides away did Pippi tip
up her head, smiling. Their eyes met and locked. *Blue,* Mischka
thought. *They're still blue.*

Pippi's face was slightly pink, as though she had been
exerting herself. "Mischka. Congratulations."

Camille threw an arm across her shoulders. "You've grown
so tall. Like your father. You look a great deal like him."

Pippi took both of Mischka's hands into her own. "You look
wonderful. And I'm so happy for you."

Mischka looked down at the pale white fingers holding her
nut-brown hands, so tanned from the sun, and realized she'd
forgotten her manners. "It's wonderful of you to come," she said
in careful German. "You both look wonderful. So wonderful. Just
wonderful."

Though she was repeating herself, she couldn't help it.
Wunderbar. The word twirled through her mind as her body
coursed with pulses of pleasure. Pippi was here. She was truly
here, in the flesh. Mischka had dreamed of this moment so often
over the years—and now that it had arrived, she didn't know
what to say or how to act.

Emil laughed and chose that moment to ask, "How do you
think they managed this great feat, little cousin?"

Mischka let go of Pippi's hands. "I assume you are the rascal
who is responsible."

Camille said, "We took the train to that little burg over the
hill, then rented this wagon from a farmer."

"I rented the wagon, Mama," Emil said.

"You may have made the arrangements, my son, but I seem
to recall that *I* was the one parting with her money."

He laughed. "This is Drina's and my wedding present to
you, Mischka. And we have another gift as well." He winked and
stepped back.

Lumi clapped her hands together. "All right now, the guests
probably would like something to eat and drink. They must be
weary from the road. You come with me, Camille."

Two mugs of cool cider were pressed into Mischka's hands
by Drina who said, "Why don't you and Pippi go off for a bit and
visit."

"I'd like that," Pippi said.

"Then later we can prepare your dress for the ceremony."

Mischka's voice wouldn't work now, so she couldn't even
thank Drina. She gave her a nod and turned toward the lovely,
golden-haired woman. Pippi carefully threaded her arm through
Mischka's. They strolled to the other side of Nicolae's wagon
and down the lane toward a grove of trees that had already been

staked out as a place for small groups to gather and chat.

"You grew very tall, Mischka."

"And you didn't grow at all."

Pippi laughed. "I just got plumper."

"You don't look plump to me. Not one bit."

"That's nice of you to say. I constantly feel I ought to be dieting."

"Dieting? I don't know that word."

"Restricting what I eat so I don't get fat."

"Oh. That's easy for me. I just get out of the cart and walk, and I can eat as much as I want."

They reached the grove, and Pippi stepped over a log. "Then there's definitely something to be said for a traveling life."

The sunlight didn't penetrate the thick bower of leaves, giving the spot a cozy, private feeling. The men had felled and split logs to make low benches. Mischka handed Pippi the mug of cider, and they lowered themselves carefully so as not to spill any. She was glad they sat next to one another and not opposite. She didn't think she could look into those bright blue eyes without becoming tongue-tied.

"We're delighted we managed to get here on time. We almost missed the connecting train out of Eisenhüttenstadt." Pippi continued on, talking about their trip, the people they had met, the landscape they had passed, and after a couple of minutes passed, she suddenly stopped. "Mischka, what's wrong?" She reached over, took the mug away, and set both on the ground, then grasped Mischka's hands. "Your hands are so cold. What's wrong?"

The tears came then.

"Look at me. What's the matter?"

Mischka could do nothing but shake with sobs. Pippi chafed her hands, and some of the warmth came back to them, but the more Mischka cried, the colder she felt.

After a few minutes, Pippi said, "Am I correct in assuming that you don't want to marry the man?"

"I don't even know him."

"What? How can you marry someone you don't know? Surely you have spent time with him — he courted you, right?"

"No. That is not always the custom."

"But Emil courted Drina, asked for her hand..."

"Arben's parents asked my parents through an emissary, and the first we ever met was last night."

"Oh, Lord." Pippi put her fingers to her mouth and sat there for a moment. "I see why you're upset. I couldn't do it. I just couldn't."

Mischka took a deep breath. "I shouldn't feel this way, I know. I have always expected to be married. All my life I knew it would happen this way, but now that the time is here, it doesn't feel real."

"I'd feel exactly the same way. But your marriage customs are so different from the way people in my village do it. You're not even seventeen yet, and already you're marrying. I plan to wait — at least until I can say I love the man I choose to marry."

"I don't have that — that — what is the German word?"

"Choice? Luxury?"

"I don't know this word, luxury, but choice is like choose, right?" Pippi nodded. "I don't have any choice. I will marry Arben, son of Luciano, and there's nothing I can do about it."

Mischka leaned forward, picked up the mug, and took a sip of the cider. She winced. "It's bitter."

Pippi took the mug from her. "I'll switch with you. Mine was fine, and I don't mind it less sweet." She picked up her own mug and handed it to Mischka.

Before Mischka could say anything, Pippi gulped a mouthful of the cider. She frowned. "It tastes exactly like mine."

Mischka snorted. "It's probably just me. Everything has tasted bitter for days." She gave Pippi a sideways glance.

"What?"

"You just drank from my mug. That's *mahrime* — considered unclean."

Pippi laughed. "Are you not the girl who ate half my apple, drank most of my wine, fingered all the jewelry I wore, and kissed me goodnight the last time I visited?"

Mischka's face flamed. For a moment, she was tempted to rise and run.

"I don't care, if you don't," Pippi said. She put an arm across Mischka's back and leaned her head against her shoulder. "I hope you'll be all right. I wish there was something I could do."

"There's nothing anyone can do. This is my path to walk, one I can't avoid."

"I'm sorry this is filled with so much uncertainty and sadness."

Mischka closed her eyes and breathed deeply. She inhaled the fresh, clean smell of the beech tree under which they sat, felt the wood of the hard log under her, and heard the birds twittering above. The pressure of Pippi's arm on her back and her head against her shoulder was calming. She wished she could sit in this shady grove until the festivities were over, then walk away into the sunset with Pippi.

If only it could be so.

Pippi sighed. *"Te' sorthene sutho."*

Mischka straightened up, startled. "What did you say?"

"Te' sorthene sutho. Did I say it wrong?"

"No, you didn't. How did you remember that?"

"Pretty good, yes? I feel rather proud of myself. I asked Emil in a letter to write it down for me—just in case. I wanted to have it right."

"Yes, you do. I'm glad you've come to my wedding, Pippi."

"Me, too. It doesn't seem right for a friend bonded forever by heart and spirit to miss out, does it?"

Mischka didn't answer. Her eyes filled with tears, but she blinked them back.

And later that night, she and sixteen other nervous girls pledged their troth to their grooms. She had a few moments of happiness when she watched Stevo marry his beloved Chavi. Mischka's dowry allowed her father to help Stevo pay Chavi's father. Once, during the sharing of the bread, Stevo glanced up, caught her eye, and smiled. His lips shone bright red in contrast to his dark beard, and his excitement was evident. She was truly happy for him and knew he would treat his girl with tenderness.

Throughout her own ceremony, she managed to fix her eyes upon Pippi, only looking away when she had to. And when it was time for Pippi to leave later that night, she kissed her full on the lips, and Pippi kissed her back.

Chapter
Eleven

Northwestern Poland, April 1929 (Seed Moon)

NINETEEN-YEAR-OLD Mischka squatted next to the fire pit, blowing gently on smoldering embers near the strips of bark she held. She willed the bark to catch fire. She needed to have a significant blaze burning by the time Zigana, her husband's mother, rose from slumber. Already the sky had lightened almost imperceptibly, and time was running out.

She hated tending the fire, knowing well that she lacked the patience. She much preferred being up and about, working with the chickens and horses, carrying and hauling wood, doing the kind of work she had enjoyed when she lived with her father's *kumpania*. Those days seemed a lifetime ago. She had not seen her family at all since her wedding. Four times she had received brief news in correspondence from Emil, along with two letters in each envelope from Pippi. Eight letters total, each well-worn from reading and the ink faded from so much exposure to firelight. Most of the time she kept them rolled up in her bundle of clothes with the few coins she had managed to keep from Arben. On their wedding night, her virginity was not the only thing he had demanded; he'd also seized her bride gifts. She'd handed over a few odd coins and all the gold from the necklace her father-in-law had provided, but she couldn't bring herself to give up the gold and silver that Emil and Drina and some members of her family had shared with her.

For a long time she had wondered why Luciano and Zigana chose her to be their daughter-in-law. Finally, she heard one of the *boria* speak to another about someone named Lousza, and Mischka asked who that was.

"Arben's first wife," was the reply.

First wife? Mischka had never been told he'd been married before, but eventually Valentina confided that no one was supposed to talk about it since Lousza had died mysteriously.

From a beating, Mischka suspected. This must be well-known by the *kumpanias* traveling in northern Poland, so they had placed their dowry with unsuspecting Roma from the south.

The other *boria*—her sisters-in-law—were working at their usual assigned tasks. Donka carried water; Terom gathered additional firewood; Simza was down at the stream washing fruit and vegetables. Valentina was best at restarting the fire, and ordinarily that was her job, but she was ill and with child, and lay in a tent nearby, quarantined. All pregnant women were considered *mahrime,* and since only the *boria* spent time with a pregnant woman, Valentina lay moaning, lonely and in pain.

Mischka understood all too well what Valentina was going through. Three times she had conceived: twice to miscarry and once to deliver a stillborn baby boy two moons early. She hoped that wouldn't happen to Valentina. Mischka hadn't yet physically recovered from the most recent pregnancy.

The sky lightened slightly. The sun was nowhere near up, and a quarter moon still shone brightly. Seed Moon, she thought. She hadn't had her bloods for four months. His seed was growing inside her again. She shuddered and felt a cold that ran deeper than the still-frigid spring weather.

The fire shouldn't have gone out, but in her exhaustion, she had slept through the night and hadn't risen to bank the embers. She had always been a sound sleeper, and fire duty was not her forté. She puffed once more, and the bark flared. Soon she had a steady flame going in a pile of tinder to which she added kindling. She let out a breath of relief. Her mother-in-law, Zigana, would have no reason to mock her today.

As if she'd heard Mischka's thought, Zigana appeared to her left, and Mischka looked up in dismay. The older woman was a head shorter than Mischka, but she made up for it in ferocity. If something a *boria* did displeased her, she was just as quick to employ a switch or log or broom as she was to yell.

"You ignorant bumbler. You're slow and unfit. My son deserves so much more. Why is he stuck with such a stupid wife?"

Mischka knew better than to answer. She bowed her head and waited to see what direction Zigana's abuse would take today.

"And you." She pointed at Donka, who was struggling to carry two giant pails of water. "You all slept late again. We'll be lucky if we have breakfast prepared in time." She spat into the fire and turned away.

Mischka relaxed a moment, thinking Zigana might be bearable today. Then a hand came around her neck and jerked her to her feet. She turned, arms up to protect her face. Arben stood barefoot in rumpled trousers and a dirty tan shirt. One black suspender was down, the other up, forming a crooked dark line down his middle. Anger twisted his handsome features. She saw the open hand coming from her left and managed to lean enough that the blow struck her on the shoulder.

"Why can't you obey my mother?" He slapped at her again, and she stumbled, trying to avoid falling into the briskly burning fire. "I wanted a prettier girl." Smack. "A smarter girl." Smack. "And I'm stuck with you, a goat-faced big mouth. Your big mouth woke me up." He grabbed the front of her coat with both hands and hauled her toward him.

Donka, Simza, and Terom disappeared from the area. Only Zigana stood off to the side, a smirk on her face. Mischka braced herself. At times like this, he usually slapped and kicked at her until he suddenly became calm. His dark eyes would shine, and he'd haul her off to the tent and force himself upon her. Devil was the word that came to her mind. He was like a devil.

He panted, and a smile started at the corners of his red lips. But before he could drag her away, she whispered, "I have my bloods."

His eyes widened in shock. He tossed her from him like rubbish. "*Mahrime.* You're dirty. Get away from me, you filthy, unclean sow."

Zigana's voice, nasally and high, cut through Mischka's desperation. "Get back to work. That fire will go out unless you tend it."

Arben moved away, heading to his *vardo,* the place she was never allowed unless he was defiling her. The sight of his dirty tan shirt reminded her of a time long past, during childhood, when the same sort of shirt was worn by a soldier who had threatened her *kumpania.* Emil had shot and killed him, and the bullet had blown a hole bigger than her fist out his back. She glared at her husband's back and imagined the same such hole, bloody and seeping. Bile rose up and burned the back of her throat. She forced herself to swallow and squatted once again by the fire.

She wished she had Emil's gun.

BY THE TIME May's Hare Moon had come and gone, Mischka could feel her abdomen shift from the child growing inside her. She covered it up at first by wearing a baggy over-blouse, then, as her midsection protruded farther, she secretly let out the waists of her skirts. She was past the point of nausea in the mornings, and she hoped that perhaps this child would survive the full term. But she hesitated to say anything. She knew it was wrong, that she could be punished severely for neglecting to admit the pregnancy, but when each month's new, dark moon made its appearance in the sky, she continued to claim the arrival of her bloods.

Today, at the side of the river, she sat on her heels, her tan and brown skirt lumping around her like foothills leading to a dark mountain. It had rained the day before, leaving a great deal of moisture in the air. She caught a faint whiff of smoke from the campfire and the intriguing scents of flowering trees and bushes in bloom. The shouts and laughter of the children sounded far away, and they were. Mischka was an eighth-mile downstream from the place the horses drank and a quarter-mile from where the women and children got their water. The men staked out a washing and drinking spot nearest to camp, and everyone else spread out downstream from there. She couldn't even see the encampment through the copse of trees over a half-mile away, and that was fine with her. She liked the solitude.

Menstruating women were considered *mahrime*—unclean and impure—as were women with child. The moment Mischka told Arben and the women of her *kumpania* that she was pregnant, she would be isolated like Valentina. She would have little work to do, could not prepare food, work with the animals, or touch the children, and she wouldn't be allowed to wander along the river or walk through the woods. Confined to a tent set apart from the rest of the camp meant she would see little of Arben, which would be a blessing, but several months of isolation from the daily activities, from watching the little children running and laughing, from being able to go off alone would be far too unbearable. She had been through it three other times, and she wasn't looking forward to it again. She took a deep breath and watched the water ripple and twist as it burbled by.

"Marona!"

Donka's call floated in and out of Mischka's ear. She heard it, but even after nearly three years, her given name didn't register the way her nickname did.

"Marona." Donka strode toward her. She was wide-eyed and out of breath. "It's Valentina."

"What about her?"

Between pants, she said, "She went into labor early, but she's bleeding."

"Bleeding?"

"Terrible bleeding. None of the men will touch her. Zigana

is at a loss. We need to get her to a doctor."

Mischka picked up her skirts and ran toward camp. Valentina had been in pain for weeks, but she was not due to have the baby yet. The child was early, which was not uncommon for a first birth, but there should be no blood. Because Mischka was supposedly menstruating, she had to circle the border of the encampment and approach Valentina's tent from the side. Huffing behind her, Donka cut straight through the middle of the clearing and past the great fire. Zigana stepped out of the tent as they arrived and blocked their entrance. "It's about time you showed up, Marona. Always off mooning somewhere and never here when you're needed." Her face was a mask of fury, and Mischka wondered what was going on behind those cold, narrowed eyes. She hoped she looked properly penitent so that Zigana would step aside and let them in.

Donka wheezed loudly and a choking sob came out. "She's not — she hasn't — "

"Don't worry. She still lives." Zigana pushed between Mischka and Donka. While Donka gaped after Zigana, looking hurt, Mischka dashed into the tent.

The air was overly warm and smelled of sweat and blood and fear. Women from several of the other households were packed into the tent, and one knelt between Valentina's legs trying to stanch the flow of blood. "Do we have time to take her to the doctor in town? Does someone know? Anyone?" The answers from the various women came rapidly, tumbling over one another.

"We must."

"Yes, we have to try."

"Have to move fast."

"This isn't right."

"No, something is wrong inside — blocking the baby's path."

Nobody moved, so Mischka said, "I'll hook up a cart."

"Yes, good idea," someone else said.

Mischka backed up and was out the door before anything further could be said. She dashed across the edge of the campground and singled out two sturdy mounts. Tack and harness hung on a rack attached to one of the carts, and with nimble hands, she got a harness on the first horse and was getting started with the second when she was interrupted.

"Marona." She looked over her shoulder. Arben's brother, Jal, stood behind her, twisting a piece of cloth in his strong hands. "What's wrong? Can you tell me what's wrong with my wife?"

"I don't know. We need to take her to a doctor."

His face twisted as though he were in pain. The women, not the men, handled birthing and midwifing, but she could tell Jal was not satisfied to be left out.

She picked up the traces and lined them up with the cart, then turned to face him. "The baby's arrival—well, it's not right, Jal. Valentina's bleeding. Too much blood. She—" Out of the corner of her eye she saw a flash of movement. Arben swept in from her right side.

"How dare you talk to my brother of blood. Of things *mahrime.*"

His palm caught the side of her head before she even saw it coming. Specks of white light flashed before her. Her vision hadn't cleared when he slammed a fist into her middle. She staggered back against the side of the cart, tasting her morning breakfast. Coughing, she choked out, "Wait. We don't have time for—"

She ducked as his fist came at her, and his knuckles whacked into the cart's worn wood near her ear.

"Aiyeee! You witch!" He shook his wounded hand and grabbed the front of her blouse with the other.

"No, Arben, no!" She struggled to slip to the side and out of his grasp, but his scuffed hand wrenched at her hair, and he drove her against the wheel of the cart. The rounded wood dug into the small of her back. A wave of hot pain shot up, and she cried out. Behind her husband, she saw Jal's shocked face as he retreated, leaving her to deal with Arben alone. Many eyes were no doubt watching from the distance, but she knew no one would move to interfere. She was on her own.

"Get off me." She brought her fists up and beat at his arms but he had too good a grip. "You are *mahrime.* Get away."

In a low growl, he said, "And you are bad luck. Bad luck of the worst kind."

"Devil!" she shrieked. "You're a devil in disguise. Let me go."

Breathing hard now, he laughed and his teeth gleamed white in the bright sun. She could smell the stench of his breath and see sweat beading at his temples. His face was so handsome, his eyes so dark and flashing, but his heart was soiled and more unclean than anything or anyone *mahrime* that she had ever encountered. With a throaty scream, she brought her knee up and shoved him away.

He let out a yowl, backed up, and clasped at his crotch. But that lasted only a moment before he launched himself at her. This time when he grabbed her blouse, it ripped. He hurled her to the ground, drew back a boot, and kicked. Her knee exploded in pain. She screamed. His boot struck her stomach, and she lost her breath in a whoosh of sound.

He unleashed a string of invective as he kicked her over and over. "Bad luck! Witch!" he shouted. She curled up, protecting her middle, letting her forearms and shoulders take the brunt of his attack. Her insides felt like they'd been ripped out. She couldn't catch her breath. *Help me. Help me...someone, please. Please.* A brown, rounded toe came rushing at the side of her face.

Just before she passed out, she remembered the German word for help: *Hilfe.* And for a moment, she saw a vision of Emil, dressed in his army uniform. The illusion was so clear, so real, that until the pain detonated in her head, she believed he had come to rescue her.

SOMETHING WARM TICKLED the side of Mischka's face, wandering from her temple to her cheekbone and toward her nose. Was it a furry caterpillar? The smell of dirt was strong. Her body felt overheated, and she couldn't draw a full breath.

A tussle was happening nearby, but she couldn't get her eyes open to see it. She heard Jal's voice. "Arben! What's got into you? Stop now. Arben, stop."

She struggled to breathe, but every move sent ripples of pain crashing through her. She managed only small snatches of air, insufficient to give her the oxygen she craved. She forced her eyes open to slits. Brilliant sun blinded her, but she couldn't reach up to shield her eyes. She flattened her palm against packed-down dirt and tried to push herself up.

Voices came nearer. She heard a shuffling. Her *boria* sisters and some of the other women struggled to carry a blanket weighted down with a lumpy figure.

"Valentina." Mischka felt a wave of panic. Doctor. Have to get her to the doctor. The horses...

Zigana's voice rose above the grunting and hard breath of those carrying the load. "Arben, what is she doing on the ground?"

"She struck me. Can you believe it? She hit me here." He pointed to his genitals.

"Move the shiftless woman out of the way." She clapped her hands. "Now. Make room. Jal, you help him."

Rough hands grabbed at her, and Mischka let out a shrill scream. Bolts of agony stabbed through her arm, ribs, and midsection, yet she was helpless to fight against the men. They half-dragged, half-carried her a few feet and dumped her to the ground.

Then Donka was at her side. "Marona. Marona, what are you doing?"

Now that she lay at a different angle, the sun was behind her. Mischka opened her eyes to see the concerned face of her sister-in-law. Her voice came out raspy and weak. "Help me."

"You're bleeding a lot," Donka said in wonderment. "Your head is bleeding." Donka's face went blank, and Mischka knew the other girl had figured out what happened. "Let me help you. Can you rise?"

Donka slipped an arm under her. Mischka tried to push herself up. It made her dizzy and she felt like she was going to throw up, but she managed to roll onto her hip, legs off to the side. A ring of silent men and women from other families in the *kumpania* stood off to the side, watching.

"Marona," Donka whispered, "there's blood—so much blood." With a look of disbelief, she held out a hand stippled with red. Mischka looked down and saw dark spots. She couldn't very well pull up her skirt in front of the men, but she felt something damp and sticky between her legs.

Donka rose. "Zigana, Marona is hurt. She needs a doctor."

"Bah. That girl is a nuisance." Zigana made a motion with both hands as if to fend off the suggestion. "Leave her lie."

A tiny, ancient woman named Antoinette, whom Mischka did not know well, approached and knelt beside her. She brushed Mischka's hair off her forehead and made a tsk-ing noise. Under her breath she said, "Vicious. He's been vicious to you."

Her face was wrinkled and tanned a deep mahogany from the sun, and the eyes that gazed into Mischka's were full of compassion. Antoinette got to her feet and waved to her grandsons, instructing them to harness a horse and get a cart ready. As the young men scrambled to do her bidding, Zigana stomped over, nearly stepping on Mischka's hand, which she hastily pulled back in time.

"Stay out of our family business, Antoinette."

Antoinette took a shiny wooden pipe out of her apron pocket, pushed her thumb into its bowl, and put the unlit pipe to her lips. "Your family business is now the business of all of us. That girl in the cart is in deep trouble, and this girl on the ground isn't far behind her. How would you like not just the one *mulé* but three different kinds of *mulé* haunting you?"

Zigana stepped back as though pushed. "What do you mean?"

Antoinette's voice went so low and raspy it gave Mischka a shiver of fear. "You better get this girl in a cart and to a doctor.

She's hurt worse than you realize."

"She's always falling down and hurting herself."

"Um hmmm...so that's what you call it. I call it a recipe for the *mulé* to haunt our *kumpania* forever."

Arben had been listening, and now he stepped forward. "You need to shut your mouth, old woman. You meddle in things that aren't for women to intrude upon."

Antoinette grinned, and Mischka saw a frightening smile that didn't reach her eyes. Two hard, cold beads of obsidian bored into Arben. "We'll see then. We'll see. You've got one *mulé* on your conscience already, little man. You want two?"

Arben's nostrils flared, and he stood up very straight, looking like he intended to come after Antoinette. His mother held out a hand and pressed him back.

Antoinette nodded slowly, still grinning. "Boy—and that's what you are because no real man would treat his women this way—you are well on the way down a path toward hell, and you will not take me with you. If you don't deliver your wife to a doctor, then I shall have my family do it. The *mulé* will not haunt us for doing our duty. And we are one moon away from the yearly meet-up. Perhaps a woman cannot call a meeting to have the leaders decide your fate, but any of us—" she made a sweeping gesture with her right arm " —can easily report this to the father of Marona. If his daughter dies, perhaps he shall petition for all of your worldly goods."

"You wouldn't," Arben said, his voice weak.

Antoinette shook her head. "If your father were alive, Arben..." Her maniacal expression faded slowly.

Zigana glared. Her next words spat out like small bullets. "Fine. Arben, get your wife into the cart."

Arben didn't move. Antoinette clamped her teeth down on her pipe and reached into her bosom to pull out a sizable roll of coins knotted in a kerchief. She fumbled with it for a moment, then stooped and pressed two coins into Mischka's hand. "If anyone but the doctor takes these coins from you, you are to return to me and say so, even if you come as a *mulé*. I will not turn you away, spirit or not. I expect a full report. Do you understand?"

Mischka said, "Yes," and Donka helped her to her feet where she stood swaying and dizzy. Something sticky rolled into her eye, burning so badly that she squeezed both eyes shut. She ran the back of her hand across her face, trembling with the exertion of lifting her arm. When she opened her eyes, she saw her fingers covered with blood. She picked up one foot and tried to step forward. If Donka hadn't been supporting her, she would have fallen.

THE TRIP FROM the campsite into the Polish town was a hellish journey of incessant bouncing and pain. Arben guided the horse. Zigana sat at the front of the cart, facing away from Yoska, one of Antoinette's sons, who perched on the edge behind Arben. Mischka lay in the cart on her left side, with her knees pulled up, and her arms holding her middle. As far as she could tell, Arben went out of his way to hit every bump, roll through every hole, and keep the horse at a jerky pace. The nausea she felt grew worse, and she finally vomited. Zigana didn't make a move to assist or check on her, but once Mischka had emptied her stomach, the vertigo wasn't so bad.

She knew something was very wrong. On the right side of her stomach, just above her right hip bone, she had no feeling at all. Her probing fingers elicited no sensation in the skin. She brought her hand up and pressed on her right rib. Pain tore through her so hard and fast that she nearly passed out. She closed her eyes and gritted her teeth.

When they finally reached the town, Arben got directions to the doctor's home, which doubled as his office. There Mischka saw the cart in which Valentina had arrived, but the doctor's wife turned them away.

"He's already got his hands full with the other woman."

Arben jerked a thumb toward the back. "What about her? Can we leave her?"

The doctor's wife looked up at the sky. "It's near noon. Old Jaworski down the lane should be getting his supper. He can help you." She pointed west. "Travel another half-mile down past the first farmhouse. Jaworski is on the right."

Old Jaworski was not old—as Mischka soon found out—nor was he a doctor. He answered Arben's knock while wiping his mouth on a yellow linen napkin and pointed them around the side of the house. According to the sign over the door, which Mischka didn't see until the men were carrying her in, Jaworski specialized in animal husbandry. Neither Yoska nor Arben could read, and Zigana knew only a smattering of Polish, not enough to read.

The room they carried her into was small, clean, and well organized. A narrow wooden table stood in the middle, and cages of varying sizes lined one of the walls. The cages were empty, except for one that contained a rumpled blanket and the tiniest sleeping puppy Mischka had ever seen. A counter ran the length of one wall with a deep sink in the middle and a row of glass cabinets above. Bottles, beakers, and tin containers filled the cabinet shelves.

Yoska tried to be gentle, but Arben threw her on the table

and stepped back as Jaworski entered through a narrow doorway that led from the main part of the house.

In broken Polish, Arben said, "She sick. Need help."

Jaworski spoke slowly. "The doctor is down the lane."

"Here they send. Busy."

"I see." He stepped over to Mischka, but didn't touch her. Steepling his hands, he tapped his fingertips against one another. "Someone has beaten this woman."

Arben looked at Yoska, but he didn't respond. Zigana hovered against the wall, looking ready to flee at any moment.

"She fall," Arben said.

Jaworski's gray eyebrows rose in disbelief. "Miss," he said, "where are you hurt?"

"Everywhere." When his face registered surprise at her use of his language, she said, "I speak Polish pretty good. Them, not so good. I think I have a broken arm. Perhaps ribs. My head hurts."

"You've been bleeding," he said.

"Yes. I feel sick inside, too."

"In what way?"

"He will tell you I fell, but it's as you said. He beat me. The kicking was bad. Now I think something is terribly wrong. I was with child, and now…I'm not so sure."

At the doorway, Zigana snorted but she shrank back when Jaworski cast a contemptuous look at her. Zigana and her violent son understood little Polish, but they obviously knew *dziecko*, the Polish word for child.

"I suspect I'll need the doctor as well, but I can help you." Jaworski turned aside and shouted, "Marta!"

A rosy-cheeked woman wearing a yellow dress and an apron covered with stitched cherries and apples appeared. "Yes, dear?"

"I need your help to undress this girl."

She nodded and advanced into the room.

"You, sir," Jaworski addressed Arben, "have you any money to pay for treatment?"

Arben looked at him blankly.

"Money?" Jaworski asked again.

Arben shook his head.

Jaworski's jaw jutted out, and his eyes flashed. "You have nothing, not a single coin to offer?"

"She clumsy. Stupid. Bad, but no I want a dying."

Mischka had already crossed the line of allegiance, and she knew it. She had no idea whether she would live or die, but she didn't want to be returned to these people to be slowly beaten to death in a week, a month, or a year if she managed to survive this time. She would rather cast her lot with strangers.

She spoke softly in the Romany tongue. "I'm not clumsy or stupid. You, my husband, are the stupid one. You killed your first wife, and now you try to kill your second wife. Was Lousza with child, too? Did you beat her to death before she could bring you a son?" With one hand she cupped her abdomen. "Your child will not live to call you Papa."

Zigana pushed past Arben, her index finger in the air. "You whore! How are we to know it's even Arben's baby?"

Mischka's head pounded too hard for her to think clearly. "He is a devil man. He deserves no sons. Or daughters. May he be impotent and all he touches barren. I curse you both."

Zigana's mouth dropped open. "How dare you? We gave you everything. We were good to you."

"You were kinder to your dogs and horses."

Jaworski spoke up. Mischka knew he couldn't understand Romany, but he must have had a hunch of what was being said. "This girl is hurt. You must pay."

Arben's face contorted into a contemptuous leer. "No money for whore."

Jaworski squared his shoulders. "I ought to call the police on you people."

At the word police, Yoska departed, calling over his shoulder, "I'll be out at the cart."

Jaworski stood between the table and Arben. "Get out."

"Mine." Arben's expression was challenging, as though he expected to have a brawl right then and there. "I own she. I take."

Mischka closed her eyes. She could barely force the words out. "I divorce you, Arben, son of Luciano. My family will go to the *Kapo* if they have to. My father will come and take your *vardo*, your gold, your horses, and anything else. He will not return the bride price. I curse you on the grave of my father's adopted father, Palko, son of Mario the Elder. You are *mahrime*— and dead to me." The world swirled before her, and she closed her eyes.

Jaworski squared his shoulders. "You must leave her, sir."

Arben shook his head. "You want she? *You* pay. Now."

"Pay?" Jaworski roared his words. "It will be you who pays. The police will arrest you. Arrest! Jail for you, you brute."

Zigana grabbed Arben's sleeve. "Come, son. Leave her. She's trash—not good enough for you. Let's get out of here."

Mischka opened her eyes as soon as they'd gone. "I had money, quite a bit of it, but I wasn't able to collect it before they brought me here." She fumbled in the front of her blouse. "Still I can pay something. I do have these." She held out two small gold coins.

Jaworski opened his broad hand, and the money tinkled into his large palm. He stared down at it for a moment as if pondering its worth, then said, "All right then. Good enough."

Chapter
Twelve

Northwestern Poland, July 1929 (Mead Moon)

MISCHKA LAY ATOP the covers of a narrow bed in a stuffy attic room. She wore a lightweight cotton shift that only came down past her knees, and still she was overly warm. Summer already, she thought. Which moon? Dyad? Mead? Through sleepy eyes, she saw a single ray of sunlight let in by a tiny dormer window. Motes of dust hung suspended in the air above her where the ray came in aslant, and she watched them hover. She felt like one of those motes — floating aimlessly, doing nothing of value.

The tune of a song Stevo used to sing came to her, but she heard it slow, and more melancholy, than Stevo had ever sung it. She spoke the words to the chorus in a whisper:

Li-lo, li-lo, li-lo lay
La la la and a happy day
He whistled and he sang till the greenwoods rang
And he won the heart of a lady

Arben could have won the heart of any lady. Why didn't he try? Why was he so cruel? She didn't understand. Why was the *kumpania* she had married into so awful compared to her family's?

After Zigana and Arben departed the week before, she'd thought she could withstand the pain of all that had happened to her. She had made it through the physical examination, through the setting of the bone in her arm, and through the stitching of the scalp wound and clean up of her other cuts and bruises. She'd even managed to block out the embarrassment of allowing the doctor and the veterinarian to intrude upon her private parts in order to attend to the miscarriage Arben had caused. Mrs. Jaworski had held her hand, clucking and tutting as Mischka listened to the men deciding what to do. After all that, she thought she was through with the indignities and pain.

But the next day, Mrs. Jaworski said to her, "It's too bad about your Gypsy sister-in-law. I'm sorry that Doctor Zajak couldn't save your friend."

Mischka was shocked, nearly unable to breathe for half a minute. She couldn't believe Valentina was dead. She spoke no more for the next day, merely turning over in the bed and burying her face in the pillow while she cried.

As the days passed, she went from sad and pensive to a despondency so strong that she could hardly make herself eat. At times, like now, she could only lie there, perspiring and on the verge of tears, wondering why she was alive and a lovely, kindhearted girl like Valentina was dead.

She wondered what time of day it was. From the angle of the light, she thought perhaps late afternoon. Her guess was confirmed when she heard the squeak of a hinge. Someone was coming up the steep stairway — more than one person. She heard a deep voice, which she recognized as Mr. Jaworski's, but his wife rounded the head post at the top of the steps first. She carried a tray containing a bowl that emitted tendrils of steam. As soon as she saw Mischka was awake, she smiled and prattled on about the food.

Mr. Jaworski followed her, a stethoscope around his neck. She didn't understand how the device worked, but he had told her he could hear her heartbeat. "You've got a good strong heart," he said each time. While his wife fussed with the tray, he felt Mischka's forehead and listened to her heart. "How is your head this afternoon?"

"Good."

"No headache?"

"It's faint and far away."

"I'm going to press on your middle now." She turned her face toward the wall as he examined her. "Does that hurt?" She shook her head. "There?"

"No."

He nodded, satisfied, and stepped back. With the roof at such a tight angle, he had to duck and hunch his broad shoulders to give Mrs. Jaworski room to pull a low table over near the bed. She said, "Now you're going to eat more than you did this morning, dear, aren't you?" Mischka shrugged. The last thing she wanted was food. "Mr. Jaworski is going to sit here for a few minutes and talk to you. You just call me if you need anything." She bustled off, leaving Mischka staring up at the gray-haired man.

He leaned over the foot of the bed, took hold of a three-legged stool, and pulled it around to the side of the bed to sit on. "Well, Mischka, it's time to choose what to do. I heard today that a troupe of Gypsies have set up camp outside town. I don't know if you know these people. Dr. Zajak says they are not the same ones who brought you here." His lips turned up in a grim half-smile. "Apparently, those vicious louts skipped town immediately. So now, you will have to make a decision."

Mischka nodded. She had a long journey to find her family far to the south. "If you will bring me my clothes, I'll go out and talk to the Roma." She emphasized the last word, but he didn't seem to notice.

He crossed his arms, brought his index finger up to his lips and sat in a pose to which she had become accustomed. When Jaworski pondered like that, she had learned she had no choice but to wait for him to speak.

Mischka closed her eyes. The thought of walking made her sick to her stomach. She wanted to fall back into a great and powerful river, let herself sink to the bottom, and bump along from boulder to boulder. Forever.

He interrupted her thoughts. "Your condition is stable now — but you're not well enough to walk a mile. Nor would I allow you to ride in a cart or on a horse." He shook his head and met her eyes again. "I will take my horse and go out to ask someone to come here to speak to you. Perhaps you can arrange to have word sent to your people." He rose and placed the stool back where he'd gotten it, then stood looming over her. "Can you tell me something?" She waited. "How did you come to speak Polish so well?"

"I learned over the years. I also speak German, some Czech, Hungarian, and a bit of French. Why?"

"I've spoken to a number of Gypsies, and they all know a smattering of Polish — like the people who brought you here — but none of them have the vocabulary you have."

"I have an ear for words and a good memory."

"I see."

"WHY DID YOU take me in?" Mischka asked a week later. "Surely by now those two gold coins have long been spent in medicine and food. So why have you not turned me out?"

"Let me answer with a question. Do you have a God whom you worship?"

She thought of the moon and the sun and the wind and the rain, but she didn't think this was what he had in mind. Still, she nodded.

"Have you read any of the Bible?" When she shook her head, he said, "It's a book of writings about how God wants us to live and to care for others. My wife and I believe in what it says and try to follow it. A great prophet, a man named Jesus who was someone with foresight and wisdom, once spoke of God's actions at the time of the end of the earth and sky, at the end of our lives. When the time comes at the end, we'll be separated into two groups — those who deserve eternal life and those who do not."

Mischka didn't understand how this applied to her. "What does this Bible have to do with why you're still helping me?"

"We belong to the Catholic faith. We follow the way of Jesus, who was our savior and prophet. Once he was asked how one could discover whether he'd be rewarded when he died or instead cast into hell. Jesus said something to the effect that those who make it to the kingdom of heaven are those who knew he was hungry and gave him food to eat; thirsty, and gave drink; when he was a stranger, he was taken in and clothed; if sick or in prison, he was visited. The people asked Jesus when they had ever found him hungry or thirsty, a stranger, or naked, or sick, or in prison, and Jesus said to them my favorite and most-treasured line in the Bible: 'Verily I say unto you, inasmuch as ye did it unto one of these my brethren, *even* these least, ye did it unto me.' "

"I'm not a brethren."

Jaworski didn't laugh often, but when he did, his amusement lit up his face, making him look kindly, a little like Nicolae when he chuckled. Beaming, he said, "To put it more simply, God asks us to care for others. Whatever we do for those who are not well off, who are in trouble, we're doing that for God, and He finds favor in it. I would hope that someday, when you have the ability to help someone else, you might think of Jesus and his message. Whatever you do for the poor and unfortunate, it's done for good and for God."

"I see." But she didn't, entirely. She'd have to think about it, and unfortunately, she didn't feel she had the energy.

"Will you eat this supper so that Marta doesn't worry about you? The soup is probably cool enough now." He slid the low table closer. "I'll let you eat in peace."

"Wait. One thing more. The word Jaworski...is that not a tree?"

He laughed again. "Jaworski means 'of the sycamores' in Polish. I think that in past times my people may have been woodcutters or tenders of orchards."

"But now you are a tender of animals."

"Yes. And of itinerant Gypsy girls." He paused. "May you

have a pleasant and nurturing meal, Mischka, in God's name. Amen."

"Thank you, Mr. Jaworski."

With a wave, he made his way down the stairs. When the door creaked shut, Mischka swung her bare feet to the floor. The wood felt warm against the soles of her feet. She leaned forward to sniff the food on the tray. The soup smelled of onions and chicken. The big chunk of bread was yeasty and warm. Bogacha *and* puyo. It smelled like her mother's cooking. That brought tears to her eyes. Even though it reminded her of home, of her childhood, she could only eat a few bites of soup and a little of the bread, then she fell back onto the bed and cried until sleep stole her away.

BY THE TIME July's Mead Moon was nearly over, Mischka's arm had healed, and she was up and around. She slipped outdoors as much as possible to wander, but every step she took seemed an effort. She moved as though wading through a stream chest-deep. Her appetite hadn't returned, and she knew she was far too thin. Even so, she couldn't fit into tiny Mrs. Jaworski's clothing. She'd taken to wearing Mr. Jaworski's work shirts and the overalls she'd found hanging in the stable. As warm as it was, she didn't need shoes.

Today, she decided to do something useful. Perhaps a little work would help her overcome the exhaustion. Tying her hair with a length of string, she surveyed the bridles and other tack hanging on rusty nails on the stable walls. All of it could use a good cleaning and oiling, but there wasn't anywhere to lay it out. With stalls for four horses and only a small open work area near the door, the Jaworskis' stable was really little more than a shed.

Mischka elected to groom the brown gelding Mr. Jaworski liked to ride around the town. She picked up a brush, but before she'd even finished currying his shoulder and withers, she was beset with such fatigue that she sank back onto a bale of hay.

She wondered why she was so tired. She slept from dusk to dawn, then again in the forenoons, and still the exhaustion wouldn't leave her. Neither the doctor down the road nor Jaworski gave her medicines any longer, so she knew those weren't responsible.

In the distance she heard the clop-clop of trotting horses. Curious, she abandoned her hay bale and sauntered out of the stable. She peeked around the corner of the house, careful not to be seen. Nothing could have prepared her for the vision in front of her. She had hardly dared allow herself to dream of such a thing, and when she did, she imagined her father, or perhaps one of her brothers, answering her summons for help. She had never expected to see Tobar, Gyorgy, *and* Emil riding toward her.

Overwhelmed, and almost frightened to believe that what she saw was real, she ducked back behind the house and leaned against the faded wood. A force bigger than her chest could contain expanded and hurt, and for a moment her breath stopped. The tears that welled up blinded her completely. She knew she couldn't face them like this, not feeling weak and defeated. Embarrassed, she pushed away from the house, wiped her eyes with her sleeve, and bolted back to the stable.

By the time the three men and Jaworski found her there, she had her emotions under control and had finished brushing the gelding as well. Yet when Gyorgy entered, relief and joy swept through her so violently, she feared she might faint. Her big brother, so strong, so smart, so solid and real. She yearned to throw herself into his arms like she had so many times when she was small. Before Gyorgy could speak, Tobar pushed his way into the room. He had to stoop to clear the doorframe, and while he paused there, he blocked a good deal of the light.

"Mischka." His dark eyes examined her from top to toe. His beard was bushier than ever, and if it were possible for an adult man to have grown taller, he had. He didn't speak, and for a moment she wondered if he disapproved of the clothing she wore, but his next words cast that from her mind. "You are whole."

Yes, she was whole physically, but she wouldn't talk of anything else.

Tobar made room so that Emil and Jaworski could squeeze in, and the four men regarded her with the kindness and concern she had taken for granted all of her life until the evil day of her marriage.

Emil looked much the same as ever, eyes the same sharp blue they'd always been, but his hair was blonder than she had ever seen it. He smiled and asked, "Is this little hen ready to come home to roost?"

Home. She had not dared to let herself hope, but maybe she would be allowed to go home.

Jaworski spoke to them in Polish, trying to explain that Mischka's injuries were healed, but that she still tired easily. Gyorgy stood off to the side, ostensibly listening to the doctor, but she felt his eyes upon her and turned her head to meet his gaze. His eyes flickered uncertainly over her attire, and a flash of realization passed through her. No matter what anyone said, she wasn't wearing women's clothes ever again. She was no longer a woman, but she wasn't a man either. She was an in-between — someone who was sexless — neither male nor female. And that was the way it would be.

Jaworski was offering them a meal and the stable to sleep in for the night. Gyorgy said, "But where will Mischka sleep then?"

Jaworski frowned. "She's settled in up at the house, and she can stay there."

Gyorgy's mouth dropped open. "You let my sister sleep in your house?"

He nodded, a surprised look on his face. "Of course. She needed medical care and preservation from the elements."

"You have slept indoors for how long?" Gyorgy asked.

"Many days." She hadn't counted. Particularly at the beginning, the days had all run into one another. All she knew for sure was that Mead Moon was nearly over and Wort Moon would soon be underway.

Gyorgy seemed amazed to hear that. Roma generally didn't take well to houses, but Mischka hadn't minded it at all. In Romany she said, "Gyorgy, he healed me using special medicines that must cost a great deal of money. I have no more coins to offer. Do you?"

"Yes. I'll take care of it before we leave tomorrow." He turned to Jaworski. "We will gladly accept your offer of food and lodging. Thank you."

"I'll let my wife know. Perhaps you can regale us with stories of your travels, of the people you have encountered, and the places you have been."

Gyorgy shrugged. "Perhaps."

Jaworski rubbed his hands together, seeming delighted. "I'll let you all talk. I'm sure you have much news to share. When the meal is ready, I'll give a shout." He left the stable, and with him went some of the stiffness the men had been displaying.

Emil was direct. "You're truly healed and all right?"

"Healed, yes. All right remains to be seen."

"What happened?" Gyorgy sat down on the bale of hay and was joined by Emil.

Mischka bowed her head. "My husband tried to kill me."

"But why?" Her brother looked truly perplexed. "Why would he do that?"

How could she explain? How could she make them understand Arben's malice, his joy in inflicting pain? She tapped her forehead. "He wasn't right up here."

Tobar leaned against the doorframe, his hands behind his

back. When he spoke, his voice was deeper and softer than she'd remembered it. "He went mad?"

"Not exactly." Mischka smacked the grooming brush on to a shelf, then led the gelding back into his stall. "He likes to hurt people. He killed his first wife, probably doing to her what he did to me."

"What?" Tobar pushed away from the doorframe and clenched his hands into fists. "That's not the way of the Roma. He must be taught a lesson."

"Tobar," Gyorgy said in a weary voice, "my father will report all of this to the *Kapo*."

"They had better not ask to get the bride price back then," Tobar said.

Emil caught her eye. "Mischka, have you any intention of returning to Arben and his people?"

Gritting her teeth, she said, "I would rather die first."

The men looked at one another and seemed to come to the same conclusion without another word. Mischka recognized the sharp bob of Gyorgy's head that indicated the topic was now closed. Tucking the grooming brush into the slot on the wall where it belonged, she asked, "What is the news of Papa, of Mama? My little sisters?" Her heart beat fast, and she was almost afraid of the answers. What if something had happened to them?

Her brother grinned. "Everyone is fine, and since we're bringing you back, you can see that for yourself. It will be a homecoming—a celebration."

She wasn't sure how true that was. Rarely did a married woman return to her original *kumpania*, and sometimes the excommunicated wife was made to feel unwelcome or was not accepted at all. She hoped it wouldn't be that way with her *kumpania*, but she didn't want to dwell on the possibilities now, or to consider the future. She changed the subject.

"New babies for any of you?"

Tobar, who hadn't quite relaxed entirely, stiffened and looked away. Emil said, "Both your brothers' wives have had babies. Drina, too. But Tobar's wife was unable to birth their child. She died in childbirth."

"Vadoma? Vadoma has died?"

Tobar's face filled with pain, and he stepped outside the shed.

This final bit of news proved too much to bear. Mischka pushed past the men, out of the dim light of the shed. Tobar stood near the house, staring up at the sky with his back to her. She took off into the apple trees behind the stable and ran on a cow path until she reached a field green with growing plants.

Skirting the rows of greenery, she slowed to a walk and let the tears come.

FOR THE FIRST time in many years, Mischka felt free. They had been riding for ten days, and once her back un-kinked and her leg muscles stopped aching, she relished the journey. They passed through villages and small towns, avoiding the bigger, less-agrarian regions. At first she had been afraid as they made their way south. What if someone accosted them? What if they happened to come upon Arben's *kumpania?*

On the second evening, Emil had pulled her aside, opened his shoulder sack, and explained that Drina had sewn it from two gunnysacks and reinforced it with heavy thread. The men did not speak of the contents of the bag, but in addition to foodstuffs, Emil showed her the pistol he had taken from his lieutenant in the trenches all those years ago. He hadn't used the gun for years but had decided to take it with him on this trip. Early in their journey north, he said, he'd bought bullets and supplies at a gunsmith's shop and later that night, outside the campfire, he'd cleaned and oiled the gun and fired three practice shots.

"See, Mischka. The gun is in perfectly good condition, and should we run into danger, I know how to use it."

"I hope you never have to take it out of your shoulder bag."

He winked at her, then tucked it away and pulled a package of dried beef from the bag. "I much prefer to use this for edibles."

The men had brought sufficient coin to purchase food along the way, and for the first time in three years, she enjoyed cooking, especially because her Roma brothers were so appreciative of the simple meals she made.

In order to raise no alarms, she traveled dressed in breeches, shirt, and straw hat. Jaworski had given her a gunnysack full of his old clothing as well, enough to last her for quite some time. She had never completely forgotten how it felt to wear comfortable, practical clothing as she once had, before she was forced to wear long skirts. Now, in the only attire she'd ever been at home in, she felt complete. Unless someone got up very close, it wasn't possible to tell she was female. For that, too, she was grateful. No longer did she care what her brother or his friends thought. She would bear the wrath of any of the members of her *kumpania*. She hoped they would not exile her, but if they did, she thought she might be able to survive on her own. Anyone willing to get her hands dirty could always find work.

At night when they camped, Mischka slept under one tree and the men slept under another with the horses tied up between. Even with nearly twenty years of Roma training regarding all the proper rules for male and female relations, Mischka discovered she could let go of these ideas without too many qualms. She would observe the cleanliness rituals to avoid any charges that she was *mahrime,* but no longer did she believe men should hold sway over women. She began to speak to her brother, Tobar, and Emil as an equal, asking questions, challenging their comments, and refusing to be in any way subservient.

She slowed her horse as they approached a grove of trees perfect for a noontime stop. As she dismounted, she asked, "Who is our leader now?"

Gyorgy said, "Still Gunari. And Bersh follows in his footsteps."

Gunari, Mischka's father's blood brother, had been in charge when she left, and she had always expected his bossy son Bersh would be the next leader. "Gunari must be getting on in years."

"He is." Tobar dismounted and led his horse under a huge beech tree. "Bersh is in charge whenever Gunari is ill, which is more and more often now."

Mischka nodded. Her given name, Marona, had been Bersh's grandmother's name. Marona had died shortly before Mischka was born, and she knew Gunari's clan had held a special place for her in their family constellation because of her name. She and Bersh had always gotten along well enough. "Bersh always liked me. He liked Papa, too."

Gyorgy said, "He still does. They spend a lot of time wandering and talking as an uncle and nephew would."

"I'm glad," Mischka said. "Very glad."

THE SIXTEENTH DAY, well into Wort Moon, they rose and ate a quick breakfast. At any time in the afternoon they could come upon the caravan. Mischka felt nervous and concentrated on the sun upon her face, the breeze at her back, and the wildflowers by the side of the road. Whatever will be, will be, she kept telling herself, but with every passing yard, her stomach knotted more tightly. Her horse's slow, patient gait belied her agitation. These were her people. Why was she afraid? She wanted to believe she would be welcomed back, but she'd seen women cast out before — women who had been unpleasant, who had broken rules and become *mahrime.* Adulterers and liars, mostly, neither of which described her, but still, she feared.

"Well, little sister, are you ready?" Gyorgy asked when they spotted a *kumpania* in the distance.

"As ready as I'll ever be." Mischka shaded her eyes as she squinted down the mild slope on which they rode. The encampment was too far away for her to make out any particulars, but Tobar seemed certain it was theirs and had gone ahead to let Gunari know of their approach.

As it turned out, Mischka was in no way shunned, and she realized it the moment they drew within a hundred yards of the encampment. She heard the commotion first. Voices called out. Chickens squawked. Barking dogs followed by a pack of small children came running toward them, shouting her name. Mischka had to rein in her horse to avoid stepping on small bodies.

One of the welcome party called, "*Beebee* Mischka!"

Beebee? Which of these called her aunt? Her eyes swept over the dark heads, the smiling dirty faces, and she didn't recognize any of them.

"Back up, little ones," Emil called out. "Make way! *Beebee* Mischka is arriving."

They all dismounted, and a little girl in a faded blue and white sack dress took Mischka's hand.

"Elena? Are you my sister Elena?" Mischka looked down into the shy sparkling eyes she'd all but forgotten. "By the moon, you have grown so big!" The tiny child laughed and skipped, pulling Mischka forward.

All around her the children swarmed, called out her name, and asked excited questions of the men. Mischka didn't so much walk as she was swept forward and into the circle of wagons. There, sitting around campfires burning brightly and standing beside a dozen *vardos,* she found the rest of the *kumpania*. The first person to reach her was the one she had most often longed to see during her years of misery.

"Mischka. At last." Lumi engulfed her in a big hug.

Over her mother's shoulder, she saw her father a short distance away, a smile of satisfaction on his face. She wished he could clasp her to him as he did when she was a small child, but that was no longer appropriate. She would have to be content just to speak with him later, quietly, when the rest of the milling tribe had settled down.

She looked into her mother's eyes, still as black as ever and shining now with happiness. The hair at her temples was shot through with streaks of gray, and her *diklo* had shifted a bit high. Tearfully, Mischka straightened it. "Mama, I'm home."

Several women rushed forward to hug and touch the

prodigal daughter. The women were all speaking at once, and much of what was said wasn't particularly polite.

"Lumi, are you glad she's returned?"

"What happened to you, Mischka?"

"Children? Did you bring children?"

"She's in *breeches*."

The din hurt her ears, and Mischka felt disoriented, as though her body were rooted to the spot but her emotions were suspended somewhere far above her.

"She's so thin."

"Thin? She's emaciated."

"They beat her," someone said in disgust. "Wasn't she a good wife?"

"Hush. Of course she was."

"How was the travel?"

"Did their men treat you well?"

"What will you do now?"

Gunari raised a hand and tried to calm the excited people. He had aged a great deal since Mischka had last seen him. It didn't seem possible that in three years his beard could have gone from salt-and-pepper gray to white. The skin around his eyes and on his forehead was lean and wrinkled like worn leather. Not until his son Bersh put his fingers to his lips and let out a shrill whistle did silence descend.

Gunari held his arms out, palms down, and gestured as though he were holding down the air. "Calm down, everyone. I am sure your questions will soon be answered." He turned to Mischka. "Marona Lovell Gallo, you have come back to us."

As Mischka nodded, Lumi's arm tightened around her waist.

"What do you seek, young woman?"

Mischka had no idea what to say. Was there a particular ritual answer expected? If so, she didn't know it, so she said the first thing that came to her mind. "Shelter and protection in the bosom of my family."

"In the absence of your husband, will you submit once more to the care of your father?"

"Yes." Her face flooded with heat as she saw Arben's face in her mind's eye.

"Mikhail, do you accept this responsibility?"

"Yes, brother, I do."

"Will you seek action on the part of the *Kapo* to protect your interests?"

"I may, Gunari. I will speak privately with my daughter, and then I'd like to confer with you."

"Yes, very good." Gunari pulled his pipe out of his pocket and set to work packing it with tobacco. Someone handed him a wooden match. Gunari struck it against the bottom of his shoe and busied himself with lighting the tobacco. He took a deep draw, exhaled, then looked around. "Does anyone here oppose the return of this woman?"

Among the crowd, Mischka spotted her childhood nemesis, Cam. He was not much taller than she was, but his black hair still curled in wild tufts just as it had when they were little. He grinned and inclined his head. She recognized Milosh and Simionce and Aladar and so many others. Nobody spoke. She heard the rustling of the chickens in their cage, and a child cried out for his mother. The smell of roasted lamb wafted her way, and still Gunari waited.

The leader put the pipe in his mouth and took another draw. "Welcome back, Mischka, niece of my heart. Let's eat!"

A great cry went up, and Mischka's knees went weak. Her eyes filled with tears, and all the colors of the campsite swirled in her vision like a kaleidoscope of reds, oranges, and yellows. The women ushered her to a log by their fire, and someone thrust a mug of cool cider into her hands. Her sister, Elena sat next to her, and for what seemed like hours, she was questioned, congratulated, patted, and stared at until finally she rose and looked for her mother.

Lumi bustled over to her. "Come to my tent." She grasped Mischka's hand and pulled her toward an area on the other side of the *vardos*. "We'll get you a new bedroll and find skirts for you."

Mischka stopped in her tracks. "No. I'll no longer wear skirts at any time except when I choose to do so."

"But — but —"

"This is the one condition I have, or I cannot stay here. I will work harder than any other woman in the *kumpania*. I will fetch water before dawn. Tend the fire all night. Care for the sick and groom every horse the people own. But I'll wear breeches doing it."

Lumi's bright green and yellow blouse rippled in the wind as she frowned and stared at her daughter. "Is this because of Arben? Did he —"

"Mother. Please. Let us never speak his name again. Never. This one concession is all I ask — that I dress as I choose." She held her mother's gaze defiantly, then let her head drop to look at the packed dirt at their feet. "Please?"

Wordlessly, Lumi took her hand, and they never spoke of the matter again.

Chapter
Thirteen

New York City, November 1989 (Snow Moon)

"DOES MY FATHER know about all of this?" Tobar asked.

Mischka said, "Yes, why do you ask?"

"I just can't believe he and Mom have never told me any of this stuff."

She met Pippi's eyes and saw the worry on her face. Pippi never wanted to talk of the times in the Old Country, and Mischka could see her discomfort. Even now, she could tell Pippi was silently beseeching her to change the subject.

"Your father does, indeed, know all about this, and that's why he named you Tobar."

"Why did my brother get a nice, easy name like Steve?" His voice sounded cranky, and Mischka bit back a smile.

"Actually, your father originally thought to name him Stevo, after my brother, but your mother favored Steven, so they compromised. If your sister had been a boy, I suspect she would have been christened Emil, instead of Emily. In a culture that doesn't think much about the past, your parents have made a simple act like naming children mean something. You can say that you're all three named after key men in Pippi's and my life."

Tobar thought about that for a moment, then turned to Pippi.

"You named my father after his father. Why couldn't I have been François the Third?"

Under her breath she said, "Oh, my."

"François is kind of wussy as a name these days," Tobar continued, "but I could have gone by Frank, you know? That wouldn't be so bad."

Pippi let out a huff and glared at Mischka. "See what you've started?"

"Come now, he's old enough to know everything."

"Yeah, Grandma, I am. Tell me about my grandfather. And about what happened to you. I want to know."

Pippi hesitated, as though she couldn't decide whether to launch into the story or leave the room. When she let out a long sigh, Mischka knew she'd given in, so she sat back to listen to Pippi's remembrances.

Chapter
Fourteen

Reims, France, May 1940 (Hare Moon)

PIPPI OPENED THE door and saw a boy on her doorstep. About twelve years old, he twirled a navy blue beret in his hands and shifted his weight from one foot to the other. His brown hair nearly touched the collar of his light jacket. He might possibly have combed the mop earlier in the day, but now the back stood up like a horse's tail. The cowlick in the front also stood on end and made him look like all he needed was a little saddle in the middle, and an elf could ride around on his head.

"Good day, Madame," he said in French. "Is the m'sieur at home?"

Pippi pressed her lips together and tried to hide her amusement. "No, I'm sorry. My husband isn't home at the moment."

"Will he return later?"

Pippi shook her head. "He's stationed north of here, with the military. He won't be home any time soon."

The boy seemed to deflate. He jammed the beret on his head. "I can't find any men at all. None at the butcher shop or the shoe store or the auto repair shop. I had hoped he would be here even though we would have to pay."

"Pay? You aren't referring to a locksmith problem, are you?"

"Yes, I need to track down a locksmith immediately, and there isn't a man to be found."

"With the German army so close now, all the able-bodied men are on active duty," she said, amazed that she would need to explain. The town talked of little else. "What seems to be the problem—can you tell me? Maybe I can help you."

"My useless little brother is locked in the basement. I told my mother that we ought to leave him locked down there until my papa comes home from the war, but she won't hear of it."

Now Pippi smiled. The boy looked so desolate, so out of

sorts, that she couldn't ignore him. "It's an inside door that won't open?" He nodded. "Give me a moment, and I'll come with you. I'm fairly sure I can help. Where do you live?"

"Five streets over."

"All right. Wait a moment." Pippi ducked into the house and went to the closet near the parlor.

"Who is it, dear?" François's mother, Richelle, rose from the settee, a fountain pen in her hand. Several letters were spread out on the coffee table in front of her.

"It's a boy with a locksmith problem."

Richelle's mother-in-law, Linette, sat in an easy chair, her feet up on a hassock. "Is everything all right then?" Her circulation was poor and her hearing worse. Richelle turned to her and said loudly, "Pippi is going to help someone with a bad lock."

Linette cupped a hand behind her ear. "Haddock? We never get any of that here in France—even before the war."

"Bad...lock," Richelle said, carefully enunciating. "Someone needs a locksmith."

"Ahhh, I see." Linette pushed her glasses up on her nose and resumed her knitting.

Richelle and Linette had been staying with Pippi ever since François and his father were called back for military service nearly three months earlier. Combining households and sharing rations seemed to be working well, and she felt closer to Richelle as each day went by. Linette was often cranky, but she was old, so Pippi tried to be as patient as she could. She and Richelle stayed up many a night after Linette had gone to bed and talked about Richelle's early experiences with her mother-in-law. After hearing some of the stories, Pippi felt lucky that Richelle was such a calm and reasonable woman.

She pulled a lightweight coat out of the closet and grabbed a rain hat as well, which she tucked into her pocket. The skies had opened up earlier, but currently the rain was at bay. Her husband's awkward locksmith bag sat on the closet floor, jammed full of every kind of tool and part that François needed on calls. Pippi hoisted it up and hurried back to the parlor. Standing on tiptoes, she brushed a kiss against Richelle's soft cheek. Her mother-in-law reminded her so much of François—tall and willowy, with dark curly hair and sympathetic hazel eyes.

"I'll be back soon," she said and headed out the front door.

The boy took the chunky satchel from her and inspected the contents. "Glory, this is heavy!"

"With any luck at all, those tools will help me free your brother."

The prospect of releasing his brother didn't seem to cheer him much, however, and they set off along the quiet streets.

The only thing Pippi regretted about marrying into the Delebecque family was that all the men were so devoted to the military. François had enlisted after he finished his mechanical studies, a course of study that made him a valuable man to have around. Not only did he serve as a locksmith, but he could do electrical work and repair small engines, cars, telephones, and furnaces. She often teased that if something had a motor or heating element, François was kin to it. He could take apart and reassemble any weapon faster than anybody she had ever seen, but she wished he'd never seen the stock end of a rifle.

Civilians had little call for gun skills, but as a soldier, his talents were invaluable. If he hadn't been so clever with motors and mechanical equipment, perhaps he wouldn't have been called up for active duty now. Pippi wished he had never been in the armed forces in the first place, but service in the military was a family tradition. When he was reactivated in February, they'd only been given three days to prepare for his departure to the Ardennes front. She missed him terribly.

Then again, if he had not been so occupied with his army duties until the age of twenty-eight, some other girl would have met him before she did and stolen him away without her ever knowing. Pippi supposed she should be grateful to the military after all.

She'd met François at a dance at the Reims spring cotillion. She and her mother had traveled to Reims five years earlier, ostensibly to spend time with Camille's cousins and aunts and uncles, but the real reason was to give Pippi time to soothe a broken heart. She'd been engaged to Dieter Strasbach for three years. For one reason or another, he'd kept postponing the wedding. On the snowy January day when she turned twenty-nine, Dieter had taken her to a picture show in Eisenhüttenstadt. Afterwards, in a snowstorm on the street corner outside the matinee house, he had pulled her up short.

"I can't go through with this, Pippi."

"Hmm?" She was looking up at the streetlamp and watching the flurries dancing against the light. She wanted to open her mouth and run like a child to let the snowflakes land on her tongue. She thought of the delightful actress, Merle Oberon, from the movie *The Scarlet Pimpernel* that they had just seen. Lady Marguerite, as played by Miss Oberon, was divine — so full of life, so beautiful. Her high forehead supported a wealth of dark, curly hair, and those eyes, so dark and mysterious. They brought to mind her childhood friend, Mischka Gallo. She wondered about her old friend. Had she remarried? Emil hadn't written for some time to say one way or another. Pippi resolved to inquire in her next letter to him.

Dieter's voice cut through her musings. "Did you hear me? I can't."

"What?" Mischka's face faded from her mind. "What did you say?"

"It's over. Between you and me." He took his hand off her elbow and jammed his fists into his pockets. When she tried to meet his eyes, he focused on the ground.

"What?" She scowled. "What are you talking about?"

"I—well, I've met someone else. I—I've wanted to tell you for so long, but, well, you know."

From the tip of her head, she felt a chill that gradually descended to the back of her neck, down her spine and legs, and turned her feet into blocks of ice. "You just sat for two hours in the movie house and shared candies, and now you're jilting me? And on my birthday?"

"I'm sorry. I haven't known how to tell you."

"Hell and damnation." The line from the movie popped up, and Dieter looked at her with shock. She wasn't going to apologize. "Who is she?" Her voice was hard and accusing.

"No one you know."

She knew his gestures, his vocal inflections, and his every emotion: whether he was happy or ashamed or frightened, and right now he sounded miserable, which served only to infuriate her. "You cad. You lousy philanderer. You've led me on *all* this time, made promises, you...you..." She didn't will it to happen, but her hand came up and smacked him across the cheek. Clad in a thick glove, it made very little impression on his face, but he stepped back, face flushing red, and nearly bumped into some passing patrons.

"Take me home."

She had wanted to strike him again and run away, dive into a snow bank and cry, but she let him take her arm and escort her to the 1928 Voisin coupe of which he was so proud. She wondered if his new girlfriend knew as much about the Voisin as she did. Did the little tramp know it had a 4.9 litre engine and four forward speeds? Did she understand the importance of applying special wax? Had Dieter taken her into the country and sped 85 miles per hour and made her laugh and shriek with glee? She supposed he had, and if he hadn't yet, he probably would do so soon, now that he had forsaken Pippi.

Tears welled up and poured down her cheeks. She wondered why in the world he had chosen to break such dastardly news in front of the movie house. Couldn't he have waited until he'd delivered her back home? Why had he taken her out for her birthday in the first place? She would never think of Leslie Howard or Raymond Massey with fondness again. She felt a closeness to Merle Oberon, though. She, too, had been duped by her charming Pimpernel of a husband. Pippi glanced at Dieter. He squinted into the blizzard, his hands tight on the wheel as if his life depended upon it. He was no Scarlet Pimpernel. She wanted to strike him again.

They drew close to home, and she felt such relief to be escaping him that she didn't even say goodbye. She stepped out of the car, slammed the door, and made her way out of his life.

And now, five years later, things were entirely different. She remembered Dieter periodically, but didn't miss him at all. She thought of him as a temporary placeholder, someone she had passed time with while waiting for the better man to come to her. But these days, she missed the company of that better man, and instead of him taking care of the neighborhood lock problems, here she was out in the elements, damp wind at her collar, as she hastened to keep up with the boy leading her to his house.

"What's your name?" Pippi hunched into her collar against the damp wind.

"Henri. Henri Bedeau."

"I am —"

"I know. Madame Delebecque. This way." He mounted the stairs to a tall, thin Tudor-style house wedged in between two cube-shaped monstrosities with mansard roofs. Before he could reach for the handle, the door was swept open.

"Where have you been, Henri? Didn't I tell you to hurry, and — well, who is this?"

Pippi smiled at the frumpy woman. "Locksmith, come to call."

The woman, Madame Bedeau, Pippi presumed, stepped back in surprise. She wore an apron decorated with pale violet-colored bluebells over a shabby dark blue dress that had seen its day. The leather scuffs she wore on her feet displayed blocky ankles and thickset calves. "You can't help us, can you?"

Pippi shrugged. "Perhaps. I'll certainly try."

"Come in then."

Henri set down the satchel and Pippi let him take her coat. "Show me the door in question, Madame Bedeau, and I'll see what I can do."

The woman led her across the foyer and through a small sitting area. Colorful wooden blocks were stacked haphazardly in the middle of the room, and Pippi stepped carefully over them. They passed through a hallway and into a warm kitchen that smelled like apple pie. On one wood counter she saw a circle of flour and some bits of drying piecrust.

Dirty dishes were piled high in the sink, and the icebox door was slightly ajar. Madame Bedeau slapped it shut with a meaty hip. The radio sat on a side counter, tuned to a news program. Something bubbled on the stove, and an array of vegetables — cabbage, carrots, potatoes, and turnips — had been tossed in a heap on the counter.

Madame Bedeau pointed at a white door. "That leads to the cellar."

Pippi couldn't help but laugh at the loud banging and muffled wails coming from the other side.

"You'd think we were killing him," Madame said. "I told him to stay out of the basement, but he didn't listen to me. Then this one," she said and pointed her thumb at Henri, "decides to be clever and manages to snap the key off in the lock." Henri hung his head in shame.

"Maaa..." the impatient prisoner wailed. "Let! Me! Out!"

"We're working on it, Vincent. Pipe down."

"How old is he?" Pippi asked.

She sighed. "Eight going on eighteen. Boys. Why couldn't I have been blessed with at least one girl?"

Pippi inspected the door. A tiny corner of silver — part of the broken key — poked out at one end of the cylinder lock. It wouldn't be much to grab, and if she could get that out, the problem was easily solved. Pippi had spent enough time in the basement with François to learn many of his tricks. She knew her way around tumblers, driver pins, and shear lines, and François's lock pick kit was extensive. The keyway just needed to be clear. She wasn't worried. If all else failed, she could use the drill.

She leaned down to examine the keyhole, but the door shook with furious pounding. "Vincent?" she called out. "Vincent?"

All was quiet for a moment. "Who's there? Ma?"

"This is the locksmith. Could you take a step back and give me a minute to deal with this lock?"

"The locksmith?" His voice was flat and toneless. "I don't believe you."

"You don't? Well, then, once I get this door open, you can pretend it's still locked and stay in the basement until you waste away."

Madame Bedeau marched over and rapped on the door. "You listen to me, Vincent Michel Bedeau! One more word from you, and you'll be quarantined to your room for a week. You sit down on that stair and keep your mouth closed until this lady unlocks the door, or I'll use your father's belt on your backside."

Pippi heard a shuffling noise, and then all was quiet. "Henri, could you drag the satchel in? I know just what I need." She rummaged through until she found the needle-nose pliers, then bent and eyed the tiny bit of the key poking out. Her hands were steady as she applied the pincers to it and squeezed tight. With a gentle jiggling, she eased the fragment out of the keyhole.

"Aha!" Henri said. "You got it out!"

"Don't sound so amazed. That was child's play."

Madame Bedeau lowered herself into a chair at the table and put her head in her hands. "Thank goodness. Now can you unlock it?"

"I think so." Five minutes later, after a deft move with the lockpicks, she heard a clicking sound as tumblers came together. Pippi watched with amusement as a red-faced Vincent Bedeau emerged from the cellar. Though his hair was cut shorter, he looked, on a smaller scale, like an exact replica of his older brother.

"There you have it, Madame Bedeau."

"Thank you." The woman sighed with relief. "Please, call me Jeanette."

"And I'm Pippi."

"Would you like some tea, Pippi?" She rose before Pippi could answer. "I've got water already hot on the stove."

"If it's no trouble."

"Not a bit. Why don't you have a seat there at the table."

Biting back a smile, Pippi watched Vincent stomp over to his brother. "You locked me in there for hours," Vincent said to Henri. "You're rotten and should be shot."

"No I shouldn't."

"I could have starved. I didn't have any water. Or a bathroom. You did it on purpose."

"Did not." Henri got to his feet, and the boys faced off. Pippi knew if she watched the faces they were making at one another, she'd burst out laughing, so she busied herself with tea and pie that their mother set out for her on the kitchen table. Before they could come to blows, their mother sent them into separate rooms.

Pippi and Jeanette passed some time talking, and she learned that the Bedeau family consisted of four children—all boys. Henri and Vincent were the youngest. Their father had been called up for military service around the same time as François, and Jeanette was plainly as worried about the war situation as Pippi.

"I've heard the Italians are itching for a fight now," Pippi said. "Have you heard anything new?"

Jeanette shook her head. "No. I don't know what to think, but wouldn't it be nice if my Marc and your husband are perhaps in the same area? Two men from the neighborhood with something in common working together?"

"Yes, indeed, it would." Pippi put her elbow on the table and her chin in her hand and gazed out the kitchen window at the boxy, dark gray house next door. The rain had come again, and she was happy to be in the Bedeaus' cozy house smelling the delectable aromas of apple pie. She was also gratified that she'd solved the lock problem. It hadn't occurred to her that she might be able to handle some of François's work. If they fell on hard times, that might prove to be an advantage.

"What was that?" Jeanette rose, lunged toward the counter, and turned up the volume on the radio. The announcer spoke in a hasty, staccato voice:

> *...I repeat, Hitler has defeated the Netherlands. The German airforce has succeeded in outflanking the strongest defenses in the low country, and Belgium and Luxembourg are expected to fall as well. Yesterday, French tanks and infantry met the German invasion at the bridgehead over the Meuse River around Bulson, five miles south of Sedan, France. A Panzer Division crossed near Dinant as well. The French could not hold the line, and German forces have now entered France through Luxembourg and the Ardennes Forest. I repeat, German forces have attacked France.*
>
> *The Dutch have come to France's aid, but Sedan is lost and the Germans are advancing. Wait a minute...this just in... The Dutch army has surrendered. Ladies and gentlemen, we have a report that our Premier, Paul Reynaud, has announced that France has lost the battle, a decisive loss, an unexpected loss. Our allies have come to our aid, but the fighting is fierce.*
>
> *German forces breached the Maginot Line and are on the move south into France. In addition, our correspondents indicate that Italian citizens are burning both English and French flags. The Italians are threatening to join the Nazi Blitzkrieg.*
>
> *For those of you just joining this broadcast, let me repeat...*

Pale-faced, Jeanette sank down in the chair across from Pippi, and they stared at one another in shock.

She reached across the table and gripped Pippi's hand. "Dear God, help us."

Pippi's eyes filled with tears. She sat for a few moments with her newfound friend and listened to the announcer's harsh voice. Soon it became apparent that the announcer had no additional news, and she rose and thanked Jeanette for her hospitality.

Jeanette clambered up and retrieved Pippi's coat from the front closet. "Thank you for your help, Pippi. Please send me a bill."

As Jeanette opened the front door, Henri appeared at Pippi's side, lugging the satchel. "I can send for that later, Henri."

"No, Madame," he said, respectfully. "I will carry it back for you."

"THIS CAN'T BE happening," Pippi said. Dreary morning light leaked in through the window, and she looked out at the roiling clouds.

Richelle slumped on her elbows over the table, her hair uncombed. "I pray for them both—and for all our soldiers." She fingered rosary beads she held in one hand. "I wish there was something more we could do."

"If only we could find some way to know what was happening—to get information."

"The radio is a poor substitute."

Pippi nodded. Saint-Saëns's "Symphony No. 3" was just coming to a close, and in the momentary pause after the music ended, both women went still.

> *This just in. Boulogne has fallen to the Nazis. I repeat, Boulogne is lost. The Allies are withdrawing from some war-torn parts of Norway, and Belgium is overrun by the German juggernaut...*

During nearly every waking moment for days on end, Pippi sat in the kitchen with Richelle, drinking coffee and listening to the radio. In between news reports, the announcers played music by Frederic Chopin, François Couperin, and Franz Liszt. One day, they sat for what seemed like hours listening to Hector Berlioz's "Damnation de Faust." The music, beautiful as well as upsetting, reflected Pippi's mood, changing from simple melodies to soaring and triumphant songs, and then to heartbreaking sorrow. She felt as though she were on a sinking ship, and both she and Richelle were often on the verge of tears. They rose occasionally to check on Grandmere Linette and to make meals, but their grim vigil by the radio went on and on, as did the unbearable reports of devastation and failure in the face of the German army.

Richelle opened the door two weeks later to receive the telegram. As though in a daze, she signed for it, set it on the table, and sank into her chair. Pippi knew she was wrong to hope that the news was of her father-in-law. Not François. Please God, not François. Richelle was shaking so badly that Pippi reached out and grasped her cold hands. Both of them began to cry.

"You open it," Richelle said. "I—I can't."

It occurred to Pippi that if this telegram contained notice of a solder falling in battle, no matter which man it was, Richelle was going to be devastated. She turned it over. The telegram was addressed to Pauline Delebeque.

A strange calm came over her. All around her, all sound ceased, and she felt as though she no longer needed air. She looked down at the envelope she held, and watched as two pale hands that seemed unconnected to her opened it. The gray printing was faint and small:

THE SECRETARY OF WAR DESIRES ME TO EXPRESS HIS DEEP REGRET THAT YOUR HUSBAND CAPTAIN FRANÇOIS F DELEBECQUE HAS BEEN REPORTED MISSING IN ACTION SINCE 20 MAY IN FRANCE. IF FURTHER DETAILS OR OTHER INFORMATION ARE RECEIVED YOU WILL BE PROMPTLY NOTIFIED.
A.E. SANSCHAGRIN, CLERK OF THE REGISTRY

The room swam before Pippi's eyes, and her chest burned.

Richelle grabbed the edge of the table. "Pippi! It's François, isn't it? Pippi!" She let out a sob and grabbed Pippi's forearms.

Pippi drew a ragged breath, and the room came back into focus. She still sat, stunned and unspeaking. Richelle took the telegram from her hands and read it with tears rolling down her cheeks. "He's missing." Her trembling voice held a trace of hope. "Only missing, Pippi."

The words got through the thick, muzzy feeling in Pippi's brain, but some part of her knew Richelle was wrong. François was gone. She could feel it in her heart—and the pain radiating from the center of her chest hardly allowed her to draw breath.

She rose from the chair and mumbled an apology, then

stumbled out of the kitchen to climb the stairs to her room — to the bed she and François shared — and lay down upon the coverlet on her side. The material was soft against her cheek. She pulled her knees up and tucked her dress around her legs. Her hands crossed over her heart, which beat a fast staccato, and she lay waiting for it to stop as surely as François's had.

Chapter
Fifteen

Poland — North of the Tatras Mountains, November 1942 (Snow Moon)

MISCHKA RODE ON the lee side of her family's wagon, and from her vantage point up on the mare, she looked back periodically to follow the progress of four men approaching on horseback. As they overtook the *kumpania*, they waved politely, slowed their horses, and cantered along the edge of the road. As they passed Mischka close to the front of the convoy, her father spoke to them in Romany and then in German. None of the men paused, so he called out in Polish, asking what news they had.

The man at the rear was splattered with mud from the hooves of his companions' horses. He slowed to a walk and wiped a splotch of mud from his face with his sleeve. "We're fleeing the Germans. A search party is scouring the countryside to capture anyone and anything that moves."

"What?" Mikhail said.

"The Germans! Their army is moving in from the west. The Russians — they're coming from the east. We have nowhere to go but south and pray that Hungary's ties with the Axis aren't so strong. Otherwise — "

"But we have papers. We are approved for travel by the Polish authorities."

"Don't you understand? They're kidnapping people like you, old man." He tightened his grip on the reins. "I'm sorry to be impertinent, but it's true." He glanced back at the wagons. "If they catch you, the able-bodied will be sent to work camps in Germany and the rest put to death." A cry from up ahead urged the young man forward.

"Wait!" Mikhail yelled. "How far are they behind us?"

The man paused to consider. "Two, perhaps three hours. They travel the back roads in fast-moving carts, and their horses are large and strong." His friends were far ahead of him now. He jammed his hat down on his head, kicked his horse, and called out "Sorry..." as he galloped away.

Mikhail wasn't the only one who understood Polish. Mischka and some of the others on horseback dismounted and waited near Bersh's *vardo*.

Mikhail handed the reins to Emil's son, little Palko, who rode next to him. He hastened past Mischka to Bersh's *vardo*. "Bersh! Bersh! Did you hear that man's report?" Running stiffly, Mikhail caught up to the leader's wagon. He gestured wildly, and his words tumbled out.

After a few minutes of discussion, Bersh whistled the signal to pick up the pace. Mikhail stepped back and waited for his own *vardo* to roll forward. He climbed up next to young Palko. When the boy offered him the reins, he shook his head and searched in his coat. Mischka could see his hands tremble as he fumbled to light a cigarette.

For a good quarter-hour, the caravan continued at the stepped-up pace, bouncing over ruts and cracking through iced-over puddles. The wind was strong, and because of the rapid pace, the entire *kumpania* was unusually silent, with only the sound of goats bleating and an occasional chicken squawk.

From the moment the Pole had warned them of the German raiding party, Mischka barely paid attention to the road, instead letting various ideas play through her mind. If the Germans were only two or three hours behind them and traveling light, they would be upon the *kumpania* long before they could reach a safe region. She knew Bersh was a slow and methodical thinker, but surely he must know that they couldn't outpace fast-moving soldiers at this rate. They needed to ditch the *vardos* and make a run for it.

Just then, Bersh sounded a whistle, and the long train ground to a halt.

Some forty men, older boys, and even a few of the women gathered next to Bersh's wagon for a hasty conference. Mischka sat on horseback near the rear of the group, between Tobar and Xavi, Emil's younger son.

Clearly worried, Bersh said, "We need speed. I regret it, but we must abandon the *vardos*."

Bersh's son, Boldor, stomped a foot and let out an exasperated gust of breath. "Oh, no! How long have I worked to have a fine wagon? And now it'll be lost."

He moved a little away from the group, hands on his hips, and Mischka studied his sorrowful face in profile. She thought Boldor such a handsome man, and she'd never seen someone work so hard to acquire a *vardo*.

"Son, son, I know," Bersh said, "but safety is our first concern."

Emil spoke from atop his horse. "Perhaps we can hide the wagons and come back for them later. Use as few horses as possible to hide the *vardos*. Send half of them one way to the thickets, and the other half over into those trees." He pointed west.

"Yes, this is my thought as well," Bersh said. "We'll take only the most essential things and make a dash for the mountains."

The deep voices of the men rose, and Bersh allowed them a minute to discuss the idea. As the din of conversation faded, he raised his hand. "This will be a difficult journey. It's the elders I worry about, so we'll put each of them on horseback with one of the bigger boys. Women will need to ride holding one—maybe two—little ones. I fear we haven't enough horses. Some men will need to run, taking turns riding and resting."

Several people let out low groans, but no one argued.

Mikhail called to Mischka, "My daughter, what is the current horse count?"

"Thirty-seven. Two are too lame to bear a man, but supplies or a light rider wouldn't harm them."

Bersh said, "All right then, thirty-five horses for eighty-eight of us. This can be done." In a loud voice he shouted, "Don warm clothes. Dress the children for cold winter. Women, go pack saddlebags of food to last at least three days—maybe a week if you can. Rich food that's nourishing but weighs little. Please, hurry."

"What about covering our trail?" Emil asked.

Tobar let out a huff. "We hope for snow for that."

Mischka said, "Didn't the Pole say the Germans are only a couple hours behind us?"

"Yes." Emil shuddered. "If we spend too much time hiding the *vardos*, they'll catch up to us."

"Perhaps we should free one horse from each team," Mischka said, "and put the women and children on horseback. Send them ahead now with some of the men and elders. That would get them started off toward safety."

"Good idea," Emil said. "And the rest of us can hide the wagons. Then we'll catch up with the others."

Tobar called out to Bersh.

"What?" Bersh said, pulling at his beard in impatience. "We don't have a lot of time. I—"

"Wait, Bersh," Tobar said. "Listen, please. This will speed things up."

Mischka didn't wait to hear Bersh's pronouncement. Instead, she was already riding to her family's *vardo*. "Mama, we're switching plans. Get food now. Pack up the grandbabies—"

Lumi's head poked out the back door. "Yes, we're already almost prepared." She vanished into the *vardo*.

For the next fifteen minutes, men raced to unhitch horses. Older children followed orders to run about collecting bags, blankets, and other items. Women gathered crying children and wrapped them and themselves in layers of clothing for the cold journey. Mischka donned extra sweaters and wrapped a wool skirt around her as well. Even the goats were laden with blankets and leather satchels. The elders, the young, and the women mounted all but fourteen of the horses. Mikhail and Stevo prepared to lead the advance party forward, with Cam, Simionce, and Aladar on foot at the rear.

Bersh said, "Godspeed to all of you. Water the horses when you can. We'll join you shortly. Now hurry."

The little children called out merry good-byes. For them, this was an adventure. The older youth and women weren't so cheerful.

As the thunder of hoofbeats faded, Mischka took hold of a horse and led the family *vardo* ahead.

"Mischka! We overlooked you," Bersh said. "You should have gone ahead with them."

She shrugged. "Who would we have left behind? My mother? One of the elders? They needed my horse."

"You could have run with Cam and Aladar."

She let out a laugh. "No, thank you. I'll help with the *vardos*. Come. Let's get to work. Then you can allow me a horse to catch up with them."

HIDING THE CARAVAN took longer than expected. Off the well-traveled path, the ground became spongy with dark mud, and the thicket they sought was a half-mile or more away. At a breakneck pace, Mischka and six of the men took the front seven *vardos* and the two chicken coops across the plain to the east while Bersh and his group steered the rest toward the stand of trees to the west. Mischka hated to leave the chickens behind, but the troupe couldn't bring them along. Besides being far too noisy, they would also slow them down too much. She could only hope that the German search party would soon retreat and she might have a chance to come back for the chickens before they all died.

They drove the *vardos* into the brambles as far as they could, then unhitched the horses, stowed the tack, and led them out. Mischka stopped at the chicken coops to spread feed all around and unlatch the doors. "Chook, chook, choo Keep each other warm."

As they hurried back through the thicket, Tobar whispered, "You came up with a good idea, Mischka. Very good." He laced his fingers together, and she stepped into his hands so he could hike her up high in the air onto the smaller of the two horses, the one named Maisie. She adjusted her baggy wool skirt, irked at the inconvenience of it, and sat comfortably on the mare while Tobar mounted Ox, the big tan draft horse.

The wind picked up, and snow began falling. Wide, flat flakes drifted all around her. "Oh," she said in wonder. "Snow. Snow to cover our tracks."

"Snow to show our tracks, you mean." She and Tobar waited as Boldor, Talpa, and Branko emerged from the thicket followed shortly by two of Branko's sons. "Hurry," Tobar said. "Let's go, men." He let out a whistle once everyone was ready, and at a steady gallop, they moved across the plain to join Bersh's men.

NIGHT HAD FALLEN before Mischka's party finally caught up with the advance group and everyone halted.

Bersh dismounted and stretched. "Everyone warm enough? Is anyone hurt?"

His wife answered. "No injuries. The horses underneath keep us warm, and it hasn't snowed for a while. We're doing well."

"Very good. Let's pause to eat something, and then we must travel on."

The majority of the riders dismounted, and Drina, Lumi, and Mischka's little sister, Elena, helped the other women pass around the food. Most of the small children were fast asleep in someone's arms and never woke to eat. After downing *bogacha* bread, jerky, and cheese, Mischka drank half a skin of water. She jumped to the ground and passed the skin to her mother, then stretched her legs. Unlike many of the others on horseback, she rode most days, and her legs would not be nearly so sore as most of theirs would be.

Some of the boys ran to and fro on the path, breaking the thin sheet of ice on the puddles, and she did the same to let her horse drink. Still holding Maisie's reins, she stood to the side of the path, one foot on the ground and the other resting on a rotted tree stump. She looked down and saw that the wool skirt over her breeches was stained with mud, but she didn't care. If she could, she would remove it completely, but she left it on for warmth. Who knew how cold it would get—or when someone else might need it. Underneath she wore wool pants, two pairs of thick wool socks, and leather boots treated with resin to make them waterproof. With three layers of sweaters and a wool coat, she was overly warm. Once they started out again, she'd be in the wind and would be more comfortable.

She tilted her head up at the night sky and said a silent prayer to the Snow Moon. *Thank you for glowing bright to light our way and for keeping us safe. Shine upon us and not above the men who would capture and enslave us.*

The waxing moon would be full in a couple more days. Only a sliver was missing tonight. A new moon indicated time to close out old issues, to let go of that which was pessimistic or hurtful, and to finish things. But a waxing moon signified a time of promise, time to call upon the goddess as Maiden and ask for the strength and understanding to begin new things and new experiences.

Mischka looked around the small clearing in which she stood. She couldn't help but smile. They were all embarking upon a new adventure, that was for sure. Soon enough, the full moon nights of the goddess as Mother would arrive, and after that, the waning moon focused on the Crone goddess. Mischka thought the cycle was lovely. She had always wondered why the Maiden/Mother/Crone Goddess was not referred to by the Roman Catholics. In combination with the Father, Christ figure, and Holy Spirit, she felt the circle was complete. The Catholic God as sun; the Goddess as moon. Both sides of the coin; day and night. She loved the sun, but she was drawn more strongly to the mysterious moon. She'd been born during a Snow Moon as a waxing quarter moon graced the sky, and that thought gave her pause. Today could be the anniversary of her birth. She must be thirty-three years old. With a chuckle, she thought, *I am old— nearly the same age as Jaworski's Christ when he was betrayed.*

Gyorgy's voice sounded softly from some distance away. "Let's go, sister. I'll give you a boost up."

Soon, they were off again, and when the moon was high in the sky they reached the foothills of the Tatras Mountains, at one of the lower passes of the Carpathian Range. Depending upon where they made their ascent and descent, they would likely pass through Slovakia, but it was less than a hundred miles south to Hungary. They pushed on as another hour passed, then two. The moon disappeared behind clouds and they were forced to slow and let the animals find the path. Mischka realized dawn was a little over an hour away.

The horses clearly suffered from fatigue, but after a brief water break, again Bersh urged them ahead. "We must get past the foothills and into terrain where it's more difficult for the German carts to travel. Come. We move on. Stay close. The path twists and turns many ways now."

Thrum...thrum...thrum... Each time her horse's hooves hit the ground, the jolt jarred Mischka and kept her awake. She was beyond tired, and her little mare must be exhausted. Mischka leaned forward, her thick hair falling down around her face and onto the horse's sweaty neck. She patted the mare, willing energy to flow to her. "Thank you, Maisie," she whispered. "Stay with me. It's not long now."

The path narrowed and went east, then later meandered and switched back to the west as they went up an incline that became more pronounced. She turned her head to look down the hill and across the valley they had fled from. Squinting, she noticed a tiny pinprick of golden light bobbing along several miles away, maybe a lantern on a cart or wagon. Perhaps a man carried it, but even from this distance, it seemed to be moving too fast—unless the man were running, and she thought that unlikely. She watched for another minute, paying no attention to Maisie, so Mischka was surprised when her mare shifted course and she was no longer able to see the light. Soon enough, they traveled southeast on the incline. The path forked, and they went to the left, then came around due east. Over her right shoulder, she watched and waited. After a few moments, from a grove of trees, the light emerged again, closer than ever.

This was not good, not good at all. To complicate matters, the blackness of the night was diminishing. She could see that the *kumpania* still had quite some distance before exiting the foothills and getting to the scrub trees around the base of the mountain. Once the sun came up, they would be in full sight unless they could make it into the trees.

They came to another fork, and this time the troupe went right, avoiding a very steep grade. Mischka scanned for the pass in the dark mountain looming ahead. As far as she could tell, her people could travel through the foothills by staying on increasingly narrow paths that led up to the pass, or they could travel along wider trails that ran parallel to the mountain's apex and periodically forked off to the south. Bersh was alternating between gradual slope and narrow path, which gave the laboring horses an easier time.

Was it her imagination, or was the bobbing light slightly bigger now? Soon its progress would be concealed by the scrub brush in the foothills, and then she would have no way to gauge how far ahead the *kumpania* was or how close their pursuers had drawn. At some point, the Germans—for she was now certain they were soldiers — were going to have to stop to unhitch their horses from the carts, but that wouldn't take much time.

She glanced behind. Three horses labored behind her bearing Aladar's son, Shandor, then Gyorgy, and finally Tobar riding with Emil's son Palko. She pulled up, and the end of the procession came to a stop as she shifted to the side and looked over her shoulder.

Shandor, obviously half-asleep, mumbled, "What's the matter?"

"Shhh..." she said. "They're closer than we think, and they mustn't hear us. Sound travels too easily up here."

Tobar said, "You've seen the light, too." It was a statement, not a question.

"What light?" Shandor whispered.

"The soldiers are only a matter of minutes away," Mischka said. "As soon as they unhitch their horses, they will race up the mountain and fall upon our families. We must draw them away — give the caravan time to get over the pass and elude them on the other side."

"How do you propose to do that?" Gyorgy cupped a hand over his mouth to muffle his words.

Tobar grinned, and his beard shook. "We take them on a wild chicken chase, right, Mischka?"

"Yes. But someone has to catch up and pass the word to Bersh. He needs to go all out, straight up the mountain. No more gentle slopes. Once the sun comes up, we'll be easy prey."

Gyorgy said, "We three men will draw them away. Mischka, you pass the word ahead."

"No, my brother. You have a family. I have none. *You* go deliver the word. Besides, we need someone strong at the end of the procession, just in case they do catch up."

"She's right, Gyorgy," Tobar said. "Shandor and I are single men. Your children depend upon you."

"Papa will kill me," Gyorgy whispered in a heated voice. "I can't leave you, Mischka. What if you're caught?"

Shandor raised his chin high. "We shall not be caught. How ridiculous."

Mischka didn't comment on Shandor's ego. "We don't have time to debate. Go. Leave it to us, Gyorgy. We'll meet you at the bottom of the mountain."

"Yes," Tobar whispered. "Here, take Palko." They quickly transferred the youth from in front of Tobar to Gyorgy's horse, and once he was settled, Tobar shook Gyorgy's hand. "Go, my friend. We'll soon be back together on the other side of the mountain."

Gyorgy sighed, then in a firm whisper he said, "Meet us at the campground in the low reaches of the south side of the mountain. We will wait—or leave a lookout for you. If you're delayed more than a few hours, then travel southward through the Slovak lands—to the farm village of Miskolc in Hungary. We'll post someone in the woods in case the town is in enemy hands. Godspeed, my sister and brothers!"

They jockeyed their horses around, and bade farewell, and almost immediately Tobar said, "They come. I hear them in the distance. We must work together now. Make a lot of noise and run west for at least two miles. Shandor, take the upper path that runs there." He pointed ahead of them to the left. "Mischka, you shall take the middle path, and I'll take the low path."

"No, Tobar," Mischka said, "you stand the greatest risk of capture."

"Don't worry about me. Ox is the strongest, hardiest horse and I have plenty of tricks up my sleeve. Shandor, do *nothing* foolish. Stay out ahead of them. Make a lot of noise to attract them to the west. Our families must make it over the pass. Once we draw them away, circle up and over to the southwest. Whatever you do, keep moving southwest and angling upwards. Understand?"

"I wish we had Emil's gun," Mischka said.

Tobar smiled a wicked, toothy grin. "We'll kill them with our bare hands if it comes to that." He took a deep breath. "All right, time to run like foxes through the forest." Palms up, he held his hands out, and his companions grabbed his big mitts. Through her leather gloves, Mischka squeezed his hand tight.

"Go like the spirits," he said. "I'll bring up the rear."

Mischka spurred her horse forward, her heart beating fast in her chest. Behind her, Shandor let out a whoop. The Snow Moon had gradually disappeared, and the bloody edge of the sun arose over the horizon, spreading a pale stain of light over the foothills that Mischka and her companions rode so furiously across.

MISCHKA WASN'T SURE how far she and Maisie traveled. The sun was up, casting rays, and she felt faint warmth on the back of her neck. Although she saw mist gushing out of her mouth with each breath, she wasn't aware of the cold. She felt only worry, extreme fatigue, the heat of exertion. Both she and the horse could see the ground better now that more light was filtering through the scrub. She heard sounds of pursuit, but far off in the distance. Should she slow her flight? What if they stopped giving chase and went back after the caravan? Torn, she decided to continue on so long as she could hear the hoofbeats and shouts.

She wondered if Bersh would be able to make the mad scramble up the mountain into Slovak territory and if soldiers would be there, too. Even if the *kumpania* managed to make it into the Slovak lands, how long would it take them to cross into Hungary? She hoped Tobar and Shandor were faring well and that the three of them had a chance of reuniting at the pass and traveling on together.

She came to a fork and angled uphill to the left, deciding she had traveled due west long enough. The little mare stumbled on the incline. Clacking her tongue against the roof of her mouth and nudging with her knees, Mischka urged her forward. So intent was she on spurring the horse that she didn't see the washout until she was almost upon it. A huge section of rock had slid down the hill forming a twenty-foot-high barricade that couldn't be crossed.

She reined in her horse, and the little mare skidded to a halt, sides heaving and sweat pouring off her flanks. Sick with panic, Mischka looked behind her. She could hear the pursuers and guessed she had only minutes to find another path to take. She had to get down to that fork and come at this from a different angle. She coaxed Maisie around and loped back down the trail to take a different route at the fork she'd passed earlier. Much to her dismay, she saw how much in the open she was and how easily her brown horse and dark brown clothing must stand out in the midst of so much gray and tan. But Maisie's hooves found purchase, and when she'd gone far enough to bypass the washout, a surge of adrenaline coursed through her. It was now or never. Tightening her grip on the reins, she tucked in behind the velvety brown head, and prodded the little horse back up the hill.

At the next turn of the trail, she broke through a thicket of low-hanging branches and yanked Maisie up short—face-to-face with a band of soldiers.

"THEY GOT HER." Shandor couldn't meet Tobar's gaze.

"Oh, no." His breath coming in rushes, Tobar took in the lay of the land. Now that daylight allowed it, he could see movement in the valley below the foothills. He counted a half-dozen soldiers and seven horses. His heart sank, knowing that there were likely more Germans they couldn't see.

Through gritted teeth, he said, "Ride like the hounds of hell, Shandor. Save yourself. I'm going after her." He turned his horse on the narrow trail, paused a moment, and looked back. "You tell her father that I will rescue her or die trying, do you hear?"

Without waiting for a reply, he left Shandor behind and spurred his horse back toward the pass.

He had no weapons other than a hammer, branches, his own brute strength—and his wits. Surely he could somehow extricate Mischka. He headed down the hill as fast as the horse could carry him, his head spinning. He tried to console himself that the *kumpania* had aimed for the pass four or five miles east of here, and because of the diversionary tactics, they may have gotten away free. He barely had time to reflect on that, when a voice yelled, "Halt!" and two German soldiers stepped out of the trees, their rifles trained on him.

Tobar did as he was told and slid off the horse with legs that felt rubbery. The soldiers came closer, speaking too fast for him to put his rudimentary German to work. They wore soiled uniforms, and they both shivered from the cold. One of them gestured toward Tobar's coat, then poked him in the forearm with the barrel of the rifle. Understanding, Tobar removed his jacket. The soldier snatched it away and put it on, prompting an argument from the other soldier. For a moment, Tobar thought he might be able to jump one of the men and get his gun, but they stopped fighting and one motioned for him to get up on his horse. They then proceeded down the trail, one soldier walking behind, his gun trained on Tobar's back, while the other took the reins and led the horse. He chose to cooperate, to wait, hoping they would lead him to Mischka and then he could free her.

They seemed nervous, reacting at every bird that rustled the trees, every small animal in the brush. Looking closer, Tobar could see they weren't much more than boys—perhaps in their late teens. He wanted to ask them why they were rounding up people like so many wild horses but he kept silent, preferring to let them think he didn't understand any of their language. When they passed the edges of the foothills and entered the valley, they encountered a middle-aged officer dressed in a much neater dark green-gray uniform. He was shouting at a group of bedraggled soldiers.

"Two riders? You've got to be joking. Two dozen horses or more have passed through here, and this is all you apprehend? You're pathetic!"

He stomped over to Tobar and sneered up into his face. "Has anyone searched him for weapons?"

The soldiers didn't answer. "My God, you men are stupid. You, over there! Prepare the wagons for travel. The others have escaped, so we may as well return with our quarry." He pointed to a trio of soldiers lined up next to a cart. "You will pursue the escapees on foot." With salutes, they broke formation and moved double-time toward the foothills.

A soldier came and led Tobar's horse away. Another searched his pockets, taking his pocketknife as well as everything else of value. As the rough hands moved over him, Tobar scanned the surroundings until he found Mischka — or the edge of her figure, to be more exact. She sat on the other side of a cart, partly hidden by the wheel. The soldier gave him a shove in her direction, and when she saw him, her mouth dropped open.

"Tobar!" She was near tears. "You should have gotten away."

Tobar squatted in front of her. "We leave no one behind, Mischka. No one."

"But now we're both captives. You could have saved yourself. One loss is better than two."

With a hint of a smile, Tobar said, "If it had been me, you would have come back. Admit it." She refused to look at him. "I could never have lived with myself if I'd run away and left you. How could I face your father? No. You keep your eyes and ears open. We'll get out of this together. I'm sure of it."

"You've always wanted to marry me," she said dryly. "Act like you're my husband now, and perhaps they'll allow us to ride together."

He lowered his big physique and sat stiffly beside her. "We *will* escape, Mischka. Wait until nightfall. We'll get away."

"I can only hope you're right." He shifted closer to her, and she leaned into his solid warmth.

BUT IT SOON became clear to Mischka that Tobar's optimism was unfounded. Tied securely to thick metal bars inside the cart, they rode for hours into the night without a break to eat or relieve themselves. At daybreak they reached a tiny dilapidated shack adjacent to railroad tracks. A row of carts waited in the late morning gloom. Most were full of civilian men, but Mischka was untied and dragged roughly to one occupied entirely by women.

Outraged, but unarmed and still tied up, Tobar could only shout at the soldiers to leave her alone. The men behaved as though they were deaf. They shoved her up into the cart, and Mischka settled heavily next to a plump blonde woman. The soldiers re-tied her, and her only consolation was that she could still see Tobar who towered over everyone near him in his cart. She stared helplessly into his dark eyes and bit her top lip to ensure she didn't cry. She could swear she saw tears running down into his beard.

Hours later they were taken from the carts and herded to a train of cattle cars. The women were pushed into one car and the men into several others. After the train set off, Mischka lost track of time. At first she attempted to look out the slats to see where they were going, so she would know their location when she managed to escape. But she soon grew too tired and thirsty to continue and sat down on the wooden floor. She fell asleep and dreamed of her family on horses, riding at breakneck pace over the mountains. She shouted, "Don't stop!" to them over and over. "Run hard, run fast."

When she awakened, the train car's door was sliding open. Soldiers shouted for them to get out, and the women stumbled out into the dusk to bring up the rear of a large pack of men, surrounded by rifle-carrying soldiers and being driven forward like a herd of animals. Mischka saw they were near a wooded area with no signs of either a town or a campfire, no farms, nothing nearby. She followed the crowd, sure-footed, but fatigued. Some of the women around her, most of whom spoke Polish, complained and cried. One kept saying her feet were bleeding while another repeatedly called out "Mercy" in Polish.

After many miles of her weeping and wailing for mercy, a young soldier yelled, "Be quiet." The Polish woman went silent.

The woman with the sore feet continued to cry out. Through gritted teeth, the soldier shouted, "Shut your mouth."

Mischka winced to hear the woman keep sobbing. Why didn't she just shut up like he told her?

But she didn't comply. The soldier shouldered his rifle and pulled her out of the group. He let loose a torrent of German, which she obviously didn't understand. She only cried more, pointing down and repeatedly screaming, "My feet. My feet are bleeding."

He lost what patience he'd had, seized her roughly by the arm, and dragged her away from the group toward the woods. Mischka covered her ears, not wanting to hear what she feared would come next. When the shot came, she shuddered and pressed her gloved fingers to her lips. The women around her drew closer; some who apparently knew one another were already holding hands. No one spoke—not a single utterance. They simply walked, their faces pinched with fear.

Running footsteps came behind them, and in an aggrieved tone, the German soldier muttered, "Now not only her feet bleed."

Mischka was glad that most of the women around her didn't seem to understand what he said—or if they did they gave no indication. A faint rain oozed from the sky, and they continued their forced march in silence.

At one point, the sea of people ahead parted, and Mischka veered to the right just in time to avoid stepping on a figure on the ground. A white-haired man lying on his side gripped his chest, his face twisted in pain. Someone should help him. This wasn't right. But Mischka knew there would be no help for him, nor for her should she fall. Placing one foot in front of the other, she didn't look back when a single shot echoed a few moments later.

Late in the night they came to railroad tracks on a flat plain. The soldiers ordered them to halt, then motioned for them to be seated. The ground was wet with rain, and Mischka didn't wish to soak her skirt or the wool pants underneath, so she squatted and arranged the skirt around her. No one spoke, but she heard sighs and a few grunts of pain. A peculiar clicking noise began to her right, and she hazarded a glance. The plump, blonde woman who had followed her all day was so cold her teeth were chattering. She wore only light shoes, a thin dress, and a shabby jacket.

The soldiers were paying little attention, so Mischka removed her coat and pulled off her top two sweaters, which she handed to the woman.

The woman's stunned eyes filled with tears, as though she could not believe the kindness offered. In Polish, she whispered her thanks and hastily pulled on the thick sweaters.

"What's your name?" Mischka asked.

"Aurora Wolnick. And yours?"

Mischka hesitated a moment. "Marona Lovell Gallo. Please call me Mischka."

"Pleased to make your acquaintance, Mischka. Thank you for the sweaters. They took me from my yard and left me no time to dress in warm clothes."

"Are you alone?"

"No. My husband and two sons are up ahead somewhere."

"How old are your sons?"

"Fifteen and sixteen. I have two grown daughters and another son, but they live over the mountains."

Mischka brightened, feeling a tiny thread of excitement for the first time in two days. "Over the mountains? They are safe in Hungary?"

"They're in Czech territory. Why do you ask?"

"My family and relations are headed for Hungary. I just wondered if I could be allowed the luxury of believing they would make it to a safe realm."

Aurora put her face in her hands, and when she raised her head, tears glittered on her cheeks. "We were so far south, we thought our farm was safe. But the Germans are relentless. They took our horses, our cattle, all of our pigs. Pigs and chickens rode in carts while we walked. This is the third day we've walked."

"Any food?"

"No. None."

"Where can they be taking us? I don't understand."

"Before they separated us, the men from my village said we're being taken to work camps."

"We won't be able to work if they don't feed us soon," Mischka said in a hissing whisper that was loud enough to attract the attention of a soldier smoking nearby. He looked in their direction with suspicious eyes. He obviously didn't want to bother with the chore of abusing them and instead began talking with a comrade nearby.

Aurora huddled closer to Mischka and said, "I hope you don't mind me sitting so near."

Mischka, sad at heart, shook her head. "No, I think human warmth may be all we have left."

Chapter
Sixteen

Tatras Mountains, November 1942 (Snow Moon)

WHEN SHANDOR CANTERED up behind the line of horses on the snowy trail, Emil breathed a sigh of relief. They were returning. Somewhere up the line, a cry went up, which was hastily muffled. They couldn't afford for sounds to travel through the crystalline air and be heard by sentries anywhere ahead or behind.

Shandor drew closer, and all the hair on Emil's arms stood on end. The young man's eyes were wild. "They're lost."

"Lost? What do you mean, lost?"

"The Germans got Mischka. Tobar went back for her. They're lost." Gyorgy was suddenly standing next to Emil. "What happened?"

Emil saw that Shandor was doing all he could to keep from crying. His dark eyes, haunted and welling with tears, wouldn't meet Mischka's brother's gaze.

Gyorgy grabbed Shandor's boot where it rested against his mount. "I knew I should have been the one to go. I knew it was a bad idea."

Emil said, "It was the only thing we could do, Gyorgy. The only thing. We've lost two to save more than eighty."

"Yes," Shandor whispered.

Gyorgy pulled Shandor off the horse. Through gnashed teeth he said, "You tell my father, then. You be the one to share news of this most excellent trade-off. What will we do without Tobar? Without Mischka—" His voice broke.

"I'll tell Mikhail," Emil said. "And we have to go on now."

"No. I'm going back to get them."

Shandor said. "It will do no good. You'd have to kill fifteen or twenty soldiers."

Emil met Gyorgy's gaze. "For the sake of the children—your children and mine—we must move on."

"I'll be the one to tell my father then. And you—" He gave Shandor a scathing look. "Stay out of my way." He turned and walked off toward the front of the convoy.

"It's not your fault," Emil said.

Shandor turned his face into his horse's withers and would speak no more.

EMIL STOOD WITH Mikhail on the side of a snow-covered slope. In a few short hours, this man, who had always seemed like a kindly uncle, had gone from a lively sixty-year-old man to a stooped and defeated one. Emil stood shoulder to shoulder with him, wanting to allow Mikhail a measure of privacy in his grief.

Mikhail said, "It was one thing to lose her to the marriage vows all those years ago, but when she came back, she was like a gift to her mother. I've been selfish, keeping her here with us all this time. And now...now what will we do without her?"

Emil had no words of comfort for his friend, no calm assurances. Nothing he could say would change things.

Suddenly, he reached over and grabbed Emil. "You're German. What will they do to her? What will they do to Tobar?" His voice was laced with desperation.

"I don't know, my friend. I don't know. I've been gone so long from that society. I haven't a clue what happens when they take people East."

In a strangled voice, Mikhail said, "But no one we have heard of has ever returned. No one."

Emil didn't know what to do or say. Over the last few months, they had heard reports of people being taken from homes, from churches, from towns. Whole *kumpanias* had been swept up, leaving behind broken crockery and smashed *vardos*. No one could say what happened to any of the people forcibly taken by the Nazis. Few were exempt. Jews, Gypsies, Catholics, Poles—even tramps with German papers weren't safe. Emil could only imagine what the authorities would do if they caught him. A clean execution would be a blessing.

Bersh approached them, panting. "We must move on." He put a hand on Mikhail's shoulder. "Thank you for the offer to lead us to your family's farm, but I have decided we should move west to the Czech lands. We'll head for Brno."

The expression on Mikhail's face went from hopeful to shocked. "But Bersh, traveling south into the Slovak lands will be warmer and easier. Going all the way to the Czech lands— that's an incredibly long journey."

"Don't you think I know that? However, Hungary is occupied, and I believe the Czech lands will be safer. We have no assurance that your father's people even live in the area any more. A *Kapo* I know and trust travels in the upper Czech region. We will go to him."

Mikhail looked thunderstruck, so Emil nodded and thanked Bersh. He put an arm around his grieving friend and guided Mikhail to his wife. Lumi was inconsolable as were Mischka's younger sisters. Drina, Emil's wife, sat astride a mare and held her sleeping son, Xavi, in front of her.

Lumi's head rose and she looked blindly at Emil, then to Mikhail. "We should never have let her be so headstrong, so willful. This is our fault."

She broke down into sobs, and Emil turned away, tears in his eyes. Little Mischka—such a joy. So exuberant and loving. She had lost a lot of that exuberance after her husband's beatings, returning from the ill-fated marriage as a quiet and enigmatic woman, not quite herself anymore. She was smarter than Bersh—smarter than most of the men—but to be heard, she had to speak through one of her brothers or Emil or Tobar. Now she was gone. He couldn't believe it.

He hastened to his horse at the rear. Shandor was already astride his mount and looked like someone had knocked the wind out of him. A memory of one of his friends, a man named Gruenwald, came to Emil just then. Gruenwald had shared the last foxhole with Emil in the Great War, and the man had known so many naughty jokes—enough to keep several men chuckling through long, cold nights. He had been gut-shot in an unexpected assault and died a slow, painful death at Emil's side

More than two decades had passed, but Emil could still picture Gruenwald's face, see his reddish hair, and recall how he pinched damp cigarettes between thumb and forefinger while trying to remember limericks. He realized that in surviving, he and Shandor had something in common, and he hoped he would get the opportunity to talk about this with the young man one day. He hoped they would live to have idle conversation over a hearty meal. To love their sons and daughters. To tell their stories to grandchildren. Such miracles could happen. Emil, of all men, knew that.

Chapter
Seventeen

Southern Poland, November 1942 (Snow Moon)

THE MORNING SUN rose as a new train arrived belching black smoke, and the captives were loaded aboard for yet another stage of their torturous journey. The doors closed before everyone had chosen a spot, but they managed to seat themselves comfortably enough, if sitting on the floor of a cold train could be considered comfortable.

Aurora leaned into Mischka, snuggled her back against her for warmth, and both of them eventually fell asleep. Mischka dreamed she rode in the back of a swaying *vardo*, the sound of horses clopping along ahead and behind. A spray of long blonde hair fanned out on the thick rug on which she lay. Mischka lifted her hand and reached out to touch it. She collected up a hank of hair and let it run through her fingers. It wasn't as thick as her own curly hair and felt soft against her palm. She leaned to the side to see who lay with her and saw the face of a young woman who looked achingly familiar, but she couldn't be sure who she was. *Open your eyes. If you open your eyes, I can be sure.*

As if reading her mind, the woman stirred and awakened. She looked up at Mischka with a frown on her face. She didn't open her mouth to speak, but Mischka clearly heard her say, "I know you. You're my friend, my love, bonded by heart and spirit."

Mischka awoke, surprised to find not Pippi, but a strange woman, snuggled into her arms. She slowly came to recognize that she sat in a damp, dimly lit train car, not the back of her parents' warm, dry *vardo*. She thought she had been asleep for a long while, but she didn't feel refreshed.

The rhythm of the clacking wheels changed, and she peered through a crack in the boards. The train slowed to a halt, and Aurora awoke and sat up. A few minutes later the door was wrenched open. Bright sunlight poured in. Mischka blinked and her eyes watered. She made out the bleary image of a soldier with his rifle pointed at them, and several women let out gasps. Mischka sat, tense, awaiting instructions, but no words were said to them. Instead, soldiers shouted, and a mob of women swarmed up into the dirty car, crowding against the current occupants. Mischka frowned as she and Aurora had to shift along the wall. A shivering girl who smelled of sour milk pressed up against her other side. Mischka knew she dared not speak, but she grew angrier by the moment. What were they to do? Levitate to make room?

As abruptly as the door opened, a soldier slid it shut, leaving everyone in semi-darkness.

"My God," a voice whispered, "what have you done to us?"

"God has nothing to do with this," another woman said. Her nasally voice was loud and accusing.

"Shhh! Stop it." This plea came from someone seated on the floor near the door. "Just find a place to sit."

"As if there *were* a place to sit," the nasal voice said. "This place stinks."

Far ahead a whistle blew, and the car jerked forward. Women stumbled and fell causing angry complaints from those trampled.

"Ouch! Get off my hand," someone called out. Other women groaned.

The nasal-voiced one said, "I need to pee."

"Well, don't do it here, Petronela," a woman said. "I'm sitting below you."

Aurora squirmed into a more comfortable position, shoulder to shoulder with Mischka. "This is such a big train. Why do they cram us all into one car?"

Mischka shrugged. "I suspect that all the cars are filling up."

"Good Lord. How many people have they captured, I wonder?"

"I don't know."

Over the next several minutes, the original occupants shifted and made room for the newcomers until they were packed shoulder to shoulder, hip to hip. Mischka's back and neck were cold, but the cracks in the wood walls brought fresh air and helped to clear away the stench of sweat and urine and fear. After a time, she closed her eyes once more and drifted into a half-sleeping state where minutes passed slowly and the hours lingered.

Mischka thought about her family, seeing them in her mind's eye as they made it over the mountain and down into safer territory. She prayed that none of them had been taken prisoner. Squeezing her eyes shut tight, she imagined the horses carrying all of the *kumpania* down the hill and into the forest region below. She saw her mother's face, her father's smile. She knew they would be frantic with worry, but as soon as she could escape, she would make her way back and join them once again.

LATE IN THE day, the train pulled to a stop on a flat plain near a stone station house and a makeshift outhouse. Mischka watched through a narrow gap as a half-dozen soldiers marched toward the train.

Chains rattled, and the unlocked door opened. A man pointed a rifle at them while another gestured and in German said, "Get out."

Mischka rose, softly whispering "get out" in Polish, Hungarian, and French for good measure. The women piled out onto the hard dirt like a stream of lemmings. The smell of burnt coal was pungent, as was another smell, something cloying and rotten. Mischka wrinkled her nose and breathed through her mouth.

A soldier said, "Move. Over there." He pointed toward the front of the shack. "You will line up in rows of eight, one behind the other."

"Rows of eight," she said in various languages. "Over here."

Mischka found it hard to believe how many human beings had been crammed into so few train cars. Men staggered from the other six cars and were directed to either side of the shack.

Her companions hurried along with her, but as they moved, she walked on tiptoe searching to the right and the left, hoping to catch sight of Tobar. She stopped and women hastily formed a line on either side of her. "Eight across," she said.

Women squeezed past and behind, and when she looked around, there were eleven rows. An angry argument began outside the women's car. Puzzled, she looked out toward the train. A soldier appeared in the doorway, kicking a large bundle of rags. The conglomeration teetered on the edge, then fell the four feet to the ground. Only then did Mischka see spindly arms and legs windmilling out the door. A woman. Oh, no. Oh no. Her breath caught in her throat. That could just as well have been her. She tried to swallow, but all the moisture in her mouth had dried up, and she thought she might be sick.

Frantically, she looked left and right...and then she saw a tall figure in the front row of the group lining up ten yards to her left. He waved, and she called out, "Tobar!" first feeling relieved to see him, then fearful that they would be separated again.

Soldiers ordered the men into formation at gunpoint, shouting, "Quiet! Quiet!"

As she heard this, Mischka was shouting, "Are you all right?" Tobar shrugged and put his hands up, palms out. A soldier turned and strode toward the women.

"Who spoke?" No one answered. He halted in front of them, rifle gripped loosely, butt down toward the ground. "If no one admits to it, I will shoot one of you at a time until someone confesses."

Mischka knew that most of the women did not understand his fast, loud speech, but she did. She looked into the soldier's flat blue eyes and in a weary tone said, "It was me."

"Step out here."

She took one tentative step.

He shrieked, "Here! Now!" He grabbed the front of her coat and jerked her forward. "On your knees."

He pushed her to the ground, and Mischka closed her eyes, waiting for the shot. An image came to mind. She sat high on a black stallion, looking back at her brother Stevo who knelt in the coarse dirt under a blood-red sun. Was this how he had felt? This cold fear?

She heard a shout, recognized a voice. "No! No! No! You must not — no!"

Her eyes popped open as Tobar's shouts drew nearer. Sick with dread, she watched as the Nazi turned his rifle on Tobar and two other soldiers, guns aimed, rushed over. Tobar stopped and put his hands up.

In broken German he said, "Please not hurt her."

"Stop!" a soldier bellowed. "On your knees. Right now."

The look on Tobar's face changed as he raised his chin high, and she knew he understood the command. "Tobar," she whispered. "No."

The big man's eyes never left the Nazi. "Never on your knees, Mischka. Never. You get up. Get up. If they put you on your knees, they mean to kill you anyway." He stopped and spread his arms wide. "Be brave, little one. Be proud and full of courage. I love you, Mischka."

"On your knees," the soldier repeated as he inched closer.

"*Nein*," Tobar said softly. Then he closed his eyes. "You can bury me standing. I've been on my knees my whole life."

Mischka opened her mouth to scream, but nothing came out. Instead, the crack of the rifle took her breath away. Tobar stood a moment, a stain of fuschia spreading from the center of his chest, then he fell.

A scream ripped from Mischka and she rose, beating her fists against her chest. "No!" The tears she had been holding so long burst from her. Stricken with horror, she could only take in small gasps of air. *I'm drowning.* She felt herself float down and down into a suffocating abyss.

A door slammed somewhere behind her, and a well-dressed officer shoved her aside and marched over to the soldier who had shot Tobar.

"What in *Der Führer's* name do you think you're doing?"

"Ah, Commander — "

"You idiot! The Fatherland has gone to huge expense to bring these vermin to work, and look what you've done." He kicked at Tobar's shoulder with the toe of his black boot. "This brute is the biggest one here. He could have done more work than a dozen oxen, and what do you do? You kill him." The commander's face grew redder by the second. "I have a deadline for this project. I will write you up myself for this insubordination."

The soldier stood at silent attention, his face entirely white.

"You will personally deliver this body for disposal."

"Yes, sir. Heil Hitler." He made the Nazi salute, right hand outstretched, not meeting the eyes of the officer scowling at him.

The officer addressed the rest of the prisoners in reasonably fluent Polish. "Get back in formation — all of you. If there is any more trouble, I'll shoot every one of you myself."

In a daze, Mischka stepped back. Hands reached out for her and pulled her back into line. Waves of shock and disbelief rolled over her. Her stomach, tight and empty, roiled, and the only thing preventing her from being sick was the fact that she had nothing to vomit. A roaring in her ears gradually abated. The group around her moved, and she shuffled along automatically. Her skin crawled, and a painful pulse beat behind her right eye. Tobar, she cried out in her mind. Tobar, not you, not you.

When she closed her eyes, she saw the big man's face. Tobar smiling; Tobar laughing as he pulled at his thick beard; Tobar picking up a small child and swinging him round and round. And then she heard his voice, over and over, speaking the very last words before his death: "Bury me standing. I've been on my knees all my life."

She couldn't bear it, and her mind went blank. Rhythmic strides. Shallow breaths. The sound of tramping all around. A peculiar woozy numbness settled over her, and later she could remember nothing at all about the five-hour march from the site of Tobar's death to the next train.

MISCHKA CONCENTRATED ON moving one foot forward and then the other. As every mile passed, the entire group with which she traveled seemed to slow more and more until she felt they shuffled through waist-high water. Next to her, Aurora huffed and wheezed, and air puffed from her mouth like chilled white smoke. All that could be heard was the creaking of shoes, the thud of footfalls, faint moans, and muffled exhalations.

Mischka drank from puddles when the soldiers allowed them to stop. This happened seldom, and they'd been walking since dawn. She couldn't remember being this physically tired or experiencing such extreme emotional lassitude, except after the last terrible beating her husband had inflicted. She stepped over a puddle covered with a scrim of ice and yearned to break through it and cup some of the liquid to her parched lips. On either side of their column, perhaps thirty yards away, grew stands of pine and spruce trees. Stalwart and old, they shifted in the wind, their branches covered with dull green needles. Something was off. Many things were off, Mischka thought, but she felt a void. The reason came to her in a rush—no birds. She had heard no birdsong, seen no birds in the trees, and none were in the sky flying south to warmer climes. In November, surely some birds remained? But no, she could not recall seeing a single bird in two days. Nor had she seen many ground animals. Where were they? What was this land that seemed a living hell?

They drew near the crest of a hill, and as the line of men in the front topped it, Mischka heard a collective gasp. The soldiers on either side moved in, cursing and shouting directions, and the prisoners limped forward.

Aurora grasped Mischka's hand as they came over the hill. "My Lord."

About a mile ahead, down in a valley, a vast camp spread like a malignant growth between the rolling hills on either side. As far as she could see, row after row of one-story oblong barracks marred the valley. Mischka tried to count them, but they blended into one another and she couldn't tell how many there were. Beyond them, two multi-story buildings belched out black and gray smoke.

Every step they took brought them closer to a huge structure in front of a fence that surrounded the camp. Through the bobbing heads before her, Mischka eyed the building. Out front sat three vehicles the likes of which she had never seen. Two were big, like train cars on wheels, and the third resembled the few automobiles she had seen, but looked like a squatty, all-green *vardo*. A soldier sat in the front seat. Even from five hundred yards, Mischka heard the sound of the engine turning over, and the vehicle jerked toward them, dirt spitting out from its rear wheels.

"Halt," one of their guards called, and Mischka and the others came to a standstill.

Suddenly the soldiers around them grew edgy, and their hands gripped their weapons tightly. The soldier nearest Mischka was close enough that she could see him scowling. His watery blue eyes glanced from side to side.

The man brought the military vehicle to a stop and stepped out. Mischka knew little of military rank, but he was clean and neat in his dress uniform, and he was older than the soldiers who had traveled with them. In her mind, she designated him the boss man, the *Kapo*.

He conversed briefly with one of the soldiers, then they broke off their discussion and the *Kapo* put his hands behind his back and addressed the exhausted prisoners in German.

"Men will line up to my left, women to the right. Six across." He didn't need to add that there would be dire consequences for disobedience. Everyone had already discovered that their captors did not answer questions or tolerate slow responses.

They started with the men. The first six were just barely in formation before the *Kapo* went down the line, nodding, pointing, considering. "Yes, yes, yes, yes, yes, no." An elderly man in a dark blue pinstriped suit was sent off to the side near two soldiers. He stood there wheezing, with the wind blowing his white hair off his forehead. The others were sent down the hill.

This process continued with most men being sent toward the camp and the few remaining assembled under guard.

The *Kapo* then stepped briskly along the rows of women. The hardier women were definitely in the front, and no one in Mischka's row was singled out, but behind her, a woman in a fancy fur coat was sent to the side.

As Mischka plodded down the hill, Aurora reached for her hand and gave it a squeeze. Mischka knew she shouldn't look back, but she watched as the *Kapo* came to the final row of prisoners. All but about a dozen men and women hastened down the hill like a pack of frightened animals.

A shot rang out, and everybody jumped, then began to run. Mischka's heart stuttered as a trio of shots was fired. Someone screamed, and Mischka looked back and saw most of the culled prisoners trying to escape down the hill. The soldiers took aim at them. Mischka seized Aurora's arm and steered her to the middle of the pack to avoid being shot if the soldiers missed their targets.

Another volley sounded, and gradually it registered with Mischka that the escort soldiers were shouting and pushing people on the outside of the group. A rifle butt thudded into the woman next to Mischka, and she would have gone down had Mischka not grabbed and righted her.

The soldiers continued to yell at them to slow down, and eventually they came to a stop. She heard laughter from up the hill, and when she looked back, all of the outcasts were so many heaps lying on the ground. Only one man was moving—trying to crawl forward—but a German was on his way over to him. He pointed his rifle, and the sound of the shot reverberated in the cold air.

One of the soldiers near her mumbled, "Damn them for opening fire before we were ready."

"Yes," another said in a bitter voice. "Hecht thinks he is so funny."

The Germans shouted more commands, and Mischka hastened to do as she was told. They were about halfway to the gates of the camp, and Mischka saw a line of people far below. Soldiers? She thought so. With every step, the group appeared larger.

Her hand hurt. She looked down and realized that Aurora still gripped it so tightly that her fingers weren't getting any blood circulation. Tears rolled down Aurora's face. Her lips moved silently.

"Are you praying?" Mischka asked.

"Yes."

"Will your God hear and help us?"

"I don't know. Truly, I don't know." She let go of Mischka's hand and wiped her face on her sleeve. "I'm not praying for me, but for my husband and sons. I hope they're not harmed. I wish they were with me."

For one brief moment, Mischka thought of Tobar, then forced from her mind the image of his stricken face just after the bullet tore into him. She couldn't let herself think of him, of his death. Nothing she could do would change what had happened, and she needed to save all her strength for what lay ahead.

Aurora found Mischka's hand again. "I've known you only this short time, and you are the closest friend I've ever had the honor to have. You must be my sister."

Mischka allowed herself a smile, the first since she was captured. "That is very kind of you. Thank you."

"No, I mean it literally," Aurora whispered. "Do you have papers?"

"Papers?"

"Identification papers."

"Some time ago, my people were all forced to declare themselves," Mischka said. "We were each given sheets of paper with special stamps. My father carries them."

"I see. That's not good. What will you tell them when they ask who you are?"

Mischka raised her head proudly. "I will say I am Marona Lovell Gallo, daughter of Mikhail Gallo who is the adopted son of the late, highly esteemed Palko Petulengro, second son of the brother of the Roma *Kapo*."

If Aurora's face could blanch any further, it did. "You're a Gypsy? A member of the Roma?"

"Yes."

"Mischka, you must listen. You cannot tell them that or they'll kill you."

"That makes no sense."

"They will murder you. You have to believe me." Aurora reached into her sweater and rooted around in her blouse, then pulled out a folded packet. "You must take this. You are my brother's Hungarian wife, Anna Zelman. My maiden name before Wolnick was Zelman. Your maiden name was Kozma. K-O-Z-M-A."

Mischka took the thin packet. "I don't understand..." The men at the head of the group were now only a hundred yards from the line of soldiers who were standing shoulder to shoulder in front of a barbwire gate.

Aurora leaned close, put an arm around Mischka. "I don't have time to explain. Please trust me. My husband Janek and I, we have been providing aid to those fleeing. Mostly Jews, but some political dissidents and even one Gypsy man who had been shunned by his people. We get identification papers through the underground, but these are copies of real papers. My brother is indeed married to a wealthy Hungarian. They fled to the United States when the troubles began in 1939. These Germans have no way of knowing that. Just listen to me, will you?"

Mischka heard the panic in Aurora's voice and saw the concern on her face. "I cannot deny my heritage."

"Yes. You can. And you must if you wish to stay alive. Look back at those people up the hill. What was their sin? They were older, foreign, sickly. These soldiers have no heart, no compassion. Please, Mischka, do what I ask. I cannot see another person murdered before my eyes."

Aurora's tears threatened to fall, and Mischka slowly nodded. "All right then. I am Anna Zelman nee Kozma. Do I have a middle name or a family name? Don't Hungarians list their names differently?"

"Anna and my brother Albin lived in Poland since they were married over ten years ago. They observed Polish custom."

"Where did I grow up? What if they ask about family?"

"Look at the papers."

Mischka unfolded the stiff paper, a Polish document with several circular stamps. The flowing writing must have been done in indelible ink. The edges of the paper were damp, but none of the writing was smudged. "I don't read Polish so well..."

Aurora pointed at the lines and read them aloud.

Anna Sapphira Zelman
Date of Birth: 13 March 1913
City of Birth: Budapest
Husband: Albin Dominik Nicolas Zelman

The address and other citizenship information listed were too much for Mischka to memorize quickly. "Why do you have this, Aurora?"

"A woman who was captured was supposed to —"

"Halt!"

Weary men and women staggered to a stop all around her as Mischka stuffed the papers into her sweater. Her mind was abuzz with questions and worries. She knew the Germans did not care for the Roma people. They'd pushed them out of Germany's borders several years earlier, but surely they would not murder someone in cold blood for being identified as "Gypsy"? How was that possible? What right did these sadistic soldiers have to take her, to shoot Tobar, to kidnap Aurora's family, to kill those poor unfortunates up on the hill? The Polish authorities would not allow it — would they?

Then she thought of Tobar standing tall, his arms spread wide. His hands had always been large and strong as two vises. Rope and axe calluses had scarred his palms. In her mind's eye, his huge hands beckoned to her as she heard his final words: "Bury me standing. I've been on my knees all my life." She saw the blood, heard his body topple. She couldn't prevent the gasp that came to her lips.

"Be quiet," a soldier's harsh voice called out.

She would be quiet. She would work. She would call herself by another name. She would do whatever it took to stay alive. Every day, she would think of Tobar, how he sacrificed his life that she might live. And live she would, even if it took every ounce of cunning she could summon.

Chapter
Eighteen

Tatras Mountains south of Poland, November 1942 (Snow Moon)

THE ONLY THING that kept Emil from falling asleep on his feet was the pressure of Drina's horse nudging him forward. Voices carried on the mountain, sometimes for many miles, so when Drina shifted the sleeping Xavi in front of her and leaned down, she whispered, and he almost didn't hear it. "We can't go on like this, Emil."

He jerked fully awake. Emil knew she was right, but what were they to do? Throughout three days and nights they had forged on, resting only twice for less than four hours each time. They'd descended at least a thousand feet in elevation as they followed the zigzagging trail, but were still surrounded by Stone Pine and snow. As long as Bersh continued to guide them southwest on these deer trails, they were not likely to find any place where they could bed down safely for very long. There were too many of them, and so many people were too easy to see.

Emil closed his eyes and tried to envision the topography of southern Poland: the Tatras Mountains, the Czech territory to the southwest, the Slovak region, and Hungary to the south. The farther west they went, the more deeply they would find themselves in the Czech territories, an area he didn't know at all. He frowned, wondering if Bersh's route was best — or if they ought to skip the Czech lands entirely and head south into the forests below as Mikhail had suggested.

Emil felt a touch on his shoulder and turned to find Mikhail behind him.

"None of this bodes well, Emil."

"No, it doesn't."

"We need to convince Bersh to stop traveling in a westerly direction. We can make it through the Slovak lands to the wooded area north of Miskolc. That would be an easy place to hide. But on this course, we'll be plodding for days along the Polish and Slovak border. Where will we get food? How can we make it all the way to Brno?"

Emil leaned close to Drina's horse and felt a small measure of warmth from the animal's flank. "We need to separate into smaller groups and rendezvous somewhere south in a fortnight. We could hide and rest more securely in groups of ten or twelve."

"I agree," Mikhail said, "but I don't think Bersh will. Still, let's go try to talk some sense into him."

But when Mikhail proposed they head to Miskolc for safe haven, Bersh said, "It's been what? Five decades since you left your homeland?"

"Yes, but I've heard plenty of news over the years from Hungarian travelers. Miskolc might be our only hope."

"Mikhail, we cannot operate on hope. I need certainty. There are eighty-eight—" He stopped and a shadow passed over his face, then he went on. "Eighty-six people depend upon me for the proper decision now."

Mikhail said, "That's true, Bersh. Our lives depend upon your wisdom. At the very least, you'll want us to descend more quickly—get out of the snow, right?"

Bersh looked away, lost in thought.

Emil passed his hand over his bleary eyes. "I'm dead on my feet. Everyone else is, too. We need rest. We need hot food. We need it badly."

"Don't you think I know that?" Bersh's voice was louder than it should be. "What do you expect me to do? Snap my fingers and produce a heated *vardo* for each of you?"

Emil said, "The shortest distance between two points is a direct line. Let's go south and travel the fastest route we can to Hungary. It would be warmer, too."

"How can you know Hungary is safe? The Germans have taken over so many cities and towns, so much territory. Everywhere we go is fraught with danger. Who is to say that Miskolc or any other village there will be safe?"

Mikhail grasped Bersh's arm gently in his leathery hands. "That train of thought takes us only toward disaster. Let's pick a destination and travel there. If, along the way, something better pops up, we will take advantage."

"No. I lead this *kumpania,* and I don't want to travel in Slovakia. A large contingent of Roma live in Brno so we will travel to the Czech lands." Bersh turned to go forward to the head of the line as Emil met Mikhail's eyes. No words were exchanged, but Emil glanced at Gyorgy, then Stevo. Mikhail's younger son whispered, "I didn't catch the plan, but wherever Papa goes, Stevo goes."

"I, too," Gyorgy said.

Mikhail clapped Gyorgy on the shoulder, and looked at Stevo. "The next place the path splits, we need to think about traveling due south."

The four men nodded and dispersed. Emil looked up at Drina, who sat wearily holding the sleeping Xavi. "Did you get all that?"

"Yes."

A short whistle signaled that Bersh was ready to go, and Emil nudged Drina's mare to follow.

They plodded on and on. An hour passed, and Emil wiped his forehead, which was perspiring despite the cold.

Drina leaned down and touched his shoulder. "Emil. Ahead."

He stared blearily into the last of the light from the sun. With dusk falling so fast, he had difficulty determining what she was pointing at, but then his eyes focused on the path, which forked.

"Emil." He turned to locate Mikhail's hoarse whisper. "Emil."

Mikhail hastened forward, slipping once on the snow. He caught his balance and edged past Gyorgy. Emil nudged Drina's mare to a stop, and the horse following walked blindly into them. My God, even the horses were asleep on their feet.

Mikhail, trailed by Gyorgy and Stevo, reached Emil. "It's now or never. We're going to have to find shelter or bed down off the trail. The women and children can't go on like this."

Gyorgy, too, was plainly uneasy. "I agree. We need shelter soon."

Emil took a deep breath. "I'm ready. I hope this is the right thing to do."

"As do I," Mikhail said. "I have never gone against the will of the leader. Are you sure you wish to follow?"

Emil's gut told him something that his fatigued mind could only partly grasp. He couldn't explain why, but he believed going forward was a mistake. He knew nothing of the Roma at Brno, but the thought of continuing on to Czech lands repelled him. So much travel, so many miles, and they lacked food. Above all, he knew his tired brain and body needed rest. But what if Mikhail's father's family had moved away — or died out?

West or south — either direction was fraught with risk.

Emil made his decision. "I'm going with you, Mikhail."

"I, too, choose to travel south," Gyorgy said. "Let's head for warmth, Papa."

Someone whistled up ahead. Emil gazed up into Drina's dark eyes. He was the head of his family, but for a brief moment, he thought of his mother, of how she had always encouraged him to treat women fairly and with respect. Drina did not expect that of him, but he expected it of himself. "Drina, if we travel south, you know your father will go with Bersh. Do you wish to stay with the *kumpania* or come with me?"

Drina's mouth turned up into the tiniest of smiles, and her dark eyes seemed to drink him in. She looked at him with love in her eyes — that was the only way to explain it. "My father is my past, Emil, but you and our children are my future. I'll stay by your side."

Even before she finished speaking, he had known what she would say, and that made his chest expand and his head feel light. He didn't know what he'd ever done to deserve the love and absolute devotion of such a good woman, but he vowed never to take it for granted.

He pulled the reins of Drina's horse and moved toward the fork in the path. When he stepped from the well-trod path into pristine snow, he realized that a tear in the fabric of his life — of all their lives — was about to occur. He thought back to his arrival and acceptance by this troupe. He was adopted and claimed, and yet, though he was one of them, sometimes he still felt like an outsider, a *gajo* whom they politely put up with.

Many changes had taken place over the years. The families had expanded. The *kumpania* had split twice. So many of the daughters had been married into other clans. His own daughter — his oldest child — had been married last year and was gone from him. Time had passed with a mind-numbing swiftness that Emil had never expected. He was forty-three years old. More than half his life was over. In a few years, his two sons would be of marriageable age. Did he want to remain on the road, always traveling, always on the move, suspected in every town, and disrespected wherever the *kumpania* went? He would rather settle somewhere, have a house, fields to grow things, peace. When he thought of the future, he didn't see himself dying in the woods somewhere, surrounded by the traditional draped tents and a dozen curious faces watching his death throes. He imagined a warm bed, indoors, the warm hands of loved ones, and quiet dignity.

He hadn't thought about church for years, but suddenly he remembered himself as a young boy, standing in front of the regal church at Reims, the cathedral of Our Lady, in the Champagne-Ardennes region of France where he and Pippi and their parents had lived in his childhood. He recalled the intricate stone carvings and the three giant portals with their High Gothic sculptured engravings. Inside was always dark, lit only by candles and any light that streamed in through the stained glass windows. His favorite was the large rose window, and during church services, he had often stared up at it, lost in the swirls of color. He wished he were there now, safe and warm, looking up at that multicolored window.

The snow crunched beneath his boots. The cool wind blew snow off an evergreen branch into his face. Lumi's horse nickered and followed Drina's on the wide path that led downhill.

He silently counted: Mikhail, Lumi, their daughter Elena; Gyorgy and his wife and fifteen-year-old son Mario; Stevo and his wife and their nine-year-old Tem; and his and Drina's two, Palko and Xavier. Thirteen total. He couldn't help thinking that it should be fifteen, for Tobar and Mischka ought to be with them. The realization made him heartsick.

He waved to Gyorgy, and the Gallo clan separated from the *kumpania.*

"Stop! I command you to stop."

Emil couldn't see Bersh, but his voice traveled well in the mountain air. So much for stealth and advancing quietly. If there were any soldiers up there, the whole troupe was dead.

"Where do you think you're going?" Bersh shouted. "I'm the leader of this *kumpania.* You may not usurp my command. Get back up on the trail."

Emil didn't think he'd ever seen their leader's face so red. In contrast, Mikhail's face was pale. Red and white. Anger and fear. Emil handed the reins to Drina and stepped to Mikhail's side.

"I'm sorry, Bersh," Mikhail said, his voice quiet yet firm. "We're going to Miskolc."

Bersh heaved like a horse that had just run miles at full gallop. "This *kumpania* will stay together, protect each other. The safety of the group depends upon us all following the same plan and working together."

"We're too many," Mikhail said. "The closer we get to the foot of the mountains, the more vulnerable we'll be. Any time now, this long line of horses and people will become visible to those below. We need to split into smaller groups and travel due south to bed down."

"I'm leading us forward to that very thing." Bersh stomped closer and raised a gloved hand. With his index finger in the air, he punctuated each of his words. "You...will...obey." Mikhail shook his head and didn't say anything. "You think you know better than me?" Bits of saliva sprayed from Bersh's mouth, and a few flecks landed in his beard. "I am the son of Gunari who was the son of Palko, your adopted father. You defy me? You defy one who was your father, God rest his soul? He would come back as a *mulé* from his eternal resting place if he knew what you are doing. You're no Roma — never have been. Imposter!"

Mikhail took a step back as though he'd been struck. He stammered when he finally spoke. "I — I must do what I think is right. My family's lives are at stake."

"*All* our families lives are at stake!" Bersh's eyes raked over the small group and came to rest above Emil's shoulder. He pointed, his arm making hatcheting motions. "You will not take the horses. Those don't belong to you."

Mikhail's mouth dropped open.

Emil said, "Wait a minute, Bersh. Someone ahead is sitting on the five horses we do own. You can't deny us these two."

"You! My father took you as his son. I've treated you as a brother, you *gajo*. And now you do this?" He spat on the ground. "You are both nothing to me. When we reach safety, I'll ask that the *Kapo* declare you dead to all of us. If you walk away now, you're nothing to me. Nothing."

Though he hadn't eaten for hours, Emil felt something from his stomach come up and burn the back of his throat. He swallowed and couldn't answer Bersh.

"This is your last chance, Mikhail. You will rejoin us. Now."

Mikhail let out a long sigh, and a stream of white smoke flowed from his nostrils and vanished into the frigid air. "We will meet again, Bersh. After the war. When we're all free to travel again, we'll meet at the yearly celebration. I will pay my respects and ask for your forgiveness. You're still my brother."

Bersh drew in a sharp breath. He stood for a few moments as the wind lifted his beard and worried at his cap. His expression grew less wild, and for the briefest moment, Emil saw tears spring into his eyes. Grief and anger and fear all pressed in on the leader. He set his lips into a hard line and didn't resist when Nanosh took his arm and pulled him back.

Emil stood gulping air as the men negotiated the icy slope. Bersh no longer seemed so towering, so bulky. With his head hunched down into the collar of his coat, he looked like a frightened turtle. Mikhail started downhill, but Emil watched their leader a moment longer. Across the distance, his eyes met those of Nanosh, and he gave the older man a final nod. Nanosh raised a hand and waved, then he, too, moved away.

Emil couldn't bear to watch anymore. To anchor himself, he hooked his fingers into the top of Drina's boot. When he looked up into his wife's eyes, he saw her face was covered with tears. She didn't hesitate, though. She tightened her grip on Xavi and urged the horse down the hill.

He heard Bersh's far-off whistle and the sounds of footfalls and harnesses creaking as the *kumpania* resumed its westward trek. With every step Emil took, the sound grew fainter and less distinct until at last he no longer heard a single sound over his own rough breath.

EMIL STIRRED FROM sleep as a horse whinnied. He sat against a giant spruce tree with Drina nestled on his right. His younger son Xavi lay sprawled across him and Drina, with his face frowning in sleep. Palko slept on Emil's other side, between Emil and Gyorgy, his shoulder warm against Emil. Next to Palko, and arrayed around the side of the tree's thick trunk, Gyorgy's son Mario nestled between his father and mother, all of them huddled for warmth.

Emil squinted through bleary eyes. The bulky shoulder bag he carried in the front of him had afforded him some warmth, but even with blankets spread over the space between tree roots, the back of his legs and his rump were cold, and his face felt numb. He heard the nickering sound again. The big red stallion stood at the edge of the evergreen tree's boughs, his profile dark against the light of the gradually rising sun. He flicked his tail and a tumble of snow fell from a low branch.

Mikhail's and Stevo's families huddled across the way under another spruce. Usually men and women slept separately, but that was neither wise nor practical now. Drina, Lumi, Tauna, Chavi, and Mikhail's daughter Elena were the only females. Left on their own, Emil doubted they could generate enough warmth to last all night. Perhaps it made the other men uncomfortable to go against Roma rules, but Emil would just as soon have his wife and two sons at his side. At heart, he was a practical German. Keeping them all alive rose far above the need to adhere to social mores.

The war had changed a lot of things, and he was sure there would be more to come. This damn war! And that Hitler was crazed and evil. What was wrong with the world? Had the politicians gone mad? He had lived among these people more than two decades, and they were good people. Just because they were different from Germans or Poles or any other nation's citizens didn't mean they should be hunted and enslaved or killed. He suddenly realized that he was thinking of the Roma separate from himself, as though he were not one of them. Well, he wasn't anymore, was he? Bersh made that clear yesterday.

As he thought about it, though, Emil marveled at the realization that he'd been undergoing a subtle change for many months, ever since the numerous edicts had come down restricting the Roma. If there had been no war to contend with, he thought he would have been ready to leave the *kumpania* and settle someplace. He wasn't too old to find a position as a schoolmaster or teacher. They could go to France, live with his father's people, and he could teach geography and world history. If an opportunity arose to do that, he would explore it.

He turned his head and nestled his face into Drina's hair, which smelled faintly of smoke. He wondered whether Drina would like living in a house.

Emil heard a sigh. He looked across the way and squinted. Mikhail was awake and looking toward him. He gave a toss of his head, Mikhail waved, and they both struggled to their feet.

Oh, good heavens. He felt a hundred years old. When he leaned forward, his back shrieked with pain. He rolled his shoulders and stamped his feet to try to get feeling back in them. He wasn't frozen solid, so he guessed that meant something.

Drina awoke and shifted Xavi away, then slowly got to her feet. Emil started to say something, but she shook her head. "Let me pass. I must wash."

Emil couldn't help the chuckle. Surrounded by miles and miles of snow, he wondered where she thought she'd find running water, but she walked a little way down the trail, removed her gloves, and squatted to wash her hands in a snow drift. "Old habits die hard," he whispered. It sent a shiver through him.

Emil yawned and reluctantly stripped off his own gloves as he made his way into a stand of trees to relieve himself. Afterwards, he cleaned his hands in the snow. *I pray for a safe day of travel — for us, for Bersh and his people, and for my little daughter, who is far away from my protection. Also for Tobar and for Mischka, wherever they may be.*

Chapter
Nineteen

South Poland, November 1942 (Snow Moon)

IN THE COLD barracks, Mischka lay on one of the three-tiered sleeping pallets. She was glad she had chosen the top of the three shelves, even if there wasn't much headroom. Aurora had originally staggered toward the lowest bunk, but Mischka convinced her to climb the rickety ladder to the top. "Heat rises," Mischka had told her in a whisper. "If there is any warmth at all, it will be near the ceiling." Aurora accepted that and climbed up with her. One of the women across the barracks cried out for blankets and a pillow. Their guard marched to the middle tier, grabbed the woman by the collar of her coat, and threw her to the floor.

The woman—really no more than a girl—let out a shriek when her plump bottom hit the floor. She scrambled to rise, but the guard kicked at her. "Stay right there. Perhaps you would enjoy sleeping on the floor for your first night here at our lovely hotel." She looked around at the frightened faces watching the scene. "Yes, you shall sleep here this night, and—" the sharp-faced female guard looked accusingly around her "—if any of you assist this filthy, greedy cow, you shall sleep beside her each night for a week."

Now Mischka lay closest to the wall, her back to Aurora who was wheezing slightly as she slept inches away. Beyond Aurora, two other women, scared refugees from central Poland's Warsaw area, also slept. They were packed onto the six-foot-wide shelf with little room to spare.

The room smelled of mold and sweat and something else rotten—a death-like stench that the dozens of occupants of the barracks hadn't brought in with them. In the distance, someone made a snuffling sound. Someone nearby turned over and muttered angrily about not having enough space. Below Mischka, a woman wept, breathing raspy gulps of air and obviously unable to keep a quavering whimper from escaping.

Mischka surveyed what she could of the long, narrow room. Wall to wall misery, that's what this place was. From this wall all the way to the other end, two long rows of the same three-tiered wood frames held four or five women crammed on each pallet, all of them uncomfortable and cold. When they had arrived earlier in the day, each woman's hair had been shorn off. They'd been forced to disrobe and had been herded into a cold and damp communal shower. Mischka had never bathed in such a room. How could eight showers run simultaneously? She thought there must be a mighty river somewhere nearby.

The water had been tepid and the soap harsh, and her skin had dried out so much that tiny bits flecked off any time she scratched. She touched the stubble on her head. In all her life, she didn't remember her hair being much shorter than an arm's length. Now her scalp felt naked, cold, crawly. Strangers had touched her hair, seen her unclothed, applied some sort of powder to her private parts, and then given her clothing that was shabby, thin, and ill-fitting. If she hadn't been so afraid of the hatchet-faced guard handing out the clothing, she would have demanded her own garments back. But one look into the woman's angry, steel-blue eyes shut Mischka up. She accepted the sack dress, thin cotton coat, and shoes and socks without comment.

For the first time in days, Mischka had time to think in stillness. She wasn't the slightest bit sleepy. Even though she lay motionless in her little slice of space on the rough wood, she had the peculiar feeling that she was still in motion. She had walked for so many miles and been shaken around in trains and carts for so long, she experienced a strange vertigo, as though she were drunk. Perhaps the lack of food added to it. After receiving mismatched garb, each woman had been given a battered tin cup half-full of a thin broth that was in no way nourishing. Mischka downed the tepid liquid without question or pause.

"All of you, keep your cups," the woman with the ladle said. "If you lose it, that'll be your tough luck."

Mischka tucked the tin cup carefully into the pocket of her coat. Small, and nothing like the flowered clay bowl she used on a daily basis with her family, it held little. But it was all she had, so it would have to do.

The thought of home, of the wagons, of her father and mother and the horses and the *kumpania* formed a lump of hurt behind her breastbone. She stiffened and squeezed her eyes shut, holding back the pain, willing herself not to call out, not to cry. She drew a labored breath and clenched her fists.

Next to her, Aurora stirred. The Polish words were so soft, Mischka nearly didn't hear them. "Hush, now. You must sleep, my sister-in-law. Save your strength."

A hand slid along Mischka's waist, patted her on the hip, and remained. "Hush. There's nothing we can do. Try to sleep."

Mischka willed herself to relax. She opened her hands, flexed her fingers. With one long inhalation, she realized Aurora was right. Nothing could be done to change their circumstances. Not right now anyway. They were all trapped, at the mercy of these rage-filled, dour-faced Germans. She wondered what kind of work the women would be forced to do. When they had come down from the hills, she hadn't seen any farms in the valley — just black smoke. She had never been in a factory, but perhaps that was where they would work.

Chapter
Twenty

Foothills of the Tatras Mountains, November 1942 (Snow Moon)

EMIL HAD BEEN on his feet so long that with each stride, he wondered how he could force himself to take another step.

The way had grown harder as they descended. The higher the sun rose, the more the snow melted, and by late afternoon, the path was a spongy, slimy mess. Hillside springs had cut down the mountainside for years; now additional streams of water trickled from above. At one point, a shower of small rocks and mud slid from an overhang and struck Drina's horse's legs and those people at the back of the line on foot. The horse skittered before Drina could bring him under control.

"Yowch!" Palko cried out. "I thought I was dirty before, but look at this!"

Emil reached down to brush away some of the dirt from Palko's breeches. His sons—both of them—looked like ragamuffins. Dirty and perspiring, everyone was mud-splashed and unkempt. Even the shoulder bag Emil carried had a splotch of dirt on it. He wiped drops of water from his neck and found grime and sweat. Anybody with a good nose would be able to smell them coming.

The farther they traveled down, the thinner the scrub pine became. The foothills bled into ridges, which led down into a wide valley flanked on either side by stands of deciduous trees. The trail, now wide enough for two to walk abreast, zigzagged down the hillside, and Emil could make out a bridle path a half-mile below. Mikhail led the motley group, closely followed by Stevo, his son Tem, and Gyorgy and his son Mario. Lumi rode one of the horses with Elena, and Drina handled the other mount with a very sleepy Xavi in front of her. Behind them were Gyorgy's wife Tauna, Palko, and Stevo's wife Chavi, and Emil brought up the rear.

They were so fatigued that each step was slow and

measured. Occasionally Emil stopped to listen, letting the group ahead of him move on. Earlier he had sensed nothing unusual, but now, with the late afternoon sun no longer overhead, something didn't feel right. He looked back up the slope, toward the mountain pass where the trees were thick with melting snow. To the left, a mountain saddle accentuated the height of the peak. He gazed back the way they had come, then slowly finished turning full circle. He shaded his eyes and peered out to the skyline. He couldn't see a town, but smoke billowed far ahead, along the horizon. One's eyes played tricks, so he couldn't estimate how far they would have to travel, but surely now that they had eaten the last of their provisions, if they didn't find an animal to kill and roast, they would travel two days or more without food before reaching a village.

They were more consistently exposed now than at any time during their journey, but no matter where he looked, he saw nothing unusual. Still, Emil felt the hair at the back of his neck stand on end, and such a feeling of dread washed over him that his head pounded. A split second later, a chestnut-sized rock tumbled down the side of the hill and bounced on the springy earth in front of his feet. He slung an arm around his shoulder bag and ran, heart beating fast. He was still seventy-five yards from the group when he heard a shout.

"Halt!"

Emil dropped to a squat. The guttural German order echoed and faded, then was repeated. Emil wasn't sure if it came from above or below. It seemed to come from somewhere behind him, but his hasty glances didn't reveal anyone. He rose and took off running.

"Hal-l-l-l-t!"

He saw Drina rein in her horse and look back.

"Don't stop!" he called out, waving frantically as though lobbing energy her way. "Run!"

Panic went up the line as the sleepy travelers jerked awake and pressed forward. The horses lumbered on, and everyone gradually gained speed. Ahead, the trail veered to the right and broadened, leveling out into the bridle path Emil had spied. Drina's cantering stallion sped up. Great clods of dirt flew from his hooves.

Emil slipped. He heard distant cracks. Then a volley of echoes. His knee hit the ground and burrowed deeply into a muddy spot. For a brief moment, a foxhole, mud, and the mad crush of frantic men appeared in a swirling fog. He looked up, expecting to see planes overhead, but the sky was clear. He shook off the eerie memory and took a deep breath. As he pushed himself up, the muck separated from his knee with a squelching sound. Another rifle shot cracked as he rose. Someone far ahead screamed.

He rushed forward, panting, slipping, and sliding down the last rise before the bridle path flattened out. Run for the trees. Get out of the open. Emil wished he could shout these instructions loud enough for the others to hear, but they were too far ahead. He heard another gunshot and looked back, filled with fury. You cowards! You scum!

On the zigzagging path far up the hill, he finally saw movement. The soldiers were shooting at them like they were wild game. His anger fueled his mad dash. The ground was still boggy, but not nearly so slippery as the incline had been, and he started to narrow the gap between him and his family. He heard no more shots and wondered why. Perhaps their attackers were merely getting into better position.

Up ahead, Lumi's horse charged into the stand of trees, followed by Drina and Xavi. Soon the first three on foot also made it, but he could still see them as they staggered into the brush, their dark-colored clothing visible against the naked trees.

He saw someone fall before he heard the report. "No!" For a moment he thought the small body that hit the ground was Mario, but when he drew nearer, he saw the dark blue and white of Tauna's *diklo* against her black hair. Mario ran toward his mother and reached her before Emil did.

"Mama!" he screamed. He fell to his knees at her side. "Mama?"

"Run," Emil gasped out.

"But Mama—"

"I'll get her. Run to your father *now!*"

The boy rose and charged off. His booted feet carried him in a straight shot toward Gyorgy who had turned back to get him. Emil scooped up Tauna and gripped her high against his chest. He hurried as fast as his legs would carry him. Something damp trickled from the hollow of his neck and into his shirt. Afraid that any minute a bullet would knock him down, he burst into the jack-pines and dove into the low brush. He landed hard. Tauna rolled away from him, a limp collection of lifeless limbs.

Gyorgy was suddenly there and lifted his wife into his arms. "Tauna. Tauna." Mario stood beside his father, his face pale and mouth gaping open.

Emil scrambled to his knees, still breathless and gasping. He looked down at the front of his coat and saw it was dark and glistening. He touched his neck and drew back fingers red with blood.

Gyorgy's raspy voice was full of anguish. "She's dead, Emil. Dead."

"I'm so sorry, Gyorgy." Emil stood and scanned the grove. He hitched up his breeches and adjusted the shoulder bag, then leaned forward to catch his breath. A deer trail led farther into the thicket. The rest of the group continued to crash forward, leaving broken branches and trampled plants. Emil looked back. "They're still coming. We need to get away."

Mario's lips moved, but no sound came out. Emil cupped his hand behind Mario's head and leaned down. "Let's go. Run." Mario didn't respond. "Listen to me, Mario. We have to go." He met Gyorgy's eyes, not daring to ask the big man what he wanted to do. Roma custom did not allow for leaving a body behind, unburied, but Emil didn't see how could they carry Tauna for long.

Gyorgy turned slowly, his wife cradled face-up in his arms. His voice was pitched low, in a hopeless tone. "Come, Mario. Follow me."

"Hurry," Emil urged. He went forward on unsteady legs to lead the way for the grieving man and his son. In less than a hundred yards, they came upon their group. Drina's riderless horse whinnied and moved restlessly, blocking Emil's line of sight. Until he stepped off the narrow path and pushed past the horse, Emil had no idea why everyone had stopped. Stevo and Lumi knelt on either side of Emil's wife. Drina's head rested in Elena's lap, and she held Xavi tight against her, face down against her breast. Mikhail stood panting with the other horse's reins wrapped in his fist.

Emil met Drina's pain-filled eyes. "What happened? The horse threw you —"

"No," she gasped out.

Emil shouted, "Give them some room." Everyone leaned back, but nobody moved away. Emil stalked over, rage fueling his jerky movements. He didn't want to look, didn't want to confirm his suspicion, but he knew. Tears of rage and grief burned in his eyes.

"My son?" He fingered a ragged circular tear in the lower section of the boy's tan coat and brought his palm close to the back of Xavi's head, afraid to touch him. He was startled when Xavi lifted his head.

"Papa." His dark eyes bored into Emil's. "The gun."

"Yes, my boy. They shot at us, didn't they?"

"Gun."

"Xavi, my son." He choked out the words as tenderly as he could.

"Papa, the...gun..." His voice grew faint and his eyes closed.

Shocked, Emil looked at Drina. Tears formed dark rivulets that ran down her cheeks. "I'm sorry, Emil. I should have ridden faster." Her cold hand gripped his. "I'll miss you. I'll love you. Always. I'll keep the *mulé* away."

"What? No, no..." As if he were an eagle, he suddenly had a vision of the bridle path, the horses, the running people—and the image was clear. His son had been shot in the back while sitting in front of his wife. She, too, must be injured. With gentle hands, he pushed Xavi to the side, and there it was: an exit wound and blood all over the front of Drina's coat.

"No," he whispered. "This can't be happening." He looked up toward the heavens. "God, no! How could you let this happen?"

He hooked his arm under Drina's neck, pulled her up toward him. "Don't leave me. Please don't leave me, Drina." He rocked her against him.

"Shhh..." She breathed against his neck. "Run, Emil. Get everybody out of here. Take care of Palko." She coughed. "Find our daughter. Leave this land."

"I can't leave you. I won't." He searched around until his eyes lit upon Stevo. "Get the horse, Stevo. Bring it over here. We have to get her to a doctor."

"Shhh." Drina raised her hand to his cheek. "There's nothing to be done, love of my heart. This is my destiny, to die in the month of the Snow Moon. But...not your fate. Live. Live on, and we'll be together again one day." Her voice grew weaker. "Please don't let those killers get the rest of us. Please...run."

She took a deep breath, her eyes on his. Her chest slowly sank as she exhaled. She didn't inhale again.

"Drina?" He shook her. "Drina?" She seemed still alive, her eyes upon him, but then the light faded from them, and he saw she no longer focused.

A guttural and mighty scream left his throat. He closed his eyes and heard it echo over and over in his head. Hands grabbed his shoulders, and voices said soothing things.

His wife, his son. It was too much. Too much. He gently settled Drina on the ground next to Xavi and rose to his feet with his hands over his face. His legs shook, and he was having trouble breathing.

A cold fear clenched the back of his neck and shivered through his body. The murderers would soon be upon them. Drina was right. They were probably already near, perhaps within earshot. "Quick. Put our dead upon the horses and get going. Now!" He pushed past Gyorgy and grabbed the stallion's bridle to pull the horse forward. Instead of leading the horse, though, he moved off the path, stepped through the dead vegetation, and circled the big animal.

Stevo scrambled through the undergrowth and grabbed his arm from behind. "Emil! Emil, listen. What are you doing?"

"What I have to do."

"No, no. Don't you dare sacrifice yourself. We need you."

He continued to plead, but Emil wouldn't listen. "I'll kill them with my bare hands."

"No, please help us escape. Come with us, Emil. Help us."

Emil ripped his arm out of Stevo's grip. "Take care of my son." He lurched back along the path.

When he glanced behind, everyone was gone, the wide spot on the trail flattened and stained with patches of blood, but otherwise bearing no evidence of what had just happened there. Emil's sense of disbelief was so great that everything around him seemed to warp and wave. Trees appeared crooked. The ground wasn't level. A thin branch smacked him in the face and left a stinging pain across his cheek.

His son was too young to die. His wife... Tauna... Xavi... How could they kill his family, his people? If he lived fifty more years, he would never forget the look on Drina's face or how fiercely Xavi peered at him, even though he must have been in pain. His son's last words — he knew he was dying. In his agony, he wanted to tell what happened.

Or did he?

Emil stopped. A cold breeze blew into his face. His limbs felt like lead, like they would no longer obey the commands his mind sent. And then, as though under a spell, he brought up one hand to search in his shoulder bag. Below his gloves, beneath a rolled cloth, under a pair of socks too small for anyone but Xavi, wrapped in a piece of leather, he found his gun. Unused for so long, the tip of the tapered barrel had rusted. The bullets lay scattered at the bottom of the satchel. One, two, three... His cold hands fumbled for more of the cold little lumps of steel. He found five shells and inserted them into the magazine with trembling fingers.

He closed his eyes and pressed his feelings down, past his throat, below his breastbone, and deep into the center of his being. Later he would have time to take out those emotions and examine them. For now, he was merely an avenging angel. His vision cleared and he straightened his spine. The world righted itself, and the ground felt solid under his feet. He saw branches undulating in the wind, felt the bite of the early evening wind, smelled pine in the air. Not so far away he heard huffing and the sound of voices.

Without vegetation, the trees didn't hide him well, so he hastened back the way he came to the spot on the trail just beyond where he'd held Drina. The brush was thicker there, and the hornbeam branches formed hedges in and around the larger beech trees. He squatted among the lattice of branches, his face against solid hardwood. He steadied his gun hand in the V of the beech's trunk and waited. In the dim light, he was sure to stop at least some of the pursuers.

German voices floated toward him, growing louder by the moment.

"I got the one on the second horse."

"Maybe not. Might have been my shot."

"No, you're wrong."

"This bunch wasn't as easy as that other group."

"Sitting ducks, those were." He laughed.

Somebody coughed. His voice came out raspy. "We'll catch up to these vermin, and once we've dealt with them, we can finally go back to camp."

"Certainly will give us bragging rights."

Emil couldn't believe what he was hearing. They discussed murder as though it were entertainment. His throat constricted, and he broke out in a sweat. The first man came into view. He wore a field-gray sidecap and a long gray coat that parted as he walked, revealing dark breeches tucked into boots. A canteen hung at his waist, a leather satchel under his left arm, and an ammo bag on his right hip. He cradled a rifle in his arms and carried a pack on his back with a combat helmet strapped to the top.

Two more soldiers followed.

Wait until I can see the buttons of his coat...

The man was young...clean-shaven...drawing closer...and now less than twenty feet away. Emil pulled the trigger and his target slammed backwards and went down.

"Oskar!" the second soldier shouted.

Emil took aim and shot him where his neck met his chest. The third man dove into the brush, and the next bullet went wild. Emil pulled the trigger again, but the gun misfired. He hunched behind the tree and grabbed the hot barrel, frantic to clear the jammed shell. His breath came out in short, sharp gasps. His vision wouldn't quite focus.

The soldier rose and pitched himself forward. His shadow blocked Emil's light as the pistol's locking mechanism clicked shut. The soldier's rifle blasted. A brief flash of fire temporarily blinded Emil before the German came at an angle around the hornbeam tree, his bayonet tip glistening. Emil jerked to the side. The bayonet missed him by inches. A solid body knocked him back, and the soldier fell upon him, pinning Emil's gun against his chest and between them. An elbow struck him in the face. He twisted and bucked trying to get the bigger man off him.

"No! No!" the German cried out. "You can't—"

Emil slammed his fist into the side of the man's jaw. The soldier grunted and shifted enough that Emil was able to twist the pistol and jam it into the man's middle. He pulled the trigger. The gun bucked between them, and the soldier let out a high-pitched yowl. He collapsed upon Emil, and his breath spurted out in ragged bursts. Emil struggled to push him off, then seized the rifle and threw it near the dead Germans, overhand, like a javelin.

The man rolled onto his side, his cap on the ground next to his head. His pack prevented him from resting on his back. He lay there panting, then he got a second wind and tried to dig in his heels and lever himself away.

Emil stuck the pistol into the waistband of his pants. He gazed down at the man below him. The insignia on his uniform showed him to be an *Obergefreiter,* a corporal with six or more years of service. His face was lined, and Emil thought him to be nearing forty. His eyes were clear blue, and his dirty-blond hair was longer than German soldiers usually kept it, so he must have been in the field for some time. He would work the field no longer. Emil grabbed for the strap of the soldier's pack, but the man fought him for it.

"No." The soldier's voice was strong, and his arms, despite the wound, were surprisingly powerful. Working around the man's feeble attempts to ward him off, Emil searched him. He carried no sidearm, but Emil pulled an army-issue knife from a sheath at the soldier's belt and held it close to his neck. "Stop fighting."

The corporal looked up at him, anger in his eyes, then let out a groan and relinquished the pack. It contained no weapons, so Emil got to his feet and searched the two bodies near the path, removing the men's belts, boots, knives, canteens, and other items. When he discovered that each soldier carried a cloth bag containing bread, dried meat, and fruit, his stomach spasmed and he stole a moment to wolf one crusty chunk of pumpernickel. In the near-darkness, he stumbled quite a bit before he located the three rifles. He piled everything in the middle of the path.

He stamped back toward the looming hornbeam to collect

the corporal's items and was surprised to find the soldier still conscious and breathing. With one hand grasping the rough wood of the hornbeam, Emil stood over the dying man. A wave of fatigue washed through him. With the toe of his boot, he kicked lightly at the soldier's leg. "Why? Why did you kill my people?"

"My duty. It's my...duty."

"But you take such pleasure in it."

The soldier let out a strangled cackle. "What's wrong...with that?"

"These are people! My wife, my son, how could you kill them like so many deer or — or — rabbits."

"Gypsies," the corporal said in a voice filled with disgust. "Even deer are worth more."

Emil had no time for thought. He took a step and kicked. The man let out a pained gasp, and Emil's next maddened flurry of kicks propelled him back a yard.

"Stop. Please stop."

"Like you stopped killing my family? Stop like that? Is that what you mean?"

"Please." He held up his hand. "Please. I'm dying. Just leave me."

All the air went out of Emil, and he fell to his knees. Tears welled in his eyes. "But how could you do this to other human beings? I was a soldier once, long ago, but I could never do what you've done."

"You? A soldier? I don't believe you." He waited a moment. "But you do speak decent German for a Gypsy."

"Roma!" Emil roared the name. "We're Roma. And I'm also German. As was my son. You killed a German."

The man scowled. "A half-blood. Nothing more. I don't regret it." He shifted into a fetal position and tightened his grip on his middle. "My life is fulfilled with the work I have done. Not just to your party, but also dozens of others last night."

Emil suddenly felt cold all over. "What? You killed other Roma?"

"Yes. A very profitable day."

Emil dove at him, grabbed the lapels of his coat, and screamed in his face. "You killed several dozen helpless souls up on the mountain?"

When the soldier smiled, blood oozed between his teeth. "Actually," he grunted out, "I killed more than my comrades put together."

"Did any escape you?"

"Maybe, maybe not."

"What did you do with the bodies?"

"They lie where they fell in a ravine up the mountain many miles from here."

Emil let go of the man and pushed himself back, squatting three feet from him. "And you're proud of this?"

"I'm achieving the work of *Der Führer*."

"You're lying. I don't believe you. They had horses, and—"

"Not anymore." He let out a choked-sounding giggle. "My men relieved them of their livestock. Those animals now serve the glory of the Third Reich. Heil Hitler." His hand came away from his body in a weak attempt to perform the salute, but fell instead to the ground.

Emil pulled the pistol from his waist and pointed it at the soldier's head. "You deserve worse than death."

The man's eyes went wide and he let out a whimper.

Emil pulled the trigger. Click. Click. Click. "I'm out of bullets. So you shall lie there, dying slowly after all." He stomped away, nearly tripping in some prickly gorse.

Now the night was fully dark, and if not for the moon shining aslant through the trees, he wouldn't be able to see a thing.

The heat of anger and energy had passed, and Emil felt as tired as he had ever been. He made his way back to the stack of items piled on the path. One body lay near him, and it sickened him to touch the man, but he made himself do it. He couldn't bring himself to take their tunics or breeches, but once he had removed coats and field caps from both men, he dragged their bodies ten yards into the trees and left them.

As he picked his way between the beech trees, he heard a twig snap. Instantly his heart beat like a jackhammer. He shouldn't have left all the clothing and supplies right there in plain sight. If other members of the corporal's army came now, he was dead. His handgun was out of bullets, and the rifles would be little to hold off advancing soldiers.

"Emil?"

The whisper was so faint, he almost didn't hear it.

"Emil?"

"Stevo?" He heard a whistle and a rustle in the bushes up to his right.

"Where are you?"

"Here." Emil made his way out to the path, and Stevo and Palko materialized like ghosts, then became solid as they moved closer.

"Papa!" Palko threw an arm around Emil.

"I'm fine. I'm all right. What are you two doing?"

"We've hidden everyone," Stevo said. "They're safe for the moment. We had to come back. I—I, well, we couldn't leave you. I thought you might—might—"

"Might be dead?" Emil grimaced. "God smiled upon me. But not upon these three worthless bastards. I've scavenged food, weapons, clothing. There's even a pup tent. Help me bundle it all up. We can use it."

Stevo put his hands up, palms out. "Something makes my skin crawl. Do these Germans have evil *mulé?*"

"Probably. We will cleanse ourselves of them soon. Please tell me there's a stream ahead."

"There is."

They worked together for several minutes to pack and organize things, then Emil rose and stumbled behind the hornbeam. The corporal was dead. Emil stripped him of his coat and boots and picked up his sidecap, then backed away. *"Te bisterdon tumare anava!"*

"What?" Stevo asked.

"I curse them. May their names be forgotten."

"I curse them, too," Stevo said. "Now let's hurry away from this horrid place."

They donned the packs, picked up the rifles, and grabbed the ammo bags and other items. With Palko between them and Stevo in the lead, Emil followed. He tried not to think, concentrating on making his tired body move in a smooth rhythm. But soon, the events of the day rose up in his mind and overwhelmed him. Drina was gone. And Xavi, his son. He couldn't believe it. He didn't want to believe it. But even the numbness of his exhausted mind couldn't hide reality.

They reached an open clearing and waited in the shadows for a moment to listen. Emil looked up at the Snow Moon rising just over the tips of a stand of trees to his left. Wisps of clouds scudded in front of the waning moon, giving it a peculiar rippled effect. *If you can hear me, Drina, give me strength. Send spirits to protect us — to protect these last of our troupe. Show us the way.*

Chapter
Twenty-One

Southern Poland, December 1942 (Oak Moon)

"HEY, STUPID. STOP that immediately."

Mischka froze. The crate she was wrestling off the back of a truck in the loading area was heavy, and the rough wood cut into her callused palms. She stole a quick glance over her shoulder, and was relieved to see that the German guard with the deep, guttural voice wasn't coming her way. He was scolding some other woman. The crate Mischka was balancing shifted, and for a moment she didn't have control of it.

Then Aurora was at her side, grabbing, helping, whispering, "Don't try to do it all yourself. Let me help."

"It's so cold," Mischka muttered. She wanted to trot around the building a few times to warm up her stiff limbs, but of course that wasn't permitted.

The sun had been up for over an hour, but the loading area was on the west side of a barn-like storage building next to the main factory. Enclosed on two sides with a roof over the top, it always remained bone-chillingly cold until well after noon. Even then it didn't get much warmer.

"Just be patient," Aurora said. "If you drop this, Vogel will take great pleasure in assaulting you."

Together she and Aurora lifted the crate and set it on the cement floor, then dragged it off to the side where their work partners, Nelka and Lidia, helped them pry off the wooden lid slats. Both young women were from strong Polish stock, and since the four of them shared the same scant sleeping space, it hadn't taken long for Aurora and Mischka to unite with them for protection. Mischka was thankful that despite background and age differences, the four women had become fast friends. She didn't know what she would do if she felt the enmity for her bedmates that some of the others seemed to feel. One woman, Petronela, behaved so badly and was so rude and selfish that no

one wanted anything to do with her. Aurora had warned
repeatedly that Petronela was going to get them all killed.

In the past couple of weeks, Mischka had not only gotten to
know the names of most of the girls and women on her work
detail, but she had also taken note of which of their guards had
hair-trigger tempers and which were more patient. Vogel was
not one of the patient ones. He had obviously been injured at
some point in the war. The right side of his ruddy face drooped,
and the one eyelid often winked involuntarily. This
embarrassment clearly enraged him, and he took out his fury on
the women he supervised. Vogel limped, too, and the right side
of his body moved stiffly. Most of the time he held his right arm
against his midsection, and although he tried to form that hand
into a fist, the big mitt was gnarled and wasted and wouldn't
cooperate. So he held a long, narrow baton in his left hand and
wasn't shy about using it as he was now on Edda. The girl turned
and bore the blows across her upper back, making an occasional
yelp.

Mischka turned her attention to another heavy crate. She
lifted an unwieldy pry bar and forced the lid off a load of boots.
Aurora scrambled to grab for a nail that went flying. They saved
the lids. They saved the nails, no matter how bent. They saved
nearly everything. Once the boots were repaired or re-soled, the
crates they arrived in would be used to ship them back out.

Vogel stopped his ranting and used his baton to wave Edda
and several other women toward the side of the loading area so
that the cargo truck could pull away. Mischka examined the pry
bar in her hand. She had never considered herself a violent
person, but in only a few weeks, she had found herself
entertaining many visions of blood and havoc. Usually, two
soldiers oversaw the work of close to a hundred women in the
dock area, but at the moment Vogel was their only guard. And
he was one she dreamed of exacting a merciless vengeance upon.
Often at the end of his work shift in midafternoon, he looked
around the loading area, his eyes sharp and cruel like a rabid
ferret's, and if someone struck his fancy, he beckoned to her. He
tended to choose the young, blue eyed, blonde girls. Mischka
supposed that this did not necessarily exempt her, but she was
thankful for her brown eyes and the dark stubble on her head.
Thankful, too, that he had shown no interest in Aurora, despite
her blonde hair. She was older and seemed to think that spared
her.

No woman could object. The chosen one must meekly follow
the limping soldier through the door to the left of the loading
dock and into the bowels of the building. She would return

sometime later, eyes dull and face marked with the furrows of tears. Most often, a friend or sympathetic older woman would comfort her with warm words and encouragement. Mischka knew she would not be so kindhearted if Vogel were to touch her or Aurora. She was afraid of what she would do. She had already been down that road, and she didn't want to travel it again.

Vogel beat his baton on the side of a crate. "Get to work, you sluts. You're like sleepwalkers. Move."

Eight arms reached into the crate and grabbed at jackboots, motorcycle boots, and the few officers' shoes, then dumped them into the rolling metal cart. Pairs were usually linked by laces or cording, but occasionally they were damaged too badly to be attached, and the women had to be certain to keep the right and left together. They got to the bottom of the crate and were left with one lone jackboot, and Mischka's heart sank.

"I'll report it," Aurora said.

Mischka shook her head. "Not you. I will."

Nelka stifled a laugh. "Don't be foolish, either of you. I'm the ugly one, and I shall do it. Step aside." She scooped up the boot from the crate, lifted her chin proudly, and stood to the side, waiting until she could catch Vogel's eye and give a respectful wave.

Mischka didn't know why the guards were always so suspicious about the receipt of one shoe or boot. The women couldn't help that whoever packed the boxes erred or that perhaps some of the footwear had been deemed irreparable and was disposed of before shipping. The guards acted like the workers had somehow hidden giant pairs of jackboots on their persons, as if they could be used as weapons or worn as one overshoe to facilitate escape. Where would anyone hide a size 14 boot under her thin coat and cotton dress? Mischka wasn't even certain where in Poland they were; how could they use a lone boot to escape? How ridiculous.

Vogel lumbered toward them, and Lidia, Mischka, and Aurora turned away to work on the lid to another crate. None of them wanted to draw his attention, and Nelka was, unfortunately, correct about her face. When she had been captured, she'd tried to run, and the pursuing soldier struck her in the face with the stock of his gun, laying open the flesh from cheekbone to chin. Mischka was amazed that it was healing without becoming contaminated from any sort of poison, but the angry, red, crooked rut did, indeed, look frightening. Nelka firmly believed herself permanently ugly and therefore not of interest to Vogel. Mischka was saddened to think that she was probably right about that, and she felt terrible for the young woman whose shapely figure, blue eyes, and heart-shaped face indicated that she had actually been quite lovely, even prettier than her older sister Lidia.

Before and after. Many of the women were whole before, and now, after such bad treatment by men, they were scarred and mutilated. Once again, she wished to strike down Vogel—and all his companions.

"What is it?" Vogel called out, his lip curled.

"A single, sir," Nelka said in halting German. She kept her eyes down. To look a guard in the face was to invite a beating—or worse.

He snatched the boot from her and shook it, as if its mate might come falling out, then looked around the crate and shuffled closer to peer into the deep wooden container.

"All right then," he said suspiciously. "You may deliver it to the singles box."

When she returned, Lidia whispered, "You're brave, Nelka."

"I suppose you never thought your little sister had the strength to face a man like that." Nelka picked up a boot and tossed it in the cart.

Lidia shivered. "If he comes after me, I won't be brave."

Mischka leaned into the crate near her companions and spoke in a low voice that all three of them could hear. "You don't have to be brave—just smart. We must do whatever we have to in order to stay alive in this hellhole, and that means doing what he says. We can still protect ourselves if we turn off our minds and go to another place."

"I couldn't do that." Lidia shook her head, and Mischka saw the fear in her face. "Where would I go?"

"I don't mean to actually *go* somewhere else, Lidia. You have to think of something else, a place of refuge. Some place where your mind can safely go while your body stays behind and endures. This will work for beatings as well as other indignities."

"How can you be sure?" Lidia asked. "How do you know?"

"That's of no importance. I just do. I'll show you how tonight."

All three women paused, each holding at least one boot, and Aurora frowned, her brow furrowed with wrinkles that became more accentuated each day. "How can you show something like that?"

"It's easy. You and Nelka shall pinch Lidia, and I'll help her go to a better place. You'll see. It works. You'll understand immediately."

Lidia closed her eyes and shuddered. Mischka wanted to put

her arms around the young woman and tell her everything would be all right, but she knew that was a lie. Instead, she said, "It's so cold. I wish the wind would stop whipping through here." She tossed a pair of mud-encrusted boots into the cart.

Nelka picked up the pry bar. "We've got to figure out how to get on a work crew inside the building. It can't possibly be so wintry in there. Or even better, the big factory. With all the steam coming off the roof, it must be warm in there. I heard everyone working on one of the upper floors gets to sit while they sew uniforms."

"I thought this place was a boot and glove factory," Mischka said.

"Oh, no. It depends on what the army processing center decides to send. Apparently they have a shortage of fabric at the moment. Usually this factory makes new uniforms for the army."

"How did you learn this?" Lidia asked.

"In the latrine. If you sit there long enough, you hear all sorts of conversations between the guards. Once even the commandant came out and spoke to the guards, talking all about the war. He was looking for someone to drive him somewhere because his regular driver was sick."

Aurora lifted her head. "Have you heard anything about the war?"

Nelka shrugged. "It's hard to tell what's going on. They were excited about some big aerial victory, but they were also cursing about the Americans joining the war. So I'm not sure."

Aurora's shoulders slumped and the air seemed to go out of her. "I can't take this place anymore."

Mischka shot a look at Vogel. The man stood at the rear of a cargo truck, partially turned away from them with one foot up on the back bumper. He held his bad arm tight against him while he used a toothpick to dig at his teeth. Mischka put an arm across Aurora's shoulders. "We shall get by, living through one hour at a time."

"I just wish I knew about Janek and my sons. Where are they?"

Nelka said, "This place is enormous. You probably don't even realize that north of our barracks there's an entire town. If you go out and look around after dark—"

Lidia's jaw dropped. "Nelka!"

Vogel glanced their way, and all four women dipped simultaneously to grab boots. Nelka came up smiling, the red gash of her scar making the grin crooked and somehow elfin and mischievous. Though Mischka was old enough to be the younger woman's mother, she felt a real sisterhood with Nelka. She was a woman of her own heart. And she had been braver than Mischka if she had gotten out after dark and explored. Mischka had noticed that Nelka had sometimes left their sleeping platform in the night, but she had thought Nelka was using the latrine. In her restless sleep, it hadn't occurred to her that Nelka was gone for any length of time.

Mischka retrieved more boots. "So you've gone out on nighttime searches?"

"Yes, I call it reconnaissance."

"I don't know that word."

"It's French. Something soldiers do to survey the battlefield and the enemy. Someone goes ahead to learn the lay of the land and the power of the forces before all the troops are committed."

"Ahh...a scout."

"Mm-hmmm."

All her life, Mischka's people had apparently been doing reconnaissance without knowing that was what it was called. "What did you find out?"

"The enemy is cautious and well-armed. All exits that I was able to find on this end are locked and guarded. The food and supply storehouses are also locked."

"So you've searched for food?"

"Among other things. There are some areas I've yet to look at. Too bad the fence is so heavily guarded between our side and where the town is on the men's side."

Mischka tossed a pair of boots toward the cart, and they flew end over end, hit the side wall of the cart, and fell in.

"Hey," Vogel hollered from across the floor. "Watch it."

Mischka ignored him. They wanted the workers to move swiftly, but none of the tactics Mischka would have used for speed were allowed.

She looked around the loading area. Twenty other teams of four to six women worked on crates just as she and her crew did. If the guards would let them organize in a different manner, Mischka was sure they could do the work in half the time and have time to rest and maintain their strength. She was acutely aware of how hard it was to be on her feet from sunup to sundown, especially since they were given food only in the morning and evening. A rainwater catchall sat in the corner, and they could drink at specified times throughout the day, but no one wanted to down too much liquid. They were allowed to visit the latrines only in the morning and evening and in case of "emergencies." An emergency was defined only as the onset of menstruation, though most of them had been known to lie upon occasion.

"Come on," Nelka said, gesturing with a toss of her head. Mischka followed her to the cargo truck, and they wrestled down another crate and dragged it over to their work area. "If you like, you may come with me tonight to look around."

"Reconnaissance?"

"Yes."

Mischka hesitated only a moment. Hope ignited within her, and her mind raced ahead to the discovery of an escape route. "I'll come," she said.

MISCHKA LAY ON her back with her right arm behind her head. The slab of hard wood that served as her bed felt cold, and drafty fingers of air seeped into the room at irregular intervals. Her stomach rumbled with hunger. The evening meal had consisted of a chestnut-sized stale biscuit and watery chicken-flavored soup that held a few chunks of potato, one pea, and no chicken.

Petronela, the Polish woman who constantly complained, lay two bunks down muttering in her nasal voice about the lack of food. "How do they expect us to work?" she asked of no one in particular. "We're cold. We're abused. We're underfed."

Someone groaned and said, "Shhh..."

"I'd like to speak to the commandant. This is inexcusable. None of them look underfed."

From farther down the barracks a voice rang out: "Shut up, Petronela."

"I will not. Someone needs to do something. At this rate, we'll all be dead by the new year." One of her bedmates must have elbowed her, because she made a grunting noise. "Stop that. No need to be rude."

A tired voice said, "Please hush. We need to sleep."

Petronela settled down then, and Mischka was glad of it. Despite the fact that the woman was a noisy nuisance, she had to admit that Petronela was right. But there was nothing to be done. Didn't the silly woman understand that the German guards had little patience and no mercy? Petronela's constant grumbling was dangerous to all of them.

Every two hours, all night long, a guard walked through the barracks, in through the door near Mischka's group and out the door at the other end. The little warmth that had accumulated swept out behind him, and all of them huddled closer together, teeth chattering and miserable. More than once Petronela had groused aloud, and Mischka was waiting for the day when the guard chose to attack rather than ignore her protests.

Outside, drunk voices singing "Stille Nacht" drew nearer, then passed in front of the barracks and gradually faded away. It didn't feel like a silent night, holy night, and all was not calm or bright. The only "glories" streaming from heaven afar were raindrops. The nice thing about the rain was that it meant the weather wasn't quite so terribly cold; the bad thing was the immense amount of mud everywhere. For two days the water and dirt had gotten into the cracks in Mischka's shoes, and she hated the feeling of grit between her toes almost as much as the aching chill.

The rain kept up a light patter on the roof. Mischka looked above her head at her tin cup balanced on the flat of the bedpost near the ceiling. In the pale lamplight streaming in from a nearby window, she watched as rain dripped — plink, plink, plink — into the cup. Within an hour, she would have a full cup to drink, and she looked forward to something in her stomach, even if only temporarily. Before too many more days passed, the weather would be so cold that no more water would fall. She wasn't anxious to see snow.

Some of the "round yon virgins" in the barracks were wasting away. Aurora had lost weight at an alarming rate. The roly-poly woman's stomach still maintained some plumpness, but her legs and arms had reduced in size, and her face was nothing short of haggard. Her haunted and worry-filled eyes accentuated her gauntness.

When they had first arrived at the camp, ten lackluster, emaciated women had been in the barracks to greet them. All of them had looked beaten down and wary, like animals who'd been caged and tortured. Now only eight of those original workers remained. Mischka didn't know where the other two had gone. One had fainted in the loading area two weeks earlier and been hauled off, and the other had simply disappeared when Mischka wasn't paying attention. She wondered if any of those eight could tell her how long they'd been in the camp? And what did the Germans do with those who were close to starving to death? The logical thing would be to feed them and give them rest so that they could soon work hard again, but she suspected that was not the case. The Germans showed more care and concern for the boots being processed than for the workers.

Mischka had been keeping track of the days she had been in the camp, and according to her count, it had been forty-four. She knew she might have missed a day, particularly at the beginning before she thought to make marks on the wall. But she knew it was near the end of Oak Moon, the time of the birth of the Christ, which so many Germans and Poles celebrated. So the old year was drawing to a close and the new one would soon be arriving. Wolf Moon. The time to plan a ritual of protection around home and family. She grimaced. There would be no planning, no protection, especially considering the kind of wolves who had her under their control.

She didn't often allow herself to think about her family, but tonight, with the rain showers buffeting the roof and walls and the barracks so cold, she closed her eyes and imagined the *kumpania* sitting around a fire in the dusky setting sun, somewhere warm and dry. Her mother offered a cup of milk-sweetened tea to her father, who sat on a log smoking his pipe. Emil and Drina stood nearby, examining the fetlock of Mischka's horse, Maisie...

Abruptly, the fantasy stopped there and her eyes fluttered open. Maisie. The dear horse she'd ridden for the last three years. She'd never see the little mare again. Something burned in the middle of her chest. As usual, she reminded herself that Maisie was a fair sacrifice for the safety of the troupe. She and Tobar were, as well. But it tore at her not knowing if her *kumpania* was safe. Did they get away?

An elbow poked her in the side, and Aurora leaned over and whispered, "Nelka is going now." Mischka started to sit up, but Aurora pushed her back. "She said count to five hundred, then meet her in the alcove of the loading building across the way."

Mischka's heart beat fast. Did she want to do this? Would their tracks easily be seen in the rain-soaked ground? She thought of Tobar. He'd never been a big risk-taker, but he'd always done what he had to do. She decided that she could do the same. She took down her tin cup, drained and replaced it, then lay back to count each beat of her heart until she reached five hundred.

She thought it must be close to midnight. The only noises she heard were the snores and heavy exhalations of exhausted women. Aurora sat up, and their heads nearly touched the ceiling as she squeezed past to the ladder. She hoped no one would pay attention to her, and if they did, that they'd assume she was on the way to the latrine. Every scuff of her feet, each rustle of her clothing sounded to her like a crash, a shriek of sound. But no one stirred. She opened the flimsy door and went quickly into the night's soft rain to slide along the south edge of the building, listening. Far away she heard the faint sounds of revelry. By the rise and fall of the tones, someone was singing to the north.

Above each barracks, at their east ends, sturdy posts twenty feet high were sunk deep into the ground. A string of dim lights, like tiny beads on a droopy chain, dangled near each barracks and threw enough light to illuminate the rows between. Every third or fourth light was out, and near the loading building, none of the bulbs were burning. She wasn't sure whether that was intentional or not, but Mischka took it as a sign of good fortune as she crept across the open area to an alcove where the loading building attached to the storage barn. Even when she was in the mouth of the doorway leading into the building, she didn't see Nelka. She jumped when a cold, wet hand grasped her forearm and pulled her into the dark.

"Wait," Nelka whispered. They stood listening. All Mischka could hear was her own blood rushing in her ears. After a moment, Nelka leaned out, then pulled back. "We can thank these idiot Germans for being so orderly and precise. I've never gone too far toward the north end of the camp, but I can tell you they have placed the latrines at the same intervals, after every two barracks. If you run into a guard, your only chance is to duck into the latrine." Mischka nodded, and Nelka took her hand and squeezed it tight. "Don't go to the other side of this building or the factory. There are always guards along the fence."

"All right."

"Remember, if a guard appears, head for the latrine and try to act like you're sleepwalking or sick. You can't help me if I get caught, and I won't help you either. We can't take the chance of being seen together. You know how suspicious these Germans are. They'd think there was some sort of plot or rebellion. So I'll go first, you follow. We're looking for food or supplies or clothing — probably in a storage building. If either of us finds anything, let out one faint whistle."

With a final squeeze, Nelka slid away along the side of the building. Mischka counted to ten, then peeked out. If she stared up and to the right, in her peripheral vision she could just barely make out Nelka's dark shape, and then she couldn't see her any longer. She took a deep breath and stepped into the drizzle. Her coat wasn't going to do much to keep out the cold, but it was surprisingly water-resistant. Too bad she didn't have a hat or hood.

Behind the building where they worked everyday sat a motorcycle with a sidecar, a cargo truck, and two *Kübelwagen* vehicles, which could carry a driver and three passengers. Mischka paused and scanned the area. When she saw and heard nothing, she crept forward across the muddy open space. She felt exposed here, like a hungry mouse caught in the middle of the kitchen, and she hastened to the shadows of the factory wall. An overhang, far above, shielded her from some of the rain. She stopped again to listen, then went on, trailing the fingers of her left hand along the blackened, gritty bricks. The wall seemed to go on and on. Every so often, she stopped to determine where the latrines were, though looking toward the light tended to slow her down because for at least another minute, her vision was clouded. When she came opposite a brick, two-story building, she squatted down. The main floor was ablaze with light and the windows in the second story were curtained. The front door, painted white, was closed, but the windows on the ground floor—two on either side of the door—sparkled with the glow of a candle in each. Beyond one window and back some ten feet or so in a corner of the room, sat a green tree decorated with little bits of something silver and shiny.

Someone moved into the far right window, and Mischka started so violently that she very nearly fell back. She caught herself by grabbing the factory wall. They couldn't see her. No need for fear. The house was too well-lit inside for them to see out. A blond-haired man in a dark uniform lifted a glass high in the air, then tipped back his head to drink from it. Afterward, he made a grand gesture with his other arm, as though he were asking someone to dance.

To the left, out of the corner of her eye, Mischka caught a blur of motion as a figure emerged from the dim light of the back of the factory. Nelka cut across the expanse of mud and disappeared into the darkness next to a shed to the left of the brick quarters. A moment later, Mischka heard a quiet whistle. She willed her legs to stand, but for some reason, they did not, and a split second later, she realized her instincts had served her well. Behind her she heard the rev of an engine and stared in shock as a vehicle came weaving its way down the muddy row between the factory and the barracks. Though she was crouched low, in a few seconds the headlights would surely illuminate her. She had no hope of not being seen.

With a squawk, she lunged to the left, around the corner of the factory. She landed on her knees and folded down into as tight a ball as she could manage.

A *Kübelwagen*, its leather roof glistening wet, careened around the corner. Water and mud sprayed behind like a rooster tail until it came to a stop close to the doorway of the building. A soldier leapt from the driver's seat and ran around to open the passenger door.

As if they had been waiting, the front door of the quarters opened, and a voice called out, "Sergeant Klein. Welcome."

Despite the drizzle, the sergeant stopped in his tracks,

saluted, and called out, "Heil Hitler." The man on the front porch, as well as the other two men exiting the car, repeated the greeting. A woman came to the door and Mischka recognized her. She was the guard, Braunhaus, who so enjoyed inflicting pain. For once, the guard's face was smiling and not twisted into the hateful expression she usually showed the prisoners. She swung open the door, and the men trooped in.

Mischka rose with difficulty. Her knees and calves were stiff, and she was wet and muddy. She moved as quickly as she could along the back of the factory, took a deep breath, then ran toward the shed where Nelka had disappeared. She backed up against the wooden wall of the shed with her eyes frantically scanning. Her breath came out in wheezes. Someone grabbed her arm and covered her mouth.

"Shhh. Took you long enough. Guess what I've found."

"What?" Mischka whispered.

Nelka tugged at Mischka's damp coat and pulled her around to the side of the shed. "Of course this useless hut is locked. I think it only has tools in it anyway, but this isn't locked." A metal bin, about five feet wide, sat under the shed's overhang. A steel lid, hinged at the back, covered it. Nelka pulled up the lid. "You've got longer arms than I have. Can you reach?"

The edge of the bin hit Mischka at the level of her ribs. She couldn't see well, but she smelled the ripe, rotting smell of old garbage. "*Mahrime.*"

"What?"

"It's unclean."

"Uh-huh. So what else is new? This whole camp is a filthy sty."

Mischka couldn't disagree. Forcing herself to lean farther in, she saw butcher paper, wadded up newspaper, and some empty tins interspersed with coffee grounds, bread crusts, half-eaten apples, and a pile of what looked like fried potatoes. She leaned down and plucked out one of the apple halves. It came up through the air to her mouth before she fully realized what she was doing, and she bit into it. Sweet and pungent. Chewing slowly, she savored it. Though it was certainly unclean, it tasted better than any food she'd had since Snow Moon before her capture. She offered the remaining quarter to Nelka.

"You eat it. I've found something, too."

Mischka chewed away at the apple until all that was left was the core, then tossed that in the bin. Nelka handed her a rubbery pancake. One triangular wedge was cut from it. She took a small experimental bite. Dry on the outside, but moist inside. She ate half of it, then stuck the other half in her coat pocket. "I'm bringing back what I can for Lidia and Aurora."

"Me, too," Nelka whispered as she hefted an over-ripe apple and reached back in. "Let's eat these potatoes and the peelings, and we'll take the crusts and fruit back to them."

The potatoes were cold and congealed, but they were laced through with grease. She choked them down, and for the first time in weeks, Mischka felt satiated. She hoped the food wasn't too badly spoiled. That it had been out in the near-freezing weather was a good sign.

They cautiously closed the bin's lid and crept away with food for Aurora and Lidia bundled into their clothing. When she got to the shadows of the factory, Mischka looked back to the brick quarters. Two women stood near the Christmas tree, glasses in hand, speaking to the sergeant. He stood with his back to the window, one arm behind him. She wondered if it was Christmas Eve or perhaps Christmas Day. As she crept along the edge of the factory, something seemed different and she hesitated, heart beating fast. Then she realized the rain had stopped. At least it had washed the mud off of her clothing. The clouds roiled in the sky, sailing along like wisps of smoke, and the moon, nearly full, smiled down upon her.

Chapter
Twenty-Two

Outside Eisenhüttenstadt, Germany, February 1943 (Storm Moon)

PIPPI SAT AT the sewing machine, piecing together two panels for a shroud. She pumped the treadle and her shoulders hunched tight as she strained to make the seams as perfect as she could. On the floor at her feet lay a pile of woven cloth and a stack of folded shrouds. So many men—boys, some of them—were being killed in the war that the two morticians in Eisenhüttenstadt could hardly keep up with the number of funerals. They'd placed a special order for burial shrouds for families unable to afford caskets.

"Pippi," Camille called out from the kitchen. "You must stop and eat something. Your soup is getting cold."

The machine chose that moment to jam, and Pippi let out a huff of frustration. "Sometimes I just hate this sewing machine. That second thread is always getting tangled."

"It couldn't have anything to do with the fact that you've been going without a break for three straight hours."

"All right, Mama, all right." Pippi rose and clumped into the adjoining kitchen. "I'm sure it's not me causing the problem."

Camille poured tea into their china cups from the flowered teapot. "Someday, maybe after the war is over, we'll be able to get a chain-stitch machine. Perhaps even one that runs on electricity."

"If this horrible war ever *gets* over." Pippi sat down and examined her cabbage soup. She was sick of soup. She was sick of rationing. She was sick of the gloomy weather and of the constant talk of war. Ever since she'd moved back to Germany from France, her life had indeed seemed dismal, but her mother had needed her far more than Richelle, her mother-in-law, so here she was, stuck sewing for the war effort and praying for an end to this nightmare.

As was the norm over meals, her mother regaled her with

the latest speculation. "At the shoe shop yesterday, Herr Galt and Herr Hofstetter both predicted that the war will go much longer and be much bloodier than we were first told. Hitler wants Italy, and the Americans and British won't let him have it."

"Oh, that fool Mussolini. I can't believe Skorzeny and those fascists rescued him from that old hotel. They should have bombed the Grand Sasso and done away with him as soon as Italy surrendered."

"Pauline Stanek! I can't believe you're wishing death upon someone."

"Mother, it's fascists like him and Herr Hitler who are wishing death upon all of us. They don't deserve to lead our country. This war is one hundred percent wrong and the world is in chaos because of it." She spooned up some of the thick broth. "I suppose I should be glad we have food and a warm house, especially when others don't. Still, who will be left when Hitler gets done pillaging and killing? Some of the elderly, a few orphaned children, and a bunch of heavy-hearted widows like me?"

"Oh, Pippi. You're still very young."

"I'm thirty-seven years old — no longer a fresh blossom." Her tone was sarcastic. "I have nothing to lose by admitting what most good Germans already know. This war is a travesty, and Adolf Hitler is an overreaching madman."

Camille brought her palms to her forehead. "I don't think I'm ever going to get used to how strident you've become. It's not safe to be so bull-headed, Pippi."

"I lost my husband to that lunatic and — "

Camille placed a hand on Pippi's forearm. "Hush, my dear. You think we're insulated here, but there are spies and informers everywhere. Why, Frau Huber told me just the other day that her cousin's husband in Eisenhüttenstadt was arrested and held for three days — three days! He was kept in a cell with political troublemakers and accused of being a Jew."

"Is he?"

"Is he what?"

"A Jew."

"No." Camille looked startled at the question. "I don't think so. What does it matter?"

"That's the point. It shouldn't matter." Pippi pushed away the half-eaten bowl of soup. "None of this should matter. *Lebensraum* is a sin. Living space for Germans? At whose expense? Who gave us the right to seize Poland? Or Italy or France — or to invade any of our neighbors? The French are a miserable occupied country. Their economy is in a shambles, and their people are downtrodden. It's a sin." Pippi took a deep breath, then looked up into her mother's blue eyes. The lines in Camille's face had grown deeper, and she looked worried. "All we're doing is biding time, waiting until the war is over. If we lose, we'll go back to the dreariness and squalor I remember from my early years, back when we thought Emil was lost for good. If we win the war, we'll live in fear, and the world will loathe us. Both are bad possibilities, but the latter is the worst."

Camille looked at a loss for answers. "What else are we to do?"

"That's my question. I ask it every day. All we're doing is supplying the dead with shrouds. How meaningful can that be?"

"It matters to the families who have lost a son or a brother. Or a husband. It's a small thing, but it's needed. It's —"

Three sharp raps sounded at the front door.

Camille picked up her napkin and wiped her mouth. "I wonder who's come calling. I haven't forgotten a customer, have I?"

Pippi shrugged. The sound of a heavier pounding shook the walls so much that a decorative plate hanging nearby rattled.

"I'm coming," Camille called out.

From her vantage point, Pippi looked past her mother as she opened the door. A soldier, dressed in a neat uniform, stood on the front stoop. His rifle was slung over his shoulder by the leather strap. "Heil Hitler."

Her mother glanced back toward Pippi. Camille's mouth had dropped open, and all the color drained from her face. Pippi felt a shock course through her. Had he been listening to her speaking to her mother? How could he have? She had only raised her voice slightly. One day last week, she had spoken frankly to the butcher at the meat market, but he shared her political viewpoints. At least it seemed that way. He wouldn't have told anyone...would he?

The soldier removed his cap. "Good afternoon, Madam. I am Corporal Richter sent here on special assignment. May I come in?"

Camille didn't seem to know what to say. Pippi rose, tossed her napkin on the table, and strode to the door, pretending a confidence she didn't feel. "Hello, Corporal. Come in. How can we help you?"

He stepped inside, bringing with him a giant gust of wind. He wasn't a large man, but he seemed to take all the air out of the room. His eyes were a muddy gray-green, and his hair, cut very short, was light brown and thinning. His whole face smoldered with the fire of one pledged to carry out his duty, no matter what.

Pippi straightened up and nudged her mother with an elbow.

"I've forgotten my manners, Corporal," Camille said. "Please come into the kitchen and have a seat. Would you like a refreshment? Some tea? A cool drink of water perhaps?"

"No, Madam, but thank you." He didn't make a move toward the kitchen, instead turning to examine Pippi. "I assume you are Fräulein Pauline Stanek?"

She didn't comment on the fact that her married name was Delebecque and "Frau" might be the more appropriate address. "Yes, I am," she said, even as her heart threatened to thud right out of her chest. He reached for his low side pocket, unbuttoned it, and removed a folded packet of papers, which he thrust at her. "These are orders for you to report to Reich headquarters at Eisenhüttenstadt for transport cross-country where you will be employed as a supervisor at the textile plant."

"What?" Camille's mouth dropped open. "My daughter isn't a soldier. She cannot be ordered—"

"Excuse me, Madam. Each and every citizen must contribute to the war effort. No one is exempt. Your daughter possesses skills critical to *Der Führer* and the Fatherland. It is a great honor for a woman to be selected to provide such help."

Camille brought her fingers to her mouth for a moment. "But—but we have a business we're running here."

He gave a curt nod. "Yes, and thankfully all of your good work has brought Fräulein Stanek to our attention. She comes highly recommended by many prominent businessmen in Eisenhüttenstadt."

Pippi's mind raced. She didn't want to work at a textile plant. However, she could think of no way to protest, so she stood, fingers interlaced in a grip that hurt her knuckles. They couldn't force her. Could they?

"Corporal, my daughter isn't trained as a soldier, nor does she have a factory background. You cannot expect her to pack up, leave her home and family, and go off to some unsafe region on the war front."

"The area to which she has been assigned is in Poland, which is now German territory controlled by our troops. It is safe, and the factory is modern, but understaffed. Fräulein Stanek is needed, and she will receive compensation for her work." He looked at his watch. "I will be gone for approximately one and one half hours. I will return at two o'clock. You will be ready for transport."

"Today?" Camille bent forward, taking the news as though the soldier had struck her in the stomach. "You can't mean today."

"Yes. That is exactly what I mean. Fräulein Stanek, you will pack one suitcase and perhaps a purse or shoulder bag. Another soldier and I will accompany you. We will arrive in Eisenhüttenstadt this afternoon. There will be some paperwork and an opportunity for you to shop for any travel necessities, and then you will catch the six o'clock train to embark upon a trip of approximately three days."

In disbelief, Pippi said, "It'll be all right, Mother. Don't worry." She wondered if this was all a ruse. Was he speaking the truth, or was she really being taken somewhere to be punished for her radical beliefs? She unfolded the papers in her hands, but before she had a chance to read them, the corporal came to attention, his chin held high and eyes focused on the wall behind Pippi's head.

"Have I made myself understood, Fräulein Stanek?"

"Yes, Corporal, you have."

"Very well, please be ready when I return for you. Heil Hitler." He executed a crisp about-face, turned the doorknob, and was gone. Pippi felt as though a train had just chugged through their living room.

"Oh, my God. This is terrible." Camille pressed her fingers to her mouth as tears coursed down her cheeks. "You must run. Hide somewhere."

Pippi let out a sigh. "There's nowhere to run — or hide."

"To France. To my people —"

"No. I couldn't find safe passage. Besides, it's no safer there. Remember? That's why I left."

"But what if —" Camille couldn't finish the question.

Pippi pulled her mother close. "Don't cry. Listen to me. You don't have time to cry."

Camille pulled back. "What do you mean?"

"Look at that stack of sewing over there. You're going to have to work double time to get all that done without me."

"Are you kidding? Those morticians in Eisenhüttenstadt are probably the 'prominent' businessmen who opened their big mouths about you. If they think I'm going to rush their order, then they've gone crazy."

Pippi tried to smile, but she knew it came out looking grim. "The whole world has gone crazy. There's nothing for us to do but accept it."

Chapter
Twenty-Three

Southern Poland, February 1943 (Storm Moon)

FOR WEEKS ON end, Mischka and her three companions had worked hard at the loading dock, each day managing to get by on scavenged food whenever they could as they submitted to every indignity their keepers threw at them. But the day came when Vogel's eyes lit upon Lidia, and with one toss of his head, their bubble of protective security burst. Vogel beckoned, then turned, dragging his bad leg as he made his way to the side door.

Mischka's heart sank. She sought out Lidia's frightened eyes and tried to send her a silent message of strength, but the terrified girl didn't seem able to focus on anything or anyone. Nelka made a gurgling sound. Mischka turned and her eyes widened. Nelka stood, hands in fists and arms shaking. Her face was red — so red that her scar hardly showed up. Mischka stepped in front of the girl. "Shhh...shhh. She'll be all right. There's nothing we can do."

Vogel glanced over his shoulder, then wheeled around with a frown on his face. "You! Get over here. I gave you an order."

As if in a trance, Lidia stepped forward looking like each step required a psychic shove from behind. Vogel resumed his weaving path. Braunhaus hadn't been paying any attention, but when she looked their way and saw Aurora, Mischka, and Nelka standing idle, she hollered, "Get back to work," and slammed her baton against the side of a cargo truck. The hollow-sounding bang startled Mischka. She bent and reached into a crate. In a moment she heard Braunhaus shrieking at someone else in the far corner, so she tossed a pair of boots into a cart and looked at Aurora whose eyes glistened with unshed tears. Nelka *was* crying — hot, angry rivulets cutting down her face.

The waiting was terrible. Every nightmare vision Mischka could imagine flashed through her mind's eye. For the first time in years she had a visceral memory of Arben — of his rough hands and the violent way he had so enjoyed taking her. But then, mercifully, another vision filled her mind — of Tobar's face and his kind eyes and bushy beard. She thought of Emil, laughing, and of her father and Gyorgy and Stevo. Even Cam's face flashed into her memory, and she was surprised. He had tormented her when they were children, but he became a good man. There were many good men who would not hurt women. Vogel just happened not to be one of them.

Though it felt like time had slowed to a crawl, no more than ten minutes passed before the side door opened and Lidia emerged. Mischka realized that they had all been holding a collective breath. She took a gulp of air and waited, standing still, just as Nelka and Aurora did.

Lidia, unmarked and not looking any different than usual, walked like an automaton toward them, her gaze on the ground. She stepped past Aurora and lifted a jackboot out of the crate, then stuck in a hand to hunt for its mate.

Nelka muttered, "Are you all right?" Lidia didn't answer. She grabbed her sister's arm. "Lidia! Did he hurt you?"

Lidia lifted the uncomprehending eyes of a whipped puppy.

Braunhaus came up behind Mischka and smacked her baton against the back of her legs, then Nelka's. Nelka whirled to face the guard, and Mischka had no trouble recognizing the blood-lust in the young woman's eyes. Once again she stepped in front of the Polish girl, but it was Aurora who addressed the guard. "This young one," Aurora said, pointing to Lidia, "would appreciate a few moments to visit the latrine."

"I'll bet she would." The look of disgust on Braunhaus's face was evident to anyone in eyeshot. "I saw her go off for special treatment. The slut gets no special favors from me. Get back to work. All of you." She raised the baton, and from the expression on her face, Mischka thought she was begging for someone to give her an excuse to rain down blows.

Throughout the exchange, Lidia had continued to bend and reach, sort and drop. She was going through the motions of pairing boots, but none of the items she picked up matched. She snagged a pair of jackboots, both right feet, and wound the laces together to prepare to tie them off. Aurora took them gently from her hands. "Let me help." She didn't look Braunhaus in the eye, but politely said, "Thank you for the reminder, ma'am. We're back up to full speed now."

"You'd better be," Braunhaus said. Someone near the doorway of the loading area stifled a surprised yelp, and Braunhaus squinted toward the entrance. A soldier was backing up a cargo truck, but the way he weaved, he must have been a novice. She stomped across the floor calling out, "Halt. Halt! You're driving like a moron. Watch out there..."

Nightfall couldn't come soon enough. The three women worked carefully at shielding the ineffective Lidia from the eyes of their guard. When Braunhaus finally blew her whistle, it was well past dark. Going through the motions, they'd all been stumbling and ineffective for at least twenty minutes. None of them could see to match two boots to save their lives. Mischka was glad the workday was over.

Later, after they had eaten runny porridge and a half-slice of bread, Mischka lay on the platform in their icebox barracks. As usual, she was nearest the wall, then Aurora, Lidia, and Nelka closest to the ladder. The entire barracks was quieter than usual. The cold and fatigue continued to take its toll, and for most of the women, slumber was their only escape. But Mischka couldn't sleep. She heard the whispers of Nelka and Aurora as they tried to get Lidia to speak, but Lidia wasn't cooperating. "She's gone to that other place I told her about," Mischka said.

"What?" Aurora asked.

"She's blanked everything out, Aurora. But it will pass."

Nelka whispered, "How do you know? How can you be sure?"

Mischka shrugged. "I can't, but it would make sense." She thought of Valentina, her favorite sister-in-law from her days with Arben's *kumpania*. Donka and Terom had never been very sympathetic, but sometimes after Arben beat her, Valentina and Simza had been kind to Mischka, bringing cool compresses for her bruises and stanching any blood flow from her face and nose. Valentina was always the gentlest. A few times she had stayed the night in the tent with Mischka, lying close, comforting her.

"Hold her," Mischka told them. "Just hold and soothe her, and that's all you can do."

MISCHKA DIDN'T FUSS over Lidia as Aurora and Nelka did. She watched the girl closely, seeing little signs of life: an increasing focus on the never-ending pile of boots, a quiet thank you when Mischka scavenged and brought back a piece of coffee cake for her, and eyes that gradually lost their vacantness. Lidia took many days to emerge completely from her self-induced walking coma, and by then Nelka was nearly mad with worry. Mischka kept telling her to be patient, but Nelka would hear none of it. Finally one day, behind one of the cargo trucks, Nelka got into Mischka's face and said, "He didn't take *you* back there and savage you. How the hell would you know?"

Mischka gazed down at her. She admired Nelka's spirit, but her sister didn't have that same fire. Lidia was a softer, gentler person who had been wounded by a crude, thoughtless animal. Lidia saw no way to fight back, not like Nelka did. Nelka had made it clear that she would sacrifice her life in order to strike out at Vogel or anyone else who came at her or her sister again. "Lidia isn't you, Nelka. She's not a fighter at heart. And sometimes there is no fight to be fought anyway."

"That's ridiculous."

"Sometimes there's nothing to be done. You have to close your eyes and endure the pain."

"That's not acceptable! And it's oh-so-easy for you to say. You've never had to deal with such an abomination."

Mischka shook her head sadly. "A thousand times have I borne it."

"Oh, please." Her tone was mocking.

Mischka sighed. She wondered if it was important for Nelka to understand her life with Arben. "Every day, sometimes twice a day, except when I got my bloods, my husband dealt with me as Vogel used your sister."

"That's preposterous. He was your husband."

"Should husbands be allowed to beat their wives senseless before seeking their pleasure? Most of his attacks were fueled first by a beating, then by using me as though I were nothing and nobody. He gave no thought toward my comfort or pain. Nor did he ever seek my permission to use my body in such a cruel way."

Nelka stared at her in horror. "Daily?"

"Yes, which is why all of our focus must be on keeping Lidia out of Vogel's line of sight. Instead of wishing him death and staring daggers at him day in and day out, you need to work to make her as unobtrusive as possible. If you don't, he'll do it again. In fact, we may not be able to prevent it—but perhaps we can keep it from happening so often."

For the first time since Mischka had known her, Nelka burst into tears. She squeezed her eyes shut and contorted her face into a mask of such pain and despair that Mischka wanted to reach out for her. Instead she crawled into the cargo truck to wrestle out the next crate.

Nelka crawled in next to Mischka. "It's not fair, Mischka. It's not. Without this scar, he could have taken me instead of my sister, and I would have been able to kill that lazy, crippled bastard."

Mischka smiled at the ferocity in her friend's voice. "No, you wouldn't. That would endanger every woman on this work detail, and you wouldn't do that to all of us."

"I can't bear it," Nelka whispered through her tears. "I can't. If I knew where he bunked I'd sneak into his quarters and slit his throat. It's all I think of, all I dream of. I can't restrain myself."

"Yes, you can. They'd catch you and kill you, and that would hurt Lidia much more than anything else could. She needs you now, Nelka. Be solid, be angry for her, be strong. You're keeping her going. You're helping to keep us all going with your fire. Don't let them put that fire out."

"What are you two doing in there?" Vogel stood behind them partially blocking the light. Mischka gave a mighty pull, and the crate slid a few feet toward her. "If I catch you napping in there, I'll beat you to within an inch of your lives."

"Yes, sir," was all Mischka said. She pulled at the crate as she crawled out of the truck. Vogel lost interest and wandered away. Looking back at Nelka, Mischka grinned. "I was sure you were going to shove the crate on top of him and try to crush the life out of his useless carcass."

"I hadn't thought of that. What a good idea. I'll have to try it next time." Nelka wiped her tears on the dirty sleeve of her coat and leaned into the crate.

Chapter
Twenty-Four

Southern Poland, First Day of March 1943 (Chaste Moon)

THE LAST FEW days of Storm Moon passed quietly. When March's Chaste Moon was not yet two days old, the first of many storms blanketed the camp with heavy, moist snow that was at first sloppy. Then the multitude of footprints and the indentations from car tires formed frozen ridges overnight, making walking slippery and treacherous. More than one woman fell on the way to the loading dock.

The snow fell drier and harder as the days of bitter cold continued. It slipped into collars, blew against bare calves, stuck to uncovered heads, and made everyone's lives miserable. The sun had not yet risen when Mischka awoke on yet another freezing morning, lying on her side, pressed against Aurora's back, with her hands tucked under her armpits. The front of her was adequately warm. But her calves and feet felt like blocks of ice.

Mischka tried to absorb what warmth she could for a few minutes, then crawled over the three women next to her, descended the ladder, and made her way to the latrine and back. She was often the first to rise. Usually she grabbed the broom and swept the barracks. The tidier they kept it, the less the guards had to attack them for. The angry blonde woman, Braunhaus, had been assigned to them since the beginning of the new year, and it took little to set her off.

Mischka swept with vigor while occasionally stopping to hop in place and flex her legs. Just to get the blood to flow was a struggle, but her feet were gradually feeling warmer.

She was at the back end of the barracks when the front door slammed open, and Braunhaus stepped in, yelling, "Awake!" She followed this with her usual whistle blast, a sharp, shrill burst of painful sound, and strutted down the center aisle rapping her baton against the sides of the wood platforms. "Up. Up, you lazy hags. Up, up."

As she drew near, Mischka stepped to the side, her eyes lowered.

"Tsk, tsk—why are you the one always sweeping. Give me that." Braunhaus wrenched the broom from Mischka's hands. With the wooden end, she jabbed the midsection of a groggy woman just emerging from a lower bunk. "You. You shall sweep." She prodded Mischka with the broom. "You are not to sweep."

"No, ma'am. Thank you."

"That's right, you should thank me. I don't know why they've forced the job upon you, but you're relieved of the duty for the rest of the week. Let some of these other ne'er-do-wells take a turn. Now, go get ready for *Zählappell*."

"Yes, ma'am."

All around, women were crawling from their bunks and moving sleepily toward the doors. They had very little time to visit the latrine, and as the moments passed, they moved more quickly.

Mischka could not understand why the Germans were so obsessed with morning and evening *Zählappell*, when the prisoners lined up outside and were counted. Based upon the location of their sleeping pallets, they were made to line up in rows up to twelve. Because Mischka and her three friends were near the door, they were in the front row, along with the women who slept in the middle pallet below. Row two consisted of the women crammed in the bunk across from them, and rows three and four were for the next two bunks and so forth. Some of the women trod out immediately and stood shivering in the snow, but Mischka waited in the barracks for as long as she could. The temperature outside was at least twenty degrees colder.

When she could stall no longer, she stepped through the door and found her spot, fourth in row one. The wind from the north wasn't very forceful, but it was bitterly cold, and she hunched over, her hands in the useless pockets of her lightweight coat. The other women gradually assembled, standing silently, waiting for Braunhaus to send them to a shed where their meager rations were distributed. They were expected to consume them quickly on the walk to the loading dock.

Braunhaus wore sturdy black leather boots and an olive-colored wool coat that nearly reached her ankles. Under the heavy coat, Mischka knew she was clad in a long skirt and tunic, both made of wool, over a white blouse. Black, lined gloves covered her hands, and her neck was swathed in a drab-olive muffler. Perhaps her ankles would feel some chill, but there was little chance that she would suffer ill effects from the weather. What interested Mischka the most was the leather and animal fur hat Braunhaus wore pulled down low and over her ears. None of the other guards had such a hat. It resembled the style of headgear that Gyorgy had been very good at creating, and looking upon it made her lonesome for her brother.

She forced her mind away from that painful train of thought and stared up at the colorless sky. She could just make out the Chaste Moon, still lingering in the early morning. The Storm Moon had passed before she thought about planning for the future as she normally did in February. She wondered if she would even have a future. Would any of them survive this? What would happen when the war was over? The Germans were obviously going to prevail, and wouldn't they keep them all here, wasting away, working until their deaths? The prisoners were nothing to them. Nothing. Her anger burned, the slight warmth moving up from the middle of her chest and into her face. Too bad that couldn't keep her warm through the night.

Braunhaus blew her whistle and jerked Mischka out of her thoughts.

"The count is off. One of you is missing. Who is missing?"

Mischka felt a hysterical giggle and forced it down. If someone was missing, how could the person answer that it was she?

Braunhaus walked along the side of their formation. "Row one, row two, row three. I believe there should be eleven in row four here. Who is missing from this row?"

Mischka stared at the ground, willing someone to speak up and identify the missing woman. If someone had escaped, it would go badly for all of them.

As if to echo Mischka's thoughts, Braunhaus stomped her booted foot in the hard-packed snow. "By God, if you have collaborated to help her escape, you shall all suffer." She shouted, "All of you!" Gripping her wood baton in her right hand, she smacked the end of it against her left palm, and Mischka could tell the German was growing angry. "Where is she?"

A little slip of a girl at the end of the row whispered, "Excuse me, ma'am, but I believe her name is Basia."

"Where is she?" Braunhaus said, her voice low and ominous.

"I don't know."

The guard tapped the girl in the middle of the chest. "You will go search the barracks." The girl turned and ran toward the door. "The rest of you will stand here in the cold until this Basia is found. If she isn't found, you will stand here all day, through snow and storm."

The barracks door slammed open, and the girl trotted out, wringing her hands. "Oh. Oh."

"What is it? Report immediately."

"I think she's dead. She's just...lying there. With her eyes open."

"Very well." Braunhaus tucked her baton under her arm, obviously relieved that she wouldn't be found derelict of duty. "I shall adjust my count. You are dismissed."

They knew well enough to proceed line by line toward the soup shack, but since they were the last barracks to arrive, only half of them received a whole bun. The other half had to split theirs. Mischka had eaten a potato and two burnt pieces of toast the night before, so she allowed Aurora to have her half of the bread.

Petronela clucked her tongue and made a whining sound. Mischka turned to make her way to the loading dock, and whatever Petronela muttered Mischka did not hear.

DAYS OF BITTER cold passed, and Mischka did not know how each of them managed to stay alive through the nights. The weaker and thinner women and girls on the lower pallets suffered terribly and were most likely to be found frozen stiff in the morning. More than once Aurora said, "Thank God you steered us to the top rack."

Petronela slept on a top pallet between two other women. One of the sad-eyed girls, Jannie, who now slept alone on the bottom shelf of Petronela's bunk, pleaded to be allowed to move up with them, but Petronela refused her saying, "This is where we were assigned, and you aren't allowed to get us all in trouble by moving."

No amount of begging by Jannie would change the obstinate woman's mind. Mischka thought it sheer cruelty on Petronela's part and was relieved when three women on a middle pallet made room for Jannie.

As each day went by, it grew harder to differentiate between any of the women, so none of the guards, Braunhaus included, knew who was who. Each prisoner wore the same defeated, wan look, and stayed hunched over in a perpetual attempt to stay warm. Each woman's hair had grown out an inch or two, so some were obviously blondes or brunettes or with a chestnut tinge, but that didn't help the guards keep track. None of the guards ever called anyone by name. "Hey, you," coupled with a pointed finger was the most common address followed closely by "Hey, stupid."

One night, as she lay in her bunk, Mischka realized that no new prisoners had been brought to the camp for some time. No one had to sleep on any of the bottom shelves now. Women in all the barracks were falling ill, starving, dropping dead. With a quick calculation Mischka counted forty-six in their building. From over sixty healthy women down to these scrawny, half-dead wrecks. The forays with Nelka into the garbage were nowhere near enough.

Aurora moved from her side to lie on her back and was humming a tune.

"What music is that?" Mischka asked.

"A psalm."

'I don't know what that is. Psalm."

"It's from the Bible—words set to music. Or they can merely be spoken as well."

"I see. Are there words?"

"Yes. Want to sing it with me?"

"I have no voice, never have. You sing it for me."

"The refrain is easy—mostly all on three notes. You can sing that." She took a breath and sang:

> *You are my refuge, O Lord;*
> *my portion in the land of the living.*

"Try that."

They sang it together once, then again, and on the third try Nelka chimed in, then said, "I'll sing that part with you, Mischka, so you'll know when to sing the refrain." Quietly at first, Aurora sang the first part:

> *I cry to the Lord with my voice;*
> *to the Lord I make loud supplication*
> *I pour out my complaint before him and tell him all my trouble*
> *When my spirit languishes within me, you know my path*
> *Where I walk they have hidden a trap for me*

With a raspy voice, Nelka sang the refrain heartily along with Mischka and Lidia. "Good," Aurora said, then went on:

> *I look to my right hand and find no one who knows me*
> *I have no place to flee to, and no one cares for me*
> *I cry out to you, O Lord, I say,*
> *"You are my refuge, my portion in the land of the living."*

Now the women nearby sang with them, and their voices rang out loudly. Someone else farther down the row voiced the next part in harmony with Aurora:

Listen to my cry for help, for I have been brought very low
Save me from those who pursue me,
for they are too strong for me
Bring me out of prison, that I may give thanks to your Name
When you have dealt bountifully with me, the righteous will
gather around me.

Mischka wasn't sure she believed in this Lord they sang of, and she had little hope that they would all be bountifully dealt with any time soon. Still, she sang the refrain one last time.

You are my refuge, O Lord;
my portion in the land of the living.

The voices from other bunks faded, and Lidia said, "The psalm makes me feel sad." No one disagreed, and the absence of the music left a hollow emptiness in the air, but no one tried to fill it.

"I'm glad we're still in the land of the living," Mischka said.

"And I as well." Aurora's voice cracked, and Mischka knew she was weeping.

"Don't cry, don't, Aurora."

"But my boys, my husband..." She choked up. "I think it's likely that I'll never see them again."

Mischka said, "Don't think that way. We don't know."

"Just keep praying," Lidia said. "It's all we can do."

Mischka threw an arm across Aurora's waist and found Lidia's arm already there.

They lay huddled like that until Aurora's breath evened out, and Mischka knew she was asleep. The face of an older man, gray-haired, came to mind, and for a moment she wasn't sure who he was. Then she remembered. Old Jaworski. The farmer-veterinarian. She wondered why he'd come to mind after all these years, and then she recalled him talking about his God and the prophet Jesus. *Verily I say to you, whatever you do to the least of us, that you do unto the Christian God.* She knew her memory of the words wasn't quite accurate, but the sentiment was right. Their captors must be godless, and no refuge would be found here, in the land of the uncaring.

After that night, Mischka didn't ask Aurora to sing again.

Chapter
Twenty-Five

Southern Poland, March 1943 (Chaste Moon)

PIPPI STEPPED OFF the train into cold gusts of snow-swept wind. She had no idea where they were, but she'd been on the train for two days, and the fresh air, despite its frigid temperature, smelled good. The interior of the train stank of sweat and old, dirty laundry. The compartment in which she rode was tinder-dry from the furnace in the corner that cranked out far more heat than they needed. The furnace was either completely off or on full blast, and when turned off, the car grew cold and unbearable far too quickly. So she and her three compartment mates suffered the swelter.

She pulled up the collar of her coat against the wind and walked briskly from one end of the wooden platform to the other. A wind-battered roof covered the middle section of the platform, but that was it. She went to the end of the wooden planks and stood staring out across a vast expanse of snow. Other than the snow-encrusted train tracks, the area was empty — no trees, no houses, no visible roads, just endless white drifts of snow for as far as Pippi could see.

A boot clumped on the plank behind her and she turned slightly. A tall, blond man in a dark brown uniform moved next to her. He carried his hat under his left arm, but his posture was not as stiff and upright as she was used to seeing from other officers. She hadn't yet figured out what the various stripes and slashes on uniforms meant, and she really didn't care. His blue eyes met hers respectfully as he gave her a nod. "Be careful there, Fräulein. If you went over the side in this wind, we might not see you buried in all that snow."

"Yes, sir." She stepped back a few inches.

"Actually, it's Major. Major Friedrich Fischer. And you are?"

"Pauline Stanek. Pleased to make your acquaintance,

Major." She reached out, and their two gloved hands grasped briefly.

He smiled, revealing small, straight teeth with one chip on the left front tooth. He had a cleft in his square chin, and he was so clean-shaven that his face had the appearance of being wind burned. She thought he was probably about thirty years old.

"May I assume that you are on the way to the factory along with some of these others?"

"Yes, I am, Major, but I'm not aware of who else is going there." She had purposely kept to herself. She had no idea whether any of the other travelers were spies or rascals, and she wasn't taking any chances.

"What is your skill, Fräulein?"

"Sewing."

"Very much needed. I'm glad that you, a civilian, were willing to come to the aid of the Reich during these trying times."

"Yes, of course." Pippi wondered if all soldiers were given some sort of special training to phrase things in that unbelievably ridiculous manner, as though the German war machine was gifted by God above. The major sounded just like the corporal who had conscripted her.

"And since you did not correct my address of you as Fräulein, am I to assume that you are unmarried?"

"Widowed." She shivered, and he gave a nod. Pippi thought he probably assumed her husband had died in the war. Well, he had — just not on the side of Germany.

The train whistle blew twice. "Time to resume our journey," Major Fischer said as he took her elbow and guided her back. As she passed the porter and stepped up onto the box to the entrance stair, the train belched out black smoke. It wafted back her way, engulfing her for a moment, and smelling sooty and dank. The wind carried it away, and she glanced behind to see the major grab the rail and pull himself up the stairs, his left arm held tight against his stomach.

AGNES BRAUNHAUS LEANED against the doorframe of Pippi's tiny bedroom, smoking a cigarette. Pippi hated the harsh, acrid smell and was appalled that she was stuck with the rough, hard-faced woman as her roommate.

The metal edge of the narrow bed frame dug into the back of Pippi's legs. She swept another quick look around the drab room, little more than a cell. Two tiny beds hugged adjacent corners, and a tall bureau sat between them. The window was very clearly painted shut, and whatever wallpaper had once adorned the walls had been painted over in an ugly dun color. Even the ceiling was the same dismal tan. She felt for the center of the bed. The sheets and blanket had been pulled tight and the corners made square, but underneath, the center of the bed sank into a deep depression.

"It's not much, I know," Agnes was saying. "Not any too comfortable, but we've got three hots and a cot, as those damn British Royal Marines say, and it's the best we can expect. Where are you from, Pauline?"

"A village on the edge of Eisenhüttenstadt—on Poland's western border."

"Lucky you." Agnes took another drag. "When they brought me here a year ago, I had to travel from Duisburg. Western Germany, that is—near the Netherlands."

Pippi knew her German geography and didn't need the explanation. She found the woman annoying and didn't reply.

"Long hours here. We've lost so many of the men in this camp. They let them work light duty out here while recovering from injuries, then snatch them away a few months later. A regular revolving door. How about that Major Fischer? Handsome, isn't he?"

Pippi didn't like the predatory gleam in the woman's eyes. She tried to smile, but between physical fatigue and her disgust, she must not have looked very convincing.

Agnes sucked hard one last time on the cigarette, then put it out by jabbing it against the doorframe. "I'll let you get unpacked now. I've got the top three drawers. The bottom three are clear for you." She pointed to the wall near the foot of their beds. "As you can see, I have the hooks there on the left. Yours are on the right. If you need anything, give me a call. I'm always Agnes-on-the-Spot. You'll see." With a bright smile, she turned and tap-tapped down the hallway.

A sense of bleakness overwhelmed Pippi, a hopelessness so soul-wrenching that it was all she could do not to rise and run from her quarters. But where would she go? Her view of the camp had revealed little—a well-guarded front gate, row after row of snow-covered barracks, their grim-looking, square quarters, and an immense and dirty building which coughed out more black smoke than the train had.

She rose and went to the one window in the room. Through a haze of lightly falling snow, she could see nothing else. How long would she be stuck in this horrible barren place?

THE NEXT MORNING, Pippi appeared in the dining room at the appointed time. The meal was served family style from chafing dishes at a table that seated twelve. The meal times had been staggered in ten-minute increments, and Pippi didn't have to wait when she entered the room. The various members of the household slipped into seats, ate quickly, then excused themselves. The chafing dishes held oily sausages and scrambled eggs slimy with sausage grease. She took small amounts and choked down what she could. At least the milk was cold and rich. As she pocketed an apple for later, Agnes swept into the room.

"Good morning, all." Agnes smiled at a tired-looking man who was just leaving the room. Pippi looked at him, wondering who he might be. With his terrible posture, he obviously wasn't a soldier. He brushed by, a linen napkin in one hand.

Thomas, the cook, pushed past with a fresh chafing dish to replace the near-empty dish of eggs. His belly hung far over his belt, and no apron could possibly disguise the rolls of fat he possessed. "There you go," he said, and waddled back into the kitchen.

Pippi moved her chair closer to the table and watched Agnes lean in and take the lid off a pan of eggs. They looked as greasy and congealed as the last batch, but Agnes didn't seem to notice. She served herself an enormous helping, speared four sausages, and sat down. "Looking forward to your first day, eh?"

Pippi nodded, feeling queasy from more than just the food. She waited in her chair and listened to the others around the table as they spoke of the weather and the war. She wasn't sure what to do next, and then the man with the linen napkin came back into the room and tossed the napkin on the table by his vacated seat. He wore a wrinkled dark blue business suit that looked none too fresh.

"Fräulein Stanek." She rose, and he held out a hand. "I'm Felix Schuster, the manager of the two factories here. I'm prepared now to escort you to your workplace. Would you please come with me?"

She found her coat crowded among others in the front closet, and he led her across the snow-packed area out front.

"It would be much easier if we had a door on this end of the building, but it's a pity, we do not. So we must walk around to the side." He led her toward the fence, a monstrosity of barbed wire and metal some twenty feet high. They walked near the dirty brick building with the fence a stone's throw to their right. At about fifty-yard intervals, armed soldiers stood inside wooden shells that would give scant protection from the inclement weather. She looked back over her shoulder. Shells lined the fence as far as she could see.

Schuster led her up some slick cement stairs. "Here we are." He wrenched open the door and allowed her to step ahead of him into a huge, drafty space. She saw scores of crates, some partially unpacked and others stacked nearly all the way up to the 18-foot-tall ceiling. "Storage here," he said. "Mostly you'll find leather and boot-making materials which end up being used at the other factory. You won't have anything to do with that. Follow me."

He led her down a short corridor to a stairway, laid his hand on the banister, and looked back at her. "This is the staff-only stairway. None of the laborers are ever to use these steps." He strode up the long staircase, rounded the top at a small landing, then went up another flight. He paused at a small alcove and gestured toward a door. "Second floor is where leather goods are assessed, cleaned, and recommissioned or sent over for repair to the leather-works building on the men's side of the camp."

After two more flights to the third floor, he said, "Storage, packing boxes, and the like. If any of your seamstresses need replacement clothing, this is where you can find it."

By the fourth floor, Schuster was huffing and not moving nearly so quickly. He stopped at the landing. "I try not to trot all this way too often. Whew! It always seems the steps grow steeper these last two floors." Pippi, too, was a bit out of breath, and she noticed a strange, rank odor. Schuster was wheezing and pushing at his knees with the palms of his hands. He paused to inhale and exhale several times and then said, "On this floor, we warehouse sewing goods, mostly yardage and thread. You and the other girls will spend a lot of time getting the supplies you need from here. There's a dumbwaiter you can use, too." He took a deep breath and continued up the stairs.

The fifth floor landing was dark and dingy. The smell of dust and something burning assailed her nose. With every step she took, whirring and grinding noises grew louder. She followed Schuster into an alcove outside a double-wide doorway. He strutted through the doorway into a room no less than fifty yards wide. Pippi had seen pastures smaller than this. But she'd never seen a pasture with row after row of sewing machines humming and clacking. She stood in the doorway, amazed at the number of workers hunched over the machines. At first guess, there must be at least two hundred. Two women in gray sweaters and olive green skirts walked slowly along the walls, watching the workers.

A pair of desks sat to the left of the door, a few feet from the wall, providing anyone who sat at them with a view of the workers from behind. Next to the desks were huge folding tables loaded with packaging materials. The dumbwaiter Schuster had mentioned was built into the rear wall. She assumed it was used to transfer goods to and from the various floors.

The entire east wall was made up of long, narrow windows that started four feet from the floor and stopped about two feet from the ceiling. Sunlight, dulled by an overcast sky, cast pallid beams through the dirty glass.

"Herr Schuster, are the windows our only source of illumination?"

"Unfortunately, yes. Lightbulbs are in short supply, so the seamstresses work only from sunup to sundown. That's all the time we can manage."

"And my task here is to do what?"

"Improve speed and efficiency. That's it in a nutshell."

IN THE THREE days that Pippi spent observing the seamstresses, she discovered a number of unpleasant facts. For one thing, the room stank to high heaven. She could smell the unwashed bodies from the stairwell by the time she reached the fourth floor, and the closer she came to the sewing workroom, the stronger and more sickening the odor became. The women were ill-clad, dirty, and apparently never allowed to bathe. This troubled Pippi almost as much as the haunted looks in the workers' eyes. And how frightened the women were! Few ever raised their heads much less looked at her.

She quickly learned that the majority didn't speak much German beyond basic phrases. Polish, Hungarian, French, Czech and Slovak dialects, and even Russian were more likely to be their native tongues. Two French women at side-by-side machines nearly fainted when she tried out a few French phrases near them. If only she knew more languages. Simply shouting louder in German didn't help any of them understand instructions.

As she wandered out on the floor, she saw the women ranged from young to middle-aged, and she quickly learned that they possessed widely varying skill levels. Some worked the cloth through the machines with agility, while others fumbled. About a dozen rarely seemed to jam up their machines, while the majority were constantly stopping to untangle spools of thread or rip out badly sewn seams. She wondered how much of the inefficiency had to do with dehydration and lack of nourishment, and she planned to ask about that after she got better acquainted with how the operation ran.

An endless stream of torn or damaged tunics, breeches, and coats arrived for repair, but there were also daily orders for new uniforms. Looking over the records, Pippi quickly saw they were weeks behind in production.

It took her a while to figure out that the other three German women who supervised the area didn't know much about sewing, but they were able to process the orders received and ensure that the completed projects were properly crated and sent off. And they meted out discipline, but other than keeping the workers quiet and at work, Frau Greta, Fräulein Bernadette, and Frau Elke were unable or unwilling to correct the problems Pippi could so easily detect.

She thought them an odd lot. They had been conscripted much the same way as Pippi had. Greta was in her late twenties, while Pippi guessed Bernadette was near forty. Elke had mentioned that she'd just celebrated her fiftieth birthday. The latter two had been working at the factory since it was captured shortly after 1939, when the assault on Poland began. Greta had joined the staff only a few months ago.

Not only because of their looks — blue eyes, blonde hair — but also because of their behavior and lack of drive, Pippi thought all three could have been sisters. They barked orders and were unsparing with the use of the batons they carried. They didn't wield heavy-duty soldiers' batons, but thinner wands of wood about a meter long. Felix Schuster proudly presented Pippi with a matching baton, and she accepted it with trepidation. If she carried it around with her, she'd have nowhere to put it when she stopped to untangle a bobbin or correct the sewing of any worker. No wonder everything moved so slowly and poorly. She quickly learned that Greta, Elke, and Bernadette did little other than yell and threaten.

Near the end of the third day, as the sun went down in the late afternoon, Pippi had had enough. She sat at one of the desks and pondered the changes that needed to be made. Two hundred and three seamstresses worked in the giant room. Just in front of the supervisors' desks, the sewing machines were arrayed in three groups of four, with each seamstress facing the far wall — just like students in school. Twenty-two rows total started at the back and went to the far end. Twelve times twenty-two, Pippi thought...but not all the machines were in use. Sixty-one units sat empty, and Pippi asked why. "Are we short on seamstresses?"

Elke, who sat at the other desk sorting buttons, said, "No, there's plenty more where they came from. The machines are broken."

"Broken?" Pippi asked. "Broken in what way?"

Elke shrugged. "I'm no mechanic."

"Have we had a mechanic up here to look at them?"

Bernadette came to stand by Pippi, then slid a hip along the side of the battered gray desk, leaned her weight there, and crossed her arms. "The soldiers are busy, and Felix is less mechanical than we are. He's great with sums and totals, but he knows next to nothing about sewing machines."

Pippi looked out the dirty window nearby. "I see scores of barracks out there. Aren't they full?"

Bernadette frowned. "Yes."

"Surely there are men—or perhaps even women—who are mechanics. Why don't we get someone in here?"

Elke rose. She was half a head taller than Pippi and a decade and a half older, so Pippi wasn't surprised when she lifted her nose in the air and said, "You've been put in charge. Feel free to stroll through the barracks and ask."

Pippi smiled politely. "I have another idea." She looked at the sea of backs hunched over their machines. Before she could speak, she heard Greta let out a string of criticism. Greta stood several rows up, squeezed between two of the sections of four. The pale wood of the switch whisked through the air three times and struck a dark-haired woman. The hum of the sewing machines wavered. Greta shouted, "This is none of your business. The rest of you attend to your work."

Pippi raised an index finger and beckoned Greta. The young woman strutted toward them as though proud of her performance. Anger burned in Pippi, but she didn't dare express it. Instead she said, "I've got some productivity ideas, and I hope you'll all go along with me and help me try them."

Greta looked her up and down, then shrugged. "What's it to me. This job doesn't matter. It's awful work. These ungrateful women are impossible to motivate. I hate them all." Elke and Bernadette murmured agreement.

"That may be so," Pippi said, "but if we can get additional workers, we can produce more."

"Yeah?" Greta said, one hand on her hip and the other flicking the switch. "How do you propose to do that?"

Pippi didn't answer. She called out, "Halt. I'd like your attention. Now." She had to circle the room once before she was able to get everyone to stop. When the room was silent, she said, "I know some of you may not understand me, but those who do, try to communicate with those around you. I want you all to stand." About a third of the women rose hesitantly. After a lot of whispering and hand motions, the rest of the women rose and faced the far wall.

Pippi strode to the windows and walked along the little aisle to the far end of the room so that she faced the workers. "Turn around your sewing machines and chairs." With both hands, she made circular motions. Greta stood near the doorway at the other end of the room, a look of disbelief on her face. Pippi clapped. "Now, please. Spin your sewing machine the other direction—toward Fräulein Elke." Pippi stepped up to a terrified little slip of a woman, pulled her chair back, and grabbed hold of the sewing machine. "Turn your machine to face that way—like this."

She had to walk around the room and up the middle aisles and keep urging them to follow the directions before finally they understood. A few looked like they might faint, but nervously they all turned their machines 180 degrees. *Scarecrows in dresses* was the phrase that came to Pippi's mind as she helped one woman. "Good," she said. "Now resume your seats." She patted the nearest chair, motioned for the woman to sit, and rejoined the supervisors in the front of the desks.

Elke said, "Fräulein Pauline, what is the use of this?"

"Now we can see which of the machines are running and which aren't."

"Couldn't we have just turned the broken ones? There would have been less of them."

Bernadette said, "This is ridiculous. I don't want these tramps looking at me all day!"

Greta stood to the side frowning. "Couldn't we merely have put signs on the unoccupied machines that are broken? Is this really necessary?"

Pippi shrugged. "I suppose we could have, but actually, I'd like to be able to see the faces of the workers anyway." Pippi turned back to the seated women. "See these other machines that are broken?" She pointed at the units that still faced the other end of the room. "Does anyone know how to fix them?" She repeated the question in German and French, then used her limited Polish words to try to get the idea across.

She waited for a low murmur to die down as the women consulted with one another, and then they were silent. A few looked up at her, but the majority stared down at their sewing machines.

Pippi hadn't examined any of the broken units, so she didn't know what was wrong with them, but she had a hunch she'd be able to fix some of them. Out of 203 people, there must be someone who could help her, though. She said, "Tell me who is mechanical and willing to help me, and you shall receive a small ration of food."

Again, a murmur of discussion went on, and some of the women on the right side pointed to a scrawny, brown-haired girl in the middle.

"You." Pippi pointed. "Yes, you. Come here. The rest of you may get back to your sewing." It took a minute for people to get their material in place and adjust their treadles, but soon the room was humming as usual.

The girl who had been called forward stood with one fist on an unused machine. Pippi saw that her knuckles were white from gripping it so tight. The loafer-style shoes on her feet were at least two sizes too big, and her pale peach housedress was thin and specked with dirt.

"Your name?" Pippi asked. The girl looked up, wide-eyed, and clearly terrified. Her eyes were dark brown and her face very pale. Pippi repeated the request.

"Mariel."

"You speak French?" The girl nodded. "Excellent, Mariel," Pippi said in French.

Greta made a grumbling sound. "You don't need to know these sluts' names, Pauline, that's for sure. Believe me, you don't want to know their names."

Pippi gave her what she hoped would pass for a sincere smile while wishing she could rip the switch from Greta's hands and use it on her. She pulled the unused sewing machine into the walkway in front of Elke's desk and motioned for Mariel to sit. The girl grabbed the chair and lowered herself into it. Pippi handed her a scrap of material about six inches square. "Give this a try."

Mariel pumped the treadle but the needle didn't move. When she met Pippi's eyes, she looked like she expected to be beaten. Pippi waited. "Well? What shall we do?"

The girl lifted the metal unit from the wooden frame and rolled it back to look underneath. Pippi barely heard her next words. "Treadle belt is off."

Pippi could see it and nodded. "What do you do?"

"Nothing."

"What do you mean, nothing?"

"I have to punch out the plug and feed the belt over that groove in the hand wheel and down to the drive wheel."

"Show me."

If it were possible to get any paler, Mariel did. "I—I would like to...to help, but I have no tools to do it with."

Pippi let out a cackle of surprise that obviously startled the girl. "You're joking, right?"

Mariel shook her head. "No, this is the problem many of the broken machines have."

"Let's get to work then. Elke, where are the tools for tinkering with the machines?"

Elke, who sat slouched behind her desk, said, "I've got a pocketknife and a screwdriver." She unlocked a desk drawer and rooted around, then came up with both and slammed the drawer shut.

Pippi took them and held out the screwdriver to Mariel. Greta and Bernadette rushed at Pippi and pulled her aside. "Wait a minute, Pauline. You can't give her that."

"What? Why not?"

Greta grabbed Pippi's elbow. In a sharp whisper she said, "It's a weapon. You can't let her get hold of it."

Pippi sighed. "What's she going to do with it? Stab all of us and run? And if she did, where would she go?"

"Why do you think these women are here?" Bernadette tapped her temple. "They're not quite right up here. Or else they've been arrested for crimes. You can't trust any of them."

"I'll carefully supervise her, Bernadette. Stop worrying." Pippi wrested her arm away and returned to the sewing machine. "Mariel, you punch out the plug with this, and I'll help you pry the belt onto the wheel."

With a nod, Mariel accepted the screwdriver, and in two minutes of tugging and coaxing, they fixed the belt. The girl tried out the machine, and now the treadle moved the needle up and down. "I'll have to adjust the tension for the top and for the bobbin case, too. Is that all right?"

Pippi grinned. "Of course." Five minutes later, the machine was back in place and running smoothly. Pippi stood holding the screwdriver and knife and feeling satisfied. "Good work, Mariel. Turn it around to indicate it's running, and please take a look at the next one over there. If you need my help or the screwdriver, please wave or call out 'Fräulein Pauline,' and I'll be there."

When she headed over to Elke's desk, she wasn't prepared for the resentful looks the three women shot at her. She chose to ignore them. "I'm going to run over to quarters. Does anyone need anything?"

Scowling, Greta shook her head, and Bernadette and Elke did the same.

Pippi handed Greta the screwdriver and knife. "Please let Mariel have these when she needs them, all right?" Greta's eyes narrowed, and she didn't give her assent, but she accepted the tools.

Feeling rather pleased with herself, Pippi took the stairs and headed out of the factory. When she found the cook in the kitchen of the quarters, she said, "Herr Thomas, I need a biscuit or cracker for my workers."

He pointed at a small package of shortbread cookies on the counter next to the coffeepot. "I know Elke likes those a lot."

"No, not for them. I mean for the seamstresses."

"What?" He looked at her, amazement on his unshaven face. His dark eyes raked her up and down. "We don't feed the camp from our stores."

"Where do I go then?"

"There's an outbuilding where their food is prepared. I'm not quite sure where it's at. I haven't been here long enough."

"Look, Thomas, I've seen the pantry. We've got more stuff in there than we could eat in a year. Just this once, will you let me have some of it? I made a promise."

He shook his head. "I cannot let you do that."

She let out a gasp of exasperation. "What if I help you with kitchen clean-up after the meal tonight?"

Thomas examined her face for a good five seconds, then wiped perspiration from his forehead with a meaty, fat-fingered hand. He slipped out of the heavy-duty apron he wore and waddled for the door. "I'm going upstairs for a cigarette and much-needed ten-minute break. I won't be back for ten minutes, and in *ten minutes* you'd better have cleared out of here. I look forward to chatting with you over pots and pans after the evening meal." As he passed through the doorframe, he looked back and winked.

Pippi scuttled into the pantry, which was nearly as big as the kitchen. She quickly examined rack after rack, each shelf jammed full of packages and bags and dried foods and staples. In one corner she found neat stacks of almost a hundred boxes of German tea cookies. She picked one up and looked at what was printed on the front. Forty count. The women could have two apiece, and Mariel would receive most of a box herself. Pippi grabbed a gunnysack from a basket on one shelf, stuffed in eleven boxes, and headed back to the factory.

ON HER FIFTH day at the sewing factory, Pippi was down on one knee working on a broken machine with Mariel and another woman named Pilar. They had repaired seven machines by taking parts from two other units that had metal pieces literally broken. Pippi didn't know how anyone could completely break off the foot, but someone had. They'd dragged those machines aside and cannibalized them for screws, bobbin assemblies, and treadle belts. After having some success, they'd been stymied by three unrepairable units in a row.

"What do you think the problem is, Mariel?"

The girl put her thumb to her chin and shrugged. "I can't tell. It feels like something with the tension of the foot and treadle, but nothing I've ever seen before."

Pippi shook her head in frustration. "I guess we move on to the next — come back to these later. We need someone who understands mechanical devices better than I do."

She heard heavy steps outside in the hall, and a young soldier, his face ruddy from the cold, appeared in the doorway and announced, "Message for Pauline Stanek."

Pippi rose, wiped her hands on her dusty skirt, and wended her way past seamstresses. She accepted the paper, a thick bond, folded in half. She opened it and saw a Nazi swastika embossed in the upper left-hand corner. Below, in a smooth, flowing script, was written:

> *Fräulein Stanek,*
>   *Unless you are otherwise engaged in critical work, please come at once to camp headquarters to receive further instructions regarding your assignment. The soldier who delivered the message will accompany you.*
> *Regards,*
> *Major Friedrich Fischer*

Pippi controlled the expression on her face, making sure to display the slightest wisp of a smile. "I must go see the major now, Elke. Please monitor the workers for me."

Elke inclined her head, her eyes glittering, and Pippi turned away wanting to scratch the malicious blue right out of Elke's head. She took her time donning her coat and gloves and wrapping a muffler around her neck. Outside she found the soldier standing at attention.

"Soldier?"

"Yes, ma'am. Please follow me."

They marched down the stairs and out into the cold. She slipped her gloves on, and the sharp wind whittled away at her face like a woodcarver's knife. Everything around her was gray or muted brown: the sky, the buildings, the dirty snow packed into slick furrows. She gazed into barracks windows as they passed, realizing for the first time how spartan they were. The only furniture she could see through the icy panes were wide, three-tier bunks with no bedclothes or blankets anywhere in sight. Pippi assumed that the occupants must be required to place their linens and bedding in a closet or chest during the day.

The soldier led her on a long journey of perhaps a quarter-mile before they stopped at a high line of fencing that cordoned off one side of the camp from the other. "Excuse me," Pippi said to her guide's back. "Why is there a checkpoint like that right in the middle of the compound?"

The soldier looked over his shoulder. "The men's side here is partitioned from the women's side."

"I see. Thank you."

Pippi had been able to look out over a portion of the camp from the fifth floor sewing area, but the factory's sightlines didn't show all that much on this end. Now, from the ground, she had the sense that it stretched out much farther than she had imagined. Far in the distance she saw another multi-story brick building much like the factory she worked in. The endless lines of barracks petered out, and off to the left, a paved street with a line of shabby little bungalows cut through what must have once been a town. How odd. A village right in the middle of this giant compound. Beyond the cottages were larger houses that became progressively more lavish.

The soldier led her along a neatly shoveled sidewalk that led to stairs up to a wide, covered porch, then asked, "Is there anything further?"

Pippi shook her head. "Thank you."

He turned on his heel and marched off. She looked up at the three-story stucco house. A Nazi flag, rippling in the sharp wind, hung from the second story and blocked much of her view. She mounted the stairs and stopped in front of a wood door so dark, it was nearly black. She touched the wood grain, rough with deep ridges, and her glove snagged a bit. Pippi reached for a brass knocker, but before she could lift the gold boar's head, the door opened.

A thin man, bald on top, and wearing a shabby dark gray suit, addressed her in German with a thick Polish accent. "You are here for the major or the captain?"

"Major Fischer."

"Right this way."

He didn't offer to take her coat but simply turned and took short mincing steps across a foyer. Black beams bisected the ceiling at regular intervals. The walls were a dingy gray, and the wood of the staircase and banister was dark and dull. Many booted feet had obviously crossed the hardwood floor. Pippi thought it would take more than one mopping to clean it, and first someone would have to scrape up and sweep out the dried mud and pebbles.

The man led her down a short hallway into what looked like a waiting area, then stepped to the side next to a double set of doors, both of which were closed. He leaned back against the wall like a limp marionette, face gray and slack. Pippi thought he must be ill.

She paced slowly around the antechamber. The fireplace on the far wall was so large she very nearly could have walked into it. The ornate wooden mantle above it was empty of any items, and above the mantle the wall was streaked with soot—except for a very large, perfectly square light spot. She wondered whose portrait had been there and where it had gone.

The ceiling was at least fourteen feet high, and unlit brass sconces hung at regular intervals around the walls. A dusty chandelier hung from a *trompe l'oeil* decoration around a multicolored, flowery ceiling medallion. She stared up for a moment, wondering how long it had taken to painstakingly paint each of the roses, orchids, and red poppies along with the flourishes of green stalks and tendrils.

At one time, townspeople probably came to this fine house and were shown into this anterior chamber to wait for someone important—a high official? The mayor? Pippi could only guess. The place had fallen upon hard times.

Packed tightly along one wall sat a dozen or so velvet-covered Queen Anne-style chairs and Dutch smoking tables. Before the war, each of the smoking tables would have held a humidor, an ashtray, and perhaps a match holder or old-fashioned lighter, each made of shiny brass or silver. Now all that remained was dusty furniture shoved to the side. Slipping her hands out of her gloves, Pippi inquired of the bald man, "Sir? What am I to do?"

He glanced up, opening heavy lids, and she realized he seemed to be in pain. He slid back his cuff and examined a wristwatch. "We are not to disturb the major before ten o'clock."

Pippi scowled. "That makes no sense. He summoned me, insisting I drop my work and hurry. Now I've rushed here and I'm made to wait?"

"I'm sorry. Please be patient."

"Nonsense." She took three steps to the door and raised a fist.

"No!" the man whispered. "Please. They'll beat me again."

Too late. Pippi's knuckles had already made contact.

A muffled voice called, "Come."

The servant stood at attention with difficulty, still looking wan but now frightened as well. Pippi turned the leaded crystal knob and stepped into a grand study. The wall to her left was lined from floor to ceiling with books. A doorway interrupted the bookcases, and through it, Pippi caught sight of a row of file cabinets, but she couldn't see what else was in that room.

Slightly behind her an alcove contained a divan, two smoking chairs, and a glass table with an old-fashioned hurricane lamp resting on a doily. To the right, along the wall was a long mahogany table and chairs. Straight ahead, across a sea of plush maroon carpet, Major Fischer sat behind one of the largest, most ornate desks Pippi had ever seen. Neat piles of paper lay in an orderly fashion across the fine wood surface, and as she watched, the major finished writing something with a flourish, picked up the sheet of paper, and put it in an out-basket.

"Ah, Fräulein Stanek. We meet again." He looked past her. "That will be all, Klaus." Pippi heard the door click shut behind her.

Fischer turned off an antique desk lamp. The curved stem matched that of the medallion in the ceiling in the other room. The alabaster glass diffuser looked exactly like one from a set on her mother-in-law's desk in Reims, and Pippi was assailed with a strong feeling of homesickness.

Major Fischer rose, back-lit by a bay window that took up much of the wall behind him. The drapes were open, but sheers masked what little light came in. Still, with the light at his back, she saw him in shadow and couldn't read his facial expression.

"Hello, Major. How is your health?"

"Fine, thank you, quite fine." He gestured to his left. "Shall we be seated at the table?"

She shrugged out of her cloak and unwound her muffler. She stuffed it and her gloves into the coat's sleeve, then laid it over the top of a Queen Anne-style chair at the table. She didn't want to feel afraid, but her heart pounded. All she wanted to do was grab her things and run out, but she waited for him to direct her. He pulled out a chair.

"Thank you." She lowered herself onto a most uncomfortable walnut chair with cabriole legs and a drop-in seat. The needlework on the back was beautiful, but obviously the stretcher underneath was broken or too loose to hold up the seat. She sank so low that she felt like a child at the big people's Christmas table.

The major slid into a chair directly opposite her. "Are you finding your accommodations to your liking?"

Pippi held back a smile. What was she supposed to say? No, they're abysmal—and apparently even worse for the camp workers? Instead she chose tact. "It's war time. No one is entirely comfortable, Major, but we shall get by."

"Yes, that's the spirit." A stiff smile revealed teeth that were small and pointy, feral like a cat's. She wondered how he'd chipped the left front one. Smile fading, he said, "Let me get to the heart of this business as I know you're in a hurry to return to your responsibilities. How is the work going at the factory?"

"I believe well, sir."

"It may come as a surprise to you, but if you were a soldier under my command, you would have been disciplined for your actions two days ago."

Heat rushed to Pippi's face. She scrambled to think of what she could possibly have done to warrant punishment, but nothing came to mind.

"You are not, however, a soldier, and in fact you have been left in charge of a function about which few soldiers know anything. I consulted with Herr Schuster, and he admitted that you have had little oversight. We have no one to train you, Fräulein Stanek, and the administration here has little time to attend to matters. So your use of scarce stores and the complete and utter disregard for protocol will be forgiven. This time only, though, and you shall forfeit amounts commensurate to the cost of the staples which you squandered." His eyes narrowed and his lips pressed together so tight that the cleft in his chin smoothed out. "Am I understood?"

"Yes, sir. Very clearly."

"Now, on to another matter. I understand that you have very quickly become too familiar with the resident workers."

"What!" Pippi knew where this was coming from, and she didn't know who to hate more, Elke or Greta. She didn't think Bernadette would have said anything, but the other two were vindictive enough. "I believe you have received inaccurate information, Major." She tried to sit up as tall as possible in her chair, but failed miserably.

"Please explain, then, why you provided the seamstresses with provisions meant for camp personnel such as yourself."

"I considered it a gesture of goodwill."

"You confound me. We don't need to show goodwill to these laborers, Fräulein Stanek. They are criminals and deviants, lawless, homicidal and depraved enemies of the Third Reich. We owe them nothing."

Pippi looked into Fischer's angry eyes. She didn't know him well enough to evaluate whether he was dangerous to her physically. Would he hit her? Hurt her? Someone had beaten the doorman, and he looked like a civilian just as she was. For the briefest moment, she remembered the Roma fortuneteller from her childhood, who, all those years ago, had warned her to "beware of the fisher." Pippi wondered if this was the Fischer the woman had had in mind, and she bit back a smile.

"Major, I have analyzed the sewing operation. I have 203— no, 202 workers. One did not appear for work today. Unless there are sewing machines hidden away somewhere that I don't know about, I have approximately 262 machines to employ. That means I have some five dozen machines idle."

He sat back in his chair with barely suppressed impatience. "I was given a report indicating that a quarter of the machines were broken."

"Because of my gesture of goodwill, five have been repaired, two have been scavenged for parts, and even as we speak, the remaining units are being worked on."

"I authorized no repairs."

"Major Fischer, the military personnel in Eisenhüttenstadt sent me here because I am a sewing expert. I am able to supervise the repair of sewing machines without wasting precious resources that the Reich is currently in need of due to the war efforts."

"I see." He cleared his throat and met her eyes reluctantly. "I'm sorry that we have no repairmen available to assist you." He paused. "I must say, it would be helpful if we could assign more seamstresses to the factory."

"I reviewed the manifests," Pippi said. "At our present rate of production, we are backlogged two months in creating new uniforms and perhaps three months in mending and reconditioning the hundreds of pieces stored in the lower floors of the factory. I can offer you a plan to initially increase output by ten percent with an approximate twenty percent increase in four weeks and fifty to sixty percent within eight weeks."

A flicker of interest registered in his cold eyes. "How is this possible?"

"I've been told there are many women in the barracks who could be made available to work for me. I already require five more seamstresses at this very moment, Major. They could be sewing even as we speak, turning out as many as twenty-eight new uniforms today for trainee soldiers or for existing troops badly in need of replacement garb."

"I wonder how it can be that no one has informed me of this." He raised his voice, sounding more furious with each word. "I run the day-to-day operations and am expected to produce results."

"As you already said, Major, I'm not a soldier. I was brought here to do a job, shown to my room, taken to the factory, and told to get to work. Until today I had no idea you were the man in charge. Do you understand? I have been given no guidance or information beyond the obvious."

"You and I arrived simultaneously," he said curtly.

"Had you been here before to know the lay of the land?"

"No. I came from — directly from combat."

His hesitation made her watch his face closely. She intuited that there was more to the story than he was telling her, but she could not inquire about that now. "Have you toured the camp?"

"But of course. I can't run day-to-day operations without understanding the scope of what I command."

"Yes, yes, Major, that's exactly what I'm getting at. I lack knowledge, partly because I am a civilian, but even if I were a soldier and had been given so little information, I couldn't do my job properly."

Fischer took a deep breath and held it in. She thought for a moment he was going to explode at her, but then he sighed. "All right, what do you want to know?"

"What is this place?"

"Poland, of course."

Pippi smiled. "No, no. Whose house is this? Who possessed it before the army took charge of it?"

"Ah, well, you didn't make yourself clear. This was the home of the industrialist who built and ran the factories."

"What happened to him?"

The major raised his nose in the air and looked down at her, his blue eyes piercing. "Who knows. This house belongs now to our *Führer*."

"It's a beautiful building."

"That it is. Dining and banquet halls, a music atrium, and a kitchen are here on this floor — along with the parlor out there and this study. The floors above have eight bedrooms and two lavatories each. We use the middle floor as offices and to store records. My staff and I have quarters on the top floor."

"You must be quite comfortable."

He looked at his wristwatch. "Fräulein Stanek, may we get back to the matter at hand?"

"Why certainly."

"What do you need to increase production?"

"I'll need to gradually add another fifty or so seamstresses. Five or six by tomorrow."

"Easily arranged."

"I shall need a few tools and perhaps some sewing machine supplies."

"I will try to get you what you need, but I may not be

successful. Many items are hard to come by."

"My workers need better nourishment."

"That isn't possible."

Pippi debated how to approach this and opted for sheer utilitarianism. "Major, it will take me several weeks to train new girls to sew with speed and finesse. If they fall over from hunger, they cannot work. If they cannot work, we cannot do our part for the war effort. If we fail to provide sewn goods, we are failing our troops."

"Providing your workers with larger rations means others will have to go without. We are rationing, Fräulein Stanek," he said with some heat. "Rationing."

"There must be some way."

"There is not!"

She didn't speak for a few moments, allowing him to get his temper under control. "Perhaps, then, as spring draws nearer we'll see some improvement in our stores. In the meantime, I'll do the best I can to increase output. You will allow me to find some more workers and train them?"

He got up stiffly from the chair and moved over to the desk to take a piece of paper and pen. He came back to the head of the table and leaned over it to write something, signed it, and slid it across to her. "Tell Felix Schuster to take you to Sergeant Vogel. Give this note to Vogel. He'll assign you as many workers as you need, whenever you need them."

Pippi summoned up as genuine-sounding a voice as she could. "You've been very kind, Major. Thank you for your guidance and your honesty about the situation here. I will do all in my power not to let you down. Is there anything else?" She donned her coat and muffler and pushed the gloves into her pocket.

Fischer stood at attention, though his posture was not as erect as most soldiers managed. "We have concluded matters, Fräulein Stanek." He looked down at the hand she extended, then took it gently. "I forget that civilians do not salute." He let go and stepped back, his face flushing pink. "You will report to me personally each week, Fräulein, starting a week from today. Before noon. I would like to be kept abreast of every improvement."

"It would be my pleasure, Major."

"Shall I find you an escort or are you able to find your way back to the factory?"

"I'll be fine. Thank you."

She headed for the door, acutely aware that his eyes were on her. At the threshold, she looked back and raised a hand. "Good day." He still stood in place and gave her a curt nod.

The house doorman was nowhere to seen, so she let herself out. She buttoned her coat over her muffler and stuck her hands into her gloves. Though it was cold, she took her time strolling back to the factory, carefully picking her way through the snow-encrusted ruts. What a strange situation she had got herself into. Major Fischer was a loose cannon, and she would definitely heed the Roma fortuneteller's advice.

Chapter
Twenty-Six

Southern Poland, March 1943 (Chaste Moon)

MISCHKA SQUATTED IN shadows next to the little shed, her forearms on her knees, and waited for an unexpected guard to shuffle past the fence sixty feet away. With every breath, puffs of white mist wafted from her. She hoped they weren't apparent from the distance. She tightened into an even smaller lump, pressed her forehead against her forearm, and waited, her heart pounding. Soon, all was quiet, and she rose slowly. The moon was out, shining on the embroidery of sparkling snow.

Nelka had already cut across the open space for the safety of the factory shadows. Now Mischka made her way over. Tonight they'd found little food in the bin. Mischka had eaten half a piece of toasted bread and the white of a hard-boiled egg. In her dress pocket she carried half a biscuit for Aurora, and that was it. Her stomach ached with hunger.

She crept along the side of the factory and stopped often to listen. The bite of the wind and the heavy air presaged snow. Just what they needed. More cold. More snow. More misery. She had gotten to the point where she no longer summoned up outrage that resulted in a physical response, but her mind still rebelled and puzzled over the unfairness of it all. She looked up at the moon. How could there be a God if such terrible people, such terrible experiences were allowed? How could any God stand idle through all this?

Now came the risky part of the evening reconnaissance. Mischka stood in the gloom of the alcove across from the barracks. She would wait until clouds obscured some of the bright light of the moon. Most nights the snow-laden clouds cooperated, but some nights — like tonight — the moon peeked through and shed more light than Mischka was comfortable with. So she waited.

The day before, she'd been shivering in the loading area

when the door next to the dock opened and a blonde-haired woman emerged. Mischka was off to the side, near the wall on the opposite end of the area, so she couldn't hear what was going on. Vogel limped over, suddenly very animated. He made a grand gesture with the hand holding the baton, and the small woman moved a few more steps. She wore flat black shoes and an unbuttoned, dark blue wool coat over a forest green dress. Before she had said more than a few words, she shivered and pulled her coat over the front of her.

Vogel preened and smiled, somehow managing to puff out his chest like a wounded peacock. He dragged his leg a few steps and grabbed a girl by the elbow, jerking her around in front of the woman. He pointed to another girl and crooked a finger. She dropped the armload of uniforms she held and approached. Even from the distance, Mischka could see the young girls were terrified. She turned her attention back to the woman, puzzled that something was oddly familiar about the turn of her head, the line of her jaw...

"Mischka?" Aurora whispered. "What is it?"

Mischka dropped a boot and took a step, then another, her heart pounding in her chest. She slipped around a crate and inched her way toward Vogel.

"Do you know how to run a sewing machine?" the woman was asking in German.

"Yes, ma'am, a little."

"Come with me then. You, too."

Mischka stopped. Pippi Stanek? It couldn't be. She stared, drinking in the sight of her friend. But it most certainly was Pippi. She willed her to turn, to glance up and look her way, but Pippi was directing more girls toward the door. The sound of it slamming echoed through the loading area.

Vogel tucked his baton under his arm and coughed into his glove. Most workers bent back to their work. "What are you looking at? You. You there." He pointed toward Mischka. "Get to work. Now." Mischka stumbled over toward her friends.

Nelka frowned, the scar on her face a red slash against her pale face. "What was that all about?"

"I thought I knew that woman."

Nelka grinned, and her expression looked savage. "After a while, everyone starts looking like someone I know — most of whom are dead. I'm thinking it's a cruel little joke to play on all of us — to make me think I see people I love. My father, my older brother. Why, yesterday I saw my grandmother coming out of the latrine — and she's been dead for six years." She giggled and elbowed Lidia. "I'm thankful I've got my big sister with me. At least I know she's not a ghost."

Lidia's expression was one of fright. "Stop it, Nelka. Work. Don't draw attention to us." Her voice was pleading, and she shook from more than the cold.

Nelka scooped up a handful of boots all knotted together. "Yes, work. Work, work, work. That's all there is here. I hate it. How much longer do they think we'll last? I ought to die just to spite them. We all ought to. Let that fat flatulent whore's son do this work himself."

Nelka had continued to rant on about their situation yesterday, but Mischka had tuned it out then and concentrated in her mind's eye on the fair-faced, blonde woman—just as she was doing now, hiding in the shadows trying not to end up dying for the sake of a crust of stale bread.

What was Pippi Stanek doing in this godforsaken labor camp? Where had she taken those six girls? They hadn't come back. Was Pippi responsible for their deaths? It couldn't be possible. Could it? No. Mischka wouldn't believe it for one moment. She wished she knew how to find Pippi. Where in the camp was she staying? She certainly wasn't a laborer. Her hair had been long and shiny, her clothes warm, clean, and well-kept. No, Pippi Stanek wasn't a laborer.

A gust of cold curled around the edge of the alcove in which Mischka stood, and she shivered and let out an involuntary gasp. The slight noise almost covered another sound—but not entirely. She held her breath and peeked out. Two guards, their rifle barrels poking above their shoulders, were on the move, walking briskly. They passed within fifteen feet of her hiding place and angled away from her, toward the front barracks—her barracks.

Mischka stood frozen for a moment. She knew she had to do something. With a glance to the left and right, she saw no one, so she took off across the road, careful not to trip over the frozen ridges and arriving breathless at the latrine near her barracks. She unfastened the leather loop, pulled open the flimsy door, and stepped in. It smelled so badly of shit that her eyes smarted and watered. Outside she heard running footsteps—boots, not shoes. She wondered where Nelka was. Had she made it back safely?

Though it was painful, she hiked up her skirt, pulled her undergarment down, and forced herself to sit back on the frigid cold wood. Not a moment too soon. The door wrenched open. Mischka looked up in shock and fear. A hand reached in, grabbed the collar of her thin coat, and tossed her out onto the hard, icy ground.

A guard shouted, "What are you doing?"

Mischka struggled to her feet, pulling at her undergarments. A large form loomed to her right and she cowered.

"For God's sake, Rolf. The stupid woman was in the latrine — what in hell do you think she was doing?"

The guard pointed an index finger in Mischka's face. "Get back to your bunk. Now."

Mischka didn't need to be told twice. She turned and ran, her breath coming out in wheezes. She nearly overshot the door, grabbed it as she slipped on the ice, then twisted the knob and burst in. She hit the top of the ladder, and her friends pulled her up so that she lay along the outside.

Aurora gripped Mischka's forearms. "What happened?"

Mischka panted, impatient for her eyes to adjust to the dark. "Where's Nelka?"

Lidia's face came into focus. "Isn't she with you?"

"We split up."

"What?" Lidia sat up. Her face hovered close to Aurora's. "You have to go get her."

"No," Aurora said. "We all have to stay put. They're on the move out there. Something's wrong."

The squeak of a door at the other end of the barracks signaled someone's approach. Mischka heard a murmur, then a sharp, angry yelp.

"Get away!" someone said.

Someone else hissed, and then Petronela's voice could be heard quite clearly complaining. Before Mischka could figure out what was going on, heavy boots stamped in. Braunhaus and two armed soldiers stood, dark outlines against the light of the moon shining in behind them.

A plaintive voice whined, "It's not our fault."

Mischka peered down the line of bunks. She heard a scuffle, some mutterings, and then suddenly a bundle of rags appeared on the floor — a bundle that squirmed and reconstituted itself into a person, crouching, waiting.

"Who's there?" one of the guards shouted. "Come this way — into the light."

Oh, no, Mischka thought.

With every step she took, Nelka's physique became increasingly identifiable. She kept her hands away from her body, palms out. "Please do not shoot me. I mean no harm."

When Lidia heard her sister's voice, she sucked in a big breath of air as if she were going to scream. Aurora got her hands over the girl's mouth before Mischka could.

Lidia thrashed, and Aurora whispered, "No. Stop it. Shhh. Shhh. Shhh."

The guard's deep voice was sharp. "Where's your partner in crime? Two of you were observed. Where's the other?"

"I'm not sure I know what you mean," Nelka said.

The butt of a rifle hit Nelka in the chest, and she fell to the floor. The guards stood over her, ready to strike again.

Braunhaus said, "Wait." Her voice was calm and cunning. "We can always talk some sense into her."

"Or we can skip the talk and beat it out of her." The soldier laughed. Standing in profile to Mischka he pulled something out of his pocket, then squatted. A golden light flashed, and for a moment his face was illuminated by the flame of a cigarette lighter. He was young, perhaps no more than twenty. The lighter made a clicking sound as it shut, and he tucked it into his breast pocket. The scent of tobacco floated up, and the man let out a sigh.

"Who is your accomplice?" His head came up and he surveyed the bunks. Mischka made sure not to meet his eyes. He grabbed the front of Nelka's coat and yanked her to her feet. "Tell us who you were with, or we shall put to death each of these women here. Every one."

"Who would do your dirty work then?" Nelka spat out.

The guard's hand was quick. A solid thud was all Mischka heard, and Nelka was on the floor again.

"You will tell us or—" He grabbed a woman from three bunks down from Mischka. She fell to the ground, shrieking. Nearly every woman in the barracks was cowering against the wall, many of them moaning and crying. The guard blew out cigarette smoke. "Tell me, or she dies."

"All right," Nelka shouted. "Now you may let her go."

Mischka took a deep breath and closed her eyes. She felt a calm come over her even while feeling frightened. She didn't know what they would do to her and to Nelka. Perhaps it didn't matter any longer. She'd cheated death once already with Arben. She'd lived through her marriage, long enough to escape and be with her family for a time. That was enough.

And now it was all over. She regretted that her life would end at this squalid, dismal camp.

"Please. I promise I'll cooperate." As Mischka made a move to sit up, Aurora sprang at her and burst into tears. Both she and Lidia clutched at her, sobbing, trying to keep as quiet as possible.

"It's over for me," Mischka whispered.

The guard's voice was impatient. "It's the middle of the night, and we have better things to do than wait for your cooperation, you Polish hag. You will get your comrade, and we'll go."

Later Mischka thought she must have been mistaken, but she swore Nelka smiled and winked at her. And then all Mischka could see was the back of Nelka's head, moving away. She stopped halfway down the barracks and said, "Come on out, now. We can't jeopardize everyone. Let's go."

Mischka heard a collective gasp of inhalation that was not followed by an exhalation. Every woman in the barracks held her breath, waiting.

The guard with the cigarette demanded, "Dammit, point her out. Which is she?"

Nelka's arm came up, pointing. "Her. Come along, Petronela."

A shrill scream sent a shiver down Mischka's spine. "Wait a minute!" Petronela screeched. "She's lying. She's—she's—it's a lie!"

The second guard hauled her out, and Petronela shrieked all the way to the door and out into the yard. Nelka followed, walking on her own next to Braunhaus, her head held high as the guard with the cigarette brought up the rear. After they were gone, someone got up and shut the door, and the chill night wind stopped blowing through.

Aurora had stopped crying, but Lidia continued to sob. "What will they do to her? What will they do?"

"Shhh..." Aurora said. "I don't know. I don't know, Lidia."

Mischka lay on her back, stunned. She couldn't stop shaking. What had Nelka done? How could she have done that? Certainly by morning Petronela would have convinced the authorities of her innocence, and the guards would return. She slid over the side and down the ladder.

Aurora grabbed at her shoulder. "Mischka, where are you going?"

"I'll wait somewhere by myself."

"No."

"I can't take any chances. No need for you and Lidia to suffer for my sins."

Aurora hissed something, but Mischka couldn't make out her words. She disregarded it and shuffled down the aisle, peering into the semi-darkness, until she found an empty lower bunk. She curled up on the cold, rough wood, her fists under her chin. No sleep came for the rest of the night.

THREE DAYS PASSED before Mischka finally believed that they weren't coming for her. In some ways that realization was worse than the terror of waiting to be taken away. Now all she could think of was Nelka's proud, scarred face and the way she had sacrificed herself to spare all of them. On the third night, she returned to the top bunk with Lidia and Aurora and lay with them, feeling the heavy weight of guilt choking her.

She hadn't cried. Lidia had wept enough for both of them. No matter what Aurora said, the girl was inconsolable, and it was all they could do to keep her working. Mischka and Aurora took turns standing next to Lidia, encouraging her to go through the motions, to bend and sort, to at least appear to be focused on the never-ending crate deliveries.

On the fourth day, they were sent to the other side of the loading area and put to work with three women she didn't know. Small windows set high in the wall let in a trickling of sun, and it felt somehow warmer. Mischka lifted her face to the sun and realized it was now Seed Moon. April. Spring was on the way.

A voice close to her ear whispered in Polish. "We don't miss her. You need not feel badly."

Mischka straightened up and looked into the face of a middle-aged woman. Her face was deeply wrinkled, and a line of grime was smudged along her hairline and temples. Huge haunted eyes dominated her narrow face. "What did you say?"

"It's not your fault."

"What are you talking about?"

"Petronela. She was a nasty, mean woman. Spiteful. Cruel. Much better her than you."

Mischka felt the blood drain from her face, but before she could say anything, the woman went on. "Did you ever find a way out of here?"

"What do you mean?" Mischka hefted a stack of uniforms and dumped them in the rolling cart.

"You often left in the night. You were looking for a way to escape, right?"

"I—I never found one."

"I thought as much." She picked up the pry bar and went to work on another crate. "You realize that your friend, the one they took away, would not have been compromised at all if it were not for Petronela?" Mischka stood staring at the woman, not understanding. "Your friend slipped into our bunk, and if Petronela had kept her rude mouth shut, nothing would have happened. But no—she had to dump her out. What was her name?"

"Nelka. Her name is Nelka."

"Yes, right. Nelka. She would have been safe, except Petronela thought she was some sort of high-class person who deserved better than the rest of us." She let out a grunt. "Betrayer. That's what she was. I don't miss her a bit. Neither do they." She gave a toss of her head toward their coworkers. "She's Magda, and the short one is Jolanta. I'm Klaudia, and you are?"

"Mischka."

EVEN WITH NEW friends helping Aurora and Mischka keep Lidia on track, Mischka felt numb, as though she'd frozen to a block of ice on the night Nelka was taken, and had no capacity to thaw. Each day she felt more—not less—frozen. The weather continued to improve as spring came on full force and headed toward summer, but it made no difference for Mischka.

Over half the women in the barracks had "disappeared" over the winter. Each morning as Mischka stood in formation and looked around at their dwindling numbers, she felt less and less hope. Without Nelka's prodding and bravado, she hadn't left the barracks in the night—except once for the latrine—and it showed in her energy level and rapid loss of weight.

One evening, about a month after losing Nelka, Mischka crawled into the bunk with Aurora and Lidia and turned on her right side to face the wall. As the walls had thawed, mildew showed up, and she stared at spots of dark green. She was half asleep, dreaming of floating in a brook, cool water on her naked skin, when something jerked her awake.

Aurora grasped her shoulder and whispered, "Mischka. Are you asleep?"

"Not now."

"Turn over."

Mischka rolled onto her back and looked up into the outline of Aurora's face. Though very little light came in through the far window, Mischka was able to see her friend's eyes sparkling in the low light. "What is it?"

"You can't leave us."

"What?"

"Don't leave us." Aurora slid her hand down and cupped Mischka's face. "You drift farther away each day."

Mischka's eyes filled with tears. "I can't help it."

When Aurora spoke, it came out choked. "You're the strong one, Mischka, not me. I can't do this without you. Please—please don't leave me."

The bitterness in Mischka's heart showed in her voice. "I'm not going anywhere."

"That's not what I mean. Don't die inside. Please, I beg you to stay with me." She lowered her head and pressed her lips to

Mischka's, lightly, then pulled back and peered down into her eyes.

Mischka was filled with longing—for what, she didn't know. She lifted her hand and smoothed a lock of hair from Aurora's eyes, then pulled her into her arms. Aurora sank against her and let out a sigh. They adjusted so that they were lying comfortably with Aurora's head tucked under Mischka's chin.

Mischka didn't know what to say. Even though she'd lain with these other women all these weeks and months, she hadn't ever felt so intimate. Always before, despite their proximity and the need to huddle for warmth, there was always some small measure of separation: an averted gaze, a turned head, a hand's width of space. She'd been reminded of when she was a child, lying below the *vardo*, snuggling with Mimi and Nadja and hearing Stevo leading late-night songs around the campfire. But this was different. Now she felt laid wide open, vulnerable. She closed her eyes and swallowed as a peculiar warmth washed over her.

Aurora tightened her grip, and Mischka realized that her friend was crying in silence. "What is it?"

"I don't know how to go on. I feel like God has forsaken me."

Mischka wanted to blurt out that yes, of course, Aurora's God had deserted her—had deserted all of them. They were all left to their own wits, unable to escape their captors. What kind of God would put them in such a situation and expect them to stay alive and hopeful?

"Why, Mischka? Why? Why would God forsake us?"

"I don't know. But we have each other, and I will not forsake you."

Aurora stiffened in her arms. "Do you promise?"

"If you will."

"Oh, I promise. I feel I already owe you my life."

"What?"

"Every step of the way, you've given me heart, kept me going. I'd have been dead back on the first day if it weren't for you."

That wasn't how Mischka remembered it. She shook her head slowly, but didn't refute Aurora's comment. Instead she wondered why they had survived at all. She thought of the work that their jailers needed done and realized that was why. "I have to keep telling myself that one day the war will be over, and Aurora, if there's a God, the Germans will lose."

Aurora whispered, "I'll know there's a God if my husband and children are spared. If not—" Her voice broke.

Mischka's heart hurt. She thought of her family, of the *kumpania*, making their way over the mountains and into the safety of the Czech lands or Hungary. "I don't know if I can even hope for that for my own family or for yours. But if I knew how to pray, I'd plead with your God to keep them all safe."

"Yes," Aurora choked out.

"All we can do now is help each other and try to outlast these heartless bastards."

Aurora stifled a sob. "Heartless bastards — good description." She relaxed against Mischka and lay quietly.

After a minute or so, Mischka realized Aurora had fallen asleep. She closed her eyes, too, but sleep wouldn't come. Many faces passed through her mind's eye: Mimi, Nadja, Pippi, Valentina, Donka, Simza, Aurora...and then Arben, her blight of a husband. Any one of her childhood girlfriends meant more to her than Arben ever could or would. She'd never loved him. She'd loved Tobar as a brother, and Emil as well. But only once in her whole life had she ever felt anything approaching the tenderness and excitement that one simple kiss from Aurora had elicited, and that was on her wedding day when Pippi kissed her goodbye.

Mahrime, she thought, but it was a reflex response. Two women lying together was *mahrime* — but why was that? Who had made up that rule? And why wasn't there a rule providing that a bigger, stronger male was not allowed to assault anyone smaller, including women in general and his wife in particular? Had some things been wrongly labeled *mahrime* — or had she perhaps been misled?

As she drifted off to sleep, still holding Aurora in her arms, Mischka came to a decision. If she made it out alive, she would find a woman, someone who would honor her and share a love the way any two married persons should.

Chapter
Twenty-Seven

Southern Poland, October 1943 (Blood Moon)

PIPPI NEVER GOT any time alone. There was nowhere to go. She missed the solitude of walking by herself through her hometown, down to the narrow brook, seeing chipmunks scrambling, listening to the birds chirp, and smelling fresh air. At home, she and Camille had worked companionably and had only paying customers to please. Working with these frightened women, most of whom were inept, was a daily trial. She'd never realized how much it meant to her to be her own woman, in charge of her own business. The war had changed everything. All she held dear had been taken from her. She wasn't even mistress of her own destiny anymore. Instead she was an unwilling cog in a machine she hated. But what was the alternative?

She knew she was fortunate compared with so many others. Her situation could be so much worse. She reminded herself of that every day. This war reduced the usual complexities of life to stark and simple choices. Imprison others or face imprisonment yourself. Obey or accept the consequences of disobedience. Bully or be bullied. For those worse off than she was, there was an even more basic choice: live, however you could, or die.

Pippi wiped her wrist across the perspiration that dampened her forehead and tried to be patient as she untangled a giant knot from a spool of thread. The factory remained hot and airless even now, in October, with the worst of the summer heat behind them. The windows were open, but no breeze and very little fresh air made it into the stinking sweatshop.

She finally grew aggravated, slipped a pair of scissors from the pocket in her dress, and cut away the knot.

Greta sauntered by and as usual couldn't resist a comment. "Tsk, tsk...cutting again."

Pippi wanted to cut Greta. The woman never lifted a finger

to untangle anything or make sure any real work was done. At least Bernadette and Elke could be counted on to give a hand occasionally. Greta lived to report Pippi, and she surely would do it again today. It had become a joke between Pippi and Major Fischer. Behind closed doors they laughed about Greta's eagerness to get Pippi in trouble.

"She's just jealous," the major kept telling Pippi, and she thought he was right.

But Greta was not nearly so troubling as Agnes Braunhaus. Agnes usually worked the graveyard shift. When Pippi came downstairs each morning, her roommate often sat in the dining area, sipping coffee and looking awful. The summer months, with temperatures often over one hundred degrees, had not been kind to her. Agnes hated the heat, and obviously had a difficult time sleeping during the day. She grew short-tempered, so much so that she looked for any opportunity to needle Pippi. Most of the early evenings Agnes spent in their shared bedroom, but some days, from dinnertime until Agnes left for her shift, she hung around and smoked. Worse, she followed Pippi from the dining area to the small front room and made snide comments.

At those times, Pippi was most desperate to find a place she could be alone. Her one solace was that one morning each week she walked over to Major Fischer's headquarters. The opulent home provided an oasis from the filth and stench and unfriendliness she saw every day. She wished her sleeping quarters were there.

Bernadette, Greta, and Elke were idle for most of the same hours Pippi was, and there were numerous other civilian workers, including Felix Schuster and his assistant, crammed into the crowded quarters. The camp itself was dry, barren, dirty. The frightened, beaten-down laborers marched from place to place during the course of the day, and Pippi was sickened by their condition. She could think of nothing she could do, so she preferred to avoid being anywhere near the barracks. Sometimes she went outside and walked along the fence line next to the factory, but everywhere she went was hot and stank of sweat and rot and something else that drifted on the wind—a bitter, stinging aroma Pippi couldn't identify. She couldn't escape that pervasive stench and sometimes even thought it had made its way beneath her skin. When she perspired, as she was now, she could smell it on herself.

Pippi discarded the cut thread, moved to the far end of the room, and surveyed the backs of the seamstresses. She had almost two hundred and fifty operational treadle machines, five of which were extremely temperamental. She put her most ingenious workers, girls like Mariel, on those units because they did the best job of nursing them along. They had gotten through a lot of the uniform repair backlog, but still, they weren't turning out any new uniforms yet. Overall, production had stayed steady for the last couple months, but she hadn't been able to improve output by the leaps and bounds it had increased through the summer. It didn't help that all the women were dehydrated. And malnourished. As if to confirm this thought, there was a flutter of motion ahead on the far left, and Pippi heard the thump of someone hitting the floor.

Greta was at the skeletal seamstress's side quickly, her baton prodding. "Get up. Get back to work, you lazy slut."

Pippi hated the language Greta used and the way she treated the prisoners worse than dogs. Hurrying over, she said, "Greta. Back away. Give her some air."

Pippi didn't know the woman's name. She lay on the floor on her side, twitching. A wet stain appeared on her skirt, and Pippi backed away a step, smelling urine.

"Not again," Greta said, and she and Bernadette looked at one another in disgust.

Pippi hid her shakiness. In an authoritative voice, she said, "Greta, go tell Herr Schuster. I'll see Sergeant Vogel."

Behind her, one of the guards—she wasn't sure which—made a comment under her breath. "Well, that's unusually cold, coming from her."

She left Elke and Bernadette staring at her and headed for the stairs. Her rapid departure had nothing to do with being cold-hearted and everything to do with feeling sick. Don't vomit. Don't vomit. She tried to keep breathing. She hurried down to the fourth floor where the sewing notions were stored. Panting and forcing down the taste of her breakfast, she burst into the welcome darkness of the large, musty room. She paced for a minute or two and willed herself to regain her composure.

Shutters covered the windows, and the place smelled of cigarette smoke. No one was allowed to smoke in the factory building. The place was too much of a tinderbox, and they had all been cautioned against it. She crossed the floor to the nearest window, wondering if Bernadette or Greta was sneaking down here—or maybe even Agnes Braunhaus, who broke rules when it pleased her.

She crossed the floor to the nearest window and pulled open a shutter. Bright sun blinded her, and she closed it quickly, then leaned back against the window frame, blinking until her eyes adjusted to the dim room. Whoever last came down for thread had left the giant cupboards in disarray. In fact, everything in the room—on the shelves and in crates—was a disorganized jumble. Greta. She was sure of it. She hated that woman.

Pippi drew a slow breath, still smelling the horrible scent of the dead woman. Four women had died on the floor in the last two months. Pippi's three coworkers took it in stride, but each death upset Pippi more. She hated feeling so helpless to change what she witnessed, and the indifference she had to show shamed her. Often she wanted to protest, particularly at Greta's cruelty, and sometimes she had to jab herself with a pin so she could remain silent. Every time she did so, she felt diminished. Had she no courage?

She hated feeling so helpless, but she saw no alternatives. And she couldn't stand here all day. Someone would come looking for her, probably Greta, if she were absent too long. Her nerves had settled enough to get by, and her heart no longer beat out of her chest, so she left the storage area and continued her trek down the stairs to find Vogel.

When she reached the door to the loading dock, she hesitated. Pippi avoided coming down here if she could help it, instead sending a prisoner when she wanted to get a message to the odious sergeant. Bracing herself, she opened the door and waited in the doorway, watching women unpack crates and sort the contents. They moved as though half-asleep. Not a single woman had hair any longer than three inches, and many were emaciated, like the dead girl upstairs. These women were starving to death.

Tears came to her eyes, and she forced herself not to cry. She couldn't afford to show weakness or sympathy. Strange how no one had actually said as much; they didn't have to. All she had to do was watch how the camp functioned and how others behaved, and she knew the unspoken rules.

Sergeant Vogel was leaning against a muddy gray cargo truck, with his back to her. She took a few strides into the work area and avoided a wooden crate with black boots spilling out. Her foot came down on the top of a ruined leather boot, and her ankle would have turned except her elbow and shoulder were suddenly supported. She felt a flash of fear as she caught her balance, then looked up into the face of her savior.

She took a step back as the other woman did. "Excuse me," Pippi said. She blinked. Mischka. The name echoed in her head, and she recalled the face of her friend—her long, curly hair, dark brown eyes, the square chin. The woman reminded her of Mischka—though she was much older, of course.

Pippi nudged the boot aside and walked on more carefully, all the while aware of being watched. When she glanced back, she saw the dark-eyed woman staring at her, a pleading look on her face. There was no way that could be Mischka, but she looked enough like her to be a sister. Her emaciated older sister.

"Sergeant Vogel?"

The soldier spun around. A wide smile broke across his clean-shaven face. "Why, it's Fräulein Stanek."

"Ah, yes. So sorry to disturb you."

"Not at all. You bring a ray of sunshine." He tucked his baton under his bad arm and fished in his breast pocket. "Perhaps you would like a cigarette?"

"Oh, that's so kind of you, but no. I don't smoke."

He slid a cigarette between his red lips. "You don't know what you're missing. Very calming to have a good smoke." He clicked open a silver lighter and lit up. "So you have come for a visit, to keep me company?"

Pippi didn't like the man. She didn't know why and scolded herself, thinking she should be more magnanimous because of his physical affliction. But just being a few feet from him made her want to back up and get away. She forced a smile. "No, I'm sorry. I'm here to spirit away a worker."

He made a harrumphing sound and tapped ash off to the side. His light blue eyes glittered through the haze of cigarette smoke. "None of them are any good. I hope they bring a new load of workers in soon. These stink." Giving a flourish with his baton, he said, "Take what you need."

"Thank you, Sergeant Vogel."

"Franz. Please call me Franz."

She hoped her expression looked open and genuine as she backed away. She couldn't make herself say his first name, much less tell him her own. She bumped into the corner of the cargo truck and hastily righted herself. Brushing dirt off the shoulder of her dress, she gazed around as if considering which prisoner to take.

The woman who looked like Mischka was bending over a crate, but Pippi saw she was watching closely. Catching her eye, she beckoned. "Please?"

The woman was tall and scrawny, but she moved toward Pippi with grace and stopped five feet away. "Pippi." Her mouth formed the name silently.

The word hit Pippi like an electric shock. "Oh, my God." It was not a question, and if it hadn't been her name, Pippi would have assumed the woman was muttering to herself. She moved a step closer and said softly, "You can't be Mischka."

"I can't? Why is that?"

Pippi was struck dumb. She stared up at the dark eyes.

Despite her natural coloring, Mischka was pale, her skin stretched taut over high cheekbones. Pippi whispered, "Why are you here?"

"Why are *you* here?"

"I was forced."

"As was I."

Swallowing with difficulty, Pippi tried to make her sluggish brain think. Despite the warm autumn breeze, she realized she was cold with fear and worry. She needed to hasten back inside the factory, gather her thoughts, figure out what to do. "Come with me."

"Where?"

"What do you mean 'where'? Somewhere safer than here."

Mischka stood her ground. "I can't leave my friends behind."

Pippi stared at her, then looked over toward Vogel. "You must come now. Before Vogel notices—"

Vogel cleared his throat and called out. "Is that woman giving you trouble, Fräulein Stanek?"

"No, Sergeant. Not at all." Smiling sweetly, she gave him a little wave before asking Mischka, "How many of you are there?" She glanced around, worried that Mischka meant all five dozen women, most of whom were surreptitiously watching them.

"Six of us."

"Get the others and come with me." She returned to the door and waited, grasping the metal doorknob as Mischka assembled a bedraggled group like little ducks all in a row. Pippi opened the door and ushered them through. They huddled inside, illuminated by the low-watt bulb hanging down from the ceiling

A young blonde girl elbowed Mischka, and Pippi heard her whisper something in Polish, something about being executed.

Mischka shook her head. "No. This is—" Mischka looked at Pippi. "How do we properly address you?"

"Fräulein Stanek will do."

Mischka looked at Pippi oddly, then pointed to the women. "This worried one is Lidia. Here is Magda, Jolanta, and Klaudia. And Aurora has traveled with me since first we were captured. We look after one another."

Pippi bit her lip. What should she do? She needed only one of these women. She looked at her watch. Three o'clock. "Do any of you sew?"

Aurora and Klaudia said yes, and Pippi asked if they could use a treadle machine. Yes, again. "You wouldn't lie to me now, would you?" They shook their heads. "You all speak German?"

Mischka said, "These are Poles, but they all speak and understand sufficient German."

Pippi had to make a split-second decision. "You, Aurora. We'll start with you. Everyone follow me."

The hallway was so narrow that they followed in single file. At the fourth floor, Pippi hesitated, but she didn't dare leave the group unsupervised. Someone could come along and assume they were up to no good and injure or kill them all. So she led them on to the fifth floor. At the top of the stairs, she said, "Wait here. Aurora, come with me."

In the sewing room, Elke sat at the desk near the front while Bernadette and Greta paced in front of the windows, as far from the site of the woman's death as possible. The dead woman had been removed.

Elke looked up. "Took you long enough."

Pippi ignored her sarcasm. "Elke, here's a new seamstress. She has some skills with treadle machines. Can you get her started?"

Elke rose reluctantly as Pippi backed up toward the door. "Where are you going?" she asked.

"The storage room is a mess. There's thread everywhere. It needs to be tidied."

"Send Greta. She's probably at fault."

"No, that's all right. I have to get an inventory for the major anyway."

Without waiting for a response, Pippi sped from the room and led the others down to the untidy cabinets and shelves on the fourth floor. "Please organize this, and do not rush. Take your time. You can see some rudimentary order. Please straighten it all up. And Mischka, come with me."

At the far end of the room, several crates were stacked against the wall. Pippi set a couple down on the floor and gestured for Mischka to sit. "Two letters from my mother have made their way to me here," she said, feeling awkward to find herself facing her old friend under such circumstances. "She hasn't heard a word from Emil. Where is he? He's not here in this camp, is he?"

"I don't think so. We were fleeing from the soldiers across the Tatras Mountains when Tobar and I were captured. The others got away. At least, that's what I hope."

"So Tobar is here?"

Mischka shook her head, but didn't elaborate. Pippi scowled. Was she going to have to pull every bit of information out of her? She longed to reach over and touch her, to quell the fear in Mischka's eyes, but she didn't dare. Anyone could walk in on them at any time.

Instead she asked, "How long have you been here?"

"Since Snow Moon."

"Remind me which month that is."

"The one before your Christmas."

"Oh, my God. Nearly a year?" Pippi broke out in a sweat. "I've been here since March. Why have I never seen you?"

Mischka shrugged.

"You're terribly thin." That was an understatement. Mischka actually looked like a stick figure with extra large eyes.

"We aren't fed well."

Pippi gazed across the expanse of the factory floor and watched the women working at the cabinets. One—the blonde girl—stood to the side and was re-rolling thread onto a spool. The others were arranging things on the shelves. Some of the open cardboard containers on the floor had been emptied, their contents stacked up on the shelves. Every woman was as thin as Mischka.

Pippi vacillated, wondering how she was going to shift six warm bodies onto her labor detail. She heard a noise in the hall, and Mischka was instantly on her feet.

"Fräulein Stanek." Felix Schuster came striding into the room. He glanced suspiciously at Mischka, then back at Pippi. "Are you all right?"

Pippi rose slowly from the crate and smoothed the front of her dress. Her heart beat double time. "Yes." She sighed. "My head got to me for a moment. It's so stuffy in here." She turned to Mischka and in a haughty voice said, "Your assistance is no longer required. Get back to work. Now."

"Vogel said you've gutted his work detail," Schuster said.

Pippi wondered who attempted to iron the wrinkles from his dark suit each day. He rarely looked well turned out. "Gutted is somewhat of an exaggeration, isn't it?"

"You need all these workers to sort and organize these sewing materials?"

Pippi bit her lip, then made a quick decision. "Actually, they're to be used as pattern cutters. However, before they can start, this room must be tidied, and no one else was free to do it."

"Patterns?" Schuster looked puzzled.

"I'm sure you'll agree it's time we start turning out new uniforms. I know the major considers this a priority as well."

Schuster looked around the room. "We still have all these crates of damaged pieces."

"True, but so many are beyond repair. As the work on them

winds down, we need to increase work on new garments. Our men fighting for the glory of the Fatherland deserve the very finest uniforms, do they not?"

"Does Major Fischer approve?"

"The major has given me free rein, and I report to him personally each week." Pippi spoke in a sharp tone, as if she were insulted by the stupidity of the question.

Like many of the camp personnel, Schuster was aware that she had regular contact with the major. Pippi had overheard enough whispered conversations to know some people thought she had special privileges.

"You should not be alone with these unpredictable scum," Schuster said. "At any time one could attack you."

Pippi's face flamed with heat. She was suddenly so angry that she wished to strike the man. Forcing down her emotions, she said, "Thank you so much for your concern for me, Herr Schuster. You are kind to fret on my behalf. But don't worry about this lot. They're harmless. I'll be fine."

"I should hope so. I'll be down on the second floor if you need me."

She bade him farewell and sank down to the crate, her mind racing. She hadn't considered machining new uniforms so soon, but the idea was a good one. The trick would be figuring out who from Mischka's crew could cut, who could sew, and how to quickly train anyone who could do neither. The other civilians wouldn't much care, but Greta would complain about all the trouble, and Elke would be angry about being left out of the decision-making. Nothing she could do about that. Everything had happened willy-nilly, and she had no time to plan. What could she do? How could she make this work?

She ran a hand through her hair and felt some of it separate from the loose braid. As she tried to repair it, she became aware of a strange hush and looked up. Her charges stood near the storage shelves and watched her covertly as they waited for more instructions. All of the spools were put away, and the packages of bias tape, needles, buttons, and other items had been neatly organized. Pippi rose and met Mischka's gaze, and a calmness came over her as she crossed the floor.

"We're going to go upstairs now," she said. "Whatever happens, just stand there, look at the floor, and let me do the talking."

And so began the subterfuge.

WITH GRETA ALWAYS hovering and Bernadette and Elke nearby, Pippi had a difficult time communicating with Mischka. She couldn't write notes because they were too easy to intercept, and there was nowhere to meet. Her only option was to lean down to look at the material Mischka was cutting and say a few words here and there. Once when they ran out of fabric she was able to point at Klaudia and Mischka and instruct them to follow her. Down on the fourth floor, they loaded a crate onto the dumbwaiter, and Pippi took that opportunity to speak. "You look terrible, Mischka. You're much too thin."

"We all are."

"I've wracked my brain, and I can't figure out how to hand over food without being caught."

"On the road-side of this building there's an alcove about ten hands wide. Do you know of it?" Pippi shook her head. "The alcove is perhaps two strides deep and leads to a door that I believe goes to the cellar below here. If you get that door open, you could leave food, perhaps even medicines should we ever need them."

"I'm still at a loss. It won't be easy to smuggle out even small amounts."

"You don't need to bring a lot, and it's best if it's not wrapped. We must eat everything or be able to easily dispose of it in the latrine. We can't leave rubbish lying around for others to question. When it's cooler and you can wear a coat you'll have more places to hide things."

Mischka touched Pippi's forearm. "Under no circumstances should you do anything to risk your safety, Pippi. Promise me you'll be careful. They're not forgiving here."

"Don't worry. I've never lied so much in my life."

LATER THAT EVENING, Pippi raided the pantry. She thought she could feed the entire seamstress detail for weeks on all the food stuffed in there. She looked around, trying to decide what was compact but of sufficient richness and finally decided on crackers, three apples, a small loaf of bread, and a large chunk of butter.

She reached under her button-up dress and removed a drawstring bag she'd tucked into her belt. She filled it, slid it between her knees, and ran the string up under her skirt to her belt. If no one looked closely, they'd never see the string. She practiced walking and found it easiest to walk a little bow-legged with her toes turned out. She thought she could manage.

Bernadette was reading in the parlor, and she looked up.

"Are you off to bed?"

"No, I'd like to read for a while, but I forgot my glasses in the shop." She fingered some wire and a screwdriver in her dress pocket.

"It's dark out. You're not going over there now."

"There's enough light to see, and no one's out and about."

"Pauline, any one of these laborers could accost you. You could be hurt."

"Everyone here is always so concerned about the laborers. In all the time I've been here, none of them has posed a single threat. They won't even look at us."

"But it could happen."

"I don't think so. Those poor pathetic people are all exhausted and wasting away. Not to mention thoroughly cowed by fear." Bernadette looked doubtful. "Go on. Finish your book. Don't worry about me. It's cool outside now, and I may even take a walk."

"Oh, no, you mustn't."

"Bernie, dear, you worry too much. I'll stick to the fence line, maybe stop and chat with some of the soldiers."

"Ohh... so that's it."

"What?"

"You've got your eye on one of the guards."

Pippi restrained herself from laughing out loud. "And what if I did?"

Bernadette reopened her book. "Find out if he has a brother."

Pippi grinned. "I'll be back before you know it, Bernie." She ducked out into the cool night air.

A guard shouldered his rifle near the factory stairs. "Good evening," she said.

"Oh, it's only you." He settled the gun butt on the ground.

"I'm heading in to the factory for a bit."

"All right, then."

She hurried in. The bare lightbulb illuminated little in the entryway. She wished she had a flashlight or a candle as she wandered around the main floor trying to find a stairwell down. Crates and boxes lined so many of the walls that she wasn't able to find the door. She finally decided she'd have to look another time when there was a lot more light.

What could she do now with the little bag of goodies? She exited the factory and went down the stairs, then gave a wave to the guard. She walked along the west side of the factory, waved to those guards as she went, and skirted the loading entrance on the south side.

"Halt. Who goes there?"

"Just me, soldier, taking a walk. I'm Fräulein Stanek from the factory." The advancing guard gave a nod and dropped back. She turned the corner and walked along the road-side of the big dirty building. She squinted in the low light, but it was so dark she couldn't see the main gate or the soldier who had just hailed her. She moved on. She nearly passed by the alcove but a low hiss brought her to a stop and she stepped back.

"Pippi."

"What in the world are you doing here?" Pippi looked all around, terrified that they would be noticed. She dropped to one knee and pretended to tie her shoe.

"I thought you were going to open the door."

"Couldn't find a way down in the dark." She untied the string at her belt, grabbed the bag, and tossed it into the dark recesses. When she stood back up, something soft hit her ankle.

"Take the bag. I can't be seen with it."

Pippi picked it up and tucked it inside her dress. "I'll look again tomorrow for the door to the basement."

"Thank you."

She didn't want to call attention to herself, so she walked on, feeling faint. Mischka had risked being out of the barracks, and it wasn't even ten o'clock yet. That frightened Pippi, and when she had the opportunity, she meant to speak to her about it.

Back at the house, Bernadette looked up as Pippi entered. "Find them?"

"What?"

"Your glasses."

With a start, Pippi shook her head. "No. I'm not sure where they've gotten themselves off to. I'll look in the morning light. But I did have a very nice walk. I think I'll do that more often."

Bernadette wrinkled up her nose. "It's ugly and threatening out there. I think you're crazy."

"Oh, well. Maybe I like living on the edge. Good night, Bernadette."

"Pippi?"

"Yes?" She paused and turned back.

"It's all right if you call me Bernie, but not in front of the workers."

"All right then, Bernie."

"Sleep well."

THE NEXT NIGHT, Pippi returned to the factory. After a quick stop on the third floor to root through clothing and find a coat, she hurried to the basement door, which she had located earlier in the day. She pushed the white button on a light switch that illuminated one bare bulb at the foot of the stairs. She descended to a dark basement with a low ceiling. Something light and gauzy tickled her nose and wrapped around her face and neck. She strangled a squeak and wiped a cobweb off her cheek.

With an arm up in front of her face, she stepped around some packing boxes and a crate big enough to hold an elephant. She came to a rickety-looking, waist-high table, and set all she carried on its battered surface. To her right stood a huge, unlit furnace with multiple octopus arms. Through a double-wide doorway she could just barely make out a dim room which contained a coal bin twenty feet wide and deeper than she could see. A line of four shovels leaned against it. Pippi figured the factory must be due for a coal delivery because there wasn't much in the bin. No wonder the building was so cold; nobody minded the boiler during the night. Perhaps they were conserving what little coal was left.

To the left she saw an indentation in the wall—the coal delivery chute. The wooden steps up to it were blackened with an accumulation of packed-down coal dust. She took off her gloves, reached into her coat pocket for the piece of wire, and set to work on the lock. The loose, old tumblers clicked open on her first try.

Mischka appeared suddenly in the doorway. "Pippi," she whispered, managing to sound delighted.

"I feel like such a success for actually getting you in this door."

Mischka's cold hands closed over hers. "You've always been a success at everything you've done."

"You possess a great deal more confidence in me than I do."

Mischka smiled, and her eyes sparkled, even in the shadows. The sharp angles of her face softened, and her gray pallor wasn't so apparent. If her hair had been more than two inches long, she would almost look like she had on her wedding day. Pippi stretched a hand up and touched the short black hair. "Your curls are gone."

"Nobody's hair really grows much here. We need meat. We haven't had any since summer."

Pippi laid a hand against Mischka's cheek and found it surprisingly warm. "I don't have any meat at all for you tonight. But I'll get what I can in the coming days. I don't know how you can stay warm."

"I'm lucky. I'm used to cold weather and sleeping under the *vardos*. Of course, we had bedrolls then, but it's not so bad for me in the barracks. If not for Aurora and me, I don't think Lidia could stay warm enough."

"She's tiny. No fat on her for insulation."

"Unfortunately no."

Pippi took Mischka's hand. "Follow me." She led her to the ancient table in the next room. "First, I found this long, lined coat that will keep you much warmer than that rag you're wearing." Mischka shrugged out of the dirty one. "You'll probably want to dirty this up, maybe put a rip or two in it so nobody pays it any attention."

"We all need coats like this—and warmer dresses, better shoes."

"Best if we replace items gradually. If you and your friends get up tomorrow morning wearing hardier new outfits, the others will question why Saint Nicholas has visited you and not them."

"Nicholas?"

"You've heard of the saint?"

"No."

"Never mind then. Take this food. I made sure I got you a coat with deep pockets to hide it. Now here's my plan. If you come this way, to the other end, the dumbwaiter is here." She led Mischka through the gloom. "I can't risk coming down here very often, but I can put food on the dumbwaiter, and you can get it any time during the night."

"But—the guards. I can't enter the building."

"We'll leave it unlocked so you can get through the coal door any time. I'll leave you what food and clothes I can each night."

"Pippi, how will I ever repay you?"

"It's not—"

They both froze. Footsteps clumped across the floor above their heads. "Go."

Mischka grabbed the food bag and evaporated into the dim recesses of the other room.

From her coat pocket, Pippi pulled matches and half a pack of Imperials that she'd lifted from Agnes's bureau drawer.

A soldier clattered down the stairs. "What are you doing down here?" His eyes swept the area.

She gave him an embarrassed smile. "Didn't want to smoke upstairs with all the cloth and flammable materials. Thought it was safer down here. Care for one?" She held out the orange and white package.

He accepted it and tamped one out. "Thank you. That's very nice. It's cold out, and a good cigarette warms my lungs. Too bad we're forbidden to smoke on the fence."

She handed him her cigarette, and he lit his from it, all the while eyeing her. She pegged him at well over sixty, and he looked tired. Over the banging of her heart, she introduced herself, and he spent ten minutes chatting about toy trains, which he told her were his life's passion.

Pippi finished her smoke and ground it out with her heel on the cement floor, then followed him upstairs, all the while musing that she had developed nerves of steel. She thought she must have been on overload for so long that she was no longer the slightest bit nervous.

Half an hour later she got the shakes in her room and only just made it to the bathroom in time to vomit. Twice.

Chapter
Twenty-Eight

New York City, November 1989 (Snow Moon)

"Wow. I'm named for someone who saved your life, *Beebee?*"

"Yes, you are," Mischka said.

"I can't believe all this happened and no one ever told me."

Pippi said, "These are not many happy memories, Tobar. It was a shameful, painful time."

"But Grandma! Why didn't you wait until dark and steal someone's keys so you could get *Beebee* Mischka and her friends and drive out of there in one of those Kübelwagens?"

Pippi laughed. "But where would we go?"

"Somewhere. Anywhere else. Hide in the woods for a while until you could somehow get to Hungary and find Emil."

"Hmm. I'm not sure your concept of distance is very good." Mischka said, "Have you had much geography in school so far?"

"Some. It's not very interesting. At my last school, we were learning about Latin America. I haven't been at the new school long enough to know what we'll be studying." He brightened. "But in eighth grade, I had to do a report on the Po Valley in Italy with maps and charts about the agricultural information. I still have it."

He sounded so proud that Mischka said, "I would like to see it. I never set foot in Italy. I'm not sure Pippi and I are doing a very good job of explaining how lost we were. Hungary was worlds away from the labor camp. I didn't even know the name for the camp, much less where on earth we were. I was certain we were in Poland, but that was the extent of my knowledge."

"And we may not be explaining how completely the Germans trapped us in the camp," Pippi said. "We couldn't find a way to get past the guards. Perhaps alone I could take a walk outside the gates, though I never did. The soldiers might have allowed me that, but they would have kept close watch on me.

There was no possibility of me helping Mischka and her five friends escape."

"Oh," was all Tobar said.

Pippi rose. "I think we could all use a refreshment. I have chocolate milk. Do you both want it?"

Tobar said, "Yes, I'll have some, but what I really want to know is how you found Uncle Emil again."

"Did we find him?" Mischka gave him a sly look. "I'm not sure about that."

"You must have. Emil—Uncle Emil—he's the one with Gyorgy and Stevo, right?""

Pippi said, "I'll be right back. Mischka, please go on. I'll listen from the kitchen."

Chapter
Twenty-Nine

Southern Poland, Early January 1945 (Wolf Moon)

WALKING FROM THE mess shed with the rest of the seamstresses, Mischka finished the porridge in her tin cup and used her thumb to scrape out every last drop. She tucked the tin cup in her dress pocket. They hadn't been given any bread for two days, and the lukewarm porridge hadn't made a dent in her hunger.

She shivered and pulled the dirty coat around her, feeling every bit of the thirty-degree temperature. Lidia stumbled and nearly spilled her porridge. "Careful," Mischka said. Don't dump that. There's no more where that came from."

Dull-eyed and exhausted, Lidia looked up at her. "You take it."

"You need the nourishment. You finish it up."

"No. I don't want it. Take it."

Aurora echoed Mischka's comments, but Lidia shook her head. "If one of you won't eat it, I'll toss it."

Aurora accepted it from Lidia's shaky hand and asked what was wrong.

"I don't know. I just want to go to sleep. For good."

Mischka shared a glance of unspoken concern with Aurora, who quickly downed half of the sticky glop and handed the cup to Mischka as they trudged up the factory stairs. Halfway up, Mischka took one of Lidia's elbows and Aurora the other. By the fourth floor they were nearly carrying her.

Mischka looked out the window into the gray sky as they entered the sewing room. Just another day, another tiring, endless day. Yet she sensed something in the air. She had noticed darting stares from the normally smug guards at the mess shed. They seemed to be sizing up the prisoners, their eyes speculative. Mischka wondered if the looks had anything to do with the change in rations. For the past two days they hadn't been given any bread. Maybe everyone was placing bets on how long the prisoners would last on so little.

The food Pippi smuggled out each night didn't go very far when there were six of them to split it, and even the addition of Lidia's lukewarm porridge hadn't come anywhere near to assuaging her hunger. Still, Mischka thanked her lucky stars that she was no longer stuck in the cold on the loading dock. The sewing room was chilly, but nothing like the outdoors. Soon, body heat would warm the temperature by several more degrees, and once Mischka began working, she could ignore the cold.

She purposely avoided seeking Pippi's eyes, but she knew exactly where Pippi stood, near the dumbwaiter and by the windows. She noted the position of the other two overseers as well, careful always to know where every threat was posted. Quickly, she made her way to the table at the far end of the room where she had been cutting material for shirts the day before. The scissors, of course, were under lock and key, so she leaned against the wall next to another worker and waited to be noticed. The hum and buzz of the machines gradually increased as the seamstresses picked up their sewing where they'd left off.

Pippi threaded her way forward with scissors. Mischka smiled each time she saw the old metal shears. Someone had snipped off the points of every pair of scissors Mischka had touched. She thought that was ridiculous. But everything at the factory was ridiculous. Pippi handed them to her and looked up with a smirk on her face. She whispered, "Have you heard the news of the advance of the Russians?"

"No." Mischka bent and carefully cut along the edge of a piece of material.

"All along the Vistula River in Poland, the Russians are breaking through on their way to Warsaw."

"The Vistula." Mischka smiled in memory of the river and of happier days traveling with the *kumpania*.

"Rumors are that the war is winding down. I hope it's over soon."

"Is it possible?" Mischka restrained herself from reaching over to touch Pippi, though she very much wanted to.

"I hope so. There surely is a lot of action these last few days. *Kübelwagen* come and go, officers in and out. Everyone's on edge."

Mischka watched Pippi's face go from animated to flat and impassive, as though she possessed two personalities. A sidelong glance revealed that the guard named Greta was watching them.

Mischka bent close to her task and concentrated on cutting

out the cuff perfectly. It was too easy to err, and making mistakes would only result in screaming, or even worse, being beaten around the head and shoulders with a baton. Mischka wished to forgo attention of either kind. She forced down a bubble of laughter though. Aurora had informed her that every item she worked on lately, she sewed a flaw into. The night before, she'd made Mischka laugh out loud as they lay atop the bunk.

"I most enjoy doing what I can to shorten up the material in the crotch," Aurora had said. "Not an item leaves my machine without something included to make that German soldier as uncomfortable as possible as he tries to hurt innocent people."

Mischka finished cutting out the shirt at the same time the other cutter finished hers. Pippi came to them with a thick roll of trouser material. "Let's work on slacks for a time."

"Yes, ma'am," Mischka said.

Pippi rolled out the material. In a loud voice, she said, "Oh, look, we'll need more twill tape and buttons. You. Come with me."

Mischka followed Pippi, her head down. As they approached the desks at the front, Elke said, "I surely hope we have better output today than the last few days." Mischka felt Elke's eyes on her, but she concentrated on standing still and appearing stupid.

"Oh, yes," Pippi said. "We will. Keep an eye on the cutter back there, will you? I'm going downstairs for supplies. You. Come along," she said curtly to Mischka.

Once they reached the fourth floor, they hustled to the cabinets and shelving and stood close to one another while sorting through containers of buttons.

"Have you noticed there are fewer guards now than at any time?" Pippi asked. "They haven't got anyone at the middle of the west and east fences at all." She shoved the can back on a shelf and looked up into Mischka's eyes. "We're not told much, but I'm frightened for you. They've been sending some of the infirm laborers out of here."

"To the east?"

"Now there's a euphemism. 'To the east.' To death is more like it." She grabbed Mischka's forearm and turned toward her. "Listen to me. You're not safe. Your friends aren't either. If the war ends, I'm afraid of what will happen to all you laborers."

Mischka surveyed her friend's worried face. "Pippi, I can never thank you enough for all you've done for us. If it weren't for you, most of my friends would be dead by now. With food, with this job, with your caring—you've kept me alive longer than I ever expected."

Pippi's face blanched. "You sound like you're ready to be laid to rest."

"No, but I have no control over that. I live from day to day." She reached up and straightened the collar on Pippi's wool dress. "Seeing you each day keeps me sane. It keeps me going. *You* have kept me going. Just having had this time with you has been enough."

"No." Now Pippi's face went red. "It can't be this way. I can't watch someone I care about be mishandled or—or die." She choked the last word out as she tipped her head forward, so close that her brow came to rest against Mischka's collarbone. Mischka's heart beat fast, but she didn't move. She gazed toward the door to the hall and stairs. No one was in sight. She ran her fingers along the circle of Pippi's blonde braids. They were soft against her callused hand.

In a muffled voice, Pippi said, "This place is a hellhole, and it's only going to get worse."

"You don't know that for sure, but if you're right, I'll hold my head high like Tobar did."

"You've never told me what happened to Tobar."

"They shot him. For no reason."

"Oh, my God." Pippi's mouth dropped open, and she stared into Mischka's eyes. "See. We've got to get you out of here. Soon."

"To where? The country's occupied. There's nowhere to run."

"There has to be somewhere." She bit her lip. "Oh, Mischka. We have to figure out something."

"Even if we did manage to escape, we have no papers, no money, no traveling clothes."

"I can get you those things."

"You can?"

"I'll try." She stood up straight and glanced at her wristwatch. "We've been gone too long. Grab what we need, and let's hurry upstairs. But we still need to talk more, to plan."

And in the coming days, each chance she got, Pippi spoke to Mischka about escaping, but always they came to the conclusion that the danger of leaving outweighed the risks of staying. Still, the topic never strayed far from Mischka's mind.

PIPPI HAD NO trouble passing through the guard gate between the men's and women's sides of the camp. Even though it was well after dark, the sole guard recognized her and merely touched his helmet in greeting. She strolled through, her heart beating fast, and made her way to the major's house. As she mounted the stairs, a breeze chilled her. She pulled her coat tighter and looked up at the moon.

Moving to the front door, she tried to listen. She didn't want to enter and startle anyone who might flinch and use her for target practice. Her hand shook as she reached for the knob. It turned soundlessly, but as she pushed at the heavy wooden door, the hinges let out a loud shriek. She stopped, shock coursing through her veins.

When no one sounded an alarm, she opened the squeaking door another four inches, which allowed her to slip in, wincing at all the noise. She stood in the darkened entryway and waited, thinking that not a creature was stirring, not even a mouse. The old house settled and creaked, sounding alive, like a hundred small mice scratching. After a moment, she realized that a tree branch was scraping against a window in the parlor to the right. Get on with it, she thought. She must go forth and take her chances. She swallowed her fear, crept across the entryway, and tiptoed down the hallway to Fischer's office. She stepped in and went immediately through the doorway to the left.

Eight file cabinets loomed in the shadows. She hoped none of the records she sought were in the top drawers because they were too high for her to look into. She wished she could somehow illuminate the room, but the moonlight shining in a window to the right would have to do. She didn't dare turn on a light and attract any attention.

Pippi fumbled with her hair, letting it down in order to pull out two hairpins. She took a deep breath and went to the first cabinet. *Dear Papa and François, if you're angels or have any influence with the Lord at all, please help me.* The hairpins went into the lock smoothly, and with only minor manipulation, she was able to unlock the second drawer from the top. Ha! So much for German ingenuity. Who had made these locks? A thief?

She flipped through file after file, all filled with sheets of paper she didn't take time to look at. Same with the next drawer down, and the two at the bottom. She pulled the top drawer open and angled around to the side on tiptoes. No luck. Shutting the drawer, she fumbled for her hairpins to re-lock it, then decided to lock them all one after another when she was done.

A cold bead of sweat rolled down her back, and she shivered, but she squared her shoulders and unlocked the next file cabinet. The middle drawer was crammed so full, it opened with difficulty. Voilá! This is what she needed. She picked up a stack of folded papers and a handful of little booklets. The first booklet had ÚTLEVÉL embossed on the front, and the second, PASZPORT. She opened another drawer, and it too was stuffed full of passports. Hundreds and hundreds of thick papers and little booklets.

She was now faced with a new problem and shook her head in frustration. None of the drawers were organized in ways that made sense to her. How was she to find the proper papers for Mischka and her friends? Further, if she were to make it out of the major's house safely and past the guard's post, she couldn't very well carry a handful of passports in plain sight. She wished she had brought the string bag. Think. What could she do? She realized that the women were all Polish, except Mischka. But Mischka could pass for Polish. Or Hungarian. She certainly spoke both languages well enough.

Pippi heard noises that sounded like footsteps overhead. Time was running out. She bit her lip and tried to still her shaking hands, then picked up a handful of the smallest books labeled PASZPORT and put them into her left coat pocket. She still had an empty right pocket, so she stuffed more in there, then crammed in two more embossed with ÚTLEVÉL until there was no more room.

It took her longer to lock the drawer than she hoped, and before she could go back to the previous ones, she heard the shriek of the front door. *Oh, no. Oh, no!* She stuck the hairpins in with the passports and moved toward the casement window through which moonlight was pouring. Tugging on it didn't work. Some lazy worker had painted it shut.

A distant male voice rumbled in the entryway and was answered by another's deep tones. Pippi slipped out of her coat and strode into the office. The plush carpet muffled her steps. She laid her coat over one of the velvet chairs near the open door and sank down upon the divan.

What little dinner she had eaten was doing backflips in her stomach. She had to force down the bile threatening to erupt. She took great big gulps of air and tried to still her heart. Please, God, let them all go upstairs to their quarters so she could sneak out. Please...

But she heard heavy boots coming her way. The footsteps stopped, but that was because they'd hit the carpet and were now nearly silent on the way into the office. Up and to her right she saw Fischer's outline as he stepped in and headed toward his desk.

"Friedrich."

Her voice was soft, but he pivoted on his heel, one hand on the pistol at his hip. "Who goes there?"

"It's me, Friedrich. Pauline."

He leaned toward his desk and flicked on the desk lamp. "Pauline." His voice was gruff. "You startled me." He sagged back against the edge of the desk, and she realized he had been frightened a great deal more than he was letting on. "What are you doing here?"

She ran her hands through her long, loose hair and swallowed. "I heard there's been bad news. I—I thought you might—might need me." She couldn't see his face in the shadows, but he moved his hand from the gun and laced his fingers together in front of his belt buckle.

"How long have you been here?"

She decided to be truthful. "Not long, perhaps fifteen minutes. I didn't see Klaus anywhere, and no one answered my knock, so I let myself in."

"I see." He was quiet for a few moments. She watched his chest rise and fall. "So you heard that Budapest fell to the Russians?"

She produced a small, horrified gasp. "I heard they'd pushed back our troops. I didn't know they'd come that far."

"Yes, they have. Now they're marching on Berlin. So none of tonight's news is good. The commander came personally to speak to us. We've been instructed to clear out the camp and — and we are to — to dispose of any threats. This is why Klaus is no longer here." He put a hand to his forehead, then let it slide down to cover his mouth. "It's a terrible business."

Even though her stomach roiled at the thought of poor old Klaus being "disposed" of, Pippi rose and moved through the thick carpet until she stood in front of Fischer. She forced herself to reach out and pat his forearm. "I'm so sorry, Friedrich."

He looked away. Whether it was the chill in the room or her distaste for him, she trembled. He immediately stood upright and took hold of her wrist. "You're freezing cold." She didn't answer, nor did she resist as he pulled her to him. "I shall warm you, little Pauline."

His breath was hot on her neck. She shut her eyes tight and placed her hands on his ribs, gently embracing him in return.

He groaned. "You have been the only bright note in this horrible assignment. The only good and true thing." His voice broke as though he fought down a sob, but before she could consider that further, his lips found hers.

She thought of François, of his warmth and gentleness. Tears sprang to her eyes, and she was glad Fischer couldn't see that in the low light. She pressed François into the back of her mind, not wanting to think of him or his death. In his place, she pictured

Mischka's dark eyes and how her mouth looked when she laughed. Mischka. This was for Mischka. Whatever happened, she would keep that in mind. Fischer lifted Pippi and carried her to the divan. She squeezed her eyes shut and remembered a summer night in a tent under a full moon. That night she was half-drunk with some sort of homemade apple wine, and she slept cradled in Mischka's arms. She hadn't thought of that in many years. She remembered the smell of leather, the feel of a scratchy wool blanket against her cheek, the creaking of the tent in the breeze. She wished she knew the songs she'd heard that night. So much laughter and dancing and happiness then...

Fischer's attentions were blessedly short-lived. When he cried out and slumped upon her, she opened her eyes and allowed herself to return to the present. She stroked his back and made soothing sounds.

After a few moments, he lifted his head. "I'm sorry. So sorry."

"Shhh, it's all right."

He slipped off her, on his knees next to the couch, which gave her the opportunity to straighten her clothes and sit up. She didn't watch as he fumbled with his trousers. He moved to settle next to her on the divan, and Pippi shifted, her hands in her lap. She focused past him at her coat. Something white stuck out of one pocket, and her heart went into her throat.

"I am truly sorry," he said. "I shouldn't have—" He shook his head.

Struggling to think of something, she said the first lie that came to mind. "I wasn't unwilling."

He enfolded her hand in his warm palms. "I'm the one who should have been unwilling. This is another of the many, many things that my wife must never know about."

"I'll never tell."

"Sometimes I think it would have been better to stay at the front, to have died in battle."

"Oh, no." If that had happened who knew what sort of awful bureaucrat would have been here in his place. She pressed her lips together tightly.

"When I was wounded—" He paused. "I don't like to speak of it, but I was wounded in May of '42. I was in hospital for months in the Ukrainian city of Kharkov. I hate the Russians. I hate them. And they're after me yet again. If it weren't for the Russians—and those cursed Americans—*Der Führer* would be the supreme leader of Europe, perhaps of the world."

"Are you saying this is the end?"

"I don't know. But the Russians will be at our backs, and

much as I hate to do it, we must retreat. Pauline, when the time comes, I can't take you with me."

"I understand. Your wife wouldn't accept that at all." She squeezed his hand.

"No, that's not what I mean. We are to leave all civilians behind."

"Oh."

"I argued against it. Please believe me."

"Are we to be disposed of?"

He inhaled a gasp of air. "Of course not."

"That's good news then. How long do we have before they come?"

"A few weeks. We have much work to do to clean up records and pack the military goods and cargo."

She rose. "I should go then. You'll need your rest."

He scrambled up off the divan. "Pauline, please. Mention nothing of my indiscretion to the others at your quarters."

"Don't worry, Friedrich. I never speak of you or the details of our meetings. You can rest assured that I'll keep this to myself."

"Thank you." He engulfed her in a bear hug, then leaned back and bent his head to place a kiss on her cheek. "You are a good woman, Pauline Stanek. I wish for you all manner of fine things."

"And I wish for you the same." She stepped away and picked up her coat. She turned the side with the white cover sticking out, hid it against her dress, and nudged the passport completely into the pocket. "I shall see you Thursday, Friedrich." She pretended not to notice his attempt to help her, and she donned the coat.

"Until then." He walked with her to the front door and opened it. "Shall I send an escort with you?"

"No, I'll be fine. And the walk will clear my head. Good night."

His smile was wide, and his teeth sparkled in the moonlight, like the teeth of a wolf on the hunt. "Pauline, Pauline, you must try to understand. I never knew it would be this way."

The anguish in his voice sounded real, but how could she tell? Pippi plastered a pleasant look on her face, but she couldn't prevent her distaste for Fischer from intensifying. She felt unclean, and she'd been on edge for so long that the thought of standing with him for one moment longer made her feel physically ill.

"Yes, who could imagine these terrible things could happen," she said ambiguously.

With earnest concern, he responded, "If you are ever asked about your work here, remember — you were just following orders."

"I will remember." Pippi turned to walk away. "Just following orders."

Chapter
Thirty

THE CROUPY COUGH that Lidia developed overnight had both Aurora and Mischka worried. More than half the women in the sewing detail were ill, and so many from the loading dock had died that only eighty laborers answered the roll call. In the early morning light, Mischka saw that Lidia was pale, and her eyes were rimmed with red. They had tried to keep her warm between them throughout the night, but when they rose just before dawn, Lidia couldn't stop shaking. It didn't help that they stood in three inches of snow. Lidia refused to go get her porridge or drink any water.

Mischka pulled her aside and leaned down to try to meet her eyes. She didn't seem to be focusing. "Lidia. Lid, you need to eat."

"I don't want any." Lidia bent double, coughed, and spat out phlegm. "I just want them to take me away to be with Nelka."

Aurora put an arm around her. "Oh, no, sweetheart. That's not wise. They probably wouldn't send you anywhere near Nelka."

"But they might. I want Nelka." Lidia's pout would have been comical if she wasn't so feverish and the topic hadn't been about life and death.

Mischka patted her on the back. "You're ill, and you need sustenance. You can't get stronger if you don't eat."

"No."

Suddenly Braunhaus stood at Mischka's side. "What's going on here?"

Mischka straightened up. Aurora hastened to explain. "Nothing, ma'am. She had a small piece of food caught in her throat. She's fine now."

"See to it. We don't have time to coddle the lazy or the shiftless."

Mischka eased Lidia back and away. "Yes, ma'am." Braunhaus, dressed warmly in a long coat and a furry hat, stomped off.

Under her breath, Aurora said, "Nobody's as lazy or shiftless as that hag."

Mischka fought back a grin. "Why, Aurora. You're always so kind, never a bad word. And now you call our fine overseer a hag."

"She most certainly is a hag. She's a disgrace to humanity, a boil on the underside of a pig."

Mischka laughed. "I have to admit that your German certainly has improved by leaps and bounds. If we ever get out of here, you can refer to our time spent in this place as language school."

"Aren't you the funny one today." Aurora took the tin cup from Lidia's hand and held it out. "Go get the porridge. If she won't eat it, then we can't let it go to waste."

No matter how hard they tried to convince Lidia, she refused to eat, so Mischka split the lukewarm porridge with Aurora. This was happening too often.

Moments later, Mischka heard the whistle to get to work. Aurora put an arm around Lidia and guided her forward. Mischka tucked the tin into Lidia's pocket and waved at Jolanta who fell in step with her. Jolanta shivered and let out a squeak. "I'll be glad to get into the warmth of the factory. My feet feel like bricks of ice."

"Mine, too."

But it wasn't much warmer in the building. Mischka had no way of knowing the temperature outside, but it was unusually cold, and whatever warmth they generated on the fifth floor was sucked right outside, replaced by numbingly frigid air. The windows were rimed with frost. In some places, the ice was a half-inch thick.

She could barely make her fingers guide the fabric into the sewing machine. Next to her, Lidia stared off in the distance for so long that the youngest supervisor, Greta, came down the row and whacked her on the back with her baton. "Get to work."

Lidia bent her head and pushed the material under the foot of the sewing machine, but it jammed immediately.

"You stupid sow. Look what you've done." Lidia pulled at the material, managing only to tangle it further. Greta struck her again. This time Lidia didn't even flinch.

Mischka wondered where Pippi was. But she couldn't rely on Pippi for everything. "Ma'am, might I help?"

Greta turned to her in a fury. "Mind your own business."

Mischka winced, her panic rising. But there was nothing to be done. If she interrupted again, it would only result in a beating. She cocked her head and glanced back at Aurora who sat three machines over and one row behind. Aurora shook her head fiercely. Ah, Aurora knew her too well. But what did she have to lose? She'd been beaten before.

She pushed down on the sewing machine and stood. Her stiff legs were sluggish to respond, but she stepped over next to Greta. "I'll fix this for you, ma'am."

The short supervisor didn't have much room to draw back, so her first blow was feeble and glanced off Mischka's left shoulder. The second time, the seamstress in the next machine ducked out of the way, so Greta's recoil was stronger, more powerful. The blow struck Mischka on the collarbone. A line of heat, like a bolt of lightning, ran down to her hand. Then her arm went numb. She cried out in pain, bit her tongue, and tensed. The next blow drove her back. She tripped over the metal leg of one of the machines and went down on her backside. She heard Elke call out Greta's name.

As the baton cut through the air, Mischka caught sight of Lidia. Her mouth was open, her eyes wide and shocked. The thin club made a whistling sound just before it struck Mischka above the left ear. She let the momentum carry her sideways and to the floor where she lay stunned. The pain ricocheted in her head, and keeping still seemed a good idea. A vision of Arben's dark hair and sparkling cruel face flashed in her mind's eye before merciful darkness blotted it out.

PIPPI HAD OVERSLEPT. She awakened feeling sore and fatigued. Emotionally, however, she felt a lightness and sense of hope she hadn't felt for months. She thought of the cache of passports hidden in a slice of the mattress at the head of her bed. Now if only she could figure out a way to get Mischka and her friends away from the camp to someplace safe, they could sit out the rest of the war with papers that could pass the scrutiny of any official they ran into who was still trying to behave as if everything were normal. She'd dreamed of escapes and journeys all night long.

She dressed, plaited her hair into a French-style braid, and tucked it under, then meandered down the stairs, greeting Thomas, the cook, who was cutting potatoes for the noon meal. She picked up a muffin to eat on the way across to the factory, put on her coat, grabbed her muffler, and let herself out.

Swirls of snow blew off the roof and sifted inside her collar before she got the muffler adjusted. The change in temperature outside from the warmth of the quarters came as quite a shock, and she hustled across the open space, finishing the last bit of the muffin. Inside the factory, it didn't feel much warmer, but at least there was no breeze and no snow fell on her head. By the time she'd mounted the ten flights of stairs to the fifth floor, her legs were definitely warm. As she approached the doorway to the workroom, the hum of the machines died off, and she heard a thump, then a grunt and a loud crack.

Puzzled, Pippi was unbuttoning her coat as she stepped through the doorway and passed in front of the desks. Few of the seamstresses were facing front. Nearly all were looking toward the back corner of the room where Elke and Greta stood.

"What's going on?" Pippi called out as she loosened her muffler.

Greta spun around. The expression on her face gave Pippi a start. Greta rarely looked guilty. Pippi strode to the windows and turned to walk up that aisle. Oh, my God. Mischka. "What happened?"

Greta's eyes narrowed. "She attacked me."

Pippi sucked in a breath and exclaimed, "She's bleeding!" She fell to her knees next to the limp figure. "Oh, hell and damnation." The skin over Mischka's ear was so thin it had split, and a gush of blood had run down her neck and dripped onto the floor. Pippi pressed her fingertips against the grayish skin at Mischka's neck. The pulse beat regularly.

Heart in her throat, Pippi looked up at the two Germans. "What really happened?" She asked the question softly, her mind in a whirl.

Elke pressed her lips together and looked away. Greta glared. "She came at me. I have the right to defend myself." She tipped her chin up. "I shall call the soldiers. They can take her to the infirmary."

Pippi had heard the expression "seeing red," but she'd never personally experienced it until now. Suddenly everything turned blood red except a small circle that held Greta's haughty face. Pippi clambered to her feet and sprang toward her. "You cruel shrew. You've been nothing but vicious since the first day I arrived."

Greta backed up and bumped into a sewing machine. "You're a sap. A weak and pathetic—"

Pippi grabbed the front of Greta's wool coat. "And you're a brute. Heartless. Barbaric. Give me that!" She wrested the baton from Greta's hand. "You are instructed never to use a weapon upon these people again."

"They're not people," Greta said with a snarl. "They're one step up from animals, and I have the right to protect myself from them." She spat on the hardwood floor. "I never wanted this job. I hate working with these stinking vermin."

Panting with fury, Pippi shoved her.

"Stop it. I'll put you on report."

"I don't care." Pippi grasped the lapels of Greta's coat so tightly that her hands hurt. "Get out. And don't come back. I don't care if they assign you to latrine duty. You're not working in here ever again."

When Pippi released her hold of the coat, Greta smirked. "I could tell she was your little pet." When Pippi surged forward, Elke grabbed her arm and stepped in front of her. Greta sauntered to the coat hook and took down her hat and scarf. "I *will* report you, and I'm also sending up the soldiers to take your little pet away."

Pippi's mouth went dry, and she couldn't make herself say what she wanted—which would have consigned her to the confessional for damning the other woman.

She turned back to Mischka and was surprised to see that her eyes were open. With the barest hint of a smile, she pushed herself up on one elbow. "Will I be punished for sleeping on the job?"

It took every bit of willpower to keep from throwing herself upon Mischka. "You've bled quite a bit. Don't touch your neck or head. I'll get a bandage."

"Luckily, Arben thoroughly conditioned my head. It may bleed, but it doesn't easily break."

Pippi whispered, "This really isn't funny." In a normal voice, she said, "Can you get up?"

In broken German, one of the French workers said, "I could help her, Fräulein." She didn't move until Pippi told her it was all right, then the girl assisted Mischka to her feet. Mischka staggered to the chair at her sewing machine.

Every worker gawked at Pippi. "Don't just sit there," she said. "Get back to your sewing. We have a lot of work to do."

In seconds, the humming and buzzing from the machines started once more.

Elke backed toward the windows. "I had nothing to do with this."

Pippi summoned her to the outside hall, out of earshot of the seamstresses. When they got there, she asked what had happened.

"I—I don't know. She just went crazy."

"But why? These women aren't violent. Greta was lying

about being attacked, wasn't she?"

Elke shifted her shoulders. "You have to understand, Pauline. Her fiancé has been missing in action for six weeks."

"My husband died in battle. Does that give me license to kill a woman?"

Elke's eyes widened, and she gulped. "No, no, of course not. I had no idea that you lost your—"

Pippi raised the hand holding the baton. "Enough. I shouldn't have mentioned it. We've all lost something or someone." She suddenly felt like sitting down.

"In her defense, Pauline, Greta is under a great deal of pressure."

"Pressure? These women are the ones under pressure." As if on cue, someone let loose with deep racking coughs. "They're sick, they're malnourished, and they're freezing. There's simply no excuse for beating any of them."

"I know, I know."

Pippi thought Elke looked properly penitent. "Where is Bernadette?"

"She was ill this morning. I don't know if she'll make it over here. She has the cough and sneezing like the workers do."

"I wish she'd been here."

"Yes, she tends to have a calming effect on Greta. I'm truly sorry that I, on the other hand, did not. It all happened so fast."

Pippi patted Elke's upper arm. "I understand." She turned at the sound of heavy footsteps on the stairs. Oh no. Did Greta do what she threatened?

Two soldiers—not guards—rounded the newel post. Both of them held pistols, pointed at the floor, in their right hands and their rifles in their left. The one in the lead said, "Good morning to you both. I understand you have had a minor insurrection."

Elke stepped to the side to let Pippi handle the matter. Pippi smiled sweetly at the soldier and rolled her eyes. "I suppose that young woman exaggerated the story a bit. We haven't got any problem. Everything is under tight control." She smacked the baton against her palm for emphasis.

"Just for the record, we would like to inspect the work area for ourselves."

She leaned toward him to look at the insignia on his coat. "Why certainly, Corporal. Be my guest." With a flourish, she stepped back next to Elke. The soldiers passed them, their boots dripping with melting snow. She didn't go to the doorway, but sagged against the wall and said a prayer consisting of only two words, "Please God, please God," repeated over and over.

A full minute passed before the two men returned. "I don't

see anything out of order, but if you have any trouble at all, please send for us."

"Oh, yes, we will." He stood a moment longer studying her face. "Something else, Corporal?"

He glanced at his companion, then cleared his throat. "I was wondering. These trousers—they don't fit properly, and I, well—"

"Oh, goodness," Pippi said. "That won't do. Can you send them over to me at your earliest convenience? I would be honored to alter them. What's wrong with the fit?"

Blood rushed to his face. "To be honest, they're too tight in the, you know—" he dropped his voice "—the crotch."

PIPPI HUDDLED IN the concave section of her bed, shivering in the blankets. She couldn't seem to get warm. Every time she thought of the events of the day, she felt like throwing up. She lay with her face to the wall and shook with silent sobs. She thought of Mischka, who right now must also be trembling on her cold pallet in the barracks. Would she be all right? Would she recover from the beating? Pippi felt she should have done something to protect her, to protect all of them.

She felt such shame—shame that she lay in a dry, clean bed with a belly full of food. If she were hungry, she could raid the pantry with impunity. If she were uncomfortable, she could get another pillow. If bored, there were books to read on the shelves in the living room. While she lived in comfort, outside her quarters hundreds of men and women lay starving and miserable in the cold. The enormity of that was difficult to grasp.

Despite the trouble she could have gotten into, Pippi had taken Mischka down to the fourth floor, sat her on a crate, and cleaned and sterilized the slice above her ear. The inch-long gash wouldn't close properly, so she'd sewn it together with the finest thread she could find.

Pippi shuddered. Stitching up the wound had been awful. Mischka sat motionless with a grimace on her face. She never made a sound, never flinched. Pippi had to stop repeatedly to close her eyes and breathe. She'd asked Mischka how she could stand the pain without any sort of numbing or sedative and received back only a shrug.

So much pain. So much horror. Pippi wondered how the laborers survived as long as they did. She didn't think she could endure—surely not for as long as Mischka had. She thought of Greta, of her cruelty and callousness. What was wrong with everyone? How had this terrible war corrupted people so grievously? The sick feeling in her stomach abated some as her anger rose. She was getting a glimmer of how an otherwise normal person could kill another human being. Rage was a potent motivator. If she'd had a weapon more powerful than a baton, she feared she might have used it on Greta. Bad enough that she so despised what Greta had done, but she also abhorred the emotions Greta's actions aroused in her. That she wanted to physically harm the other woman meant she was no better than Greta, and that was sobering.

Many years earlier, when she had talked to Emil about his experiences with the Roma and in the Great War, she had wondered how her gentle, kind brother had managed to shoot anyone. Over time, he'd made her understand the idea of protecting oneself. Self-defense is, after all, one of the few acceptable reasons for taking a life. The fact that several hundred men and women in the camp didn't rise up and kill their captors amazed Pippi. Every one of them could claim self-defense. Instead, they were treated with indignity and cruelty, and one by one, they sickened and died, never putting up a fight. How soon before Mischka joined the dead?

A shaft of light cut into the room, and Pippi hastily wiped her face. Agnes Braunhaus stood in the doorway, a cigarette in her hand. "You awake?"

"Yes."

"I heard about what happened today." Pippi didn't respond. "You're going to get yourself into serious trouble, Pauline." Pippi heard her suck in a lungful of smoke. "What do you have to say for yourself?"

Pippi didn't think there was anything she could say to explain her actions or her feelings. She wasn't a silly teenager. In fact, she thought she was probably as old as—or older—than Agnes. Agnes. How did a woman become like Agnes? She was heartless, so there was no use trying to appeal to the woman's compassion. Pippi said, "I'll be glad when the war is over."

Agnes let out a snort. "You're too weak, too helpless and faint-hearted. Pauline, you must keep the end in sight. The means may be painful, but they justify the end, and that will be a place of honor for *Der Führer* and for all those who respect his policies and follow the rules."

"That's how you see it?"

"Most assuredly."

"Under the circumstances, what would your advice be?"

Agnes let out a sigh, and the bitter smell of the cigarette smoke caused Pippi's stomach to roil. "You owe Greta an apology. She was doing what is her right and responsibility—to discipline the lazy and shiftless with whom you have the misfortune of working."

"I see."

"So you'll apologize?"

"I'll carefully consider your advice."

"Good. Very good. Well, I'll let you sleep. I go on duty in less than an hour."

"Stay warm, Agnes."

"I'll try. It certainly is quite cold out. Good night, Pauline."

She pulled the door shut leaving Pippi in the pitch-black darkness. Agnes could go to hell — and take Greta with her. Pippi would lie naked in the snow before she ever apologized for being compassionate to another human being.

Chapter
Thirty-One

New York City, November 1989 (Snow Moon)

PIPPI FELL SILENT, looking first at Mischka, then at her grandson.

Tobar said, "Did she die?"

"Of course not. She's sitting right here, still with a scar over her ear, but her hair covers it."

"No. Not *Beebee* Mischka." His face was pale, and his voice shook with concern. "The girl Lidia, who would not eat her porridge. Did she die?"

Mischka nodded. "Yes, she did. She gave up one day and couldn't go on. Without hope, no one could face that place."

Tobar frowned in anguish. "But that's unfair. Totally unfair."

Pippi agreed with him. She was—even now, forty-four years later—still amazed at what had transpired all those years ago and that she had lived to tell the tale. For a moment, she considered they might have gotten in too deep, that they shouldn't be telling him all of this. He was so young. But he took it in with grace—and with ardent interest. Perhaps they could continue.

"What about Emil?" he asked. "You haven't told me zip about him for the longest time. What happened to him?"

Mischka asked, "Do you recall anything at all that the family has said regarding your Uncle Emil?"

"I remember him a little, from when I was a boy. He was very old, and I don't remember anything special anyone has said." His face became alarmed. "What happened to him? Something bad?"

"All in good time, Tobar. All in good time."

"Grandma!"

He looked back and forth between them, and Pippi had to suppress a smile. "Don't you want to know how we got out of the labor camp?"

"Well, yes, but I want to know what happened to everyone else, too. Especially Emil and Mikhail and all their kids."

Mischka patted his pajama-clad knee. "As your wicked grandmother said, all in good time."

Chapter
Thirty-Two

PIPPI STOOD SHIVERING in the back of the factory room, her arms crossed over her wool coat. They were down to fifty-eight seamstresses, and Vogel would no longer let her recruit workers from the loading area. An aura of desperation shrouded the camp and its leaders. Major Fischer hadn't met with her for the last two weeks, and Pippi didn't have any problem with that. The last time she had seen him, he'd been nervous and wild-eyed, preoccupied with the war. He'd spoken kindly, but sent her away after she'd made a brief report. He seemed completely disinterested in whether or not the quotas were filled.

Ten days had passed since the last delivery of staples and supplies. Though occasional cargo trucks still arrived carrying clothing, boots, and shoes, there had been no shipments of fresh food. At breakfast this morning, the cook had been out of milk and had announced that he was short of cheese and yeast and would be conserving foodstuffs until future goods were delivered.

Pippi's heart fell. That would make it more difficult to sneak food for Mischka. She could only hope that a transport truck got through soon. They hadn't received the post for weeks either.

She shivered again and tucked her gloved hands under her armpits. One of the seamstresses in front of her let out a whimper, then looked up, fear etched into her features due to her outburst. Pippi sighed. Schuster wouldn't burn any of the coal, and everyone up here was freezing to death. How ridiculous.

"That's it," she said. "Mariel." The young woman froze. "Mischka. Aurora, everyone." Every woman stopped what she was doing. At the desk behind Pippi, Bernadette asked what was going on. Pippi waved a hand toward the women. "We're all far too cold. I couldn't run a sewing machine in these temperatures if my life depended upon it. I don't know how these workers are doing it. I'm going to disburse additional clothing." Bernadette frowned but didn't respond, so Pippi gave a toss of her head. "Come on, you three. Let's make this easier on all of you."

The women followed Pippi down to the third floor. Scores of crates were stacked haphazardly. Pippi went to an open one and pulled out a wad of used clothing. "Take stockings, shoes, gloves, boots, whatever you need to stay as warm as possible. You may use any of these items for lap blankets as well."

"I'm well provided for," Mischka said. "Perhaps the others—"

"There's no shortage. For once, you're all going to take whatever you need."

Mariel whispered, "But what if we're caught?"

"You will not be caught—and even if someone does make a comment, you are to refer them to me." She turned aside and clapped her hands together to get the blood circulating. "I should have thought of this two months ago. Once you're outfitted, please go upstairs and send down three more."

Mischka said, "There are some who will have difficulty."

"That's true. You three have my permission to determine what those women need. Take it up to them and try to get them fitted. Send down the next three, and let's see if we can't warm everyone enough to keep from freezing solid to their machines."

Two hours later, Pippi turned out the light on the second floor. They had made a dent in only a few crates, and there were still scores of wood containers left untouched. She should have thought of this much sooner. What an idiot she thought she was.

TIME PASSED IN a kaleidoscope of cold and fear and heightened tension. The winter winds lessened, and the temperature rose, but the cold and damp still made everyone's bones ache. Mischka slept much warmer, as did her companions, and as each day passed, she looked forward to spring.

Lidia wasted away until she resembled a small child with giant blue eyes. She no longer coughed, but moved as though in a trance. Aurora could get her to drink, but she refused food.

Walking back to the barracks after dark one day in late April, Mischka took Aurora's arm. "It won't be long now, Aurora. If Lidia doesn't get medical care and nourishment, she's going to die." They strode behind Magda and Jolanta, who held Lidia up between them.

"I know. I pray for her each night."

"Why does your God not—what is the word?"

"Intercede?"

"Step in. Save her. Save us. Free us from this frozen hell."

"I don't know."

"Does this mean there is no God?"

"I'm not sure, my friend. God is merely giving us strength, I think. I feel something — something that powers me, and it must be God. I have hope within me, and I believe it's from God. Some of the theologians speak of free will, and if we have free will, then I think that God does not entirely control our destinies. But He gives me hope."

They reached the barracks and trudged in. The autumn before, all of the women had agreed to move to the center of the barracks and to do all they could to conserve heat. No one slept alone. Three or four women squeezed together on every pallet, and the chilly bottom and middle racks were unused. Mischka huddled with Lidia and Aurora and another girl, Layla, whose friends had died the previous month. Mischka waited for things to calm down, then did her evening reconnaissance for food. After sharing the meager rations Pippi had filched, she fell to sleep quickly.

In the deepest part of the night, Mischka awakened, her neck prickling. On edge, she waited for the sound of the guard, but all was quiet in the barracks. She sat up and looked around. Muted light slanted in through a window near the south door. That door hadn't opened since they had all lain down to sleep. Mischka never failed to awaken at two-hour intervals, and unless she had lost all sense of time, no one had come for the ten o'clock, midnight, and now the two o'clock march through the barracks. That had never happened before.

She clambered from the pallet and looked out the window. She couldn't spot the soldier usually posted near the gate. The gate was shut, but the light usually burning in the guard booth was out. What was going on?

Heart beating fast, she opened the door and slipped out. She headed toward the latrine, but kept an eye on everything. As she reached for the wood door handle, she saw a tiny orange flare from a cigarette twenty yards away.

A deep voice said, "Halt. Who goes there?"

She heard the rustle of movement as two men materialized from out of the shadows. Mischka pulled open the door. "May I use the latrine?"

"Oh. Go ahead."

The two guards walked past, one saying to the other, "They have surrounded Berlin. What hope have we now?"

"We can't have lost the war," the other man said. "It's not possible."

"This is my thought as well, but..."

The voices drifted in the wind. Mischka stood inside the stinking wood structure, and glorious hope expanded in her chest. She hustled back to the barracks and climbed up into bed. "Aurora. Lidia." Aurora opened her eyes and groaned. "I've just heard good news. Berlin may soon fall."

Aurora rolled on her side. "And where did you get this marvelous news?"

"Two guards talking."

"I hope it's true."

Mischka froze, smelling a familiar odor, but since she wasn't in the latrine, she shouldn't be smelling it now. "Lidia," she whispered. "Lidia." She touched the young woman's neck and found it cool, with no blood pumping. "Oh, no," she moaned. "No."

"What is it?"

"Lidia. She's gone. She can't die now. We're on the brink of rescue."

Aurora reached across the girl to squeeze Mischka's arm. "I was afraid this would happen."

Mischka crawled halfway down the ladder. With Aurora guiding, she lifted Lidia's body and carried it to the lowest bunk. They set her there face up, straightened her clothing, and stood hand in hand staring down at her.

Aurora let out a choking sound, and Mischka put her arms around her friend and held her close. "She was so young, Mischka. Too young. Far too young. My children are her age. What about my children? Has someone cared for them?" Her sobs awakened a woman in the next bunk.

"Shhh," Mischka said to her. "It's nothing. Go back to sleep." She tightened her grip on Aurora and ran a hand over the wool cap Aurora wore. "We must be strong. Call on that God you say is giving you hope and strength."

"But it's not fair that she should die — especially if the war is nearly over."

"No, it's not fair." Because their pallet was soiled, they climbed into an empty bunk. Mischka lay shivering in the dark and thought of all Lidia had been through. A cold rage built until she couldn't help thinking that if she had a machine gun, she would go out right now and use it on every German in sight. Braunhaus. Vogel. Mow them down. Kill them all. She'd like to see each soldier and guard die slow, painful, bloody deaths. And then she thought of Pippi. She, too, was German. Even Bernadette wasn't so bad. The cook in the mess shed was a tired old man who was never cruel, so he wasn't deserving of death either.

They were all stuck here, at the whim of a madman, and there was nothing they could do but wait. And, oh, how hard it was to wait.

STUNNING NEWS CAME on the first of May. Adolf Hitler had committed suicide the day before.

Pippi sat at the breakfast table with Bernadette, Agnes, and Felix Schuster. She listened to the talk around her and thought that Hitler's death hadn't happened soon enough.

Thomas, the cook, came to the table and slapped down a pot of thin oatmeal and some stale rolls. He slid into the chair at the head of the table, wiped his perspiring forehead with the corner of his apron, and said, "Those damn Allied bastards."

Felix Schuster seemed to be in a state of shock. "Germany cannot — must not — lose this war."

"I don't think we have any say in it," Bernadette said dryly.

Schuster's eyes narrowed, and he looked at her with hatred distorting his face. "And what do you know? Women have no idea what war is like."

"*Der Führer* cannot be dead." Agnes burst into tears. "He is my guiding light, my heart, my soul." Pippi looked at her in amazement, but the anguish in her voice was real. "How could he leave us — leave me?"

"Looking out for his own hide," one of the guards said. "I expect those bastard Allies would have been merciless."

Pippi rose. She hadn't been able to eat a bite, and she didn't want to stay in the company of a group that was mourning someone she despised.

"You're not going over to the factory now, are you?" Bernadette asked. "You haven't eaten."

"I'm not hungry."

Agnes wailed and shook a fist. "How could anyone eat at a time like this? Our country's greatest leader is dead."

Pippi rushed to the closet, threw on her coat, and hurried out the door. Thirty minutes later, when the whistle blew and the first of the laborers shuffled in, she watched for Mischka, caught her eye, and smiled. From the look on Mischka's face, she knew that somehow the news must have trickled down. Pippi felt rather than saw a sense of excitement in the room, an energy that she had never sensed before. It was hope.

She stood at the window and watched the sun move higher in the sky. The sewing machines hummed behind her, providing a sense of normalcy, but the workers weren't sewing uniforms. Pippi had invited them to select materials from the storage floor to adapt whatever they needed for traveling clothes. Some of them now wore good leather boots and layers of shabby dresses and sweaters. Mischka was clad in wool trousers and a white shirt, with blue suspenders under her coat. No one had chosen the grays and greens and browns of the German military.

Pippi heard the grinding of gears and peered down. A *Kübelwagen* suddenly appeared to her right and raced along the dirt road between the factory and the barracks. Another followed moments later.

Bernadette came to stand by Pippi's side. "What do you think is going on?"

Pippi shrugged. A soldier and two guards came from the south and ran along the track below them. Pippi could see that the south gate was closed, but no one guarded it now.

From the north came the unmistakable sound of a gun being fired. Every sewing machine on the floor stopped, and Pippi found herself suddenly surrounded by women. She reached for the bottom of the window, and other hands helped press it upwards. In seconds, they opened all the windows, and five dozen heads craned to look out.

Pippi wished she could see more. The women's and men's barracks were visible, but the factory wall blocked the buildings on the northwest end of the camp.

"Look!" someone called out. Four *Kübelwagens*, two smaller autos, and three cargo trucks headed in a line toward the north gate. Five people raced after the vehicles, frantically waving. The rear cargo truck came to a halt. A soldier jumped out of the back and threatened them with his gun. The five men behind made wild gestures.

"They're the civilian workers," Bernadette said in wonder. "Isn't that Herr Schuster in the gray suit?"

Pippi squinted, but the figures were too far away to be sure. "If I don't miss my guess, Bernie, I think our brave military is in rapid retreat."

"And we're being left behind?"

"My God," a voice murmured. Pippi glanced to her right, then followed the direction a woman was pointing.

To the north, past the broad apron that surrounded the gate, far out on the flat lands stippled with new grass, clouds of dust coated the horizon.

Elke ran into the room, wringing her hands. "The Allies are coming! We're being abandoned."

Greta followed on Elke's heels, stopping behind the crush of women at the window. "What do we do? They've left us behind. What shall we do?"

Pippi looked out again. Six lumps on the horizon grew larger. Tanks. Other vehicles followed. And then she saw troops. Hundreds of men on foot, in formation.

"We're saved!" a woman screamed.

"We'll finally be freed," someone else said in Polish.

"Free!"

"*Libre!*"

"*Frei!*"

Pippi leaned out the window. The German entourage was slowing. The last cargo truck jerked to a halt and backed up in a hurry. The other trucks followed, then the cars and *Kübelwagens*. The seven vehicles passed under the windows, their engines grinding and whirring. They went to the south gate, and two soldiers jumped out of the truck and opened it. Pippi looked up the long, steep hill beyond the convoy. She wondered if the vehicles could make it through the rain-sodden earth in time to get away, but before she could consider that further, a shout went up. Tanks hit the north gate and knocked the high fence flat. Men marching double time spilled into the camp.

The first German cargo truck cleared the south gate and attempted to climb the hill. Great clods of dirt shot out from the back tires, but it mired in the mud, as did the next two trucks. Gray-clad bodies peeled out of the stuck vehicles and dove for cover.

And then the Allied soldiers were upon them.

"Surrender!" The word was shouted in German over and over, but the Germans didn't heed it. Surrender, Pippi thought. Give it up. Just stop and surrender, you fools.

One of the *Kübelwagens* passed through the gate. Instead of going uphill, the driver wheeled to the left and headed for the trees. Smoke shot from the muzzle of a launcher held by a kneeling soldier. The shell blasted through the wire fence and struck the rear of the *Kübelwagen*. The explosion was deafening. The vehicle sat there, smoking, and no one got out.

The sound of machine gun fire filled the air.

"Get down," Bernadette said. "We could be hit by a stray bullet."

None of the seamstresses moved, and neither did Pippi.

The Germans didn't fight much longer. Their men fell, shouting and screaming, and the advancing troops renewed their calls for surrender. The remaining German soldiers, at least the ones Pippi could see, dropped their weapons.

Someone put a warm hand on her shoulder, and Pippi looked back, expecting Elke. Instead Mischka said, "We haven't much time now. We must cut your hair."

"What?"

"Someone get the scissors." She guided Pippi to the nearest chair and shoved her into it.

"But—but—"

Mischka squatted in front of her. "There is no other way. Your hair will grow back. But not if you're not alive." Aurora shoved the scissors into Mischka's hands.

"I don't understand," Pippi said.

"Those are Russian soldiers." Mischka opened the jaws of the scissors. "You must become one of us. Otherwise, you'll be taken captive as their prisoner of war and a collaborator with the Nazi machine."

Pippi blanched. She hadn't thought about what would happen between liberation of the labor camp and her arrival back home. The other civilian workers had been in such a state of disbelief and denial that the subject hadn't come up. Now she needed to think fast. What would happen to all of them? The Russians would provide food and arrange for some sort of transport—but only for those they viewed as on their side. Who knew what fate their enemies would face. "Cut it."

Both Mischka and Aurora began hacking at her hair. Mariel caught the pieces and jammed them into a little cloth sack. Tears came to Pippi's eyes—not because of the loss of her hair, but because she didn't feel she deserved to be taken in by these women who had suffered so much for so long. "I should have done more for you," she whispered.

Mischka paused from her chopping. "What?"

"I should have done more."

"Quiet now. We must hurry."

Her head felt light and cool when they were done. She blushed, thinking she must look ridiculous. Someone appeared at her side with shabby but sturdy clothes and outerwear.

"Quickly," Mischka said. "You have to look like the rest of us."

Half of the women still watched what was happening outside, but the other half looked at her with solemn eyes. Pippi glanced around and found Bernadette. "Bernie, you're next." Bernadette gulped and her eyes widened, but she dropped into a seat for her haircut.

Mischka handed the scissors to someone else and called out, "You two." She pointed at Elke and Greta. "Find more scissors, and we'll take care of you."

Greta's face tightened into a grimace. "I'll just bet you'll take care of us. None of you will touch a hair on my head."

"You're even stupider than I had thought," Mischka said.

Greta pushed past two of the women, nearly knocking one off her feet. "Who are you to talk to me that way? You're nothing but scum. You're all filthy vermin, and the only thing I regret is that you didn't die when I was forced to discipline you. Degenerate scum. That's what you are."

Mischka tipped her head up and stood tall. "This is exactly what the Russians will think when they catch sight of you. I shall look forward to the show."

Hands balled into fists, Greta backed up. Her face tightened into a mask of fury. "We'll just see about that." She turned on her heel and stomped out of the room.

"You?" Mischka said, with a nod to Elke. "Are you as big a fool as that one?"

"No." Elke trembled as she sat in a rickety chair. She was so pale that Pippi thought she was going to faint. "I would be honored if any one of you would give me the same treatment as Pauline."

THE NEXT FEW hours passed in a whirlwind as Mischka and the seamstresses stood silently observing from the fifth floor window. The Russian soldiers rounded up the Germans, searched them all, and made them sit on the ground against the south fence. The Nazis who had been injured weren't given first aid. Mischka heard several shots over a fifteen-minute period. Bodies were dragged away from the stalled cargo trucks and placed in a row along the fence. The vehicles were driven back inside the gates.

The Russian soldiers scrambled through the camp like a pack of wild dogs on a hunt, calling out to one another as they found each barracks empty. When they turned to the factories and other buildings, Mischka moved away from the window. She heard the sound of footsteps and foreign words shouted far below. "I think we had better sit down and be as calm as possible."

Wordlessly, the seamstresses and their shorn supervisors sat at the treadle machines. Most of them laced their hands together on top of the machines.

Aurora burst into tears. Mischka whispered, "What is it? What's wrong?"

"I think we're about to be saved, but I'm scared to death."

"Don't be afraid."

"I can't help it. What if they hurt us?"

"They won't." Mariel spoke up, her Polish deeply accented by her French tongue. "They now get big eyeful of skinny, ugly women and a noseful of our stink. I think they will run from us."

A ripple of laughter swept the room, and then all were quiet. Mischka looked around and counted. Fifty-two, not counting Pippi and the two others. Only fifty-two had survived out of hundreds, perhaps thousands. A deep sense of sadness passed over her, sadness for Nelka, and a deep grief for Lidia, who didn't live to see this day.

She could hear them coming, systematically searching the building from the bottom up. Voices called out, but she heard no gunshots. Heavy footfalls clomped up the stairs...and when the first soldier peeked into the room, rifle at the ready, the room was so silent that Mischka could hear her heart beat. She glanced to the side at Pippi who faced forward with a frightened look on her face.

More footsteps, and then four soldiers entered the room. They were young, and each sported a couple days' growth of beard. The man in the lead asked something, but he spoke a language Mischka didn't know. The soldiers uttered a torrent of words, arguing, talking over one another. The one in the lead said, "*Sprechen Sie Deutsche?*"

No one answered.

He looked around the room, grinned, then spoke in halting Polish. "No German here, I see. Anybody speaking Polish?"

"*Ja!*" cried out many voices. The silent room was transformed—electrified—by the soldier's inquiry. Women called out questions. Someone said, "Thank you, thank you," over and over. Many began to cry.

"Wait. Stop," the soldier said. He leaned his rifle barrel into the crook of his arm and waved with the other hand. "Quiet, quiet." They calmed down. "Stay at peace a moment. We return with food and better translator."

"Oh, my God," Aurora sobbed. "My husband, my sons, I hope they're alive."

Mischka reached over and gripped her friend's arm. "They will be. They must be."

BY SUNDOWN, EVERY woman laborer throughout the camp—some two hundred ragged survivors—had been brought to the factory. They were allowed to find suitable clothes and shoes, but they weren't fed again until after dark. The soldiers led them out of the factory to the mess shed, apologizing that the food was simple. After having had runny soups, tasteless porridge, and no meat for so long, Mischka could find no fault with the meal. A soldier outside the shed handed out small loaves of bread from what looked to be a gunnysack. For a moment she was taken aback. She had this entire loaf for herself?

He gestured for her to move toward the shack, so she took a bite as she stepped along. The crust was dry and tough, but the bread inside was soft and fragrant of yeast and oats and wheat. The two men ladling the soup called it *schi*. Made with sauerkraut, chunks of carrot, and pieces of beef brisket in a thick sauce, it was delicious — almost as good as the *puyo* Mischka's mother had made. The only thing missing was the garlic.

She cradled her bowl in one hand and the bread in the other, as she hastened to squat next to a barracks wall beside Pippi and Aurora. All around them, women talked with hope-filled voices.

Aurora elbowed her. "I asked when we'll be allowed to see our men."

"And?"

"We're going over to a hall in a short while to be reunited. I'm praying."

Mischka looked up at the moon rising in the sky. Soon another month would pass, and it would be Seed Moon, time to plant seeds of desire. She desired nothing more than to find her family and all be together again. She envied Aurora. Tonight she would know if her husband and sons were still alive, but it could be months before Mischka found out about her own family and *kumpania*.

She finished the broth in her bowl and rose. "I'm going to ask for more. Anyone else?"

Pippi handed over her metal bowl. "If they'll allow it, I'd like some. And when you come back, we need to figure out how to get hold of the passports."

"Where are they?"

"In my quarters."

Mischka shook her head. "I don't think you're going to be able to get in there."

"I have to try."

"Maybe. Maybe not. Maybe we have to let them go."

"But we need them for — for travel." Her voice sounded terrified.

Mischka squatted down and put a hand on Pippi's knee. "We're all refugees now. You can be anybody you want to be."

Chapter
Thirty-Three

New York City, November 1989 (Snow Moon)

"WHAT HAPPENED THEN?" Tobar asked. "What about Aurora's family? Were any of them alive?"

Mischka smiled at him and briefly stroked his hair from his eyes. "All of them were safe. The younger son was sick with that coughing fever, but once he was given food and adequate clean water, he improved quickly. The husband could hardly believe his wife was alive. He kept remarking how thin she was, and she kept saying, 'My boys are men now,' with amazement in her voice. What a wonderful reunion. I remember it with such joy."

"But there was no one there for you, *Beebee*."

"No, there wasn't. But I had Pippi and Aurora and so many of the other girls to rejoice with."

"Did Aurora come to America?"

"No. She and Janek went back and reclaimed their land."

"So you never saw her again."

"Not after the fall of 1945," Mischka said, "but she wrote to me several times a year right up until her death in 1985. She was a fine friend to the end. I kept every one of her letters. After she died, her granddaughter sent me everything I had written to her. If you ever decide to be the family historian, you may have them for your collection."

"I may take you up on that," he said. "I'm still waiting to hear about Emil. And what happened to the mean ones, that horrible Vogel and Greta and all the rest?"

Pippi rose and settled next to Mischka on the couch and leaned into her. "This next part is not so easy, *liebling*."

Mischka gazed at her first, then at Tobar's worried face. She could read his curiosity and worry—and impatience.

He clenched his hands in fists, and his face took on a fierce look. "Oh, no. You're not quitting now. Tell me why it's not easy?"

"It just isn't," Pippi said with a sigh. "First, the Russians lined up all the soldiers—the Germans, I mean—and shot them. Yes, I know it sounds shocking. I was shocked at the time. You see, that means your grandfather was executed."

"What?"

Mischka thought the blank look on Tobar's face would have been comical if she hadn't known how serious the topic was.

Pippi reached across Mischka and patted Tobar's ankle. "Your blood grandfather was a soldier, Tobar. Wounded honorably in battle. He was Major Friedrich Fischer of the German army."

"No way."

Pippi laughed. "Yes, it was the way."

"But what about Grandfather François?"

"He died a long time before your father was born. He wasn't your blood grandfather, Tobar. We still honor his memory, though. He fought bravely in the war. Have your parents talked with you about any of this?"

Tobar hesitated. "Dad says he didn't have a father. He had *Beebee*, instead. They've told me a little about the war, but nothing like what you two have."

"I know you're not yet a grown-up," Mischka said, "but this is your family history. It's important for you to know and understand where you came from. Why your name is something to be proud of. And also why teaching language and history is so important to your parents. And travel! Your parents have the wanderlust, you know. When your father married the daughter of my nephew Mario, they vowed to see the world."

"I know that. I don't always like it."

"Some of our family have the wanderlust more than others," Mischka said. "When I was younger, I missed it, but now, not so much."

"And I never had it." Pippi shuddered. "I did more traveling than I ever wanted to do because of that damn war."

"Yes, it was a difficult, terrible time. You couldn't pay me to go back."

Pippi said, "We were caught in the midst of madness. We never spoke of it directly, but your grandfather, Friedrich, didn't enjoy overseeing the camp. He was a man with at least some principles. It must have been dreadful, his being expected to work for the Nazi regime when I'm not sure he entirely believed in it. I choose to remember Friedrich's uncertainty, not the actions that so many men like him took. What are your thoughts about it?"

"I—I don't know."

Tobar was obviously confused, but Mischka knew what was coming next. She took hold of Pippi's hand and gave it a squeeze of encouragement.

After a short pause, Pippi said, "Tobar, I walked out of the labor camp with more than my horrific experiences. When I finally arrived at the Delebecque home in Reims, France, I discovered I was pregnant with your father. Thank God for Grandpa François's mother. *Belle-mere.* That's French for mother-in-law — literally it means beautiful mother. Mother Richelle took care of me through the birthing of your father and long after."

"But — but — what about *Beebee* Mischka? Why couldn't she take care of you?"

"She was in Poland. And when we parted, I didn't even know I was with child."

Tobar's eyes were puzzled. "I thought Poland was far from France."

"It is," Mischka said. "We were separated — countries apart."

Pippi said, "Europe is big, and I don't know how many thousands of people — "

"Millions of people, I think," Mischka said.

"Yes, millions of people were on the move, trying to get back home."

"But, Grandma, how did you find each other again? How did you get here?"

Pippi patted his knee. "All in good time, Tobar. There I was among the millions who were displaced. What a mess. The Russians kept us at the factory labor camp for a week, but then we got word that Germany was truly defeated, and we could make our way home. At that point, the Russians readied us for departure, asking for addresses and family information. I couldn't say I was a German national. I told them my name was Pauline Delebecque. Which it was. And is. I gave them the address of your great-grandmother in Reims, France."

Mischka said, "And I told them I was Hungarian but that I had been married to Aurora's dead brother. I used Aurora's family address in Poland."

"Big mistake," Pippi said.

Tobar looked from one to another. "Why?"

"They transported us by train," Mischka said, "and we walked a good bit, too. But when we arrived at the refugee camp, your grandmother and I were separated, and there wasn't anything we could do. We vowed to find one another, but we had little time to make arrangements."

Pippi said, "I told her to write to Reims as soon as she got word about the *kumpania.*"

"And so I went with Aurora's family. It took two weeks just to journey from one camp to another and then make our way to their farm. By then it was mid-June, Dyad Moon, and we had scant time to plant. We worked from before first light until sundown to get crops planted in the field. Even so, we worried that the harvest would be too meager. I helped in the autumn, and once the crops were in, it was time to go find my family."

"Did you write to Grandma?"

"Yes, I did, but she never got the letters."

"Why?"

Pippi said, "Forty years ago, the postal service wasn't very efficient, Tobar, especially after a war."

"It was autumn then," Mischka said. "So I bid farewell to Aurora and Janek, and I made my way across Poland, heading for the Tatras mountains where last I'd seen my family."

Chapter
Thirty-Four

Southeastern Poland, November 1945 (Snow Moon)

WHAT IF SHE was the last Roma left?

Mischka hadn't seen a single *kumpania* in all the miles she had traveled. Where were the Roma? Where were her people? She needed to know the answer, but she was frightened of the truth.

Two days earlier, she'd managed to capture a horse that was roaming loose, reins dragging and the aged saddle twisted to the horse's side. She didn't know who the animal belonged to, but she wasn't one to ask questions. Though the mare appeared to be old, she was sturdy and looked as though she'd been well-tended. Better cared for than the women were in the camp. If only she had been fed half as well as this horse, she wouldn't be in so much pain. After two days of riding, Mischka's legs and backside were sorer than she could ever remember them being. But she was alive and eagerly thanked the gods, the moon, the sun, and any other deity deserving of gratitude.

The countryside was awash in gold and tan and orange. Most of the leaves had fallen, and what little foliage was left fluttered regularly off near-naked limbs. Some of the towns she passed were alive with commerce and activity. Others had burned-out storefronts and boarded-up houses.

She stopped at a sleepy backwater crossroads and entered a store that sold groceries, meat, some hardware, and fishing supplies. The proprietor stood behind the counter speaking about the war with three men covered in road dust. "Thank God the war's over," one man said. Someone grunted assent.

"The damn Germans gutted the country," a traveler said. "It'll be years before industry returns to a reasonable state."

The shopkeeper shook his head. "I have to admit, though, that we can thank the Germans for one thing. At least they took care of the Gypsy problem once and for all."

The glass jar of preserves Mischka held slipped from her fingers and crashed to the floor. She looked down at the mess and stepped back, then stomped out, fighting tears.

"Wait a minute," the shopkeeper called out. "Wait..."

Mischka mounted the horse and urged it out of town, her mind a whirling maelstrom of rage and worry. Where were her people?

She managed to get only a few hours of troubled sleep and rose at dawn to continue her journey. She reached an encampment near the Vistula River, and her mouth watered when she smelled the aromas from cooking fires around the area, but the people weren't Roma. The fish-smoking shacks were already busy with huge catches, and she bought two packages of smoked salmon wrapped in newspaper, enough for several meals.

She counted the money Aurora and Janek had insisted she take for helping with the harvest. With the high cost of food, she had enough *zloty* to last a few more days, and then she would have to scavenge or steal. Apples were plentiful. She picked them as she traveled and kept a gunnysack full of them strapped to the horse's saddle. Twice she'd come across edible pears and added them as well. But she had little time to tarry. Soon enough, winter would arrive. She needed to get over the Tatras Mountains and find the *kumpania*.

Many hours later, she came upon an area that had been burned. Fresh grasses and seedlings had sprouted, so the burn had occurred previous to this past spring. Across the scorched fields she saw a cluster of houses and nudged the horse toward them. A half-dozen little cottages stood in a row. The four to the west were collapsed and crumbling, but the other two were merely blackened and stood stolid, like two giant lumps of stone.

As she drew near, a drape lifted from a window, and she glimpsed a face before the curtain dropped. She rode toward that cottage, feeling the early evening air brisk against her face. Soon dusk would fall, and she entertained hope that perhaps tonight she might sleep out of the elements.

The front door of the cottage yawned open, and Mischka slowed the horse to a walk, but when she heard a click-click noise, she dug her heels in. With a startled whinny, the mare sprang forward. Someone shouted. She heard a gunshot and folded low against the horse's neck. She didn't look back until they'd covered several hundred yards. Far behind, a tiny figure shook a rifle in the air, but she couldn't hear anything more than the distant whining of his voice. Not much hospitality there.

After spending the night sleeping under a tree, she approached the foothills of the Tatras. All day long they rose before her, growing larger in her vision with every passing mile. Near evening, she came to a familiar place on the dirt road and realized she was close to the area where they'd ditched the *vardos*. It took a while, but after following the river and doubling back twice, she discovered the thicket. The *vardos* were sunk down in the dirt with hornbeam and gorse and other prickly brush surrounding them. Someone had found and scavenged from them. Much of the wood had been pulled away from the sides of the wagons, perhaps used for firewood, leaving the metal pieces looking like the ribs of enormous dead animals.

Mischka reined in and dismounted. The brambles were thick, but she pushed through until she was under the crooked branches of a hornbeam tree. The weathered *vardo* she came upon first had been picked over so thoroughly that she had no way of recognizing who had once owned it. Along with pine cones, twigs, and a lot of loose dirt, she saw the pieces of a broken mirror, the handle of a horse brush, and a sodden pile of washed out cloth. The wood frame that would have been nailed to the wall and floor to support a thin mattress had been ripped out and was nowhere to be seen. All that remained were a few nails crumbling into a rusty dust.

Mischka found all of the wagons in the same state. The carts they'd stowed were completely gone. Someone had probably used them to tote away the *kumpania's* worldly possessions. Mischka hoped that it was her family and friends who had collected the goods, but she had a feeling it was not so. She didn't sense any malevolent spirits, but she felt a wash of sadness as she stood surrounded by the overgrown hedges and rotting *vardos*.

She stepped over the tongue of a wagon and caught sight of the boxy chicken house. *Khania*. The word came to mind unbidden along with whole strings of Romany. She'd been speaking Polish and German for too long. Shouldering past prickly branches, she reached for the door. *Whap!* Something burst out of the top of the wooden house. Mischka would have fallen backwards except she was close to one of the *vardos* and managed to catch herself against it. A white bird speckled with pale gray flapped upward and away, and she followed its line of flight to the trees near the river.

The chicken house was just as empty as the ruined *vardos*. A sob rose in her throat and tears filled her eyes. She stumbled through the copse, not caring that pointy branches scratched at her face, arms, and shoulders. She could hardly see to make her way to the mare, but when she reached her, she threw her arm over warm withers and pressed her face into the soft tan neck, spilling hot tears into the dusty hide.

After a few moments, she wiped her eyes with the sleeve of her shirt. "I'm sorry, horse. I've got tears all over you."

The mare turned her head and let out a quiet whinny. So much intelligence existed in her dark brown eyes that Mischka almost wondered if she'd understood. "I suppose I ought to give you a name. Horse doesn't seem adequate. I'll have to think of something." She ran her hand along the strong neck, then took the reins and led her around the thicket, through leaves and low brush, and down to the river. "It's getting dark. I think we should camp here tonight and make for the mountains tomorrow."

Mischka pulled an apple from the fruit bag and held it out on her palm. "Here you go. Apple. That's a good name." She settled against the broad base of a tree and opened her satchel. A bird cawed. The river bubbled by. The dried salmon tasted good.

Her heart hurt.

MISCHKA AWOKE THE next morning, stiff from lying on the hard ground under the tree. She sat and stretched her neck as the remnants of a dream came to her. She had been running, searching in farmhouses and shops, calling for Pippi. Everywhere she went, the people looked upon her with such pity. "Stop staring," she'd called out. "Where is Pippi? What have you done with her?" Faces of people she didn't know went on and on, compassion etched into their expressions. No one would answer as she ran from place to place, desperate and out of breath.

The dream stayed with her all through breakfast and for the first miles of her journey. She didn't want to believe that Pippi could be dead, but was it possible? Could something have happened to her? No, she would feel it in her heart. It wasn't possible. Was it? All day she wondered.

She tried to put the nightmare out of her mind, to focus on the terrain, for she had reached the foothills and Apple was working harder. Mischka rode for an hour or so, then walked with the horse for a mile. She thought that would keep her legs stretched, and it allowed Apple some measure of rest as they approached one of the lower passes of the Carpathian Range. The saddle between peaks had been so apparent a few days earlier; now when she looked up, all she saw was the immensity of the mountain.

She couldn't help but remember the frantic race three years earlier and how panicked her *kumpania* had been. What a terrible journey. Three years. It was Snow Moon then, too. So it was three years to the month since she last passed this way. She'd never been over the Tatras mountains, had never visited the Slovak lands or Hungary. Her father had come across the mountains before he'd attained manhood, and she'd heard so many tales of his youth. She looked up at the winding path ahead and felt respect that a fourteen-year-old boy had walked over the mountain pass with only a wineskin of water and three days' food.

She wondered where her people had gone. They might have stopped anywhere to hide out; or they could have gone on to the woods north of Miskolc, the place her father had occasionally spoken of. She hoped there was still a shop in the foothills on the other side. She recalled that she and Tobar were to check there for messages.

Mischka and Apple reached the pass near suppertime. She paused long enough to eat flatbread and jerky and drink a lot of cold water. The breeze was chilly, and she smelled snow in the air when she tugged on Apple's reins and began her descent to the foothills of the Tatras. Her chances of finding the Roma— much less her own people—seemed slim, yet still she held on to hope.

EMIL FELT AS though he were suspended in time, waiting for the right moment to arrive. The last weeks, as the war ground to a halt, he'd been filled with restlessness. The war really was finished...and now what? He wasn't sure. Was it safe to go out and about? Most of the partisans in the forest camp had packed up and left, a steady trickle of men and women finally able to go home now that the soldiers were gone. Soon he and Mikhail, Gyorgy, and Stevo needed to make some decisions.

And their small group was only ten. Only ten? He had to laugh at that qualification. He hadn't thought in terms of "only ten" when they'd been scrambling for food through the last winter. Ten had seemed an enormous number to feed properly. All of them had lost weight. He thought he looked like a gaunt ragamuffin.

Around him people began to awaken and rise. Someone stoked the fire. Emil smelled the sweet smoke of a clove cigarette. Across the clearing, Mikhail's wife Lumi coughed and wheezed. She had been ill through most of the autumn— something with her lungs. All of them had been lung sick, coughing up phlegm and beset by headaches, but Lumi hadn't yet recovered. She probably needed medicine that only a doctor would have.

"I believe it's time to pack up and move out," Mikhail said.

Emil nodded. "My sentiments, too."

Mikhail had aged well, Emil thought. His hair was thin and graying, but his body was still wiry and strong, his eyes clear, and his thought processes sound. Yet change was underway. He used to seem taller than Emil, and now he wasn't. In his old age, he'd been shrinking.

Emil watched Elena working at the fire. She was a fine young woman and needed a husband. Palko would soon be marrying age, too. They all needed security, regular meals, and a warm place for the winter. "Will your cousins need any labor in the spring?"

"Hard to say. Their sympathy has been well-meant, but they haven't had much to share. I think they'll let us winter with them, and then we ought to return to Poland."

A far-off bird-whistle sounded in the forest, and Emil scanned the trees until he heard another whistle, this time closer. Someone was coming, but the sentries were signaling that it wasn't a threat. "Elena?" he called. "Do you have coffee ready?"

"Of course." Her voice was musical, and her snapping eyes reminded him so much of Mischka that for a moment he felt a pang in his chest. Mischka would have been proud of her little sister. She was a fine young woman.

Emil heard an odd choking sound and turned as Mikhail stood up.

"It cannot be." A faint puff of mist emerged from Mikhail's mouth each time he released a breath. "Am I dying?"

Emil rushed to his side. "What do you mean? You're fine. Look at me."

"I must be crossing over to the other side." Mikhail raised an arm and pointed.

Emil was startled to see a tall man leading a brown horse through the trees toward them. Emil saw leaves falling. A breath of wind blew some of them against the man's coat. Frowning, he watched the figure stride forward. He was wearing a wool coat and gray pants tucked into calf-high boots. Emil had a thought too preposterous to entertain. That wasn't a man. That was...that was...Mischka?

The visitor raised a hand. "*Droboy tume Romale.*"

The camp went silent as though everyone had stopped breathing.

Emil recognized that voice. He'd heard it call out good

morning more times than he could ever count.

Someone else said, *"Sastimos?"* but the voice was so tentative that the visitor broke into a smile.

"Is that all the greeting I get after braving the German brutes and traveling great distances across rivers, over the Tatras, and through a dozen makeshift Hungarian camps in order to find you?"

"Mischka?" The word came out of Mikhail's mouth in a whisper.

Emil saw a flare of black skirt and red shawl as a scrawny form hurtled out of the tent across the clearing, and Lumi covered a dozen yards to pitch herself into the arms of her daughter. Coughing and wheezing, she began to wail.

"Mama." Mischka soothed her. "You're not well?"

"I will be. I will be now."

Tears blurred Emil's vision, and he wiped them away with the flat of his hand. Though it had been heartbreaking to accept, he had made himself believe that Mischka was killed. After all this time, he'd been so sure of it that he'd carried the guilt and pain like a bullet wedged near his heart.

Now it was as though she'd risen from the dead. That brought thoughts of Drina and little Xavi and how they would never be welcomed home. They were truly dead. He turned away so that no one would see his tears. Composing himself, he wiped his face on his shirtsleeve and took a deep breath.

"Emil," Mischka's voice called out. "Don't be such a rascal. I have news of your sister."

THE OTHER WOMEN had retired to the tents, and Mischka sat speaking with Mikhail.

"All of them? All?" Mischka didn't want to believe what she was hearing. "I can't believe they're dead. All?"

"We think so. And now Tobar."

"Drina. Xavi. Tauna." She repeated the names reverently. "What about Liza?"

Mikhail grimaced. "We have no way of knowing what happened with her husband's *kumpania*. I don't even know where to begin searching. The old way of sending messages is lost. There's no one left to carry them."

The look in her father's eyes hurt Mischka to the core. She saw his shame and despair as clearly as lightning at night. As though it were his fault. She thought of how narrowly these few of her people had escaped the slaughter of the rest of the *kumpania,* and an anger, burning and barely contained, rose up in her. She fought it down and got shakily to her feet. "I'm going to check on the women."

Inside her mother's tent, it was dark and close and smelled of sweat. Stevo's wife, Chavi, sat next to Lumi, humming quietly. Mischka didn't like what she saw. Lumi's face was flushed, and without even touching her, Mischka knew she burned with a fever. Each breath she drew went in with a hiss and came out with a painful rasp.

Mischka dropped to her knees next to the thick bedroll. "How is she?"

Chavi shook her head slowly.

"Perhaps we should warm her, bring her near the fire."

"It won't help. She's near the end."

The end? Mischka sat back on her heels, feeling like the wind had been knocked out of her. The end? She willed herself not to cry and was grateful for her restraint when her mother opened her eyes and whispered Mischka's name.

"Yes, Mama. It's me."

Lumi let out a contented sigh. "Glad. My heart...is glad."

Mischka leaned closer, and Chavi moved out of the way. The tent flap opened, letting in a slice of light, then dimness closed around them again, and she was alone with her mother. She sat on the ground next to her. Lumi shifted and brought her hand out of the bedroll, and Mischka gripped it.

Her mother whispered, "Take care...of your sister."

"I will."

"Leave here."

Mischka sucked in a breath. She didn't want to leave, didn't want to step outside the tent, for surely if she did, her mother would be gone. "I can't."

"Yes." She coughed weakly and closed her eyes. "Leave...this...place. Find a new land...where we aren't hated. Find hope."

"Fight this, Mama. Come with us to a new place."

The smile she received nearly broke Mischka's heart. "My travels...are over. Go on...in my place. We are Roma. We seek. We find. Go on and...find hope, my daughter. Find hope."

She closed her eyes, but still she breathed. Mischka watched her chest rise and fall, listened to the painful inhalations. She held her mother's dry hand and waited with her.

And then they were nine plus Mischka.

Chapter
Thirty-Five

EMIL HADN'T BEEN sad to see the four outsiders leave when Lumi died. They could make their way back to the farming communities outside Miskolc and find work. The little ragtag band of Roma were a different matter. They would still be persecuted, and the Gallo cousins weren't so eager for another winter of dependence by Mikhail's group, no matter how few in number they were. Three days after they buried Lumi, they sat around a fire, holding mugs of coffee and discussing travel back to Poland.

Mischka had been the most outspoken. "Mama decreed that we should leave," Mischka said. "Her last words to me were to find a new place, somewhere where there's hope."

Gyorgy's voice was bitter. "There is no such place for us, little sister. No one anywhere will want us."

Mischka didn't answer for a while. She picked up a thin stick and poked it in the fire. "In my travels I had occasion to speak to many soldiers and doctors and missionaries. After the war ended, I talked each night to a woman at a Red Cross station in the displaced person's camp. She spoke Polish, but she helped me with my English. For many hours she told me of her home in a place called Terre Haute, Indiana, where they have farms and mills and raise pigs and chickens for selling. She said they seek workers."

"Where is this place?" Gyorgy asked.

"America." Mischka said the word, and a silence fell over the group at the campfire.

After a moment, Gyorgy rose and hovered over them, his face dappled in golden light. "America is an entirely different continent."

"I know that," Mischka said.

"Sorry to sound mocking, but in case you didn't know, you

can reach it only by a very long voyage over the sea."

"I'm not afraid to take the journey."

"Do you think I'm afraid?" Gyorgy shouted. He shoved his hands into his coat pockets and turned away to pace.

Emil studied the three Gallo men. Mikhail had sunken down into himself. Swathed in blankets, he sat staring into the fire. His two sons were clearly upset. Stevo kept rubbing at the scar on his head, and Gyorgy looked like a firecracker ready to go off.

Until the last few days, Mikhail had been the elder to whom everyone listened and who made final decisions. With Lumi's death and Mikhail's grief, the balance was shifting. Neither Chavi nor Elena had said a word, but they watched Mischka with an intensity Emil found fascinating. This was no longer a *kumpania* — at least not like any *kumpania* he had ever known.

The fire crackled, and Emil was warm next to it, but when he rose and stepped back just a couple feet, he felt the chill at his back. It wouldn't be long before the snow would fly. They needed to make a decision about their plans.

As he came to that conclusion, Mischka raised her voice. "Listen, big brother. If we're to leave this place, we must get over the mountain before the weather drives us back. If we decide not to journey on, then we need to make arrangements to winter here."

"Don't you think I know that?" Gyorgy's words came out in gusts of smoke and indignation.

Chavi, who had never in her life spoken up at the campfire, picked up the coffeepot. As she poured herself a cup, she said, "Stevo? I am prepared to walk. Tem is ready as well."

Stevo didn't say a word. Chavi went around the campfire and refilled mugs. When she came to Emil, he shook his head. He didn't want to be juggling a hot beverage when he said his piece. Before he could speak up, Mikhail cleared his throat. His voice was soft, barely loud enough to hear over the crackle of the fire.

"We are all that's left. Our wise and wonderful people have been hunted down like wild dogs and killed. For all we know, we may be the last few of our race." With that, his voice broke and he leaned his forehead into the palm of his hand so that his next words were muffled. "Maybe we will find other Roma like ourselves — people who hid and can come out now. But it can never be the same. Never the same."

Gyorgy stopped pacing and placed his beefy hands on Mikhail's shoulders. "Papa, you have us. We're still your family. We can start a new *kumpania* with others who hid as we did."

"Remnants. All remnants. Scattered to the wind like old rags." With that, Mikhail put his head down against his knees.

"Hungary is not my home. Poland is not my home. Nowhere is my home. Nowhere."

Emil watched through the flames of the fire as the Gallo men did something Roma women almost never saw. They embraced one another and cried. Elena, Chavi, and Mischka made no move to leave. Even the boys, Palko, Mario, and Tem watched quietly, their young faces solemn, but none of them stepped away either.

After a few minutes, Mikhail regained his composure. Careful not to meet anyone's eye, he wiped his nose, and Emil watched in amazement as the old man seemed to expand, to grow wider and broader-shouldered.

Mikhail looked up to the heavens and said, "As this Oak Moon is my witness, I no longer wish to roam these lands where we're unwanted, even though they are the lands of my forefathers. I accord honor and respect to Mikhail, the father of my birth, and to Palko, the father of my rebirth. Long may their spirits rest. But the old way is broken, and I will no longer heed the mission of long-dead travelers. Instead, we shall for once listen to a woman. My Luminitsa decreed that we seek hope, and that's what we shall do. If hope lies in America, that's where we shall go. If any man," he said and looked around the campfire, "or woman, or even any child should object, you will let me know now."

No one spoke. A log in the fire shifted, and sparks flew upward. Mikhail's gaze roved around the circle. "If we leave at first light, we can cover a great distance, especially with the horse. Mischka has brought money, and we've got meat and enough dried fruit to get into Poland. Then we travel to America."

Emil remembered what Drina had said to him in the woods, her last words before she died, and he wondered if women crossing over had access to knowledge that the men did not.

"First I want to get my sister and mother, but I'm with you, Mikhail. Your travels are my travels."

Mischka lifted her coffee mug into the air. "*Latcho drom.* To new journeys."

Emil raised his cup, and so did everyone else. "New journeys!"

Chapter
Thirty-Six

New York City, November 1989 (Snow Moon)

THE FIRST RAYS of sun were coming up over the horizon, and Tobar was yawning.

Pippi said, "You ought to get some sleep, young man. The whole household will be up before long. We have a busy day ahead of us."

"Hey, can't a guy yawn and stretch every once in a while?"

Mischka patted his arm. "But you must be exhausted."

"No. Mom says I'm a night owl, and I am. Besides, nobody's ever told me all this before."

Mischka shrugged. "People don't usually tell children horror stories. Terrible, terrible things happened during the war."

"I thought history was boring stuff that happened to other people."

Mischka couldn't help but smile. "We lived it, just as you will live yours."

"You've sure made me kind of curious about the past." Tobar yawned again. "How did you get here—to the United States?"

Pippi said, "It would take us another entire day to tell that tale. My part is easy. I waited in Reims with François's mother until Emil sent word that they were all safe. By then your father was almost two years old, Tobar, but your great-grandmother was ill so I couldn't leave. I stayed two more years caring for her, living in a comfortable house with all the luxuries one could want. I had an easy time compared to the rest."

Mischka chuckled. "Yes, that may be so. But you had to wait, always afraid that something bad would happen. Waiting would have killed me."

Tobar laughed. "That's how I feel. I can't wait to grow up. I'm ready to be a man now."

Mischka smiled, thinking Pippi's grandson was well named. "I'll tell you what we did. First, we went back over the mountain before the snows came and found the old wagons. From the remains, we managed to patch together a *vardo*. Apple pulled it to a farm town, and we lived out of it while we labored to earn money to live. Eventually we saved enough to buy another horse and cart, and we traveled to Swinoujscie on the Baltic Sea. We worked there for nearly two years, saving money, then we found a ship bound for the United States and we got jobs on board. My father and I worked the galley. My brothers and Emil were topside."

"Emil slipped into East Germany and got our mama," Pippi said. "That was when Germany was divided into East Germany and West Germany, but there was no wall up yet. From France, I could travel across the German border on the west with ease, but I couldn't get into East Germany to join Emil. Do you know about the Iron Curtain?"

Tobar shrugged. "Not that much."

"After the war, two different governments were created. The Soviet Union was in charge of the east, and it was nearly impossible to leave or to enter from the west without great risk. I don't know how Emil managed to sneak our mother out into Poland, but he did."

Mischka said, "So there we were in Swinoujscie, the men and I and young Mario with jobs on the ship. Chavi, Elena, and Camille — your great-grandmother — were booked for passage. Tem and Palko," she said, and grinned, "well, Tem and Palko were stowaways. By the time the sailors realized we'd hidden them aboard, we were five days at sea."

Tobar frowned. "You left Grandma Pippi behind?"

"We had no choice," Mischka said. "We planned to send for her later."

"So I could be growing up in Poland now if you hadn't somehow gotten here, Grandma."

Pippi smiled. "Actually, you would have grown up in France. You'd be a Frenchman today, young man. But instead, Richelle died in 1950. Heart trouble. Richelle was the mother of my husband, François."

"I remember, Grandma."

"She left me quite a bit of money. I used it to book passage on a ship for a 'visit' to America. I arrived here in the summer, and I never left."

"We learned about illegal aliens in social studies. You're not illegal, are you? They could send you away."

Pippi laughed. "Don't be silly. Back then, it was much easier to settle here. I got a job at a milliner's shop making dresses and designing patterns, and after a few years, I applied for citizenship and was grandfathered in."

"Grandfathered?"

"Yes. That's when something has been going on for so long without ill effects that the government decides to make it officially permanent. I became officially permanent in 1956."

Mischka reached out and squeezed Tobar's arm. "And I became officially permanent — and Greek — in 1952."

"What?"

"I'm a woman of many disguises, but I didn't think I'd have a chance of getting citizenship papers. I didn't read English at the time, and I didn't have money like Pippi did. I was one of the thousands of poor, money-grubbing immigrants who sneaked into the country when no one was looking. I spoke Romany, which Americans didn't know from a hole in the ground. I also spoke Hungarian, Polish, German, and some French, Italian, and Czech dialects. If they'd deported me, I'd have been sent back to the mess in Europe, and I didn't want to go."

"I'll bet," Tobar said. "You would have been alone and without Grandma."

"Yes. Perhaps there was a one in a million chance that somewhere in Poland my sister, Liza, still lived, but even today, I don't think so. It hurts my heart to remember her, but how would I have found her? And I certainly would have made no effort to find Arben or his clan. No, I needed to stay in New York, so when Mr. Giannakos offered me Greek papers, I took them. Remember Mr. G, Pippi?"

"How could I forget? Remember how when he met a person, he used to shout out his name, followed by his hometown?"

Mischka laughed and mimicked his words. "In a big booming voice, he'd say, 'Nestor Giannakos, from the city of Halkiades, in Artis, in the region of Epirus, in Greece, long may she live!' He was a big, burly Greek man with an astoundingly loud laugh, Tobar. His produce market was a good place to labor for those early years until I began working in your grandmother's sewing shop. Giannakos was a good man, a generous man. He lost his first wife in the Old Country, but he'd kept her papers. Those he gave to me. So you may continue to call me *Beebee* Mischka, but my legal name — or illegal name, if you please — is Sophia Giannakos."

"You've had a lot of names, *Beebee*."

"The name may change, but the insides are still the same. So that's the end of the story. Our journey was successful, and here we are."

"Wait a minute," Tobar said. "What happened after Grandma got here? You left out thirty-nine years."

"Ah, yes. I forgot you do math at school. Now that I think of it, there are a few other details that you might find interesting..."

Chapter
Thirty-Seven

New York City, July 1950 (Mead Moon)

MISCHKA STOOD SWEATING in the late-morning heat of the produce market. The noontime rush had not yet started. She hoped to have the fruit sections arranged perfectly before hordes of customers descended. The vegetables were all set out, glistening under the shop lights. Deep red tomatoes. Eggplant so purple they looked neon. Shiny cucumbers. Heads of lettuce and cabbage as big as bowling balls. She loved working with produce, often marveling at all the lovely edibles spread out through the store. After so much deprivation during the war, it was a comfort to be surrounded by food.

Jace and Nicolas Giannakos, the teenage grandsons of the owner, were busy unpacking box after box of fruit that Mischka expertly set out for display, weeding out the occasional damaged fruit as she worked. Her hands were quick—lightning fast, in fact. Even Mr. Giannakos commented on how speedily she could set up a display or take it down, all without ever dropping so much as an apple.

In Greek she said, "The bananas look especially good this time."

Jace let out a sigh. "English, Mischka. We're Americans here."

"I like to practice my Greek."

"My grandfather is happy to do so, but Nico and I prefer English."

"Yah, yah." She waved them aside and took hold of a tray of peaches as Jace swiped a boxcutter along the side of a box. With a laugh, she said, "Careful there, Mister English. The peaches are fragile. You do understand the meaning of *fragile*, right?"

Jace looked up toward the heavens as through praying for patience. "Of course." He bent to snatch up three heavy cardboard boxes and dragged them off toward the back room.

Jace and his brother were handsome young men, both doing well in school. They worked hard, and she liked them. On her citizenship papers, she carried their deceased grandmother's name, but they didn't seem to mind. They got along with Mischka well enough, though they weren't so kind to their four pesky younger sisters.

Mischka continued to work at a breakneck pace. She liked the feeling of speed and efficiency. There'd be plenty enough time before too long to step back and relax. She was nearly done with the last of a box of pears when she heard a jaunty whistling coming closer. Mr. Giannakos rounded the corner from the backroom, his face red and beads of sweat on his forehead. His shirtsleeves were rolled up to his elbow, and his slacks were creased. He'd been out back supervising the unloading of produce for the next day. He spent as much time unloading as even the lowliest laborer. He liked physical labor, and he respected others who did as well.

In Greek he called out, "Mischka! The stand looks marvelous."

She thanked him, feeling glad at heart. The noon whistle from a nearby factory went off as she bent to pick up the last box. "It'll be busy now."

He wiped his forehead on his shoulder and spoke in English. "Let us work then. Make big money for the day."

The next hour flew by as Mischka weighed produce, scrawled the poundage on squares of brown paper, and sent the customers to pay at the front. Some of the afternoon buyers from hotels also made their way in with orders, and she funneled their papers to the Giannakos boys.

Suddenly there was a shout, and Mr. Giannakos rushed to the front of the store, where the cashier had hold of someone. Mischka thought it strange that the person was dressed in a heavy coat when it was over eighty degrees, but she turned her attention to a customer. She was still helping the woman choose eggplant when she heard a torrent of Polish.

"Let me go, you rude and nasty dogs. Take your hands off me." The voice was high and light.

"Mischka, can you translate?" Mr. Giannakos called, and Mischka asked her customer to excuse her.

Jace was holding the woman when she reached them, and in Polish Mischka asked, "What's going on here?"

The woman in the dark coat twisted toward her, and Mischka was struck with a sense of *déjà vu*. The slim woman's blonde hair was matted and greasy, and the tan coat she wore, though once obviously finely made, was a men's double-breasted tweed with wide lapels that was far too big. But it was the face that stopped Mischka in her tracks. The blue eyes glittered, met Mischka's, and narrowed.

Mischka stared at a pale purplish scar from cheekbone to chin. "Nelka?"

"Let me go, you oafs!" She twisted and pulled to no avail.

Jace wasn't letting go. Two apples and a small bag of tangerines lay on the floor. "She was stealing," he said.

Hardly able to breathe, Mischka choked out, "Nelka? Is that you?"

The woman made a growling sound. "How do you know my name?" Panting, she kicked back. "Let me go!"

"Nelka, it's me. Mischka. From the camp in Poland."

Nelka stopped struggling and stood ramrod stiff. For several heartbeats, Mischka stared into eyes that had gone wide with disbelief, then they shifted to the side. Still breathing hard, she muttered, "Where is she? Where?"

"I'm right here. Can't you see me?"

She looked back in a fury. "Of course I can! Where is she? My sister! Where?"

Mischka felt like she'd been sucker punched. The room lights actually seemed to flicker. She couldn't get a breath in. Her throat burned and she gasped.

Mr. Giannakos took hold of Mischka's forearm and leaned in to look her in the eye. "Mischka? Are you all right?"

She couldn't speak. She managed to get in a deep breath, but all she could see in her mind's eye was little Lidia's pale white face the last morning, right before she died.

"Take her to the back office," Mr. Giannakos said to Jace. He pulled on Mischka's arm. "You need to come with me."

The office was a cubbyhole no more than eight-by-eight where the accounting work was done. Furnished with two hardback chairs and a tiny desk, it smelled faintly of ink. The hand-operated press upon which they printed flyers took up the left side of the desk. Jace delivered Nelka to one of the chairs, and Mischka settled in the other. Mr. Giannakos sat behind his desk.

"Young woman, I could have you arrested for theft. Do you wish to pay for the fruit?"

Mischka translated, but Nelka didn't answer the shop-owner's question. "I wish to know where my sister is." She looked at Mischka with insolence. "I left her in your care."

Tears sprang to Mischka's eyes. "I'm sorry, Nelka. She died before we could be liberated."

With a shriek, Nelka launched herself from the chair at Mischka.

"No!" Mischka called out as she tried to fend off the blows. Jace had to pull the screaming woman off her. Mischka understood her shouted accusations too well. She felt light-headed and had to back up and lean against the plaster wall behind her.

Nelka flailed her arms. "You killed her. I saved you, and you killed my sister." She let out a cry so loud it made Mischka's ears ring, then sank to her knees, sobbing. Jace released her.

Mischka squatted nearby, her shoulder still smarting from Nelka's bony fist. "Nelka, don't. Please."

Nelka slumped onto her side in a fetal position, facing away from Mischka. She was sweating and wheezing and still wrapped in the heavy coat, but she shook as though she were freezing.

"Nelka." No response. "Nelka!" Mischka returned to her seat in the wood chair and waited. She took a deep breath, and now, in addition to the ink, she smelled pungent body odor.

After a few moments, Jace and Mr. Giannakos left the room, and Nelka stopped sniffling and moaning. She sat up. Her face was ruddy, and the scar on her cheek looked like a fresh gash. Mischka had to look close to be sure that this was not so.

"What happened to Lidia? Did they kill her?"

"No. She fell ill with the croup. It was winter. She—she couldn't bear the loss of you. She wouldn't fight."

More tears bubbled up and poured down Nelka's face. "I didn't think any of you would make it out of there. I always thought she was probably dead. I couldn't feel her in my heart anymore. Vogel didn't—he didn't abuse her further, did he?"

"No. You'll be happy to hear that at the end, the Russians liberated the camp and he was shot by a firing squad. So was Braunhaus."

Nelka's eyes lit up with vicious glee, and for the first time, Mischka thought she glimpsed real madness. Then her scarred face went slack.

Sensing that Nelka was finished with her outburst, Mischka held out her hand. "Come. Let's get you something to eat, and then we'll take a walk. I have a great deal to tell you."

They went to a café and sat at a table for two by the front window where sunshine streamed in and the sidewalk traffic outside was a constant reminder of how busy everyone was. Mischka had a cup of coffee, and Nelka downed a plate of eggs, four pieces of buttered toast, and a piece of apple pie. She ate like she hadn't had food for days, and Mischka suspected that was the case.

When Nelka was done, she pushed her plate away and sat

back in her chair, her eyes blank. Mischka wondered what had gone wrong with her, for surely there was something very much out of order. She recalled Nelka's daring, her defiance, her unwillingness to let the Nazi guards get the best of her. This was not the Nelka she had known, the woman with whom she had spent all those months sharing a pallet.

"Nelka, how did you escape?"

"Have you got a cigarette?"

"No, sorry."

Nelka steepled her fingers, and the tips, under dirty half-moon fingernails, went white from the pressure. Her voice was flat, as though she were relating a story that had happened to someone else. "They took me away to days of travel and beatings. I can't remember how everything fits together, but in the end I was in Auschwitz, which has left its permanent mark on me."

She rolled up the sleeve of her coat, and Mischka caught a glimpse of blue numbers tattooed into the pale white skin. The figures hardly registered before Nelka rolled the sleeve back down.

"Yes, they branded us like cattle, and we waited to die in their slaughterhouse."

"But you didn't die."

"Yes, I did. I didn't know it until I saw you, but now I know it's true." The voice was so cold, so distant, that it gave Mischka the shivers.

She didn't know what to say. She swallowed down caustic bile, and pushed the coffee cup away. "What happened?"

"I became a...plaything. For a German guard. A woman."

"I don't understand."

"She called me her valet. She fattened me up, only to use me for a punching bag. She was fascinated by the scar on my face. She put matching ones on my chest, my stomach, my back and buttocks. Shall I show you now?" Nelka looked around the restaurant with a sly expression.

Mischka swallowed hard. "I believe you. I'm no stranger to the beatings of one who enjoys administering them."

"You'll be happy to know that the disgusting, horrible shrew, Petronela, met a brutal end."

Mischka couldn't help but wince.

"Yes, right up to the last moment of her life she was complaining. And then a Nazi pig put a bayonet right through her heart. That was before the Allies came to liberate the camp. Too late for priggish Petronela, but not soon enough for me, either. My keeper—the German madwoman—possessed forged papers proving her to be an Englishwoman, though anyone who heard her speak had to know she was no such thing. She used passports and other documents lifted from her victims to flee Germany and go to London, and she took me with her. She had a great deal of money as well."

"She brought you here?"

A smile played on Nelka's face. "You could say that. She very kindly provided her papers so I could book passage to this godforsaken place."

"I don't understand."

"You wouldn't. No one does."

"What happened to her?"

"I killed her."

This was so unexpected that Mischka felt her jaw drop. Nelka smiled a terrible, wicked grin, and it seemed the scar on her cheek gleamed blood-red in the sunlight that poured through the café window.

"She beat me one time too many. I stabbed her with a kitchen paring knife. I stabbed and stabbed until the blood stopped running. Desecrating her body gave me more pleasure than anything I've ever done."

Mischka took some coins from her pocket and set them on the table. She rose. "Come." She hastily exited the café, her breath coming in short gasps. She had to move, had to get fresh air or else vomit. She'd traveled two city blocks before she looked behind her, almost hoping that Nelka had failed to follow, but there she was, dogging Mischka's footsteps.

Nelka caught up with her. "You're shocked? How can you be shocked? Didn't we dream many a night of ways to murder Vogel?"

"That was—different. I know what happened to you was terrible, but I don't understand how you could enjoy murdering her."

"I needed her papers, and I took them, just as she took what she needed from me. I owed her nothing. She deserved worse than death."

"What did you do with her body?"

"Hid it in the root cellar of an abandoned cottage. I took her clothes, I took her money, I took her papers, and I escaped Europe." Her voice assumed that deadness again as she said, "I'm never going back, now that I know Lidia is dead."

Mischka stepped around a street vendor selling apples, and her mind whirled. What had Nelka turned into? A monster? How could she speak of murder with such glee? Back at Giannakos's Produce, Mischka had initially thought that she could help

Nelka—assist her in getting a job, perhaps even take her into her home. Now she felt repulsed and sickened.

She evaded the flow of foot traffic on all sides of her and backed up against the side of a building. In a calm voice, she said, "What are your plans, Nelka?"

"Plans? I have no plans. Surviving day to day is all I can manage."

"Where do you live?"

"Live?" Her smile was mocking.

"Do you want a job?"

"Work for these greedy sons of swine? I'd sooner steal."

Mischka sought her eyes and leaned closer. "Nelka, I could find you living quarters and help you get a job—something with a proper and upstanding storeowner."

"I don't need your help. I don't need you, you murdering bitch." Nelka's eyes shone with madness once more. She was so close that Mischka could see beads of perspiration along her greasy hairline and smell the reek of her unwashed body. Nelka shook a finger in Mischka's face. "You're responsible for the death of all I loved. You. One day you shall pay."

Her face went slack, and she turned and pushed through the stream of pedestrians. More than one person called out a startled "Hey!"

Mischka was glad for the building behind her. She held her palms flat against the smooth, cool surface, grounding herself, trying to catch her breath, as she watched Nelka reach the curb and hesitate.

"Oh, no. Nelka, no!" For just the briefest moment, she glimpsed the purple facial scar. Then Nelka launched herself into the path of a black coal delivery truck. The shiny metal grille in front struck her dead-center and flung her onto the street. The driver swerved and tried to stop, but Nelka's small form disappeared under a wheel.

Mischka heard a great inhalation all around. Other vehicles skidded to a halt, and car horns sounded. A woman screamed. The sidewalk emptied around Mischka as people swarmed toward the one-way street.

"Get a doctor!" someone yelled

Mischka took a deep breath. She must go help her. Help Nelka. But her feet wouldn't move.

"It's no use," a man called out. "She's dead."

Still bracing herself against the wall, Mischka took a step aside. Away from the carnage, away from the crowd, away. Anywhere but here. She reached the corner and had to relinquish contact with the building. She was shaky, but she pushed on, crossed the street, and kept walking quickly. Away, away.

TWO DAYS LATER, Mischka lay in bed and thought about her walk with Nelka. Until then, she'd believed she'd put the terrors of the camps out of her mind, but speaking to Nelka had brought everything back in a fresh rush, like an explosion of dangerous fireworks in her mind. She could hardly sleep now with all the bad dreams assailing her. Muzzle flashes of gunfire. Dead faces of girls she hardly knew. The ugly, twisted Vogel beating a tiny girl to a bloody pulp. A baton whisking through the air, over and over, slashing at her own bare skin.

The horror of Tobar's death came back to her as well. She dreamed repeatedly of his smiling brown eyes, which suddenly went vacant as the German bullet ripped through his body. She thought of hundreds of moments of brutality and malice. It seemed that everywhere she went, she was reminded of depravity. An old gentleman, shuffling along in a blue serge suit, brought her the memory of the white-haired man shot and killed as the soldiers had driven them toward the labor camp. She wondered how she had gotten such a clear picture of the man's face. She saw it now in her dreams.

Though she hadn't actually seen Nelka's body, she imagined its destruction in her mind's eye, and it horrified her. She saw blood and knives in her dreams and awakened shaking with fear. Even worse, she felt newly homesick for the *vardos* and the *kumpania,* for the laughter of the children, the high fires and singing, the spiced coffee, *bogacha,* and *puyo.* She missed the traveling, missed always looking forward to a new and different place which could be full of surprises. For a moment, she even missed the *diklo* headgear she'd worn for those years married to Arben.

She gave herself a mental shake, and tried to talk herself out of the memories.

True, the days on the road had been wearisome. She had bathed often from streams as cold as ice. Strangers sometimes threw rocks or chased them out of town. And always overshadowing her *kumpania* life, her opinion—her wisdom— had not been valued by the men.

Still, she missed a time when the world had seemed magical. *Magique.* She saw herself as a young girl, feeling the magic, running through enchanted forests or riding astride talking horses, feeling whole and in tune with nature. Unaware that she stood on the brink of a world intent upon exterminating her.

Mágikus. Magický. Zauberisch. Magie. Magiczny... Magia. She knew many words for magic in nearly a dozen languages, and now she knew there was no such thing.

Magic didn't exist. The world was an ugly place.

Chapter
Thirty-Eight

New York City, August 1950 (Wort Moon)

LITTLE FRANÇOIS STOOD on the ship's promenade deck and peeped through a slat in the metal fence to look out upon the gray, dark sea. Pippi stood directly behind him, feeling slightly light-headed. She'd been seasick the first few days of the voyage, but after a time, she finally stopped vomiting and gradually became accustomed to the movement of the sea. She had been told that the Queen Mary was such a large ship that she would hardly feel a thing. What lies. The ship was, indeed, over 80,000 tons and a thousand feet long, but it still vibrated and shuddered in the water, particularly during the fierce storm on the second night. Despite what she'd been told, Pippi was more than aware that she was at sea.

Over the sound of the wind whistling and blowing against the flags nearby, she heard the low hum of people talking. Dozens of passengers braved the wind. Standing at the rail that ran atop the fence, they looked out across the leaden sea, each eager to be the first to sight land.

François reached one pale hand up to grab the rail. Dressed like a miniature man, he wore tan twill slacks, leather oxfords, a light blue pullover sweater, and a suit jacket that was much too big for him. Pippi hoped he was warm enough. Even though she didn't think there was any possible way for him to fall from the deck into the sea, she had a tight grip on his coat collar. She constantly watched him like a hawk. Four-year-old boys were unpredictable, and more than once she'd seen her little monkey son climb surfaces that it would never occur to her could be scaled.

She was cold in the chilly breeze and growing more so every minute, despite wearing her heaviest Chesterfield coat and thick leotards under her skirt. Who would believe it was summer? Her bouffant petticoat, all the rage in Europe, merely made it easier for the brisk wind to blow against her legs and up her skirt. Her flat-heeled leather shoes had a full, rounded toe, so her feet weren't yet chilled, but she anticipated being cold through and through before too long.

"François, let's go inside."

"No, please, Mama. I want to see land." He looked up at her, his blue eyes so very like Emil's that she found herself thinking of her brother multiple times each day. His hair was tinged with brown. At his birth, it had been white-blond, but as each month went by, it seemed to darken a bit more. She was amazed to watch him grow, to see his limbs so straight and strong. He was well-coordinated and already nimble-footed, a natural athlete. He was also adept with both French and German. She wondered how quickly he would learn English. She had tried to teach him a few words and phrases, but her knowledge was rudimentary. She worried that she wouldn't be able to learn the language quickly enough, and if she didn't, how could she get a job?

"Hello, Mrs. Delebecque." A man in a fedora and topcoat paused beside her and tipped his hat.

"Mr. Faunce. How are you this morning?" She pasted on a smile.

"I'm pleased to be close to our destination. I see you have your sea-legs now."

"Yes, I do, and I'm grateful for that."

He'd been seated at her dining table the third night, and she remembered with embarrassment how sick she'd felt. She had excused herself to run to the ladies room, lost the soup course she'd just eaten, and then stood looking in the mirror, amazed that she could quite literally sport such a tinge of gray-green on her face. When she returned to the table, he'd been solicitous, his soft hands patting her, and his gray eyes constantly appraising. His dark blond hair had a touch of silver, and she guessed he was fifteen years her senior.

Ever since that night, he'd inquired about her health and constantly tried to strike up conversations with her, but something about him left her cold. His German was clear and crisp, and considering the jeweled rings, collar pin, tie clips, and cufflinks he wore, she thought he must be a man with money. But she didn't like him. His teeth were yellow and his eyeteeth oddly long and feral-looking. He reminded her of a jackal. Ever since he'd learned that she was a widow, he'd been dogging her, and it was all she could do to avoid him.

"What is the first thing you will do upon arrival, Mrs. Delebecque?"

"I hope to locate my family, and then I'll rest and recover

from this voyage."

"Ahh, I shall assist you in any way you like. I have connections to help you search."

"That's very kind, but won't be necessary, Mr. Faunce. They expect us and will find me upon arrival." She shivered.

"Oh, goodness. Are you cold?"

He made a move as if to shelter her under his arm, but she grimaced and leaned down to her son. "Let's go inside, François."

Her uncooperative son shook his head. "I want to see us get there."

"It could be hours before we get to New York. Come away from the rail, and let's go inside and warm up."

"But—"

"Please do not argue with me. I'm chilled."

"You go inside then. I'll watch."

"I will not leave you here by yourself. Come." With a dismissive nod toward Mr. Faunce, she peeled François's hand away from the rail. His fingers were cold and damp. His hands never seemed to warm up completely. "Look how chilled you are. Let's go."

He grumbled, and she was sure he'd called her *marâtre* under his breath. Yes, she was a cruel mother if that meant keeping her son safe. Tugging at his arm, she turned and stepped away from the rail just as a loud cheer went up.

François let out a squeal and jerked his hand from hers. She let him race over and peer through the metal fence. He was so excited that he quivered and danced. He turned and called out to her. "It's land! We're nearly there, Mama."

Pippi could make out a faint strip on the horizon. She didn't have the heart to tell her son that it might be many hours before they covered the distance and were able to dock. She rested her hands on François's shoulders and gazed out across the ocean. If nothing disastrous had happened, her family would be there waiting. Mama, Emil, Mischka. All of them had been on her mind for so long. Since her mother-in-law had died, she'd felt so alone. Something tightened behind her breastbone. How hard it was to believe so much time had passed. And now here she was, coming to a new country, leaving familiar surroundings behind. Once she got on dry land, she hoped she'd feel less apprehensive.

THE QUEEN MARY sailed into the harbor at Chelsea Piers in the late afternoon on a sun-drenched, sticky day, and Emil stood waiting, hands in pockets. The ship's horn emitted a deep, ear-splitting blast that reverberated through the air and shook the ground. Everyone jumped and covered their ears before the next blast rent the sky.

Everyone but Mikhail had come with Emil in the early morning, but as the day went on, Mischka's brothers had had to report to work, and Palko and Tem grew hungry and impatient, so Chavi took them home. Mischka and Elena still waited. Mario, a young man who now sported a handsome goatee on his chin and a wedding band on his left hand, stood next to Emil's mother, Camille. Emil knew that lightning could strike the waiting area, and Mama wouldn't leave.

Meeting ocean-liner passengers was not for the faint of heart. Even after the ship had been docked for many hours, the travelers had to stay on board while Customs officers searched baggage and approved each entry to the city. Such was the case today as well. Before the first group emerged from Customs, afternoon had arrived, and still Emil and the other family members waited.

It seemed to take forever for the ship to dock, and then porters carted all the luggage down the gangplank first before any passengers were allowed to depart. Hundreds of bags were arrayed on the dock by the time the first passengers descended the gangplank, holding tight to its canvas sides. Emil wished he had field glasses. More than once he saw an adult figure with a child-sized companion, but he was too far away to tell whether they were Pippi and François.

"I cannot wait seeing special friend of mine," Elena said in English. Her language skills were improving, but a lot of the time she and the rest of the Gallos slipped into Romany.

Besides Mischka, who picked up languages with untold speed, Mario was quickest at learning the language. He said, "I wish they'd hurry."

Emil's mother laughed and shivered with ill-concealed delight. Her English was abysmal, so she spoke in German most of the time. "If I had known I'd be separated from my daughter for so long, I would never have left Germany."

"But, Mama," Emil said, "you'd still be stuck in the village near Eisenhüttenstadt, and we never would have gotten you out."

"I know. It's just that I've missed her so much that my heart is pained."

Emil understood. The ache in his own heart for Drina and for his little son, Xavi, would never leave him. He still dreamed of them, longed for them. He was grateful that his mother's wish to see her only daughter could be fulfilled, but he couldn't help feeling a great sadness. He would never have the chance to wait for his beloved to return to him from across the sea. He could never visit her grave, never see his little son with the laughing eyes.

They rarely spoke of their lost families. Emil imagined that all of them still felt their absence deeply, but it was easier not to discuss. No amount of talk could bring back any of the *kumpania* or family members taken from them during the terrible years of the war.

He thought of his friends. Mikhail had been the luckiest. Both of his sons, Gyorgy and Stevo, had survived as had Mischka and Elena. Mikhail had lost Lumi and Liza, but four of his five children were still with him. Stevo's wife Chavi was healthy and pregnant again, and little Tem had made it safely across the sea. Perhaps they would never know what happened to Stevo's other four children.

Gyorgy was the unluckiest of all. Of his four sons, he had only Mario. His wife Tauna's brutal death had to weigh upon him, just as Drina's weighed on Emil. Sometimes Emil felt like their group consisted of leftovers — mismatched remainders. Almost everyone else was dead.

With the exception of Elena, who lived with a family for whom she provided domestic help, the clan lived in three flats, all on the same street. They cleaved to one another, met often for meals, and lent money and clothing as needed. None spoke of their fears, but Emil felt a fierce protectiveness for each and every one of them. Quite simply, he would die to keep any one of them safe.

Each waited with great expectation for the arrival of Pippi and her son, for they represented hope. If Pippi and François could arrive unscathed from the Old Country, perhaps later on down the road they might be surprised by the arrival of some other unexpected family member, or someone from the *kumpania*. They had a list of ninety-seven Roma, most of whom Emil believed were dead, but Mischka had spent time haunting Immigration offices to try to locate any who might have made it to America. She hadn't had any luck yet, but she kept going back.

Watching Mischka pace along the fence, he wondered why she had been so distant lately. Instead of showing delight over the imminent arrivals, she remained off to the side, glum and silent. She hadn't been herself for weeks, ever since the day she came home and told him she'd run into someone from the labor camp, and then the woman had been hit by a truck and killed before her eyes. Emil tried to get more information from her, but she'd turned inward.

What had happened to the easygoing woman who had worked so hard to help earn their passage from Swinoujscie? He had relied on her steadiness, her energy. But something had indeed happened. He hadn't seen Mischka like this since she'd returned all those years ago from the marriage to Arben.

And then on the last day of July, she'd come home to the three-bedroom flat she shared with Emil, Palko, and Camille and announced that she'd secured lodging at a boarding house six blocks away. Emil had been stunned. She packed her clothes and few belongings in a gunnysack, and the next morning she was gone. Emil felt her absence acutely. If he had his way, he would own a house with a rabbit warren of bedrooms, and all of them would live together—Mikhail's entire clan, the Staneks, and anyone else they picked up along the way. Emil worked swing shift at the docks with Gyorgy and Stevo, and so far, that didn't provide any of them enough income to afford a house. But in September, Emil would be enrolling in college to train for better work, and someday he expected to buy a home.

He heard his mother gasp and was aware of the people around him rushing forward. Suddenly, his sister was wrapped in their mother's arms, and both of them were crying. He saw tears on Mischka's face, which she swiftly brushed away.

Two porters delivered some heavy bags, and the men wrestled these out of the way, then settled to wait for mother and daughter to stop crying and exclaiming.

Emil noticed the little boy tugging on Pippi's skirts. He had a look of uncertainty on his face. The pale blue of his pullover sweater matched his eyes. Emil gestured him over.

"You are François." The boy nodded. "I'm your Uncle Emil. Did you enjoy the boat ride?"

"It's not a boat. The Queen Mary is the biggest ship on the ocean."

"Ah, I see. Were you seasick?"

"No. Of course not. Mama was. But not me. I'm going to grow up and be a sailor so I can travel everywhere."

"Emil," Camille called out. "Your sister is here, finally here."

Emil had to laugh at the absurdity of her statement—as if they hadn't been waiting for this event for hours. But he hurried over and gave Pippi a hug.

"I'm so glad you're here safe." He looked around, suddenly aware of a blond man who held a leather suitcase and hovered to one side. "And who have we here?"

The man extended his hand. "Gerhard Faunce, just arriving

here from the Fatherland." His German was crisp and precise.

Emil glanced at Pippi, saw the stiff look on her face, and said without warmth, "Welcome to America, *Herr* Faunce."

"Yes, thank you very much. I was most concerned to see that Mrs. Delebecque and her son arrived safely. Perhaps you will allow me to call?"

"Oh, I'm sorry, sir. That would not do," Emil said. "My sister is about to become betrothed. But thank you for your assistance and for watching out for her."

With a nod and an angry look in his eyes, the man sidled past. When he was out of earshot, Emil met Pippi's eyes. "I hope I read that situation correctly."

"Oh, yes, big brother. You certainly did. Thank you."

Mischka clasped Pippi's hands and said in English, "Welcome to America." She repeated the words in German, then stepped away as Pippi's mother took her arm.

Camille said, "Let's get out of this heat. Let's go home."

Emil glanced over his shoulder and saw Mischka right behind him. "Are you all right?" he asked.

"Oh, yes," Mischka said.

But the next time he looked for her, Mischka was gone. They had passed the cross street that led to her boardinghouse, and he realized that she must have left them at that point. He felt a pang of regret, but that was quickly overwhelmed by the relief of reaching their flat. He and Mario hauled the bags up two flights of stairs to their rooms, and the party began.

MISCHKA WALKED ALONG a quiet avenue and looked at the trees overhead so full of bright leaves. Birds twittered and hopped from branch to branch. She had been roaming aimlessly for an hour. Lately she'd been taking long walks through the city, acquainting herself with the area for miles around her boardinghouse but avoiding the rougher parts of town. Today she loped along, her legs overly warm in the lightweight tan slacks she wore.

She felt a curious lightness—and a thankfulness—that Pippi and François had arrived safely. But at the same time, their arrival evoked a combination of emotions she couldn't quite fathom. How could happiness be tinged with such sadness and worry? She didn't even know what she was worried about.

One thing was clear. Nobody had told her that Pippi's hand in marriage had been promised to someone. When had that occurred? How preposterous that Pippi Stanek should travel all the way to America only to be handed off to some stranger. Was it about money? Why couldn't they all band together and share their income? Mischka had been gradually salting away her own earnings, a dollar here, two dollars there. She hadn't counted lately, but she had more than two hundred dollars hidden in her room. Surely that nest egg could help Pippi get settled. Why did she have to be married off to someone?

She picked up her pace, swinging her arms vigorously. She turned the corner on Fourth Street and nearly collided with an old man shambling along.

"*Chap nit,*" he called out in Yiddish. Dark, flinty eyes stared out at her from under a flat-topped black hat. His full gray beard was bushy and might have been comical had he not raised his cane. "Take it easy, you," he said in English. "Not so fast."

She looked down at the sidewalk. "My apologies, sir."

He touched nicotine-stained fingers to his hat and limped past her with a dignity that left a lump in her throat. Up the street, she saw an old woman in a flowered dress and white gloves walking with a teenage girl. Nearby, a man in an apron swept in front of a bookstore. A newsboy on a bicycle wheeled past calling out, "Newspaper...get your news...read all about it."

All around her, the city crawled with people busy at work, busy with their loved ones, and here she was, miles from home, longing for something she couldn't explain. She turned and walked back toward Mrs. Levinstein's boardinghouse. She'd missed the party at the Stanek's, but that suited her fine. She wasn't in any mood for celebration.

SIX DAYS A week, Mischka rose before the sun came up, arrived at Giannakos's Produce by five in the morning, and was finished in the late afternoon. The two year anniversary of coming to America came and went, and all she could think of was the Old Country.

At night she dreamed of walking on dusty roads on open land, wind in her hair and springtime plants, grasses, and trees all around. She awakened one night to the creaking of the house, and it reminded her so much of the sound of a harness on a team leading a *vardo* that she started to cry. Little things such as the sound of Polish or German speech or the smoky smell of meat cooking over a fire could unexpectedly bring on tears.

She didn't understand what was happening to her. She thought to seek her father's advice, but on a windy October Sunday, a visit to the flat where he lived with Gyorgy's family held no opportunity to speak to Mikhail in private. Everyone

was celebrating the announcement that Mario's wife Sylva was
with child, and Mischka could hardly let her glumness and
depression put a damper on the good news.

She had hoped to see Pippi—perhaps share the quandary
with her—but she hadn't arrived after an hour. So Mischka
finished her cheese, wine, fruit, and *bogacha* bread, hugged Sylva
and shook Mario's hand, and slipped out.

A mile had passed before Mischka looked about, aware that
for no reason, she'd headed north. Usually she went to the river
and walked there, but this time she decided to try something
new. Cabs passed, their drivers honking and gesturing. Street
vendors hawked barbecued meats, fruit, pocket sandwiches, and
more. She strode up the avenue watching and listening to the
people: Italians, Greeks, Jews, Poles, Negroes, an Asian woman
pushing a dilapidated wooden cart, and the cacophony of
constant talk, truly a babble of voices.

She stopped and looked up and down Fifth Avenue.
Everything felt foreign. Unreal. Resuming her walk, she
wondered what she should do. Lately there had been times when
she'd felt panicky, as if she couldn't draw in quite enough
breath, and sometimes she could hardly bear her surroundings.
Huge buildings, cement sidewalks, no horizon. Busy streets,
honking cars, noise, noise, noise. Even at midnight, people were
out and about, haunting jazz clubs, returning from the cinema,
coming and going from bars and restaurants.

She longed for the Old Country, especially when unbidden
thoughts came to mind. She didn't want to remember Nelka or
think of her crumpled body lying so still on the avenue, but she
did.

Why was she alive, when so many had died? Some of them
were bright and beautiful—why them, and not her? What was
the meaning of it all?

The hard pavement under her feet and the brisk wind in her
face kept her grounded, even when tears ran down her face. She
just kept moving. She didn't know how much time passed, but
she was lost in an area she'd never been to before. Mischka
wasn't worried though. She knew all the streets ran east-west
and the avenues north-south. She could easily find her way back
home.

She was ready to turn back when she smelled an unusual
odor, like damp peat. It drew her forward another block. Then
another.

At the end of the second block she saw a fountain, which
surprised her so completely that she stopped abruptly. A
shabbily dressed young man in an old-fashioned derby hat

bumped into her. He excused himself and slipped past as she moved slowly forward.

The fountain was quite grand. It consisted of six basins, each smaller than the one below as they rose from one level to the next. On its top was a ball on which stood a bronze sculpture of a nude woman. A cloth lay over her left leg, and she held against it a basket of what Mischka thought was fruit. Her hips were broad and solid, her breasts small, her arms and legs lean and muscled. Mischka stood and stared. If bronze could be made flesh, the woman might be any number of Roma women she had known in her life, transported from the Vistula River in Poland.

Water tumbled over the edges of the basins, gray-green against the granite of the display. Minutes passed, and still Mischka stared, incredulous. She leaned forward and touched the granite of the lowest basin. It was cold and smooth against her fingers.

She heard someone stop to her right, slightly behind her, and still she gawked.

"Beautiful work, is it not," said a feminine voice accented with the sounds of Britain.

"Yes. What is this place?"

"This place? Or this fountain?"

"Either. Both." She turned and met the blue eyes of a plump woman in a pale blue skirt and blouse. She wore a jaunty Kingston-style straw hat with a bright blue hatband, and her white-gloved fingers encircled the handle of a boxy, woven, white purse.

"This is the Grand Army Plaza, and that's Pulitzer Fountain."

"Who is she?" Mischka pointed toward the bronze statue.

"I can't recall her name—but she's a goddess of plenty. The sculptor Karl Bitter created her around 1915 and modeled the fountain after one in Paris. Oddly enough, the day he finished the original model, he was run over and killed by a car here in the city."

Mischka shivered. "That's terrible. But why is it here?"

The woman smiled, showing slightly uneven teeth. "Because it's beautiful. Some things exist merely to enchant the eye, to make the heart sing, or to inspire awe. I can tell from the look on your face that you know the awe of which I speak."

Mischka nodded slowly. "Thank you. I'll have to come here often."

"You have, of course, explored the whole park?"

Mischka cocked her head to the side. "Park?"

"Yes, this is Central Park, but only the tiniest smidgen of it.

There are over eight hundred acres." She pointed north. "Head that way, and you'll see what I mean. Good day, now, my dear." The woman moved off toward Fifty-Ninth Street, and Mischka watched her until she was lost in the flow of pedestrians.

She looked about the plaza on which people strolled in the autumn sun. The branches of bare trees, angling upward, caught her eye, and for a moment, she foolishly thought they might be fruit trees. With each step she took toward them, she was more certain that she was, indeed, seeing pear trees. When she stood touching the rough trunk of one of them, a lump grew in her throat.

As if in a trance, she started along a path and again noticed that damp mossy smell. She came to a pond and was so surprised that she stepped off the path and squatted, her elbows on her knees. If not for the sound of traffic and voices, she might be able to convince herself that she was out in the country.

She walked and walked for what seemed to be miles, passing gardens and hedges, rock formations, and a memorial for World War I. She came upon passageways, benches, stone arches, and a strange granite statue of a woman and a cat flying on the back of a goose with the woman's cape rustling out as if in the wind. She wondered if she had died and gone to a strange new land, but when she took a path off to the side, she ended up on Fifth Avenue near Sixty-Ninth where the cars and buses and taxis were plentiful and pedestrians meandered about in their Sunday best.

The sun was low on the horizon when she realized she was miles from home. She didn't want to be out after dark in a part of the city she didn't know well, so she started down Fifth Avenue. She knew she could take a subway and speedily cover the miles, but in all the time she'd lived in New York, she had only once ducked down into the subway station to escape pelting hail. It had given her such a feeling of claustrophobia that she fled.

She covered four miles steadily, and her feet were hurting by the time she arrived at Mrs. Levinstein's. She ran a hot bath and undressed, then sank, fatigued, into the porcelain tub to soak. For the first time in weeks, she felt at peace.

Chapter
Thirty-Nine

New York City, October 1950 (Blood Moon)

MISCHKA CRAWLED UNDER the slanted produce bin and retrieved three yellow onions and an apple. She wasn't sure how the apple had made its way to this side of the store, but it had been dented, punctured, and seriously scuffed. She put it with the damaged fruit and replaced the onions in their bin.

At a lull in customers, she crossed the store, removed a broom from the rack, and started sweeping at the rear corner. So intent was she that she didn't hear anyone come up behind her. When someone touched her shoulder, she jumped.

"Oh, Pippi, it's you." Ever since Pippi had gotten a job at a garment shop three blocks away, she had been making a point to stop in at Giannakos's often. Mischka liked to see her happy face, but she was usually at a loss as to what to say to her.

"How are you, Mischka?"

"Quite fine, as you can see."

"I never see you."

Mischka laughed. "Of course you do. You're in here every other day."

"I mean outside the shop. Come to the apartment for dinner tonight. Sylva is making souvlaki. The whole house smells wonderful from the melange of spices."

"I can't. I'm making roasted lamb strips for Mrs. Levinstein."

"Bring her with you, then."

"Mrs. Levinstein is Jewish."

Pippi's face flushed bright red. "You're saying Mrs. Levinstein wouldn't like to be in the company of Germans?" Mischka blinked, and opened her mouth to speak, but Pippi spoke first. "I thought all people were supposed to get a new chance here in America—even Germans." She turned and flounced out of the shop.

Mischka wanted to call out after her, but Pippi moved so fast that she didn't have a chance. How ridiculous. Mrs. Levinstein was one of the least judgmental people Mischka had ever met. But she doubted whether her Jewish landlady would look kindly upon eating souvlaki, which was made with pork.

After work, Mischka considered hiking north to the park, but she didn't have the energy. She went home, greeted her landlady, and went up to her room for a nap before supper.

She was awakened from the depths of a dream where she was running and not quite able to breathe. Her body felt heavy, and she was on the edge of tears.

She looked around her half-lit room. The bureau cast an ominous shadow across the floor, and suddenly she felt closed in. She rose and went to the window, pulled back the sheers, and looked out. Lowering herself into a straight-backed chair that sat next to the windowsill, she gazed down into the neighborhood. As usual, people hastened along, calling out to one another, ducking into brownstones, hopping in and out of cars. No matter what, the world kept spinning, people kept moving, and nothing much changed.

A rap sounded at the door. She crossed the half-darkened room to find Mrs. Levinstein in the hall twisting a handkerchief in both hands.

"A working man is here to speak to you," she said. "I didn't ask his name, but he's from your family. I told him to wait in the parlor."

Mischka's heart leapt into her throat. "Thank you. I'll be right there."

She slipped on her shoes and caught up with Mrs. Levinstein on the first landing and had to slow down to allow for her landlady's more stately pace.

Mischka crossed the foyer and swept into the parlor, which was used only as a sitting room to greet guests. Emil stood at the side window, his back to her and hat in one hand.

"What is it, Emil? What's wrong?"

"No one is dead," he was quick to assure her in accented English. "Everyone's accounted for."

"What's wrong then?"

"I need to speak to you about Pippi."

"Oh?"

She gestured toward one of the chairs, but he shook his head. "My work clothes might soil the furniture. Perhaps we might talk outside? Would that be all right?"

She got her coat and joined him on the front stairs. He stood on the top step, one hand on the metal banister. The wind was brisk and blew his graying blond hair to one side. His tanned skin had lightened considerably since the days when they'd wandered the Polish countryside. His natural appearance was much more evident, and he no longer looked much like a Roma. His blue eyes met hers, and he looked at her thoughtfully.

Switching to German, he said, "Shall we walk?"

They set off down the street and had gone a full block before Emil told her what was on his mind. "You haven't been yourself since summer, and please don't pretend you don't know what I'm talking about. You're distracted and distant and very clearly unhappy. Something has happened to you. Pippi is at wit's end, and we're all worried about you."

She didn't answer. They walked slowly, carefully crossing streets and threading their way through all the foot traffic. What could she tell him? She hardly understood her feelings herself. She felt like a gray blanket had dropped over the top of her head, letting in little light, and muffling her responses to the world around her. Half the time she wanted to cry, and the other half she wanted to lie down to sleep and not wake up.

"Mischka, do you have a problem with Pippi or with what happened in the camp?"

Startled, she said, "No, of course not. She saved my life. She protected my friends. Why would you think there's a problem?"

"Something that happened today—something that you said upset her."

"Oh. She took that wrong. She asked me to supper, and when I said I was already planning a meal at the boarding house, she suggested I bring Mrs. Levinstein along. Your household is having souvlaki, though, and Mrs. Levinstein is Jewish. She doesn't eat pork."

"Ah, I see." He brought up his fedora and jammed it on his head. She wished she had a hat. The wind was cold. "Pippi thinks you're angry with her."

"Emil, I'm not angry at anyone."

"You've hardly been to see Pippi, and when you've been in a gathering, you keep to yourself. Pippi misses you. I miss the old Mischka."

"Pippi will be busy with her nuptials soon. She doesn't need me complicating her life."

"Nuptials?" Emil stared. "What nuptials?"

"Her wedding."

"Pippi isn't getting married."

"What? Of course she is. You said so when we met the ship—you told that man who wanted to call on her that she's betrothed."

Emil let out a laugh that was so forceful, it sounded like a bark. "I said those things to rid her of that barnacle who had tried to attach himself to her. I could tell she wanted nothing to do with him. So you've been out of sorts because of this?"

Mischka's face was hot, and she'd broken out in a sweat. How embarrassing that she hadn't picked up the nuances that day. How could she have misunderstood so completely? Now that she thought about it, she realized there had been no announcement, none of the usual gossip and excitement an impending wedding would bring.

"Is that all it is?" Emil asked. "Or is there something more? Something deeper seems to be troubling you."

"I'm — I don't know what's wrong."

"Mischka, you've been a force to reckon with all your life. You kept us going when we weren't sure if we'd ever get on a ship out of Swinoujscie, and without your language skills, we might not have cleared Customs. You were the first to find work here in the city. You've been steady and helpful and inspiring, and I can never thank you enough. I don't know what I would have done without your efforts. And now, I sense that you could use my help, but I don't know what it is you need."

She hunched her shoulders in her coat, turned to face the wind, and trudged forward. He fell in step beside her. How could she explain what was happening to her when she hardly understood it herself? But she had to try. She owed him that much. "Do you ever have bad dreams, Emil?"

"Yes."

"Do you ever think of bad things from the wars?"

"I try not to."

"Remember the woman from the labor camp who came into the store recently? Her name was Nelka. I didn't tell you all the details. She jumped out in front of a coal truck that day she died. On purpose. It wasn't an accident. I can't quite help but believe that it was my fault."

"Why? You didn't make that choice for her."

"But her sister died while in my care."

"Care? You were in a labor camp. How could you be responsible for her?"

"Nelka saved me from a terrible fate, and all she expected was that I look out for her sister Lidia. But she died. When I told Nelka what happened, she gave up all hope."

"And you think you're responsible for Nelka, too?"

"Yes. No. Well, I don't know."

Emil gripped her arm and pulled her to stop next to a closed-up newspaper shed. "Remember when you were little, and we were set upon by those Polish soldiers?"

"You shot them."

"Yes, I did. It was either them or Stevo and Tobar and Gyorgy—perhaps all of us. Killing those soldiers tortured me for more time than I care to admit. Eventually, I realized that I was forced to make a choice in only a split second, and I had to forgive myself for what I did. From what you've told me, you had no choices with these two girls. You were swept up in events you couldn't change or control. The German war machine is to blame. Not you. You and Pippi had no choice but to submit, to try to survive, and Nelka was wrong to blame you. She should have been angry at someone much bigger than you." He let out a sigh and released her arm. "Perhaps God, in fact."

Tears sprang into Mischka's eyes, and she turned her face away. "But she's dead now, Emil. Dead. And it's not fair. It's not right."

He rested the palm of his hand against a lamppost. "Little that happened in regard to the war was fair or right. I've lived through two world wars, and I feel qualified to relate this indisputable fact, Mischka. War is ugly, and the best thing you can do is say to yourself, 'It happened, but it's over, and I must go on living.' If you think anything else, you let *them* win—all the despots and killers and those who snuffed out the lives of so many of us. That would be the worst thing. You *can't* let them win, so you can't blame yourself anymore. That way lies madness. Do you understand? You cannot let them win."

Mischka bit her lip to fight back tears. The wind fought to get inside her coat, and she crossed her arms tight against her chest as if to shield herself. Her head felt heavy and full, as if overloaded with the facts swirling around inside.

Emil touched her shoulder. "The world is a better place with you in it, Mischka. If it weren't for you, I don't think I'd be alive today to say this to you."

"What?"

He grinned. "You were such a little scamp. Nine years old, and you had much to teach a shellshocked soldier of nineteen. I'll never forget that, Mischka. Never. Your family and Gunari, my adopted father, saved me from God only knows what. Your mother and Patia were always kind to me. I miss Bersh so much some days that it hurts my heart. And I can hardly bear to speak of Drina and Xavi."

Now her tears came, and she turned away, unable to speak.

He tugged at her sleeve. "Come, let's walk. It'll clear your head." They strode silently for two blocks before he said, "We need to honor their memories, Mischka. Perhaps we need to

speak more often of those whom we have lost. I know I don't—
speak of them, I mean. I can hardly find the words, but I have
come to believe that we must. Why should we bear this sorrow
alone? We never got to say goodbye to any but Lumi, and
perhaps that's what you're missing. Let us come together in a
family council and talk about this. All right?"

"But not tonight."

"No. We both need time to think, and I should like to
discuss the matter with Mikhail."

She slowed to a stop. "My father would not want to discuss
it, I'm sure. You know the rules. I should not speak of any of it
with him."

"But I can. And you may be surprised about Mikhail. He's
changed. We have all changed since coming to America."

Mischka wasn't sure how much of that was true, but she
would think about it. "Emil, I must return to Mrs. Levinstein's to
prepare the evening meal."

"I know." He reached out both hands and enfolded her cold
fingers in his. "You're not alone, *liebling*."

She squeezed his hands, unable to speak, then said goodbye
and headed back toward the boardinghouse. The breeze was cold
against her damp face, and she was chilled, but her heart seemed
to have expanded in a comforting way. For the first time in many
days, she felt hope.

Chapter
Forty

New York City November 1950 (Snow Moon)

PIPPI RETURNED HOME from a long day of cutting out
patterns and sewing sample dresses. She was still trying to get
the A-line right for a new dress style and was irritated not to
have succeeded. She climbed six flights of stairs to her third
floor apartment, wishing for a moment that her flat was as
accessible as the one that Mikhail, Gyorgy, Mario, and Sylva
shared on the first floor of the brownstone next door. But
perhaps as reward for the long climb, the rooms Pippi and her
son shared with Emil, Palko, and Camille were more spacious.
Still, she thought, as she unlocked the door, their living quarters
were far too cramped. She was seriously thinking of renting the
flat across the hall when the current tenants moved out at the
end of the year. In fact, the brownstone was for sale. She thought
she might be able to put a down payment on it with the money
Mother Richelle had left. She resolved to look into that.

"Hello, dear," Camille called out from the table in the nook
area that bridged the front room and the kitchen. "We have
company."

Pippi felt a small shock of pleasure when she saw Mischka
sitting at the table. Her face showed some color today, and her
dark eyes didn't look anywhere near as haunted as they had the
last time they spoke. "How are you?" Pippi asked.

"I'm fine. I hope I'm not intruding."

Before Pippi could reply, Camille said, "No, of course not.
You're always welcome."

François tugged at the pocket of Mischka's slacks, and she
said, "Would you like me to take this little monkey for a run?"

Pippi said, "Hmm, that might not be a bad idea. I'll come
with you. François, get your coat."

"I don't know where it is."

"How many places are there to hide it here? Hunt around

and find it, or Mischka and I will take a walk without you."
Pippi beamed up at Mischka, then watched as François raced
around the flat, finally locating his coat in the room Pippi shared
with him. "Mama, we'll be back once François's energy has
dissipated."

They trooped down the stairs into cool but humid fresh air.
Pippi said, "François, you know the rules. Stay out of people's
way. You can run to that lamppost, then come back."

"All right, Mama." He took off, his little legs and arms
pumping and his blond hair standing on end like corn silk in a
breeze.

Pippi observed Mischka out of the corner of her eye. Her
friend had a relaxed smile on her face and appeared a great deal
less tense than she had lately. Pippi stepped closer and hooked
her left arm through Mischka's right. "I'm so glad to see you."
Mischka blushed, but she didn't pull her arm away. "I'm sorry I
jumped to the wrong conclusions the other day."

"It's all right. I understand. You were gone so quickly I
wasn't able to explain."

"That was my fault. I'll be more patient next time."

François arrived at the lamppost and turned to run back. He
dashed around a thick-ankled woman, who dragged a metal
grocery cart overflowing with parcels, and launched himself
toward Pippi's legs.

Pippi let go of Mischka and braced herself. "Now what did I
tell you about being careful, François!"

"I'm sorry."

"Why don't you skip down to the corner and back—but not
too close to the street, all right?" He made a goofy face and took
off. She shook her head. "He's such a handful."

"No more so than any child. He's a delight—so full of life, so
curious. He reminds me of me."

"I wondered—I mean, well, I didn't know how you'd feel
about this child." The look Mischka gave her was puzzled. "You
know, his being out of wedlock."

"I would never judge you, of all people, Pippi. He's your
child, from your flesh. I hardly know him yet, but why wouldn't
I love him?"

"I don't know. I was just worried."

"That's my fault. Ever since Nelka's death—"

Pippi interrupted. "Now that was a strange meeting. Ever
since Emil told me about it, I've been having nightmares. And
daymares, too, if there is such a thing."

Mischka stared at her, wide-eyed. "You, too?"

"Oh, yes. Sometimes I'm at a sewing machine working away

peacefully, and suddenly I feel transported to the sewing room at the camp."

"Is there ever going to be peace about all that? It's the past. Why won't it stay the past?"

Pippi shrugged. "I truly can't say." François arrived back in front of them, out of breath and laughing. "Keep on running, boy." He turned around and took off again as they continued down the street.

Mischka said, "François is one subject I must admit wondering about."

"What?"

"Why didn't you tell me?"

"I didn't know. I didn't immediately realize I was pregnant." She took a moment to describe what happened on the night Major Fischer nearly caught her.

Mischka stopped. All the blood drained from her face as she said, "You never told me any of this. They would have executed you if you'd been caught."

"I wasn't caught."

"The major caught you."

"But I got away."

"Only because he forced himself upon you."

"The price I had to pay. Do you blame me?"

"No, of course not. I'm glad I didn't know at the time. I might have done something foolish."

Pippi laughed and took Mischka's arm again. "I don't think so. You were never foolish."

Huffing and puffing, François arrived in front of them again.

Mischka said, "François, I've found a place called Central Park that I want to take you to—a huge area where you can run at will. No cars to worry about."

Excited, he said, "Can we go now?"

"No, not today. It's too long a journey. We should go on a weekend and take a picnic lunch with us."

Pippi saw how intent François was. "Maybe we could go this Sunday."

"Yes, yes, yes." François danced up and down with each word, then dodged away at a more sedate pace.

"He's getting tired now," Pippi said. "It's strange how much he reminds me of my husband—and he doesn't share a drop of Delebecque blood. But he's fascinated to disassemble every clock and mechanism in the house. He's already taken off doorknobs and unscrewed all the moving parts in Mama's music box. It took me hours to put it back together. I have to watch his every move.

I don't know where he got this."

"He has a mother who was rather clever with lockpicks and sewing machine repair."

"True, but I learned that from my husband."

"The point is that you learned. You have an aptitude for it, otherwise you wouldn't have been able to learn it."

Pippi considered that, then said, "For his next birthday, I'm thinking of giving him his own set of miniature household tools."

"That's a wonderful idea, but let me do it."

"Oh, no, that's not necessary."

"Pippi, you should get him mother-like items: clothing, shoes, necessary things like that. His extended family should be allowed to bring him gifts that can be played with."

"I think it would be quite expensive."

Mischka smiled and managed to look rather proud of herself. "Don't worry about that. I'll haggle a good deal with old Stanislovski at the hardware store across from Giannakos. Practically every day I have to run over and translate for him. This will be his chance to reward me for my help." She winked and grinned. "Leave it to me, Pippi."

"You're very sweet." Pippi leaned into her friend, and they went on.

MISCHKA SAT ON the steps in front of Mrs. Levinstein's boardinghouse. Even after being in New York over two years, Mischka was still not accustomed to having Sunday off work. Her entire life, she had worked at something every day of the week, and to have free time on her hands felt strange. Mischka was sorry that Mr. Giannakos's grocery was closed on Sundays. She liked being busy, and to sit, even in the midafternoon warmth of the autumn sun was nerve-wracking. Perhaps she should take up reading. She wasn't very good at reading English, though.

Mr. Giannakos kept encouraging Mischka to practice more. "It's easy when you work at it. I come to this country aged four, and by five, I know all my numbers and letters."

Easy for him to say. Mischka stopped to calculate her age: 40. In fact, she would be 41 in a few days. English wasn't so easy to read and was a much trickier language than Romany. Or German or Polish, for that matter. She decided she would go to the library and check out some books. She would learn the language better. She would.

That settled, she was still left with nothing to do. The library was closed today. A man in gray slacks and a camel's-hair jacket walked by. He glanced her way and gave a quick nod, then continued on his way. She didn't know him. Other than Mrs. Levinstein and the two other girls who lived in the boardinghouse, she didn't know anyone in the neighborhood. She knew plenty enough people at work. She could hardly keep track of them and didn't need any more acquaintances. She should have planned something with Elena.

She was tempted to get up and take another walk, but just then she spied a familiar figure coming her way. Pippi's golden hair shone, and she carried something boxy under one arm. Halting at the foot of the stairs, she said in German, "Hello. What do you think?"

Mischka thought the afternoon might be a good one—Pippi was willing to let down her guard and speak in her native tongue. Her friend had been trying so hard to speak English, and she still wasn't very good at it. "Think about what?"

Pippi let out a huff. "My outfit."

Now Mischka looked closer at Pippi's apparel. Her jacket was yellow with black trim, and she wore a black over-the-knee skirt. The blouse underneath the jacket was white with yellow trim, and her shoes were also black. Mischka shrugged. "You …you look very nice," she stammered out, but she had no sense of fashion or what any of the clothing styles were called.

Pippi sighed as if she knew that. She mounted the stairs. "I designed this and sewed it myself. This cloth coat is lined, see?" She pulled open the front of the baggy coat, and pointed. "The blouse underneath doubles as a suit-top. It's made out of gabardine, and the pockets were very hard to get right. This is a straight skirt—nothing fancy. All I need is a decent hat to go with it. But do you want to know the best thing about it?" She didn't wait for Mischka to answer. "I showed it to the shop supervisor, and he wants me to sew more of them, in various colors. I will have a design all my own."

Mischka glanced down at her own outfit, a low-necked peasant blouse, a pair of dark, pleated slacks, and ankle-strap leather flats. She knew she looked positively dowdy next to Pippi. She'd never have the flair for fashion that Pippi did. "I'm so glad to see you happy about something."

"I'm not the only one who'll be happy. Wait until you see what I've brought you." She handed her the square object, which was wrapped in butcher paper and tied up with string.

"What is it?"

"I suggest we take it up to your room so it can be plugged in."

"Plugged in?"

"You'll see what I mean."

Outside the door to her room, Mischka said, "Lucky I tidied up the pigpen."

"Don't be foolish. Your room is never a pigpen."

Mischka looked back with concern. Pippi had said that with so much rancor in her voice. She hoped Pippi wasn't losing the good mood she'd been in. She walked over to the twin bed and set the package on it. "Shall I take your jacket?"

"I've got it." Pippi slipped it off and hung it on a hook by the doorway, then walked over to the straight-backed chair near the window. "Go ahead. Rip it open."

"I can't loosen the string."

"Just cut it."

Mischka went to the dresser for scissors, and with two quick snips, the paper fell away and revealed a brown rectangular box with two dials. "A radio!"

"Plug it in. It needs to warm up a minute or two."

Mischka practically tripped over her own feet finding the electrical outlet behind the little table next to her bed. She set the unit on the table and turned both knobs. The one on the right clicked, and she heard a faint hum. "Where'd you get this?"

"It was Emil's. He got it from somebody when he first came here. He bought a new one, and he wanted you to have this."

"What about you? You don't have a radio. You should keep it for yourself."

"Oh, Mischka, you love music and dancing far more than I ever will. I thought you should have it."

"How do you know I love music? Or dancing?"

"Oh, please. Remember when we were kids—at Emil and Drina's wedding?"

"I remember." Sadness had a way of cutting through her when she least expected, and the thought of Drina and so many others who were gone sobered her.

The hum grew louder, then a burst of static coughed out and stabilized into a steady crackle. Mischka adjusted the left-hand knob until she found a radio station playing the end of a swing tune featuring piano, strings, and horns. She twiddled the other knob to adjust the volume. As the song drew to a close and segued into a slow orchestral waltz, she swallowed the lump in her throat. "You're right. I do love it. I hear music all day at work."

"So do I, and when I go home, I like the quiet."

Mischka grinned and lowered herself to the edge of her bed. "I would leave music on night and day if I had the choice."

"And now you do. Keep Emil's radio, and you can sing and dance to your heart's content."

"I never was much of a singer."

"But you could 'cut a rug' as my American coworkers say. Get up. I'll show you the steps for this waltz. Come." She rose and reached for Mischka's hand. "Even though you're taller, I'll lead." Pippi's right hand went around Mischka's waist as she looked up into her eyes. "Now just follow me on a three-count."

Mischka didn't know what a three-count was, but she would have followed Pippi on any count of any number. Her heart kicked up to double time, and she felt her face burning. She tried to concentrate on the steps. Fortunately, she got the rhythm immediately, but relaxing into Pippi's body proved excruciating. She wondered how anyone breathed when they danced so close to another human being, especially when one longed for something from the other. A strange combination of emotions coursed through her. On the one hand, she wanted to push Pippi away and back off as though she were being burned by a hot fire; on the other hand, it was all she could do to keep from crushing Pippi to her chest and pressing her lips to her neck.

Through gritted teeth she said, "*Lavolta*."

"Hmmm?" Pippi was looking down, watching their feet.

"This is like the *lavolta*...or a slower *polska*."

"I never danced much before. I'm not the best dancer, but I'm trying to learn new things."

The waltz ended, and a new song began, this one at a medium tempo. She stopped and squeezed Mischka's waist, then looked up into her eyes, her lips parted slightly and a smile beginning. "I have a good idea. You should go to the dance hall with me and the other seamstresses some Friday night. I've gone twice now. It's great fun."

Mischka dropped Pippi's hand and backed up, shaking her head. "I don't think so."

"Oh, come now. It's fun. You'd be a delight on the floor. You pick up the steps so fast, and you're so graceful."

"No." Mischka had trouble swallowing. Heat swept through her body, and the blood in her veins pounded so hard that her head hurt. She had the overwhelming urge to kiss Pippi, and she could barely stop herself. Without thought, her next words tumbled out of her mouth. "It's *mahrime*. Not right."

Now it was Pippi's turn to flush. Her face turned a lovely shade of pink, and a spark of anger lit her eyes. "*Mahrime*? Not right? What's wrong with you, Mischka? We're dead women. We're not even supposed to be alive. It's a damn miracle that either of us is here today. Can't you see that? The old customs, the old traditions, the old rules — what's the point? I'll never get my husband back, and we'll probably never locate anyone else from your family."

Mischka's breath caught in her throat. She stumbled back, and her hand searched for the edge of the bed. She found it and sat heavily.

Pippi lowered her eyes and seemed to sink into herself. Her chin nearly touched her chest, and her hands knotted into fists. Head bowed, she said, "I'm sorry. That came out harsher than I intended." She stalked to the chair by the window and sat down. "At this point, my friend, I've decided to live life to the fullest. It's been hard to realize, to understand, but life goes on, Mischka. The past is past, and there's nothing we can do about it. What's the point of following old rules that don't matter anymore? We're in America, land of the free. I'm going to be who I want to be and do what I want to do now."

Mischka bit her upper lip so hard that she was afraid she had broken the skin. Gradually her heartbeat slowed, and her wits returned. She glanced up at Pippi, then away.

"You disagree?" Pippi's voice was full of surprise. "How can you disagree?"

She rose and strode toward the bed. Mischka felt like a small animal, cornered in the forest.

Pippi came close and stepped into the V of Mischka's legs. She bent slightly and took Mischka's face gently in her hands. "Mischka, I'm forty-four years old. I've loved. I've lost. But I never lost you — not for long. You were always in my memories, in my thoughts, in my hopes for all these years. I've loved you since I was fourteen years old, when we sat in the entrance to your tent and drank apple wine and talked. I've never met anyone like you, and I never will again, so I can't lose you. Do you understand? If you turn away from me, I'll die."

"I wouldn't." Mischka choked the words out.

"Wouldn't what?"

"Turn — turn away." She angled her head slightly and leaned into the warm hand stroking the right side of her face. Every nerve, every tendon in her body was on high alert, but this time she didn't feel the panic of the earlier moments. It helped to be seated. At least she didn't feel she'd fall over in a dead faint.

"Do you remember what you told me once, long ago, when we were girls?" Pippi's hand paused. "I know I'm going to mangle the pronunciation, but here goes. *Te' sorthene sutho.*"

"Dearest friend bonded by heart and spirit. Forever," Mischka said in a hushed voice.

Pippi smiled. "You remember."

"Of course." She brought her hands to her chest and crossed them over her heart. "North, south, east, west, by the sun and the moon—and inside my heart."

"I still feel that same way, Mischka."

"What are you saying?"

Pippi stooped so that her face was level with Mischka's, and her hands dropped to grip Mischka's shoulders. "I'm saying that we should stop playing these games, stop pretending. You feel the same way I do. Admit it."

Mischka straightened up. "I admit nothing."

The laugh that bubbled up from Pippi was infectious. "You stubborn woman. You must have been worse than hell and high water everywhere you went over these many years."

"No, I think not."

"We belong together."

"I don't have the courage."

"Well, I do."

Mischka couldn't take her eyes off Pippi's lips. She watched them part slightly. Pippi took a deep breath and let it out slowly, then leaned forward. Her eyes searching, she pressed her mouth against Mischka's. So gentle, so sweet.

A whimper escaped from Mischka's throat. Pippi's lips trailed kisses down the side of her face, to her neck. Mischka raised her hands, feeling disbelief and desire so strong her whole body pulsed. She moved her hands to the woven twill at Pippi's waist, felt the swell of her hips, the ridge of hipbone, and pulled Pippi close. She wrapped her arms around her, buried her face in the cool gabardine, and felt the tears rise.

Pippi's hands were in Mischka's hair, stroking, patting, caressing her neck. "Shhh... No need to cry."

But Mischka couldn't stop herself. The tears came anyway. She didn't even know what she was crying for. She knew the moment was perfect. She'd never felt as happy, as comfortable. Never in her life had anything felt so right. The feeling was so bittersweet that she both wished it would end so she could cherish it forever and hoped it would never stop. Her ambivalence almost made her laugh. She rose and enclosed Pippi in a full embrace, buried her face in her neck, breathed in the faint smell of Pippi's soap, and felt Pippi clasp her just as tight.

The sun shone on them through the window. Pippi whispered an endearment in her ear. The radio played a Duke Ellington song. Life went on.

Chapter
Forty-One

New York City, November 1989 (Snow Moon)

MISCHKA LOOKED AT her watch. "It's nearly seven. Are you finally tired, Tobar?" She glanced over at Pippi who was dozing at the other end of the sofa.

He yawned. "I guess I am. But it's still only midnight to me."

"You'll have to change your sleep schedule soon."

"I will. Maybe I won't go to bed now at all. That way, I'll be tired tonight." He rose and stretched. "So today's your birthday, *Beebee* Mischka."

"Yes."

"How old are you?"

"My passport says seventy."

Pippi roused at that comment. "Don't let her fool you, Tobar. She's eighty. Three-and-a-half years younger than I am."

"But my passport says—"

"Ha! Your passport also says you were born in Halkiades, Greece, as Sophia Giannakos. All lies." Laughing, she informed Tobar. "She's eighty, and that's why your parents have come all this way to stay with us and celebrate."

A rapping at the door startled them. Mischka said, "Who could that be at this hour?" Tobar made a move toward the foyer, but Mischka called out to him to stop. "Let me look. I don't know who could have gotten into our building, but lately there has been some vandalism." She rose with effort, and her knees made a cracking sound.

At the peephole, she saw several familiar dark heads bobbing, so she opened the door.

"*Beebee* Mischka. Are you watching TV?" Her sister Elena's grandson Nico leaned forward and kissed her on the cheek. His young wife Gloria patted her arm and slipped past carrying a grocery bag packed full.

"You won't believe what's happening!" Nico called out. He, too, carried a brown grocery bag overflowing with vegetables and bread and noodle boxes.

Suddenly a moving mass of small children pushed past her and dashed into the living room.

Nico said, "Sorry it's so early, but we knew you'd want to know."

"Know what?" she asked.

"Hey!" Nico yelled at the kids. "No jumping on the couch." He stepped away to lecture his unruly brood.

More people clomped up the stairs, and Mischka stood in the doorway, puzzled, watching her living room fill up.

A tousle-haired, pajama-clad François stood in the hallway looking grumpy. "What's happening?" he asked. Pippi was already going to him, so Mischka didn't answer.

Nico headed for the kitchen. "We have to call Grandma Elena," he said. "She'll want to be here, too."

"I'll go get her," Nico's wife said. "You tune in the news." She swept past Mischka and headed for the stairs. Since the hall was now empty, Mischka closed the door.

Mischka looked across the room and met Pippi's eye. Pippi shrugged. They hadn't planned on having people arrive until closer to noon, but Mischka didn't care. "Who wants spiced Roma coffee?" she called.

She helped to prepare snacks and distribute coffee. The talk and the excitement were all about The Wall.

"It's finally opening up," Nico said with glee.

Mischka hadn't been following the news, so she wasn't quite sure what he was referring to. All she knew was that something momentous was about to happen overseas. She stood in the doorway between the kitchen and living room, sipping at a mug of sweetened coffee laced with milk and almond. Pippi sat across the room on a flowered, two-person divan. She looked tired. Early morning sunlight shone through the wall of windows behind her and illuminated her silver hair.

Mischka handed her mug to Pippi before carefully lowering herself.

"I'll have a sip of this," Pippi said.

"You said you didn't want any."

"Just a sip."

"I've seen your idea of a sip. Go ahead. Have all you want. We certainly have enough people here to get us more."

She gazed in amazement at all the people. Men and women, young and old, and of many different skin tones. They sat or stood or squatted, and all of them spoke in excited tones.

Children ran through the arch leading to the front door, down the hallway to the bedrooms, and back. She counted forty-one, including the tiniest toddlers, and then the front door opened, and Nico's wife Gloria ushered in Mischka's sister Elena along with the Sanchez family, another group of five.

Ramon Sanchez, married to her brother Stevo's granddaughter, was a big man, not unlike her old friend Tobar. Each time Mischka caught sight of Ramon, she was struck by how much he looked like her long-dead friend. Even after all these years, she missed him. But today was meant to be a happy occasion, so she put Tobar out of her mind.

In years past, her people sat around a campfire; nowadays, the television seemed to be the center of their gatherings. Her TV was blaring over in the corner, but she wasn't following the program. Even though her hearing wasn't what it used to be, she could make out the patter of children's footsteps, the clinking of glasses, the guttural sound of men's laughter, and a rising buzz of expectation. Two black-haired little girls sat at her feet munching on old Halloween candy from an orange plastic pumpkin. One held out an empty red wrapper and let it flutter from her fingertips.

From across the room, the child's mother, clad in jeans and an NYU sweatshirt rose from her seat on a folding chair. She threaded her way through children playing with Legos in front of the TV, all the while scolding the girls for littering. Grabbing up the wrapper, her eyes met Mischka's. "Sorry, *Beebee*."

"It's not a problem, Liza." Mischka smiled at the young mother. Liza, who was her sister Elena's daughter, had always been her favorite—perhaps because she bore the name of someone once near and dear. She was secretly pleased that so many of those in this younger generation were named after Roma from the Old Country.

Liza frowned at her child. "Valentina, it's too early in the morning for you and Cousin Maria to be eating candy. If you're hungry, go see Gloria in the kitchen." She took the plastic pumpkin from the girls and looked toward Mischka, who smiled back at her. "Are you warm enough, *Beebee*?"

"How could I not be with these toasty little ones at my feet?"

"They're not crowding you, are they?"

"No, no. Of course not. I'm fine. We're fine." She glanced down at the head leaning on her shoulder. Pippi shifted and sleepy blue eyes opened. "Wake up. You're missing all the fun." Her sleepy companion yawned and Mischka laughed. "Look at this. Look at this family. Aren't we lucky?"

Pippi said, "Such *vielfalt*—how do you say it?"

"Variety."

"Yes, we're so lucky to have it."

A shout went up, and Liza's husband, Daniel, rushed to the television set. "This is it!" he shouted. "The people are passing through the wall to the other side!"

Tobar nestled in on the floor next to the divan and looked up at Mischka. "What does this mean?"

"Well, if the wall opens between the halves of Germany, Tobar, it means that people from the west—such as where your father was born in France—can now cross over to the east and be with family and friends in Germany or Poland or Hungary and so on. After all this time, Europe will be open again. Perhaps the travelers will once again wander the roads."

A gradual hush fell over the house as parents quieted their children. Mischka shivered. Even with the blanket on her lap and Pippi pressed close, she suddenly felt cold. The hand entwined in hers squeezed tighter, and she held her breath, not quite believing. Could it be true? Would it really happen? Daniel turned the TV up so they could all hear the news announcer:

"...is imminent. Officials from both East Berlin and West Berlin have verified to our correspondents in Germany that the border has begun to open. It's reported that Bornholmer Strasse is open. Ah, here's some footage at Checkpoint Charlie. As you can see, a stream of people—not sure if they're tourists or what—are making their way through, and the border guards aren't stopping them. The German officials have been allowing this all night..."

Footage of cheering people, some laughing, some crying, beamed out over the airwaves all the way across the Atlantic, from a land far away from New York City. Mischka thought of how far her family and friends had traveled, how long their journey had been from Europe to New York, and it was almost too much to imagine. All that time and space and distance.

"Ohhh..." Pippi said. It came out like a sigh. Mischka watched hot tears run down Pippi's face, and her own eyes filled in sympathy. The picture on the television blurred, and the room shifted to the left, then to the right. A feeling of panic hit her, and she closed her eyes.

"*Beebee? Beebee*, are you all right?" She felt hands gripping her shoulders and forearms, and someone cupped the back of her head.

Nico said, "*Beebee* Mischka?"

In a concerned voice, Liza said, "What's wrong, *Beebee?*"

Mischka opened her eyes and saw a cluster of faces all around, with her sister's grandson Nico's face closest. He tenderly supported her head. His hair was dark and his black beard neat. For a moment, she thought he looked exactly like her father. The words were out of her mouth before she could stop them. "Papa," she said in wonder.

Two dozen adults took a collective inward breath, and she knew she needed to clarify. With a tentative hand, she reached up and patted the side of his face. "Nico, you remind me of my father, that's all. And this—this spectacle brings back so many memories. So much I have not said. So much I—" she glanced at Pippi "—we have never told. So this is unexpectedly emotional for us."

Nico said, "I knew it, *Beebee* Mischka. We all knew you'd feel that way. We can't wait to hear all about it. Jan is going to bring a video camera over, and we're going to film your birthday party, and then we want you two to tell us everything."

"Yes," many voices called out. "Everything."

"But first, we'll be having lunch and cake," Liza said in her quiet voice. A chorus of children's voices cheered that idea. "It's a happy birthday to *Beebee* Mischka!"

Mischka smiled at them across the room. And then everyone went back to the TV, occasionally shouting out in exultation.

From his spot on the floor, Tobar caught Mischka's eye and winked. She turned to Pippi and whispered, "Look at him. He's more like his Uncle Emil than perhaps we realized. I think he's a teacher and future historian."

PIPPI WATCHED THE commotion in the flat. With wall-to-wall people, she almost felt claustrophobic. Ordinarily she'd be in the kitchen, making strudel, fixing sandwiches, and talking with the women, but today, she just wanted to stay huddled with Mischka on the divan, out of everyone's way.

The size and jubilance of her family amazed her. When François married the daughter of Mario and Sylva, she didn't lose a son, she gained an entire clan. Mario and Sylva had four more children after young Tobar's mother was born; Stevo and Chavi's son Tem and his wife had seven children; Elena and Paul had five; Emil's son Palko three; and her François, now an amazing forty-two years old, had three with Maria. Twenty-three in that generation. She was awed by it. Two-thirds of them had started their own families, and when she looked around the room, she couldn't even keep track of which child was which or to whom he or she belonged.

The enormity of it brought a lump to her throat. Still, she believed she had been luckier than most. When she considered all that Mischka had lost, she didn't know how her partner could face each day. Mischka had deserved a fairytale life after all she'd been through, but it was not to be. Her father died a long, slow death from cancer, and when Gyorgy and Stevo died of heart attacks the same year, Pippi didn't know how Mischka had stood it. But she had, and she became the matriarch of the Gallo clan, the person to whom everyone came for advice. Pippi looked at the white-haired woman seated so close, her eyes still clear and dark, and she loved her all the more for her endurance.

Pippi believed in her heart that these last four decades in America had made it worth the pain and suffering of her first forty-odd years. But of course, things were in no way perfect. Even after all these years, she still missed her mother. Her father seemed a distant memory that bore no pain, but her brother... Oh, Emil. She knew perfectly well why she had kept avoiding Tobar's questions about Emil.

The last time she had seen him, he'd been so frail, so weak. Ravaged by congestive heart failure, he could barely speak. He'd never married again, so she took care of him at the end. She remembered the bittersweet comfort of sitting in the chair next to his hospital bed for hours holding his warm, dry hand while he slept. Once he had awakened and looked at her with such pain in his eyes. He gasped out, "Pippi...I did my...best."

"I know you did, my dear. I know you always did."

That hadn't satisfied him. "They—come. In dreams." He closed his eyes and let out a choking cough.

"Who? Who, Emil? The soldiers?"

"No, no." It took some time for him to answer. "The Roma. They come. For me."

Those were the last words he ever spoke to her. He died in the night, after she had gone home to sleep.

The Roma come for me—not *to* me; he had said *for* me. She wasn't sure if that was a good thing, but she hoped it was. If there was an afterlife, she wanted to believe that even before Emil found their parents, he would be reunited with his Roma wife, Drina, his lost children, and with his great friends, Tobar, Gyorgy, and Stevo.

She didn't know if she could believe in an afterlife. She'd been raised Catholic, but she had fallen away from that faith a long time ago. If there was an afterlife, she prayed that one day she might be reunited with all of those people from her past,

Emil included.

A pang of regret, of physical pain in her heart and throat, brought tears to her eyes, and she reached for Mischka's hand to steady herself. Seven years had passed, but she never remembered her brother without such a feeling of homesickness that she felt unsteady. And here was her grandson, Tobar, looking exactly as she remembered Emil when she was six and Emil was twelve.

And now the family — this vast and sprawling bunch of Germans and Roma, Italians and Spaniards, Poles and Jews — they wanted to hear the story of the old days. The thought took her breath away. She realized that she wanted to leave a record. She wanted to tell the stories. Until she and Mischka had talked about it with Tobar, she'd put as much of it out of her mind as she could. All these years she'd kept it pressed back, but now she could let it out. Why hadn't she felt safe before? She didn't know the answer. All that mattered was that she wanted to share it all now.

MISCHKA STOOD AT the front door of the brownstone, waving goodbye to some of their visitors. The cold night air gusted in. She shivered and closed the door and made her way up the stairs to the apartment. People had been encouraging her and Pippi to move to a smaller flat on the first floor, but she secretly believed that walking the flights of stairs was what had kept them fit and alive all these years.

In the living room, Pippi was curled up on the divan next to Tobar, and most of the remaining adults looked sleepy.

"It's late," Mischka said. "Perhaps we should retire for the night and celebrate again tomorrow."

Nico said, "Yes, we'd love to get more footage of you."

Pippi sat up. "Tomorrow. We'll talk more tomorrow. My throat is actually sore from all the talking."

Liza, Elena's daughter, was seated on the floor against the sofa, her knees up and her arms around them. "Before we go to bed, I need to ask — how did you survive all that? How?"

Pointing her index finger in the air, Mischka answered, "The Goddess — or perhaps the moon — watched over me." She pointed to Pippi. "And that one, too. She saved my life more than once."

"No, no," a groggy voice said, and Pippi swung her legs around to the floor. "Mischka had the will to live. She had the will to go on. My *liebling* would have made it through — no matter what."

Tobar asked, "What does *liebling* mean, Grandma Pip?"

Mischka answered the question. "It means darling — or sweet one." She moved across the room to the bay windows. Reflection from inside shone off the glass, but even so, as she drew closer, she could see the moon up over the buildings. "Look. Look at the moon."

She leaned over, turned off the floor lamp, and made a gesture to Liza to do the same with the overhead lights. Her niece flipped the light switches on the wall, and the room was plunged into near darkness with only the light of the muted television in the background. For a moment all was quiet, and then she heard the rustling of many footsteps. At the same time, two small hands took one of hers, and she glanced down to see Liza's daughter, Valentina, standing to her left in the moonlight. On her right, Pippi held her other hand and pressed up against her, one arm around Mischka's back.

"Do you remember the name of that moon, Liza?"

After a pause, Liza said, "No, *Beebee*. I'm so sorry but it escapes me."

"I thought you had memorized them all."

"Yes, when I was a child I did. I remember January is the Wolf Moon because it's a time to protect your family, and Seed Moon is April for planting. I also remember other names: Barley and Mead...and Storm Moon...but not when they are. I'm sorry."

"That's all right," Mischka said. "But this November moon is a special one. October was the Blood Moon, when we make offerings in the memory of those who have gone from this world. Pippi and I have thought so much these last weeks about those we loved — and lost. But now it's Snow Moon. Time to let go of the bad or the things that soak the soul in negative ways. Here in America, the New Year celebration is for this, but that's not how the old Roma ways work. We Roma make these commitments under the light of the Snow Moon, and when December's Oak Moon rises, we do all we can to be steadfast, to be strong, and to keep those promises we made. It's a time of forgiveness. Time to let go of the past." She paused, holding back tears. "Still, I want you all, my family, never to forget. The despicable things that happened in the war must never happen again. Not ever."

All around, her nieces and nephews and Pippi's son and the grandchildren murmured. "Don't worry," they said. "No, *Beebee*, we won't forget."

Filled with alarm, Tobar's voice called out, "Look, *Beebee*, look." She turned away from the light of the Snow Moon rising. "They're attacking!"

As Mischka's heart beat wildly, the group moved with various degrees of speed toward the television set, and it was not until she stood six feet from it that she realized what was happening. Gleeful men and women, some young, some old, had rushed the Berlin Wall.

Nico darted forward to turn up the TV's sound. From both sides, the people of East and West Berlin were taking down the stone monstrosity that divided them.

The newsman stopped speaking, and all that could be heard was the sound of hammers, axes, and sledgehammers — and people shouting encouragement. The camera shifted and went aloft, giving an aerial view of the scene below. When one person tired, another stepped forward and continued to strike the wall with whatever implement was available. Soldiers stood aside, at ease, and watched, not bothering to stop a single person's effort.

Soon, as both sides worked, someone began to sing, her voice plaintive. Other people joined in until the singing was loud and clear. Mischka recognized the words. "Unbelievable. They're singing an American song, something called 'Blowin' in the Wind.' "

Mischka backed up and went to sit on the divan, joining Pippi. With tears coursing down her face, she whispered, "Well, Pippi, we can all go there now and visit or travel where we want. They can come here, and we can go there." Wonderment in her voice, she said, "So it's over, my love. It's finally, truly over. You can go home to Reims or to Eisenhüttenstadt or anywhere you want to go."

Pippi's arm curled behind Mischka's back, encircled her waist, and squeezed tight. "I am home, *liebling*. We've been home for many years."

Mischka wiped her cheeks. "I guess you're right. And now that I'm seventy, I probably don't need to travel much more anyway."

Pippi rolled her eyes and snuggled in closer. "Seventy, my foot!"

The End

The Roma Moons

January ~ Wolf Moon: A time for rituals of protection for home, family, and travelers

February ~ Storm Moon: A time to ask the Old Ones for rituals to plan for the future

March ~ Chaste Moon: A time for rituals seeking fulfillment of appropriate wishes

April ~ Seed Moon: A time for rituals for planting seeds in Mother Earth

May ~ Hare Moon: A time for rituals to look forward to goals of the future

June ~ Dyad Moon: A time to find a ritual that balances spiritual and physical desires

July ~ Mead Moon: A time for rituals of thanks to be given to the Old Ones when your goals are reached

August ~ Wort Moon: A time for rituals celebrating preservation of what one has

September ~ Barley Moon: A time for rituals of thanksgiving for all that has been received

October ~ Blood Moon: A time for rituals and offerings to remember those who have passed from this world

November ~ Snow Moon: A time for rituals to banish negative and unproductive thoughts or practices

December ~ Oak Moon: A time for a ritual to strengthen and maintain one's dearest convictions

Select Bibliography of Roma/Gypsy Resources

A History of the Gypsies of Eastern Europe and Russia
by David M. Crowe

The Gypsies in Poland: History and Customs
by Jerzy Ficowski

Bury Me Standing: The Gypsies and Their Journey
by Isabel Fonseca

The Gypsies (Peoples of Europe)
by Angus M. Fraser

We Are the Romani People
by Ian Hancock

The Rom: Walking in the Paths of the Gypsies
by Roger Moreau

And the Violins Stopped Playing: A Story of the Gypsy Holocaust
by Alexander Ramati

Gypsy Folktales
by Diane Tong

Gypsies
by Jan Yoors

The Heroic Present: Life Among the Gypsies
by Jan Yoors

Gypsy Law: Romani Legal Traditions and Culture
by Walter O. Weyrauch

FORTHCOMING TITLES
published by
Regal Crest

In Broad Daylight
by Jane Vollbrecht

Colleen McCrady, an aspiring writer, is on the verge of having her first novel accepted for publication. Elizabeth Albright, owner and managing editor of Standing in Sappho's Shadow Publishing — Triple S, as it's known in the lesbian publishing industry — gives Colleen a helping hand, and in the process, the two discover that a love for lesbian literature isn't the only thing they have in common.

Despite their romantic chemistry, Colleen and Elizabeth are at odds over other aspects of their relationship. Try as she might, Elizabeth can't get Colleen to reveal many details of her childhood and family life. Colleen is likewise stymied in her attempts to get Elizabeth to bring their relationship out into the open. The situation comes to a head when Colleen offers Elizabeth a new manuscript — one which will either take their relationship in a new direction or destroy the bonds between them.

Elizabeth is drawn into Colleen's tragic past as she discovers the long-buried secret that Colleen reveals in her new book. A mystery that is nearly a half century old is reopened when Elizabeth helps Colleen unravel the puzzle of what really happened to a lone, deaf black man who worked on Colleen's father's farm in northern Minnesota all those years ago. The story that unfolds is a multilayered tale of love and hate, bigotry and acceptance, heartbreak and triumph.

Once the mystery is solved, only one question lingers: can Elizabeth and Colleen step out of the shadows and stand together In Broad Daylight?

Coming in February 2007

Devil's Bridge
by Greg Lilly

Two friends, Myra and Topher, deal with their twisting lives. Her husband beats her, his lover ignores him, and their friendship must bend with changes of its own.

Dealing with their own problems, Myra's increasingly violent husband and Topher's unrequited love for his partner Alex, they don't realize how much their lives parallel each other.

Myra's husband Gil controls her actions with his violence. Doubts finally creep into Myra's reluctant mind. Her dream of a happy family is slipping out of her reach. Although Topher helps her build self-esteem and is the stable influence in her life, he is in a crisis over where he fits in the gay community—too old for the club life, but not in a stable committed relationship. He allows Alex to manipulate him with the future possibility of love.

Finding strength to leave their relationships, Myra and Topher decide to escape from their life and start over—together. But, Myra's husband craves revenge. At a place called DEVIL'S BRIDGE, vengeance is redeemed.

Coming in May 2007

More Lori L. Lake titles

Gun Shy

While on patrol, Minnesota police officer Dez Reilly saves two women from a brutal attack. One of them, Jaylynn Savage, is immediately attracted to the taciturn cop—so much so that she joins the St. Paul Police Academy. As fate would have it, Dez is eventually assigned as Jaylynn's Field Training Officer. Having been burned in the past by getting romantically involved with another cop, Dez has a steadfast rule she has abided by for nine years: Cops are off limits. But as Jaylynn and Dez get to know one another, a strong friendship forms. Will Dez break her cardinal rule and take a chance on love with Jaylynn, or will she remain forever gun shy? *Gun Shy* is an exciting glimpse into the day-to-day work world of police officers as Jaylynn learns the ins and outs of the job and Dez learns the ins and outs of her own heart.

ISBN 978-1-932300-56-7

Under the Gun

Under the Gun is the sequel to the bestselling novel, *Gun Shy*, continuing the story of St. Paul Police Officers Dez Reilly and Jaylynn Savage. Picking up just a couple weeks after *Gun Shy* ended, the sequel finds the two officers adjusting to their relationship, but things start to go downhill when they get dispatched to a double homicide—Jaylynn's first murder scene. Dez is supportive and protective toward Jay, and things seem to be going all right until Dez's nemesis reports their personal relationship, and their commanding officer restricts them from riding together on patrol. This sets off a chain of events that result in Jaylynn getting wounded, Dez being suspended, and both of them having to face the possibility of life without the other. They face struggles—separately and together—that they must work through while truly feeling "under the gun."

Second Edition
ISBN 978-1-932300-57-4

Have Gun We'll Travel

Dez Reilly and Jaylynn Savage have settled into a comfortable working and living arrangement. Their house is in good shape, their relationship is wonderful, and their jobs—while busy—are fulfilling. But everyone needs a break once in a while, so when they take off on a camping trip to northern Minnesota with good friends Crystal and Shayna, they expect nothing more than long hikes, romantic wood fires, and plenty of down time. Instead, they find themselves caught in the whirlwind created when two escaped convicts, law enforcement, and desperate Russian mobsters clash north of the privately-run, medium-security Kendall Correctional Center. Set in the woodland area in Minnesota near Superior National Forest, this adventure/suspense novel features Jaylynn taken hostage by the escapees and needing to do all she can to protect herself while Dez figures out how to catch up with and disarm the convicts, short-circuit the Russians, and use the law enforcement resources in such a way that nothing happens to Jaylynn. It's a race to the finish as author Lori L. Lake uproots Dez and Jaylynn from the romance genre to bring them center stage in her first suspense thriller.

ISBN: 1-932300-33-3 (978-1-932300-33-8)

Ricochet In Time

Hatred is ugly and does bad things to good people, even in the land of "Minnesota Nice" where no one wants to believe dis-crimination exists. Danielle "Dani" Corbett knows firsthand what hatred can cost. After a vicious and intentional attack, Dani's girlfriend, Meg O'Donnell, is dead. Dani is left emotionally scarred, and her injuries prevent her from fleeing on her motor-cycle. But as one door has closed for her, another opens when she is befriended by Grace Beaumont, a young woman who works as a physical therapist at the hospital. With Grace's friendship and the help of Grace's aunts, Estelline and Ruth, Dani gets through the ordeal of bringing Meg's killer to justice.

Filled with memorable characters, Ricochet In Time is the story of one lonely woman's fight for justice—and her struggle to resolve the troubles of her past and find a place in a world where she belongs.

ISBN: 1-932300-17-1 (978-1-932300-17-8)

Different Dress

Different Dress is the story of three women on a cross-country musical road tour. Jaime Esperanza works production and sound on the music tour. The headliner, Lacey Leigh Jaxon, is a fast-living prima donna with intimacy problems. She's had a brief relationship with Jaime, then dumped her for the new guy (who lasted all of about two weeks). Lacey still comes back to Jaime in between conquests, and Jaime hasn't yet gotten her entirely out of her heart.

After Lacey Leigh steamrolls yet another opening act, a folksinger from Minnesota named Kip Galvin, who wrote one of Lacey's biggest songs, is brought on board for the summer tour. Kip has true talent, she loves people and they respond, and she has a pleasant stage presence. A friendship springs up between Jaime and Kip—but what about Lacey Leigh?

It's a honky-tonk, bluesy, pop, country EXPLOSION of emotion as these three women duke it out. Who will win Jaime's heart and soul?

ISBN: 1-932300-08-2 (978-1-932300-08-6)

Stepping Out: Short Stories

In these fourteen short stories, Lori L. Lake captures how change and loss influence the course of lives: a mother and daughter have an age-old fight; a frightened woman attempts to deal with an abusive lover; a father tries to understand his lesbian daughter's retreat from him; an athlete who misses her chance—or does she?

Lovingly crafted, the collection has been described as a series of mini-novels where themes of alienation and loss, particularly for characters who are gay or lesbian, are woven throughout. Lake is right on about the anguish and confusion of characters caught in the middle of circumstances, usually of someone else's making. Still, each character steps out with hope and determination.

In the words of Jean Stewart: "Beyond the mechanics of good storytelling, a sturdy vulnerability surfaces in every one of these short stories. Lori Lake must possess, simply as part of her inherent nature, a loving heart. It gleams out from these stories, even the sad ones, like a lamp in a lighthouse—maybe far away sometimes, maybe just a passing, slanting flash in the dark—but there to be seen all the same. It makes for a bittersweet journey."

ISBN: 1-932300-16-3 (978-1-932300-16-1)

Lori L. Lake is the author of the "Gun" series, a trilogy consisting of the romantic police procedurals *Gun Shy* and *Under The Gun* and the adventure/thriller *Have Gun We'll Travel*. Her first novel, *Ricochet In Time*, was about a hate crime. She has also written a book of short stories, *Stepping Out*, a standalone romance, *Different Dress*, and edited the Lambda Literary Award Finalist anthology, *The Milk of Human Kindness: Lesbian Authors Write About Mothers and Daughters*. She co-edited *Romance for LIFE*, an anthology which is a benefit for the fight against breast cancer.

In addition to earning Lambda Literary Finalist in the anthology category, Lori has been the recipient of nine Stonewall Society Literary Awards in 2003, 2004, and 2005. *Have Gun We'll Travel* was a 2006 Golden Crown Literary Award Finalist, and *Lavender Magazine*'s readers have twice named her *Twin Cities OutStanding GLBT Author*.

With her partner of 25 years, Lori lives south of the Twin Cities in Minnesota. She likes to go to the movies, play guitar, lift weights, and get together with friends to play cards and board games. She teaches Queer Fiction courses at The Loft Literary Center, the largest independent writing community in the nation. Lori is currently at work on her next novel. For more information, see her website at **www.lorillake.com**.

Printed in the United States
62234LVS00004B/1-81